N

David Hewson is a journalist for the *Sunday Times*. He is the author of three other highly acclaimed thrillers, *Semana Santa*, *Epiphany* and *Solstice*. He lives with his family in east Kent.

David Hewson

NATIVE RITES

HarperCollins*Publishers*

HarperCollins*Publishers*
77-85 Fulham Palace Road,
Hammersmith, London W6 8JB

www.**fire**and**water**.com

A Paperback Original 2000
1 3 5 7 9 8 6 4 2

Copyright © David Hewson 2000

The Author asserts the moral right to
be identified as the author of this work

A catalogue record for this book
is available from the British Library

ISBN 0 00 651358 1

Typeset in Galliard by Palimpsest Book Production Limited,
Polmont, Stirlingshire

Printed and bound in Great Britain by
Caledonian International Book Manufacturing Ltd, Glasgow

MICHAELMAS

It was the third week of September and the harvest was late. The air was alive with the sharp, sweet smell of cut wheat and barley. Specks of straw hung in the feeble breeze, glittering in the mellow late-afternoon sun. Alison Fenway sat naked on the edge of the big double bed, trying to order her thoughts.

Miles lay on the sheets, curled into the shape of a lazy apostrophe, a cat-like smile on his handsome face. His hair was turning a touch grey over the ears now. Too soon, she thought, at just thirty-five. There was no fat on his lean, muscular body.

'Is it really only two months?' she asked and wondered how well her American accent fitted into the Georgian splendour of the place, whether the walls heard her intonation and tut-tutted inwardly to themselves.

He rolled his eyes at the ceiling, thinking. 'Good God, yes. It just flew, didn't it?'

Dimly, she could recall the day she left the hospital in the Catskills, her mind still a bitter, reeling whirl. There was a car ride, a flight, tortured sleep, then England, home for Miles, always somewhere foreign to her. The weather had been kind. The motorway began as a familiar, choking serpent of urban congestion, until they veered south, into Kent where the countryside appeared out of nowhere: flat open farmland

and, in the distance, the high ridge of the Downs. Then a final wriggle through narrow, winding lanes, scarcely wide enough to take two cars, and they were nearly there.

Her first sight of Beulah was from the valley near Wye. The village lay past a spectacular chalk horse cut high into the Downs above, at the top of the tortuous climb of Vipers Hill. She sat in the passenger seat in silence, her mind trying to embrace the idea that the city was behind them. It had seemed to make sense when Miles had first raised the notion. But that was *after*. Anything would have made sense, any escape plan from the city and its vivid, searing memories. He had inherited the house just after she 'fell ill'. He had shown her pictures in the hospital, and she had nodded. It meant she was moving again. Her dead father's voice haunted her, the Boston brogue cold and hard: *We all need a goal, Alison. Time you remembered that.*

The car had rolled over the top of the hill, dived into a sudden zigzag of sharp bends, then sauntered along a dead-straight avenue of poplars waving softly in the morning breeze.

Something was happening on the village green: colour and people, games and rituals. They had stopped outside a three-storey Georgian mansion so vast she thought it was a hotel. And, like the shining knight he was, Miles Fenway had carried her, grinning, over the threshold, into Priory House, shown her around its myriad corners and the airy, high-ceilinged rooms. Later, they walked through the sprawling rear garden of lawn, herbaceous border and errant vegetable beds, hand in hand, like children entering some secret paradise.

In each life, she knew, there was a pivotal point where a single, small decision determined the direction of everything that happened thereafter. Entering Beulah and discovering Priory House was one of these. It would have been so easy to have rejected it. To have realised that this was no way to find a new home, begin a new beginning, simply on the basis of some distant blood ties, a property deed passed on from one generation to the next. There was an instant when she could have shaken her head and said: *No. I make my own life. I choose my own places.*

The words ran through her head . . . and fell silently away. In front of the ancient, heat-blackened Aga in the vast farmhouse kitchen she had kissed Miles, grateful that he knew when to lead and when to sit back. Her acceptance, and the feeling of relief that came with it, were still etched on her memory. This *would* work out. They deserved a break, at last.

Alison took one last, long suck of her cigarette, then stubbed it out, half finished, on the ashtray that sat on the windowsill. There was no reason to smoke after sex. This was habit, a clichéd habit at that. She didn't even enjoy it these days. They needed to make love, at the right time, for all the right reasons. Tobacco had no place in the game. It tasted foul. She could smell herself sometimes. And when she lit the damned thing, when there was that brief spurt of flame from the lighter, sometimes her head caught fire too, remembering, remembering. It was time to give up. No. *Tomorrow* was time to give up.

There was a faint miaow at the door and the pale ginger form of the cat walked imperiously into the room. Miles had bought her Thomas the week after they moved in. The beast had a glorious, snooty character, spending most of the day lazily eyeing the world from a basket by the Aga. She had once opened the back door and invited him to explore the garden, with its wild creatures and feral delights. Thomas had stared at her and blinked in offended, feline disbelief.

With a minimum of effort, the cat jumped on the bed and sat between them, demanding the attention of both. She stroked it gently on the neck, then leaned over the animal and gave Miles a peck on the cheek. There was stubble there

3

already. He seemed so full of life since they had moved, as if everything inside him was running at twice its normal speed. 'Thanks,' she said.

'For what?'

'For the cat. For indulging me.'

Miles sat upright. 'Please. This is for both of us.'

She shook her head. 'You spend four hours each day in the car. You're a city animal, Miles. We both know you're just indulging a crazy woman.'

He closed his eyes in that pained fashion she recognised. 'You are not crazy. You never were. Just . . .'

She put a finger to his lips. 'Shush. I know. "Into each life, a little rain . . ."'

'Quite,' he muttered confidently, then stood up, strode away into the bathroom. Soon she heard the sound of the shower. The noise made Thomas's ears prick upright. The cat thought about the possibility of water for one moment, then dashed for the door and the safety of the basket by the Aga.

Alison laughed inwardly to herself and went to the window, hungry for the view of the village. She caught her breath. The Blamire twins had stopped watching the cricket match on the green. They had turned round and were now peering, quite deliberately, back at the house. Back into the bedroom where she stood, naked behind the glass.

'Take a good look, boys,' she said quietly, in the coarsest Manhattan drawl she could manage, and leaned forward to feel the cold pressing on her breasts, gave a vacant, innocent grin to the world, then lazily picked up the silk dressing gown from the bed and dragged it over her shoulders. It felt organic, like wispy skin shed by some mythical reptile. She sat back on the bed, lit another cigarette, then looked out of the window again. The Blamires were watching the game, broad backs to her. A shame, she thought. She would have liked to have seen their round, weathered faces, tried

4

to judge if they were a little more red now. One of the twins – Harry, or was it Mitch? she still found it hard to tell the difference – walked over to the other side of the green, skirting the perimeter of the game, and started to help a small group of villagers heaving logs into a rough pile. The noise of the shower died.

'Miles,' she said loudly. 'What's going on? What kind of Brit nonsense is this?'

He came out of the bathroom, pummelling his head with a towel. 'Ar, it be a *big* day.'

'Jeez. That must be the worst hick accent I have ever heard. Even I can do English better than that.'

'Is that so?' He seemed a touch offended.

'You're a merchant banker. You find it congenitally impossible to listen to people. I can pass as a normal human being. I *do*.'

'Fine. So what *do* they say?'

'Oh, the usual estuarial annoyances you get on the BBC these days. Some dropped consonants. *Paw* for Paul. *Goh* for got. But not the whole way. They'd never say, for example, *I goa go see Paw*.'

She thought about it. Once upon a time, a decade before, when she'd tried to pretend she could be an actress, she had studied speech. She could still turn out a passable impersonation of Gwyneth Paltrow doing English if she wanted. Not bad for someone who'd spent the first fifteen years enduring a privileged existence in Boston, Massachusetts. Alison thought of their two closest towns, each a twenty-minute drive from the heights of the Downs where Beulah sat, in isolated rural splendour. 'Ash*furrd*. Cant*urr*bury.'

He towelled his hair, looking impressed. 'Very good. The Blamire boys will take you to their hearts.'

She glanced out at the green and made a mental note: this is *not* the middle of nowhere. There are people around. You shouldn't stand naked at windows and not expect them to look. More than that, you shouldn't taunt them. 'I think they have already. So back to the point. What's going on out there?'

He slipped on a shirt, then a pair of jeans. 'As I said. The *big* day. Harvest festival. The whole thing goes back yonks.'

The group around the wood pile were getting somewhere now. And it was clear what they were building. Just thinking about it made her feel cold. 'You mean like harvest home? I thought it was all kids in church giving away apples, boring priests and "We plough the fields and scatter".'

He put a damp hand to her head and she almost pulled herself away. Miles could be deeply, infuriatingly condescending at times. '*Yonks,*' he repeated. 'Don't be so temporally parochial. It's all pagan, you know. Christmas. Easter. Everything.'

'A bonfire? This is September. Not that stupid stuff you guys do on November the fifth.'

'Guy Fawkes is mere slippage, dear girl. I bet if you went back several hundred years every village in England was doing something like this just now. The end of the harvest. Birth, rebirth. That kind of thing. You should talk to John Tyler about it. He knows everything.'

She recoiled at the sound of Tyler's name and didn't know why. It was a week since the examination. The thought of it still made her flesh crawl. 'Ah, the bedside manner from hell. How nice to have him living in the village too.'

Miles sighed and stroked her hair. This time she really did pull away. 'We may come to be grateful for that,' he said. 'You know I'll pay for anyone you want to see in London. But Tyler seems a good man. The locals *worship* him and his wife.'

A good man. She had spent an hour in the surgery in Wye, three miles down the hill. An hour of being prodded and poked, in all the familiar ways. 'There's nothing wrong with

6

you or me, Miles. We both know that. It's just a question of time.'

I will conceive, I will conceive. Why can't you understand that?

'All the same, a tame, talented doctor on your doorstep isn't something you should ignore.'

Perhaps this country doctor has cures, she thought. Spells, incantations. Birth. Rebirth. He was welcome to try them all. Anyone was. She didn't care how it happened. She just wanted to be pregnant, wanted to feel the pulse of life inside her and hear the sound of young voices echoing down the long, empty corridors of Priory House.

Alison watched the activity on the green. Correction: the *Minnis*. They were so proud of their local traditions, the odd local names. This, she thought, was the real difference between the village and the city. It wanted to stay apart, it craved its own identity. Did that mean they hated intruders? No. Not even American ones with their odd accents and dubious reasons for being here. She had never encountered anything except warmth and friendliness, not infrequently mixed with a little eccentricity. Granny Jukes, the old biddy who lived in the tidy white windmill on the opposite side of the Minnis, was a prime example. She must have been ninety if she was a day, but the arrival of some alien in their midst just made her grin, somewhat toothlessly, even more. The slightly menacing Blamires had been just as cheery, though they were a touch too oddly local for her taste.

She could see the wigwam outline of the bonfire coming together on the lush green grass of the common. And something else behind it too, being fussed around by a gaggle of village women, Granny Jukes at the centre. What looked like a huge corn dolly lay on the grass close to the pile of wood, its straw body the colour of the rich afternoon sun. It was the size of a man.

Sounds came to her through the window. The lazy stroke

of a cricket bat on a ball. Someone shouting a call for out. The mechanical whirring of insects on the breeze. And cheering. The huge prone figure on the ground was starting to move, coming upright.

Miles was watching from the window, entirely captivated by the scene.

'You should get dressed, old girl. This looks like fun.'

With a shaking hand she rolled another cigarette out of the packet, then closed her eyes and, quite blind to the world, tried to guide the lighter flame gingerly towards her face.

Nature made the Blamire boys identical; temperament undid the trick. They were born forty-nine years before, two screaming bundles brought into the world in the tiny front room of 3 Arden Cottages, a hundred yards down the lane from the Green Man. Harry Blamire senior was propping up the bar at the time. He'd finished the day on the Marley estate, walked to the door of his tied cottage, then turned round when he heard the commotion inside.

'You're early,' the landlord said.

'Whelpin' going on,' Harry senior grunted, and stuck his face into the first of several pints of Bishop's Finger. It was one of the longer sentences he uttered in a relatively brief life. When the twins were six years old, and all too familiar with the Blamire boot, belt and fist, Harry senior, worse for wear, walked into an oncoming threshing machine on the long Marley field, close to the chalk horse. The graphic description of his demise was now a part of village folklore, something to repeat on a slow, long night in the public bar when there was an over-enthusiastic incomer who was simply pleading for a touch of damping down.

Until they were fifteen, even Agnes Blamire found it hard

to tell the twins apart. Then along came Burning Man and solved the problem. The boys liked to drink by then, and she never did ask where they got the money. Old man Marley had promised them a job on the estate starting the following spring, when the planting season began. That meant they could keep the tied cottage, and it ought to bring in the cash too. Things were looking up, and that always did make Agnes feel uncomfortable.

It was the Ashford boys, visiting for the fire and unwanted too, that started it. Taunting. Shouting. Calling names. *Oik. Sheep-shagger. Numpty.* The twins were short. They had compact, round faces, with narrow, squinty eyes. If you didn't look too hard it was easy to think they were just stupid country layabouts, incapable of stringing a sentence together. But Agnes knew her boys better than that. They were smart. They could be cunning. Somewhere, in the invisible space between them, was that mysterious, binding mechanism twins have, the one that sometimes made them seem like the same person, alive in two separate bodies. Agnes could be scared of the boys now and then. If she felt that way, strangers ought to as well.

Not that the Ashford gang understood any of this. They'd had their fill of warm, strong Spitfire bitter in the pub. Dutch courage coursed through their veins. They were bigger on the ground as well. There were only two Blamire boys. The Ashford gang ran to six and a couple of unsavoury-looking girls. No one knew what started the fight. All anyone could remember was the sudden, swift ferocity of the boys. Arms flailing, screaming incomprehensibly, they turned on their attackers and beat them to the ground, might have killed them too if a couple of the local men hadn't gingerly intervened.

Then one of the Ashford kids pulled out a knife, metal glinted in the bright afternoon sun, and Agnes Blamire's twins were no longer identical. The blade gave Harry what he liked to call his lightning streak. The zigzag wound down his left cheek required fifty-two stitches at the William Harvey Hospital. It was so deep that stubble never grew in the scar, making the mark even more noticeable because of its paleness against the reddy coarseness of the rest of Harry's face.

The youth who wielded the knife saw fit, after listening to local chatter, to move to a bedsit in Gravesend, thirty miles away, get a job in the docks, and forget about Ashford altogether. Two years after scarring Harry he went out one night on his moped and never returned. Agnes was dead by then, gone in her sleep. The boys occupied 3 Arden Cottages in a state of perpetual near-squalor, living off baked beans and TV dinners in a house strewn with pornographic magazines, odd trophies they picked up from following the hunt – a pair of stag horns, a fox brush. They mellowed over the years. Old man Marley even sold them the cottage for a knockdown price before he died. But the Blamire spirit was always there. Harry's lightning streak never darkened.

Alison and Miles Fenway, knowing only a little of this tale, walked slowly over the Minnis towards the bonfire. He had held her hand when they walked through the big double gate set in the hedge of copper beech at the front of the house. Alison, not knowing why, shook free when she saw the twins. The cricketers had left the pitch and were taking tea in the little white-painted pavilion at the perimeter of the ground. Beyond the perfect grass, which the Blamires tended daily – one of their several sources of local income – the rest of the Minnis stretched over the top of the Downs towards Folkestone, a tangle of low shrubs and bracken where you could get lost for hours. Spinneys of blackthorn ran through the common, all the way to Sterning Wood. The sloes were now ripening fast. The previous day she had picked a few. They looked so beautiful: tiny wild blue plums with a handsome powdery sheen. She'd tasted one and spat it out, the fruit was so bitter. Sara Harrison, who was close by with her small, noisy dog, had noticed and promised to show her how to make sloe brandy. 'So much better than the gin.' Alison liked Sara, though they had hardly spoken. Soon she would take up the offer.

Miles was distracted, talking to the good doctor Tyler. Harry Blamire openly leered at her, sniffing the air. 'You smell lovely, Mrs Fenway. Like you was made of flowers.'

'Chanel, Harry. What else can a girl wear?'

'You got nice tits too,' he said, and winked.

Alison beamed at him, unfazed. 'And – what is it you guys call it? – the *box*?'

Harry's piggy eyes narrowed. 'Oh, nice box. Yeah. Not that we saw as much as we would have liked. Now did we, Mitchy boy?'

The other one didn't smile often. Or talk so much either. 'Box is a box,' he said finally. 'Seen one, seen 'em all. Tits are different. Tits *vary*.'

Harry shrugged his big, powerful shoulders. The twins were built like bull terriers. 'That's Mitch for you. The philosophical sort. Me, I'll gawp at whatever comes my way.'

'Darling?' Miles had his hand lightly on her shoulder. He looked puzzled. Had he heard? Or was Dr Tyler so riveting?

'Mitch here was saying that my tits are fine but my box – no, *all* boxes – are the same. Harry, on the other hand, likes both. What do you think, Miles?'

Miles Fenway looked as if he'd swallowed a fish. 'I, er, I . . .'

He was a good six inches bigger than the twins. She'd seen Miles in a fight too, long ago in a smoke-filled downtown bar. He'd been transformed into a dark, muscular shape gripped by a sudden burst of violent fury. Miles could look after himself if the occasion arose. 'I think, my dear, we should close the curtains a little more often in future.'

'These Yanks,' Harry said, beaming. 'They're all hippies,

11

you ask me. Can't blame a man for looking.' He was full of himself. He punched his twin on the shoulder, quite hard it seemed to Alison, and they went back to heaving wood onto the pile.

The straw man was beside the bonfire now. She couldn't help looking at it. Granny Jukes and a couple of women from the short line of council houses at the edge of the village were fiddling with the construction. Sara Harrison was helping, half-heartedly Alison thought, in the background. The creature had a flimsy wooden skeleton which could have been wicker or willow whips. Its skin was dry, brittle straw of the kind that seemed to litter every narrow lane leading onto the common this last week. The carcass was hollow. Two large gaps had been left in the head. When the bonfire was ablaze, she guessed, they would look like burning eyes, staring straight out at you.

'It's a harmless sacrifice.' John Tyler's voice made her jump. The doctor had walked up to stand beside her and she hadn't even noticed. 'I'm sorry. Did I startle you?'

'No, I . . .' Miles was watching her like a hawk. It seemed so important to him that these people were impressed. 'I was thinking of something else. A sacrifice?'

John Tyler reminded her of an old, inquisitive, bald-headed eagle. His face was pinched and almost bloodless. A pair of gold-rimmed spectacles perched on a long, bony nose. Two pale grey eyes watched her, always. Most doctors she knew hated being reminded of their profession off duty. Tyler, she guessed, was one of the rare, opposite kind. He would probably walk up to complete strangers at parties and advise them to go for a thyroid check-up. He looked in his late fifties, quite fit in a cadaverous way. As usual, he wore a thin wool jumper, this time in bright red with the name 'Pringle' embroidered upon it. His wife Marjorie stood by his side, smiling silently, in a proprietorial fashion. Marjorie was a huge woman with a flabby red face and a booming, bossy voice. It wasn't hard to work out who was in charge of the Tyler household.

'Purely symbolic. Nothing but straw,' Tyler continued. 'It marks the end of summer, the end of the harvest. The ritual sacrifice of this year's corn guarantees the next. The Christian church couldn't stomach *that* idea, of course, so instead we have Michaelmas, the feast of the Archangel Michael. Who was a pretty fearsome chap in his own right, but that's another story.'

Alison watched Marjorie Tyler listening patiently. She must have heard it a million times, judging by the bored look on her face. 'Anthropology was always beyond me, Dr Tyler. Why do you need a sacrifice to guarantee anything?'

He shrugged. 'You're from New England, Mrs Fenway. An old family?'

'On my mother's side, yes. She was true Boston brahmin, and earlier than that too.'

Marjorie suddenly looked interested. 'Much earlier, my dear?'

'Right back to the Pilgrim Fathers. The Parkers were on the *Mayflower*. We even had someone at Salem when all that witch nonsense was happening. Rosalind Parker. Rosalind was . . .'

She stared at the huge skeleton taking shape on the grass and went silent.

'Burned, I imagine?' Tyler offered.

'Yes,' she replied quietly. The Tylers exchanged impenetrable glances.

'Primitive people hold primitive beliefs,' John Tyler continued. 'Why do we need Christmas? Why do we drink the blood of Christ? Human beings like rituals. Still do. Although our distant, pre-Christian ancestors weren't as primitive as many think. The timing is quite deliberate. The autumnal equinox, the point at which day ceases to be longer than night, when the god of darkness moves into supremacy

13

over the god of light. There are a million stories – the Welsh Blodeuwedd, John Barleycorn – but they all tend to the same view. Renewal through a token sacrifice guarantees the return of light. And with it prosperity, the fecundity of the land. Not a lot on your side of the pond except for the Native American Corn God cycle. The Puritans saw to that. I do think America would have been more interesting if the red man had won, don't you?'

'I guess that's what they teach in class these days.'

Tyler peered intently into her face. 'Oh yes. And you need fire too. A cleansing fire. That seems to be a common thread.'

Dammit, Miles. You told him. You probably told the lot of them.

Which was, she knew, quite ridiculous. She turned her back on the Burning Man. 'So that's it? This weird cricket stuff you do? A bonfire?'

Marjorie Tyler giggled. 'Not quite, darling,' she said, in a thick, ginny Home Counties drawl. She made a little dance around them, singing in a wavering, high-pitched voice.

'Little Sir John of the nut brown bowl
And the brandy in his glass
Aye, little Sir John of the nut brown bowl
Proved the strongest man at last
For the huntsman he can't hunt the fox
Nor loudly blow his horn
And the tinker can't mend either kettle or pots
Wi'out a little John Barleycorn.'

John Tyler watched her icily. 'Traditionally one gets as pissed as a parrot on Burning Man day. And my wife, as you may have gathered, is a great stickler for tradition.'

By seven in the evening, when the sun was setting some-where over Romney Marsh, most of Beulah seemed to have joined Marjorie Tyler in her interpretation of the ritual. The bar of the Green Man was heaving with locals and a ragged band of bohemian outsiders who had hitched a ride to the proceedings.

In essence, Alison gathered, this was a village fete. But Beulah, of course, had to have its variations. A local farmer, a fierce-looking man with a bushy grey beard, had herded a flock of ducks across the Minnis, using a couple of hungry-looking sheepdogs. The long, white birds, with extended necks, like Masai women snatched from Africa and trans-formed by witchcraft, walked through tiny gates, up and down a miniature wooden bridge. A small crowd looked on mutely. They must have watched this year in and year out, she guessed. Perhaps John Tyler was right and Burn-ing Man had been here for ever. The duckherd too. A thousand years before, you could have stood on this very spot, yawning in half-drunk admiration at the same pointless ceremony.

Then the stalls were cleared away and the small, bustling crowd moved to the pub. The air had the delicious promise of autumn, overlaid with the cruder smell of charcoal and burnt meat. Miles was inside. 'Mixing,' he said. He was turning out to be a good mixer. During the week she hardly saw him. At weekends, he could scarcely wait to get into the pub and let his hair down with the locals.

She didn't begrudge this. They still made love in the afternoon, and one day the magic would work. He had even bought his own charms, the furtive collection of 'sex aids' he kept hidden in a box in the cupboard. Velvet sashes, a blindfold, tie-me-up, tie-me-down stuff. Next time, she promised herself, the curtains would stay closed.

Back in London, Miles worked hard, harder than either of them could ever have contemplated. At weekends the mantle of the City fell from his shoulders. He dressed like a country brute, got an enormous kick from charging round the garden on his new miniature tractor. He looked so young again, playing the country squire, and she loved that part of him. She loved Priory House more and more too. The three-storeyed pile was imposing without being grand. It demanded to be lived in. Sometimes she felt it quietly cursed her for failing to fill the spare bedrooms with kids and the noisy, sprawling detritus of a real family.

Even the pub had a positive effect. GPs and farmhands, lawyers and postmen, gamekeepers and the odd, stray accountant – the Green Man seemed to attract an extraordinary mix of men to its long, central bar. They stood there for hours, beneath the dried hop garlands, wreathed in smoke, talking about anything, absolutely anything, but business. Miles came back bright and sparkling, and only a touch pissed. He needed the break from the bank. They both did.

Alison finished her third glass of Beaujolais. Almost immediately another appeared in front of her face, carried by a long, slim arm encased in the loose folds of a rather dated cheesecloth shirt.

'Bottoms up,' Sara Harrison said and chinked their glasses together. 'If the buggers in there can get arseholed, so can we.'

'Thanks.'

'Don't thank me. This one's on Granny.'

The old woman was two tables away, peering at them through the crowd, holding up a half of bitter. 'Chiz!' yelled a cracked voice through the hubbub.

They both returned the gesture. 'Wow,' Alison gasped. 'I hope to Christ I can still party like that at her age.'

'Granny's a figurehead here. Has she invited you into the windmill yet?'

16

'No.'

Sara shrugged. 'Too early, I suppose. When you go in for a cup of tea there, you really have arrived in Beulah.'

'Can't wait.' Alison tried the wine. It tasted more bitter somehow.

'They've drunk the last bottle of the decent stuff,' Sara said, watching her. 'Now we're down to the cooking plonk, I'm afraid. I'll get you a gin if you want?'

Alison shook her head quickly, fearing that a second's hesitation would send Sara back to the crowded bar, fighting for a double. 'I think it may start coming out of my ears in a moment.'

'Moderation,' Sara agreed. 'An excellent idea. You don't mind me asking but you're trying to conceive, aren't you? Drink and fags reduce the chances awfully, they say. And if Miles's little wrigglers do hit the spot, the chances are they won't stick. Not if you don't give up.'

Alison tried to think straight through the booze cloud beginning to fog her mind. 'He told you that?'

'Who?' Sara was puzzled. 'Oh, you mean Miles. Good Lord, no. Doesn't have to. You don't need to be Sherlock Holmes to work it out. Either a bundle is on the way, or you're working at it. Fancy a burger? I do.'

Alison mumbled something that sounded like yes. Sara grabbed the passing Mitch Blamire by the shoulder and yelled, 'Be a darling and get us a couple of burgers off the barbie, Mitch. Pint of Spit in it for you.'

'I didn't realise it was that obvious,' Alison said.

Mitch Blamire returned swiftly with two charred lumps of unidentifiable meat stuffed inside a soft Tesco bun, then shuffled back to the bar. The burger didn't taste too bad. Alison hadn't realised how hungry she was.

'Seasons. Everything in life comes down to seasons. Been trying long?'

You had to tell someone. The secret couldn't stay locked

17

in Manhattan for ever. 'Too long. I miscarried last year. Twelve weeks in.'

Sara stared at her, aghast, then put a soft hand on her shoulder. 'Bugger. What a cretin I am.'

Sara was tall, almost six foot, and willowy thin. She always seemed to wear loose, shapeless clothes, on this occasion a long, flowing purple skirt that came to her ankles and a baggy cheesecloth top. Her hair was a mess, a big, bright-orange tangle of curls that seemed to shoot out of her head in all directions. Which was odd, because Alison thought that, underneath it all, Sara was probably extremely attractive. She had an open, honest face, lightly covered with freckles, long, with high cheekbones. And bright-blue eyes that always looked surprised, never ceasing to dart everywhere, looking for the next wonder in the world.

They seemed so different. Alison was the product of a standard, broken New England home. Skinny, smart, and scatty, she had fallen through life, tumbling from bad stage school into the black art of marketing, tumbling into beds, into marriage, all the while turning to her anxious, pale attractiveness to get her out of whatever mess happened to come along. Sara was probably her own age, no more than thirty-three or -four, but so *exotic*. Alison couldn't begin to guess what made her like this. She only knew there was something about Sara she liked.

'You don't need to apologise,' Alison said, smiling. 'Why do people always do that? These things happen all the time.'

'All the same, I was being forward. Me all over.' Sara stuffed the remains of the burger into her mouth and mumbled something utterly incomprehensible.

'Pardon?'

'I *said* . . .' Sara took a deep swig of wine. 'I'm in the same boat too. On the conceiving front. Although you're one step ahead of me. At least you know whose little wrigglers are supposed to be doing the job.'

Alison wondered how much she'd had to drink. Not that much, surely. She finished her wine, popped through the pub door, tapped Miles on the shoulder and asked him to get a couple of gin and tonics, doubles. He was part of a noisy gaggle of men, most of whom she didn't recognise. He looked happy.

'Going for the big one?' Miles asked, a slight slur in his voice. He gazed behind her. Sara was inside now too, peering at him through the smoke. 'Hope you're not leading my little girl astray, Miss Harrison.'

Sara smiled icily. 'I think your "little girl" is capable of making her own decisions, Miles.'

'Oh shit,' he barked to the grinning gaggle at the bar. 'Foot in mouth again.'

Harry Blamire was looking at them. 'Generally speaking, this is a men's area,' he said. 'When it's Burning Man, anyway.'

'Oh,' Sara said, mock apologetically. 'I *am* sorry. Back to your discourse, gents. What is it tonight? Wittgenstein? Kant?'

'Mind your language, gel,' Harry cautioned. He looked more like an upright bull terrier than ever. His glassy eyes glowered back at them, uncomprehending.

They backed out of the bar, both convulsed in hysterical laughter.

'*"Mind your language, gel!"*' Sara roared.

It was dark now, the night seemed to have fallen on a sudden lurch of gravity. Granny Jukes was fast asleep on one of the pub benches, her back to the wall. She was snoring like an ancient walrus. Alison shivered. Someone was starting to work on the bonfire, spreading petrol around the base. She could smell the harshness of the fuel. The straw effigy was nowhere to be seen.

'At least that's one set of little wrigglers you don't need to worry about.'

19

'Harry?' Sara asked, suddenly serious. 'Oh, I don't know. He's fit. And strong. And both the boys – God, why do we all call them that, they're nearly fifty – both of them are a lot brighter than they act.'

'You could not, for one second, countenance . . .' Alison was lost for words.

'I'm thirty-four. Not quite mutton dressed as lamb yet, but not far off. One reason I'm in this fix is I've been too choosy. Perhaps I should start lowering the entry barriers.'

'Not that much.'

Sara went quiet. Alison wondered if she had gone too far.

'We're different,' Sara said eventually. 'You want to have Miles's baby because it's for the two of you. I just want one for *me*. I don't care what happens afterwards. He can bugger off to Australia if he wants. Or just fall off his perch.'

Alison wasn't sure she liked this sudden serious turn in the conversation. 'You could get it done. Artificial insemination. Whatever.'

'Hah!' Sara laughed, and her wild hair blocked out the faint but growing image of the moon for a moment. 'I *could* give Harry Blamire an empty yoghurt pot and a copy of *Playboy*.'

If you were that desperate, Alison wondered, why not?

'Because,' said Sara, almost reading her mind, 'it just wouldn't be right. I want to conceive. Properly. With a man, grunting and sweating over me. I want to *feel* that happen. Not have some boring GP like John Tyler put on a pair of rubber gloves and start poking inside me with a syringe or whatever, like someone trying to spray greenfly on tomatoes.'

'You might feel differently if there were medical reasons.'

'I might,' Sara said, calming down. 'But there aren't. I just haven't found the right occasion. Not yet. But I will.

You will. Fate, darling. You found Priory House. Or it found you. Which was it by the way?'

The question echoed dully in her head. Miles had inherited the house from this dead, distant relative she had never met while she was in the clinic, struggling to regain what equilibrium she might possess. The process that took them from the apartment in Manhattan to this slightly faded mansion in the wilds of England was still somewhat hazy. She no longer cared about the details. It was right. That was all that mattered.

'I don't have a clue,' she replied. 'And, frankly, I don't give a damn.'

Sara punched her lightly on the shoulder. 'That's the spirit. We'll make you English yet. Lady of the Manor. Queen of the May.'

Alison took a sip of the gin and tonic. It tasted warm and flat. She'd had too much to drink. Her head felt heavy. She didn't feel like staying up to watch the Burning Man. It was just a bonfire after all.

'Maybe tonight,' Sara said, quietly changing the subject. 'Something in the air.'

Alison tried to work out what she was talking about. Finally, it came. 'You mean, with someone here? Someone in the pub? Just anyone?'

The bright-blue eyes were on her now, not letting go. 'Why not? You and Miles should be thinking about it too. That's what Burning Man is about, after all. I'm not exactly an expert on all these little folk customs – John Tyler is the man for that. But I'll bet you anything that there's a little legend that says this is a wonderful moment to conceive. That if you find the right man tonight, he can plant a seed inside you, and you'll feel it grow, through the winter, through the long cold nights. And then, come – when would it be, June? – you bring some life into the world. If we get our little wrigglers tonight, Alison, we'd both be as big as

21

hippos and ready to whelp by Midsummer's Eve. What do you think?'

Alison stared into the pub and couldn't help saying it. The beer was flowing. The men looked as if they'd never leave the bar. 'I think, looking at the state Miles is getting himself in, I've a fat chance tonight. And you've got even less.'

Sara Harrison turned to stare at the Minnis. The smell of petrol was becoming intense. There was still no sign of the straw man.

'Sorry,' Alison mumbled. 'It's the booze. It depresses me sometimes.'

'No offence taken,' Sara replied, smiling warmly again.

'Need to go.' Alison lurched off to the floodlit alley that led to the rear of the pub and the back door, praying it would still be unlocked. She didn't want to press her way through the throng of smoking, bellowing men standing between the front door and the loos. Even if Miles was feeling frisky tonight, she wasn't willing to oblige, not with all the blindfolds, all the wind-up gizmos in his toy box. They'd had their chance in the afternoon.

She wondered about Sara. She ought to get to know her better. Sara was like just about everyone in the village. Not quite what she seemed. Beneath the old hippie exterior she was smart, engaged, challenging to be with. She would become her friend. Maybe one day they would grow happily fat together, sit side by side on one of the benches that dotted the Minnis, waiting for deliverance.

Alison turned the corner and blinked, felt suddenly drunk. The floodlit alley led her into nothingness, a big black pool of darkness at the back of the pub. She couldn't see a thing, but there was someone there. No. More than one person. They were rolling around on the ground, grunting. She could hear the sound of bodies moving, falling painfully. And then a man began to scream, an awful scream, loud and high and terrifying.

'*Miles!*'

This was like the bad time, she thought.

'*Miles! MILES!*'

An arm on her shoulder. A scent she recognised.

'Jesus Christ,' Sara yelled into the dark. 'What the hell is going on?'

A lone security light from the car park was triggered by someone running past them. For the brief instant it was on, Alison saw . . . *what?* Men on the ground. Fighting. Trying to contain something, someone. Both the Blamires were there. She could identify their compact, muscular shapes. But the rest were impossible to recognise. The light came on and then it was gone. Miles could not have been among them. It was impossible. Impossible, too, that the effigy was there as well. The light was deceptive. It flashed so briefly.

'Sodding animals,' Sara yelled, and took her arm firmly, turned her around and marched her back to the front of the pub.

'Another drink,' Sara ordered, and thrust a glass of whisky into her hand. 'Down the hatch.'

It tasted like fire in her mouth.

'Probably the bloody antis again.'

'What?'

Sara shook her head. 'Oh. I keep forgetting. You're so new. The antis. They had the beagles running at Wye today, and that always brings them out. They come here because they know Beulah won't let the hunt through. But that doesn't mean we want a bunch of scruffy travellers on the doorstep either. Particularly not tonight.'

Alison looked inside the pub. The men were at the bar again, Miles among them. They looked tense. They weren't speaking. The Blamires were nowhere to be seen. Alison felt a flame of tipsy anger sear through her head. She strode to the bar and stabbed Miles deliberately in the shoulder. 'What the hell were you up to?'

The side of his head was grazed. His eyes looked wild. The rest of the crowd at the bar watched the two of them sullenly.

'There was a fight,' Miles muttered. '*OK?*'

'A fight?' She was outraged and she didn't know why. 'Jesus Christ! You were in a fight? What do you think you are? Eighteen years old all over again?'

He sighed, and very deliberately took a long, deep draught from his glass.

'I think,' she said, 'that's quite enough.'

'You're making a scene,' he said calmly.

'*I'm* making a scene? You're rolling around on the ground like some drunken animal, brawling, and *I'm* making a scene?'

'There was a fight,' he repeated. 'We went to break it up.'

The crowd smirked silently, as if they were waiting for this dénouement all along.

'To break it up?' she repeated lamely.

'That's right. To break it up.'

Norman, the landlord, leaned over the counter. 'Folk sometimes get a touch excited here at Burning Man, Mrs Fenway. Nothing serious. Sorry and all, but that's why we suggest the ladies watch the fun from outside. Just this one night.'

'Goddamn idiots,' she muttered, and hated the laughter in their eyes.

Miles reached over the bar and ordered a triple Scotch. His face looked a touch more conciliatory. 'It's OK, love. Get yourself a grandstand position. The show's about to start. And when it does I'll be out there with you. Promise.'

She looked out of the arched windows of the pub. The Blamire boys were struggling past with the straw figure in their arms, heading for the bonfire, making a meal of their efforts. Flames were licking at the base of the wooden teepee on the Minnis. The moon was bright and full, a harvest moon, the colour of gold. It looked like the lesser cousin of the sun, an indolent yellow giant barely able to keep its glory above the horizon.

She took a deep gulp of the Scotch, made Miles buy another just to be on the safe side, and wandered unsteadily outside.

Night in the village was a revelation. Some time soon she would sit out in the garden and do nothing but stare at the jewelled glory of the stars. Beulah was close to seven hundred feet above sea level, one of the highest points in south-east England. Here you could forget about pollution from artificial light or the internal combustion engine. The Minnis had only a scattering of sodium lamps around the perimeter. Even with the combined illumination of every one of the thirty or so houses that made up the village, the sky was still dominant. The air was so clean it felt as if it scoured the lungs. There was nothing between you and the universe, nothing at all.

She kept her back to the bonfire, trying to ignore the drunken yelps and screams, and let the sky fill her head. It had been a standing joke at school that you could always tell when someone was really wasted or stoned. They just stood outside, mouth wide open, gawping up at the heavens, trying to remember what the Plough looked like, how to tell the difference between a star and a planet, where to find Andromeda. And she never could remember. It didn't take away the sense of wonder, not one bit.

Alison fixed her attention on the rolling depth of space above her, the dark, velvety folds of the night. Then the fireworks began, and Beulah came back into her head once more.

'Drink and a bun, dear?' It was Marjorie Tyler, holding in one hand, quite steadily, a mug of something, steam rising out of the rim, and in the other a plate of cakes. She looked almost sober. Perhaps, Alison thought to herself, she had simply drunk right through the intoxication phase straight back to some semblance of sobriety. She wished she knew the trick.

'What is it?' Talk about mixing drinks. She'd been through everything from cheap Beaujolais to the fearsome strong beer called Bishop's Finger, gin and tonic, and, somewhere along the way, a Glenmorangie or four. If Sara was right and alcohol really could reduce your ability to conceive it was unlikely she would have a child this side of Christmas 2030.

'Kent apple punch. Good local cider. Spices. And a touch of our local apple brandy too. And a cake. You need a little ballast too, you know.'

Alison took a swig from the mug. The aroma of fresh apples and cinnamon raced through her head, with an afterburn of raw spirit. It felt wonderful. Then she devoured two of the buns in short order. They tasted like apple muffins with an odd herby kick.

'Good, eh?' Marjorie beamed. 'I know how to make a cocktail. You should try my whisky sour some time.'

'Not before breakfast, thanks.' Alison could hear the fire crackling behind her. One more minute and she'd take a look. 'Have the antis gone?'

Marjorie looked baffled. 'Were they here?'

'Apparently. There was a fight.'

'Oh, dear. Mind you, if it hadn't been them, someone else would have done just as well. Men and drink do not mix. In love with the world one moment. Itching to kick the living daylights out of it the next. Then they blame it on testosterone when really we all know it's nothing but Johnnie Walker and umpteen pints of Shepherd Neame. Hypocrites. Every last one of them.'

'Quite.' The reviving effect of the punch didn't last long. She was starting to feel giddy again.

Marjorie peered at her. It made Alison feel awkward.

'You are going to watch, aren't you?'

'Bonfires aren't really my scene.'

'It's not as if they're burning Rosalind Parker for a witch all over again now, is it?'

She wished the woman would go away. Her head felt terrible. The cakes had an odd, earthy aftertaste. 'What do you mean?'

'It's about us. The ceremony. Burning Man goes back centuries.'

'Yonks even, as you guys say.'

Marjorie Tyler took one puzzled look at her, then disappeared into the night without saying a word. Alison breathed deeply, hoping for a miracle, and turned around. Or rather *tried to*. Some odd kind of disconnection occurred when her brain issued the 'move' command to her feet. It took too long to arrive, with the result that the rest of her body gyrated while her toes stayed exactly where they were. This was, she realised, as the night turned turtle, and horizontal moved to vertical in front of her eyes, a classic drunk fall.

Youfuggindruggedmeyoufugginbitchyoufuggindruggedme. Did the words come out? Or just drift lazily inside her head, falling from one ear to the other and then rebounding when they hit the inner lining of her skull?

Alison rolled giddily on the ground, aware that she was making a noise of some kind, but not one she could identify. She found herself on all fours, thinking, deep down in the subterranean turmoil of what passed just then for consciousness, *I hope to God I don't crawl into some dogshit*. It could be a dream, of course. It could be like that old, old story she read one time, where they hanged a man and, in between them setting the trap of his gallows and the noose snapping his neck, there was an entire, credible episode of life, full of incident, as real as anything could be.

She crawled, slowly, towards the forest of legs by the blaze, listening to the unintelligible low mumble come out of her mouth . . . *Miles, Miles, wherethefugareyew?*

Then she looked into the flames and there was nothing else in her head. *Fire.* She wasn't dreaming. Not even the best of her nightmares had this kind of clarity. Alison could feel the heat prickling her cheeks, smell the great golden beast devouring itself, smacking its flaming, acrid chops. The burning wood sang and hissed, the air was thick with soot and embers.

Miles, Miles.

Not a dream, too uncomfortable for that. Her elbows hurt from dragging her body along the grass. The stench of the blaze was so real it stole the oxygen from her lungs. And she felt sick too, felt ready to barf everything from the last six hours on the grass (and just the thought of spewing made a stomach contents list run straight through her head, like a report from an autopsy, burgers and crisps, beer and wine, whisky, gin, Marjorie Tyler's odd little cakes, the apple punch, and the thought of that made a cinnamon burp rise deep from her guts).

Alison retched pathetically, saw a gap in the forest of legs where there were no flames behind, tried to grab one of the dark, tall tree trunks around her, failed, then pushed herself up into a crouch. This was a precious space: the heat had not yet reached her. From this odd position on the ground she could peer up through the unburned timbers to see the night untouched by flame.

And see the Burning Man.

Ofugofugofug.

It stood atop the bonfire, still intact. The flames played

28

around its lower quarters for maximum theatrical effect. The gigantic straw figure seemed to her a mile high, tall enough to let you climb to the moon through its wispy, golden hair which danced maniacally on the updraught. There was a commotion in the crowd, voices (the Blamire boys, the Blamire boys, you can always rely on the Blamire boys). Someone – a dark, stocky figure wreathed in smoke – walked up to the fire, jerked a can and petrol flew through the night air. A wall of flame shot skywards, bit into the Burning Man's legs, raced across his vast, golden torso, sent coursing rivers of fire through his head, his hair.

Two deep, empty holes in the straw head. Alison looked into Burning Man's eyes.

They looked back.

Inside the huge straw effigy something moved, struggling. She shook her head, felt a thin stream of bile fall from the corner of her mouth, struggled to make some real kind of sound, to drag herself to her feet.

Miles!

She lurched at the nearest figure, tried to hold onto its clothes. Someone moved away. Someone laughed.

MILESGODDAMNYOU!

And looked at the Burning Man again. Now he was truly ablaze. The flames raced through the straw structure, a long finger of fire pointing at the sky. Behind the orange and yellow inferno, something . . . She shook her head again, trying to clear it. *A dark shape moving.*

She wished she were sober. *'Mi –'*

Two hands came down and pulled her roughly to her feet. The familiar face of her husband looked down at her. He wore a puzzled smile.

'Oh my,' Miles said, sounding very sober. 'You did go for the big one now, didn't you?'

Alison felt small and stupid and terribly grateful for his

presence. Miles always did come to rescue her in the end. 'In the fire . . . Didn't you see?'

He laughed. 'See what?'

'*A man!*'

Miles put his big, powerful arms around her, held her tight, humming nothing in particular.

'I asked a question,' she mumbled into the folds of his jacket. He peered into her face, calm, in control. She knew that expression oh so well. It was the Fenway version of consolation.

'You still get spooked by what happened in New York, don't you?'

'*Miles, I saw . . .*'

'Shush.' He put a big, fat finger to her lips. It tasted of smoke and burnt food. 'It's my fault. I should have seen this was wrong. I thought . . .'

'*I saw . . .*'

'I thought,' he continued, interrupting her, 'that you might be ready to face things. God, I can be so stupid at times.'

She didn't say anything. It was pointless. He hugged her tight into his jacket. The smell of smoke was overwhelming. She couldn't get it out of her head. There was another smell there. Like meat, burning.

'I love you, Alison.' There were tears in his eyes. She didn't have the heart to tell him it was the drink talking, that he was wearing the biggest pair of beer goggles ever made. The world was spinning again. The fire seemed to be getting bigger all the time. Its stench hung over everything. 'I'll do anything to make you happy. I'll move heaven and earth. You're so beautiful. It breaks me up seeing you like this.'

Fugginshutupyouidiotiknowhatisaw.

It was all going again. Marjorie Tyler's cakes seemed to be growing inside her gut, getting so big they felt like a

30

false pregnancy (and I know what the real one's like, Alison thought, *I know*).

In the bonfire something exploded, with a sound like gunfire. She closed her eyes and the image was still there: blackened flesh, flames licking over its leathery surface, eyes popping out of their sockets, the last scraps of hair on fire. Then she fell, into a sea of arms, all waiting to cushion her, carry her, out of the heat, out of the night. To somewhere safe and familiar where they would wash the smell of smoke from her hair, from her skin, wash it clean out of her life.

The curtains were open. Bright sunshine poured into the bedroom. Alison Fenway rolled over in bed and looked at the clock. It was ten fifteen. She rolled back and looked at Miles. He lay on his back, naked, mouth open, emitting a rattling, energetic snore. The room was cold and stank of beer, farts and something else her wounded brain could not yet name. She dragged the duvet around her, walked over to the window and threw it open. Chill September air rushed to greet her. Alison stuck her head out of the window and took several painful breaths. There was a noise on the Minnis. To her astonishment Harry Blamire was there, driving the cricket club's ancient tractor, round and round the outfield, mowing the pitch.

'Goddamn hicks,' she croaked, and was then reduced to a fit of painful coughing. Still wrapped in the duvet she stumbled back to the bed and threw herself on it, as hard as she could. She watched Miles's dark, flaccid body bounce up and down when she landed. His face was covered in dry, animal stubble. The widget, as he was wont to call it, nestled at his groin. It was unusually red, which puzzled her.

'Smoke,' Alison said suddenly, out of nowhere. It was

31

coming back. The worst part of any hangover: the memories. Crawling on the damp grass behind the bonfire, trying to avoid the dogshit, scared to death, shrieking at the thought that there was something alive inside the straw effigy, something that moved. And screaming, mindlessly, at the top of her voice, some crap about wrigglers and antis and why *couldn't* anyone else see what was going on?

Alison took a long, deep breath and absolutely refused to utter those useless words 'never again'. Then thought about a shower. But hadn't there been one anyway, after they carried her back to the house? The room stank of smoke. She didn't. Her ragged sense of perception just might be detecting the faintest odour of soap on her skin.

She shrugged off the idea, threw her arm over her eyes in what was, she knew, a horribly clichéd expression of pain. Something soft and wispy fell across her face. Alison took her arm away and examined her right wrist. Tied around it, tightly enough to be immobile, was a cream silk sash from Miles's toy box.

Her mind beginning to work at last, Alison hitched herself up in bed and threw the duvet to the floor. There was the faint, but discernible, mark of a sash on her left wrist too, and the same on each ankle. She stared in the bedside mirror. On either side of her eyes were two light-pink bands, like faint sunburn. There was also, she realised, beginning to feel both angry and sick, a distinct redness to one side of her mouth. She licked her lips and let her tongue go to the corner. It felt like the kind of fuzzy pain you got with a cold sore, distant but unmistakable.

She got up and walked over to the wardrobe where Miles kept 'his things'. The toy box was still open. The sashes had been lazily stuffed in the open top. She counted them: five. With the one attached to her wrist . . .

Something hot and uncontrollable began to wake in her head. She walked over to the bed, stood on it with one stride

32

and looked at him. The widget *was* red. Cursing, she kicked him as hard as she could in the rear and watched the dark form career off the side of the divan. Miles rolled over once, screamed and then opened his eyes. It took, she thought, a mere five seconds for the tell-tale stain of guilt to start to form on his face.

'You *bastard*, Miles!'

'Uhhhhhhhh.' He moaned, swallowed on a dry throat, and looked sickly.

'You utter bastard.'

'Uhhhhhhhh.'

She leapt down from the bed, kicked him hard again on the backside. 'Shut up. You bastard.'

'I think,' Miles whined, 'I've got that message. Is that for anything in particular or am I just generally responsible for whatever happens to be troubling you right now?'

'You shit,' she said, waving the silk sash in his face. '*This* happens to be troubling me. Are we hearing bells now?'

He looked at the cream thing flapping through the air and groaned again.

'There are,' she continued, 'games I will play, Miles, though God knows why because, frankly, they do nothing for me. However, they do *not* include being tied up, blind-folded and *gagged*, for God's sake, while I am totally uncon-scious. Being incapable of saying no does not count as consent, Miles. Is there any part of that statement you don't understand?'

She hated him when he looked like this. He was so pitiful she ended up forgiving him anything. Men, Alison thought, could be so pathetic at times.

'Sorry,' he mumbled. Something flickered in his eyes. He was starting to look a touch alert. He was remembering, and Alison was absolutely certain she wanted to be somewhere else before he remembered much more.

She undid the sash on her wrist, with some difficulty, then

dropped it gently onto his chest. 'I am having a shower. Then I am going for a walk. I do not wish to speak with you this side of lunch, Miles. Which you will be cooking for yourself.'

He eyed her from the bed, searching for something in her face. It was a new expression, she thought. Miles still had some surprises. 'You won't complain if it works though, will you?' he said. 'Burning Man. And all that.'

'Bullshit!' Alison stormed into the bathroom and walked straight beneath the icy cold shower.

By eleven, after a breakfast of orange juice, two large mugs of coffee and a small bowl of Special K, Alison was out of the door. There'd been not a sound from Miles. She knew what the routine would be on a day like this. He would surface at one, cook an enormous fried breakfast, and be as sweet as pie to her for the rest of the day. It worked. Usually.

Alison walked out of the front gate and strode onto the green, setting a fair pace, hoping to blow away the cobwebs of booze, smoke and anything else that might be lurking inside. She felt old, tired and not a little betrayed. She could live with Miles's games. If they made him happy, that was fine. All men were boys. Boys with money. Her mother had drilled that into her in the beginning. But there had to be lines, and spatchcocking your wife *with a gag and blindfold* while she was, to all intents and purposes, dead to the world represented one of them.

Nor, for the life of her, could she understand what Miles got out of it. Was that all she meant to him? A doll to jump on? No, she didn't believe that for one minute. Miles loved her, deeply, irrevocably. She could just about remember his drunken testament to this fact the previous night. Perhaps the sashes, the gag and the blindfold were some booze-fuelled attempt at intimacy. Perhaps she ought to be grateful. At least Miles's little game pushed the horrid, deathly image of the bonfire to the back of her head. Next to the very real hallucination that someone was being burned alive in front of a village gathering in south-east England, Miles's odd little attempts at a form of necrophilia seemed mere peccadilloes.

'Penny for them.' Sara Harrison seemed to appear out of nowhere. Alison had walked from one side of the cricket pitch to the other, undisturbed, unknowing. She looked around. Harry Blamire was off his tractor now, doing something around the remains of last night's fire.

'Pipe dreams,' Alison said. 'I was praying for a total blood change and the permanent erasure of some less than pleasant memories.'

'Ah.' Sara was beaming, full of life. Not a trace of a hangover, and that was remarkable, Alison thought. She was sure they'd been matching each other, drink for drink, during the evening. 'Stop that, Yappy.'

The dog, a tense little Jack Russell, was digging away at one of the patchwork of molehills that covered the Minnis.

'Let me guess,' Sara continued. 'You had some of Marjorie's cakes.'

'And just about everything Norman happens to sell over the bar of the Green Man. As, I might say, did you.' She felt quite offended that Sara didn't look hung over. It was against the laws of nature. Perhaps this was just one of Beulah's many gifts.

'Yes, but I didn't have any of Marjorie's cakes. Come on, Alison. 'Fess up. How many?'

'God knows. Three? I can't really remember.'

'Oh, *dear*.'

Alison sighed and watched Yappy dive into another mole-hill. 'This is all getting much too weird for me. What's wrong with Marjorie's cakes?'

Sara shrugged. Her eyes weren't the slightest bit blood-shot. 'Hard as this may be to believe, Marjorie is one of your original hippies. She has, how shall I put it, a chemical constitution. Not just gin and illicit hooch. If you take a look in her greenhouse you'll see what I'm getting at. Toms and lettuce ain't growing there. Not at all.'

'What do you mean?'

'It's an open secret. Third Saturday of each month John and Marjorie catch the BA shuttle to Amsterdam from Gatwick. He . . . well, God knows what John gets up to there. I really wouldn't like to imagine. But Marjorie has a lot of friends in the *pharmaceuticals* business. She comes back with a few packets of seeds and grows them out back. Nothing for sale, mind you. If you ask, she'll just give you the stuff. Powerful weed. But then you seem to know that already.'

Alison felt drained. She simply loathed the idea of people doing something to her body without her knowing. 'You mean last night I wasn't only dead drunk but high on home-grown pot cakes served by the wife of our friendly local GP?'

'About sums it up.'

'*Damn!*'

'Burning Man, Alison. Gets a bit wild around here.' Sara was working so hard to be sympathetic.

'You might have told me.'

'About Marjorie? I didn't notice, honestly. I just thought you'd sloped off home pissed, so I watched the bonfire. Next thing I know you're crawling through on all fours screaming bloody murder about there being somebody *inside*.'

'Oh, Jesus . . . what a way to introduce yourself to the village.'

Sara patted her heartily on the back. 'Don't worry. Most people were so far gone they didn't even notice. And as I keep saying to you, it was Burning Man. It's like the Oktoberfest. Whatever you do – *whatever* – it's forgotten

36

the day after. If we had a few more Catholics, we'd probably have automatic forgiveness, available on demand, just like they do in Munich.'

'That would come in useful.' Alison was thinking of the sash.

'Enough about you,' Sara said, beaming. 'Let's talk about me for a moment. Let's talk about me and the wrigglers. Remember?'

It was amazing how the brain could bury a memory underneath half a gallon of alcohol and retrieve it in a millisecond. 'You're not serious. You didn't. Who?'

'Who cares? And that would be telling. Burning Man is supposed to be a shagfest. It would be impolite to rat. All that matters is it worked. Put your hand here.' She took Alison's hand and placed it gently on her flat, trim stomach. 'Can you feel it?'

Alison did her best to smile. 'Not exactly. But then I can't feel much at the moment.'

'It worked, Alison. It *worked*. A few weeks from now I'll be peering at the little jar of pee, watching it go blue, and then it's down to dirty John Tyler for confirmation. I *know* it.'

'Then,' Alison said, 'you must be right.' And thought: *the woman is crazier than me. At least I know what it feels like.*

'I'm not mad you know. Just because I don't want to broadcast the father's name to the world.' That unnerving prescience again.

Alison took Sara's hand and placed it on her own stomach. 'What do you feel?'

Sara looked uncomfortable. 'Something happened? Last night?'

'Something happened,' Alison agreed. 'Don't ask me what because I don't think I was quite conscious.'

'Now that *is* spooky.'

'Quite.' She wasn't going to say anything. Not unless she was pushed. 'So what do you feel, Sara?'

Sara took her hand away. 'I don't think it works with other people. Sorry.'

Alison shrugged. 'Never mind. The state Miles was in he probably didn't get there anyway. We will do it, you know.'

'That's the spirit and . . . oh God, that damned dog.' Yappy was digging up more of the cricket pitch. 'He's got so much energy. And I need to go home and make some calls.'

'I'll take him. I feel like a walk.'

'You're a real love. And when you get back I'll make you some apple tea. Guaranteed to cure all hangovers.'

Sara marched off back to her little cottage at the southern end of the Minnis. Alison found herself watching her go, feeling inwardly content. There was going to be a friendship there. She could sense it with the same certainty that Sara felt about her little wrigglers. And she needed that friendship. Miles was not enough. Sometimes there was too much of the child in him.

The dog looked up at her as if to say, 'Let's go.' There was the hint of autumn on the green. The sky had lost some of its summer fire. It was now a pale, eggshell blue, striped with wisps of cirrus. Alison clapped her hands and watched the dog turn tail and race around the perimeter of the pitch, its rear end bobbing up and down like a child's fluffy white toy. She laughed: it was a ridiculous sight. Then she followed it, feeling happier. Everyone gets drunk from time to time, everyone gets embarrassing. Even without Marjorie Tyler's unasked-for additional assistance.

Soon she was opposite Priory House. She stopped and looked at the place that was now home, thanks to the odd legacy of a distant relative who, as far she understood it, Miles scarcely knew in any case. It was, the more she looked at it, rather magnificent. They'd swapped a two-bedroom apartment in midtown Manhattan for this vast, imposing pile that stood over the Minnis like some feudal lord with a crusty countenance that was part Georgian, part Elizabethan or even earlier. The upstairs curtains were open. The smell of frying bacon was doubtless drifting from the Aga already. Miles on apology duty. It didn't happen often but when it did there was always a certain fun to be had. Perhaps she'd send him in to Whitstable for a fresh lobster or oysters. No. There was a sexual connotation there and she did not feel like facing it, today at least.

'Why do we need them at all?' Alison asked herself. 'Why can't you just press a button and have done with it? Instead of . . . all this *humping*.'

Although it was quite enjoyable usually. *When you were awake*.

She was close to the scene of the bonfire now. In the daylight it looked small, pathetic even. It was hard to recreate the image that had been so vivid the previous evening: crouched on all fours, staring up from the forest of legs, seeing this roaring mountain of flame and something living inside, suffering an agonising, fiery death.

'That goddamn Tyler woman's a menace,' Alison muttered, and toyed, only briefly, with the idea of shopping her to the local law. But this nice, new, local copper they talked about probably knew about it too. Society hereabouts was so different from the city. It was as if they made up their own rules, outside everyone else's. Then expected you to conform without even telling you what the boundaries were.

One of the Blamires – it was Harry, she could see the pale lightning streak on his cheek – was now raking away the dusty grey embers of the fire. Bull terrier number two was behind the wheel of the tractor, racing around the pitch at speed, sending up a translucent green haze of cuttings from the grass. Harry gave her a genial smile and said, 'Morning, Mrs Fenway. And how are you today?'

Then he mumbled something she didn't quite catch. It was cold, her head wasn't working properly. He couldn't really have whispered 'nice box' under his breath. It just wasn't possible.

'I feel like shit,' she admitted.

'Don't look it. You'll recover,' Harry said, eyeing her in a way she didn't like one bit. She thought about Sara. It was meant to be a shagfest. Perhaps the ever-horny Harry had provided her little wrigglers.

'Did you have a nice night, Harry?'

'Smashing, Mrs Fenway. And you?'

'Memorable,' she lied.

'Must be hard for you, being a Yank and that.'

'I'm doing my best.'

'Yeah.' He grinned. 'Don't mind me. I'm just plain stupid. London folk are outsiders here until they fit in. Why's it going to be different for the likes of you?'

She'd assumed they were all locals. That Beulah was like this, a perfect piece of rural England, the moment she arrived. 'So we're not the only . . . what's the word?'

'Incomers. Only ones in a while. Need some more, Mrs Fenway. Need kids here, not another little village dying on its feet.'

That was true, she thought. There didn't seem to be a child of school age in the place. 'I'll do what I can.'

'There's no doubt about it, now. None at all.' He was the picture of health. His ruddy face glowed in the chill breeze. He heaved a half-burnt tree trunk out of the way with one swift movement. It was ridiculous, she knew, but there was something about Harry Blamire she mistrusted. And it wasn't just this bright perkiness in the face of her hangover.

'You want some gardening doing? I took the liberty of taking a look out back yesterday. We done it for Miss Emily before she went and hit the bottle down in Spain. We know that garden better than anyone. It could be a real treat.'

'Talk to my husband.'

He stabbed his garden fork hard into the black, scarred

40

earth. 'Reckon I will. But you'll have to excuse me now. This is thirsty work. Don't suppose you fancy a beer?'

Just the thought made her feel queasy. 'Thanks but no.'

Harry Blamire nodded, and walked off purposefully to the pub. The tractor stopped and Mitch did the same. As far as she could see the twins didn't even look at each other, let alone speak.

Yappy came back from a good couple of minutes spent scrabbling in the cold ashes of the bonfire. His white fur was now dappled with charcoal, his face almost pitch black.

She examined him in dismay. 'Oh, Yappy. What will the boss say?'

The dog was seated but could scarcely contain himself. He had a little grin of pride on his face. His paintbrush tail wagged furiously from side to side, and his eyes wouldn't leave her face. Something, a piece of fabric, scorched and ragged, dangled from his mouth.

'OK, pooch, give,' Alison said, putting her hand down to his mouth.

The rag had been only partly consumed by the blaze. It unravelled as the dog let go to reveal itself as a torn piece from a hessian sack, with the fragments of two printed words on it: 'Patern –' and 'Fa –'. Caught up on the loose fibres of the matted rag was something that must have become entangled in it as Yappy rooted around the burnt earth. This thing had seen the very heart of the fire. It was about two inches long, pale grey and covered in drool and ash. Alison stared at the object. Then she put it in her pocket and started back over the green, back towards Sara's house, Yappy in tow, forcing her mind to go blank, refusing to think about this for a single millisecond or countenance sharing the discovery with another person until she understood, fully, what it meant.

Yappy's discovery was the bone from a human finger. There was nothing else in the world it could be.

41

HALLOWEEN

October was glorious, warm and sunny. The cricket season
came to a close. The Minnis fell into autumn, deserted most
days except for solitary dog walkers, parties hunting for late
blackberries among tangles of brambles, and the cognoscenti
who knew where to track down the sloes and obscure wild
edible fungi. Alison took to solitary strolls in the wilder parts
of the common, relishing the way the bracing wind blew
straight off the Channel and made her feel alive. The finger
bone, or whatever it was (the longer she did nothing about
it, the more her doubts grew), was secreted in cotton wool
inside a matchbox stored very carefully in a tiny cupboard
above the Aga. A decision was required, and a careful
one too. Her outburst at the bonfire was too erratic, too
emotional to give her much credibility. She was reluctant to
start shouting murder without some forethought or further
evidence. Then, while these thoughts were settling in her
head, the earth began to shake.

Miles had been lying in bed at eleven in the morning
reading the business section of the *Sunday Times*. Suddenly,
he jumped up with a frightened yelp. Alison had rarely seen
such an expression of terror on his face. It was as if someone
had died. The paper had an exclusive. The bank's great
rival, a Frankfurt house, was rumoured to be launching
a take-over bid. If it went through, it meant that the

three-hundred-year-old traditional house of Mersons would be no more.

Over a late breakfast of French toast and maple syrup, the ginger cat twining between their legs, Miles poring over every one of the broadsheets, fielding calls from colleagues, rivals and the media, she asked, 'What's going to happen?'

He slapped a big dollop of syrup onto the bright yellow bread. 'Darling, if this goes through, one of two things: the Germans will either fire me or ask me to run the whole show.'

'Will they win then?'

'In all probability,' he admitted. 'Frankly, we need global partners. This has been coming for some time, although I rather hoped your fellow countrymen would get in first. A nice, distant American owner would be wonderful.'

She picked at her food, wishing she understood more of the place where he spent most of the waking day. Even in New York his job at the Wall Street branch of Mersons had been a mystery. 'But if they're going to win, why don't you save yourself all this money and effort and negotiate the best deal you can?'

Miles gave her his best condescending smile. 'I wish it were that simple. If we roll over and ask them to tickle our tummies they'll think we're all wimps and fire the lot of us. Quite right too. We have to put up a decent defence just to show them what we're made of. The trouble is . . .' He scratched his chin with a forefinger and fed Thomas a morsel of sweet toast. 'The trouble is judging it correctly. If we throw ourselves into the whole thing too enthusiastically we look like bolshie Little Englanders. And so we're out that way as well. All a question of judgement.'

'Could you get another job?'

'Dunno,' he replied immediately. 'Norman would probably let me pull pints at the Green Man for a while.'

'*Miles*! This is serious.'

'I am being serious. I haven't a clue. I've worked at Mersons all my adult life. I get head-hunted from time to time. But head-hunting rather depends on your status. They get brownie points for pinching someone in a high-profile job. It doesn't count for quite the same thing when you're out of work.'

She was oblivious of the state of their finances. 'What do we have in the bank?'

'Oh.' He made a show of mentally calculating the figure. 'About five grand . . . New York was expensive if you recall. Cost an arm and a leg moving back here. And I shelled out close to a hundred on a loan to get the house in order. Dear Emily may have given us the place for free but it needed a lot of work before I could let you see it.'

She felt guilty. 'I never asked, did I? Just left it to you as usual.'

'No complaints. I could reschedule the loan if it comes to the worst.'

'All the same, it's not enough, is it? Not if you're out of work for a long time.'

He reached over and took her hand. 'Alison, my love. I'm not bright at many things but I do understand money.'

'So what does it mean?'

'On the one hand, I could come out as the new chief executive of a German-owned subsidiary office. That would put me on, say, half a mill basic, plus bonuses and options that ought to take me well over the mill mark. Which, in case you don't recall, is more than double the pittance I earn at the moment.'

She stroked the cat and smiled. 'I like the sound of that, Miles. Do you?'

'Absolutely. And once I get my feet under the table you can bet that the modus operandi will be adjusted to suit our lifestyle. No way would the buggers get me back living in London.'

'Alternatively?'

'Alternatively, I'll be out on my ear with a pay-off, I guess, of 600K or so. Take the effing tax out of that and, theoretically, we end up with enough to live on for two years, two and a half perhaps, without earning a cent. After that it's the milk round or the bar of the Green Man. And, at some stage, bye-bye Priory House. We couldn't afford the upkeep on a place like this.'

Thomas yowled for attention. She got up and opened a tin of cat food. 'We could economise.'

He shook his head gently and laughed. It was at times like these that Alison remembered why she took to Miles in the first place. He cared so much and it was all so selfless, never asking a price.

'We could economise but you have to see the whole picture. We want to live too. No. If I lose the job, I need to get another, on equal or better pay, within six months. If not, we sell the house, downsize to something with a more sensible mortgage, and try to work out what happens next. Leave it any later than that and we could see our equity disappear entirely before long, and that is not something either of us would relish.'

'Do we stop trying?'

'Trying what?' He was genuinely baffled.

'A child, Miles! Can we really afford one if you might be out of a job?'

He seemed amazed. 'Good God, Alison. Either of us could walk under a bus tomorrow. Why should we let a stupid thing like this stand in the way of a baby? You're not having second thoughts for other reasons, are you?'

'No!' She was happy here. She was making friends, starting to meet people on those long walks across the Minnis.

'Good. Then let's carry on as we intended. As soon as the phone stops ringing, if you like.'

'That might be next year.'

45

'Not so long. Have you seen John Tyler again?'

She was starting to hate doctors. They all said the same thing. 'I'll make an appointment if you like.'

'It's your decision. But think of it this way. We know I'm firing live bullets. We know your pipework's all connected right too. If he can't solve that particular riddle we'll find someone who can.'

'Tomorrow,' she replied with a smile. 'I'll phone him tomorrow.'

Then Andy Moorside, the Mersons chief executive, was on the phone and talk of babies disappeared altogether. Battle was about to be joined. A war committee of Mersons' senior personnel was being assembled. There was not the slightest possibility of an agreed bid. A brutal hostile take-over was in the making, and one that could run on well into the New Year. It would entail tactics and strategy, dirty tricks and millions spent on PR. Miles was to be in command of black propaganda, spreading rumours about the Farber group's liquidity, its record on the environment and minority hiring, anything and everything that could darken the name of the Germans. He was to have access to private investigators and tame politicians. No expense would be spared.

And this would take time. So much time. It was soon obvious that the daily trek from Beulah to the City was not one he could make reliably. A £300-a-night suite had been booked for him at the Tower Hotel. On an open-ended basis. Until the battle was won or lost there was no clue when he might make it home in the evenings, or even at weekends.

Alison listened to the calls and, at the end of the afternoon, to Miles's gloomy analysis of the mountain of work ahead. The papers painted the Mersons-Farber battle as one of the great conflicts of the international financial world. Even the Saturday afternoon ritual, in the soft, broad bed overlooking the Minnis, seemed in doubt.

Miles understood her sadness, she knew. It was not a situation of his choosing. 'Pecker up, old girl,' he said, kissing her on the nose. 'It only needs one little soldier to hit the mark. We'll get there. And this time next year we'll be wondering how to spend all that lovely moolah too.'

In the meantime, she thought, only half bitterly, there would be Beulah for company. And the cat.

When she phoned the Wye surgery there was a cancelled appointment later in the week. Miles had already warned her that he faced a long day, and there was no guarantee he wouldn't be staying in the hotel. He left Priory House with a small case of clothes and a resigned expression on his face. They kissed in the drive and Alison was happy. If he'd suggested she go back on the pill, wait a while for the child, she would have done it like a shot.

At ten, Sara phoned. They'd been meeting since the debacle of Burning Man. Sara's business – which revolved around importing fabrics and other design objects – seemed to soak up a lot of her time.

'News?' Sara wondered.

'Why do you ask? I sometimes think you're a witch. Miles's bank may be taken over. Either he winds up the boss or out on his ear with a pay-off and not a clue about how we manage the debt on this place.'

'He can do my accounts. Come round for tea. Please.'

Ten minutes later she was ringing the bell at Crabtree Lodge, the tiny half-timbered cottage at the southern end of the Minnis where Sara lived. It was an exquisite house, she thought. If she ever found herself single again, Alison swore she would murder Sara and take her place. The Lodge was like a miniature from a Constable painting.

White-walled, with the timber unpainted so that the wood sat pale brown against the plasterwork, it stood in a perfect circle of greenery: lilac, a small walnut tree, a forest of dog roses now shedding flowers for bright, red hips. There was a small barred gate at the front which separated it from the gravel path leading from the Minnis. A ramshackle garage to the right, covered in clematis, just about managed to swallow Sara's ancient 2CV. At the rear, pheasant and partridge foraged noisily, sending up a flurry of feathers and commotion the moment they heard a human footfall.

Alison had been inside four times now, and on each occasion she could scarcely contain her joy. Sara, with extra-ordinary taste, had crammed the interior with an eclectic collection of belongings: Indian rugs, odd African furniture, bright, colourful paintings from Haiti, and a selection of sideboards culled from local boot fairs. She had packed the tiny place with stuff on the grounds that the fuller it was with junk, the bigger it would seem. And it worked. Alison adored Crabtree Lodge. Even the faint but discernible aroma of damp had some character to it, a hint of apple scent or Earl Grey tea.

Yappy lay on an old hessian throw in front of the lead-coloured duck's nest fireplace, fast asleep. The two of them sat next to each other on a shapeless, battered sofa and sipped fruit tea, Alison waiting for the inevitable.

'You're pregnant,' she said, unable to contain herself any more. 'I can tell. It's obvious. You look so goddamn healthy.'

Sara responded cautiously. 'Now let's not jump the gun, dear girl. I have been doing certain calculations and I believe Burning Man may have made a contribution to the game. Nevertheless, one missed period does not an infant make. I'll give it a week or two before I go to see our friend Tyler. But I got the preggers kit from Boots and it went the right colour. Also I have, this very morning, yakked a good bowl of Weetabix down the bog and found myself screaming vile abuse at a perfectly innocuous news item on the *Today* programme.'

'You're knocked up, darling. With child. Expecting. Possessed of a bun in the oven. Most definitely in the family way. And . . .'

Suddenly damp-eyed, the pair of them hugged like sisters on the sofa. The uncertain cushions heaved between them.

'I am *so* delighted for you, Sara.'

'Oh God.' Sara wiped away a tear that threatened to make a dash for her right cheek. 'Blubbering too. I'm going to be a mass of hysterical hormones for the next eight months, aren't I? What a thought.'

Alison felt strangely proud of her. 'You'll be fine. You've got such . . . guts.'

'I'm going to need them. It seemed such a good idea when I'd tucked a few under my belt that night. I guess I'd been thinking about it already, subconsciously anyway. But now . . .'

'You are *not* regretting it.'

'Absolutely not. Just thinking about the implications. How I actually manage things.'

'Ask the father to help. You can get some money from him, surely?'

Sara looked shocked. 'Certainly not. For one thing, I lured him here. The state he was in I doubt he even remembers much about it anyway. Seems a bit rotten to ask the bloke to fork out for the next twenty years for a drunken shag he probably wouldn't have bothered with under normal circumstances.'

Alison stroked Yappy, who was now awake and panting in front of the needless fire. 'No clues? You'll have to write it on the birth certificate you know.'

'No clues,' she said sternly. 'You're my friend, Alison. Part of friendship is knowing the boundaries.'

'Apologies. Never again.'

'Quite. And as for the birth certificate, I'll just write "man in red Ford Escort, Watford Gap services". If they want to send me to jail, that's their prerogative.'

Alison felt the pot. 'Shall I make more tea?'

'Please. You know where everything is. I can blabber at you from here.'

Alison got up and walked into the kitchen, a few steps away, through a rickety open door. The fruit tea was from Istanbul, stored in a brass urn that looked as if it had escaped from a pantomime version of Aladdin. She opened a couple of cupboards and the knife drawer. No two cups, mugs, plates or pieces of cutlery were the same. Sara lived in a delightfully ordered form of perpetual chaos. As Alison washed the old mugs, she wondered what a baby would do to proceedings.

'You do have people hereabouts, don't you?'

'Distant cousin in St Albans. She's the nearest. My parents died years ago. I was an only child, a late accident. That's one of the reasons I was starting to panic, I imagine.'

Alison came to the kitchen door, idly drying one of the mugs with a threadbare tea towel. 'But you must know someone. What happens when you need something? What happens when the big day arrives? At three in the morning?'

Sara shrugged her shoulders and smiled. 'Something will work out. I can't help thinking that I've got a lot better deal than most women who've lived in this cottage. I mean, it's three hundred years old. What sort of maternity care do you think people got then?'

'I imagine Harry Blamire's great-to-the-power-of-zillion grandpa took a break from birthing a few pigs and wandered over with a pair of forceps and a grubby rag.'

'Exactly,' said Sara, eyes glittering. 'And he probably sired it too.'

Alison wondered if there was a point to that statement,

then remembered her promise. 'I'll do what I can. Of course. What about the business?'

'That's the easy part. I do most of it on the computer these days anyway. Buy something in Turkey, sell it to a nice network of hippie stallholders, anywhere from Camden Lock to Amsterdam.'

'What sort of something?'

'Crap, mainly.' Sara smiled. 'But high-quality crap. Carpets. Djibbahs. I have a nice line in Indian brasswork if you ever need some.'

Alison looked at the tea canister and said, 'I'll bear that in mind.' Outside the kitchen window the back garden of the cottage was almost completely overgrown, a tangle of brambles and dying balsam. 'All the same, you need to maintain your income.'

'Ten e-mails a day and I'm done. All the stock goes in and out of a bonded warehouse in Hounslow.'

'You need to run the house.'

'Got a woman comes up from Wye. Best cleaner in the world.'

'Well,' Alison said, 'what *do* you need?' She walked back into the room carrying two mugs of tea.

'Support. Advice. Someone to talk to.'

'Consider it done.'

Sara put her mug on the small teak table in front of the sofa. 'I'm so sorry it didn't work for you. It would have been lovely. The two of us getting plump together.'

'Not to be. Don't give up hope. I'll be right behind you.'

'I know. I *know*!' Sara was wearing her best batty expression. 'And, um, Miles is doing his part?'

Alison thought about the sashes and the blindfold. There were some things that were a little too private, even for Sara. 'We'll get there.'

Sara saluted. 'Yes, boss. You sound just like a husband.'

'Thank *you*.'

'No offence meant. And there was something else.'

Prescient again, Alison thought. 'Was there?'

'I thought so. It was written all over your face when you walked through the door.'

Alison clutched the small bone tucked deep in the pocket of her Barbour. It didn't feel quite right yet. Sara was so wrapped up in the baby.

She hesitated. 'Not now.' Then she kissed Sara softly on the cheek and looked into her bright-blue eyes. 'And you will look after yourself, my girl. No drinking. No smoking. No nonsense at all. I have a fancy to be called auntie before long and you are my best, my only, bet.'

She drove down the hill, past mountains of leaves shed by the overhanging trees. The forest that covered the lower levels of the Downs was now a deep, rich mix of autumn colours. Jackdaws and jays swept out of the branches cawing noisily. There had been a frost that night, the first of the winter. It left a light sheen, like sparkling, dewy talcum powder. The weather forecast said there was more to come. Around eight, after she had eaten a lone breakfast, a curious and bold pheasant had appeared in the back garden, near the vegetable patch, begging for crumbs, its winter plumage a rich riot of orange, gold and red. Gingerly, she had walked towards it, throwing pieces of bread. The bird had cocked its head at her, stared with a bright, beady eye and pecked them eagerly off the ground. Alison had smiled at the creature, talking to it in a foolish way. It made her feel accepted somehow.

She waited in the practice's small, modern surgery for fifteen minutes and was asked to go to Tyler's room. He had his jacket slung behind his chair and was wearing a neatly pressed white cotton shirt and a red silk tie. Alison couldn't help but wonder if he did the ironing himself. Marjorie might have difficulty getting that kind of perfect finish while high as a kite on home-grown dope or dripping with gin.

'Well, Mrs Fenway,' John Tyler said with a professional smile, 'six weeks since we last had the pleasure of a visit from you, I see. So is it good news?'

'No,' she said, and wished there wasn't such an obvious note of accusation in her voice.

'Fine . . .' he continued. 'So what *is* the problem?'

'You mean it's not obvious? *That's* the problem.'

He grunted and looked at the file. 'Remind me, my dear. You were pregnant last year, for the first time, and miscarried. We never spoke about this in any detail when you first came. Perhaps you could fill me in now.'

It came straight out of the blue, with a sudden, vicious immediacy. 'Th – there was a fire,' she stuttered. 'They said it was stress.'

He just looked at her expectantly. Damn doctors, she swore beneath her breath. They always want you to pour out the most awkward moments of your life just like that, not a pause, not the slightest hesitation.

'Where I worked. In New York. There was a fire.'

Just the words brought the taste of the smoke into her mouth. And the memory, vivid in her head, of what followed.

'Go on.'

She closed her eyes, then quickly opened them again. It was astonishing how rapidly the images flickered into life out of nowhere when they felt like it.

'I worked in this cheap little office block. On the forty-eighth floor. There was a fire on the floor below. I was on my own. The elevators didn't work. So I stood on the roof. It happened there. While I was waiting for the firemen.'

'You were injured?' Tyler's bald head shone beneath the fluorescent light of the surgery.

'No, not really. Just smoke.'

'It must have been dreadful. Go on.'

She didn't feel like going on. This wasn't why she came to the surgery. Doctors behaved as if they had some god-given right to your secrets. They didn't. Sure, she'd stood on the roof. Stood there yelling, screaming, watching the curious faces at the windows of the surrounding blocks. Wondering why they couldn't help. But that wasn't the whole thing. What the firemen found when they finally arrived was some crazed woman, ready to throw herself off the ledge. 'They took one look at me and sent me off to hospital.'

'Do you remember that? What happened precisely?'

She closed her eyes, saw the nightmare start to replay on cue, then opened them quickly again. 'Not precisely. The next thing I remember is Miles standing by the side of the bed looking as if I was about to die. The poor man was in floods of tears. The doctors told me I'd had a miscarriage. Like I hadn't guessed.'

'Shock-induced, I imagine. No physical reason. Not uncommon.'

No *physical* reason. Tyler would never, she imagined, pass a sympathy course. But that wasn't, she reminded herself, what he was there for. He was paid to heal the sick, not amuse them. Some of the finest doctors she'd met in New York were as perfunctory as hell when it came to everyday politeness.

'You still feel guilty?'

She sighed. Was it so obvious? 'It goes around in my head from time to time. I try to remember what happened and it's all a jumble. I think . . .'

'If only . . . If only you'd popped out for lunch. If only you'd tried the stairs. If only you hadn't turned up for work that day at all. Don't feel ashamed.'

54

Tyler made a passable effort at an understanding expression. 'Everybody feels that way about accidents. It's no use my telling you to think differently. You have to do that yourself. One day it stops. Or not. Whatever. I see they put you into . . . what is the euphemism? Ah yes, "residential care".'

'We have very expensive insurance,' she replied. 'You'd be amazed what it pays for.'

'Hmm,' he grunted. 'I have my own opinions about that.'

'I had a breakdown.'

'Hardly surprising,' he said briskly. 'People get sick. People get well. The way of the world. You are well. Believe me. And since then you and Miles have been trying? Regularly?'

'Regularly.'

'Meaning?'

'Three times weekly. After meals.'

Tyler wrinkled his nose, ignoring the facetious remark. 'Hmmm. Have you tried any special timings? Positions? Pregnancy is always a case of the happy accident, of course, although there are ways in which you can try to improve the odds. Technically human beings are fertile only two or three days each month, but the body doesn't read textbooks. If you get depressed, you get colds more easily. It makes sense to me to believe, therefore, that if you wish to conceive, a frame of mind that revolves around procreation, perhaps a touch obsessively, is no bad thing.'

She took a deep breath. 'My husband leaves home at six thirty and gets back at nine or ten at night. The chances are that his hours are going to get even worse for the foreseeable future. Unless he can e-mail me his sperm, special timings are out.'

'Ah yes. The Mersons situation. I read about that in the papers. The Germans will win in all probability. We are *all* Europeans now, I suppose.'

'Thank you. As I was saying, the chances of our making out to schedule are about on a par with Harry Blamire making the next Pope. I need something rather more efficacious than that.'

John Tyler leaned back in his big leather chair. His brow furrowed. The grey autumn light filtered through the rapidly balding beech saplings by the window. 'There is no physical reason why you or your husband shouldn't conceive. It's much too early for any clinical intervention in my opinion. I could do that, but you'd regret it. Later.'

'I think that's for me to judge.'

'Not at all. I'm the doctor here. You are a perfectly fit young woman. A touch skinny, nothing wrong with that. Regular sex is all you need. Try a little variation. It stops the boredom creeping in.'

Alison felt her blood begin to boil. 'What goddamn difference does that make? It's all the same process, isn't it?'

Tyler looked thoughtful. He brought his hands up to his face and gently tapped his fingertips together. 'No. It isn't actually. We always like to think of ourselves as mere machines these days, just a complex set of chemical reactions. But it isn't true. Or if it is, there are still large areas of the machine which are beyond our understanding. Two perfectly healthy, virile people may couple daily for an entire lifetime and never produce offspring. Two sickly, anaemic specimens may do it ten times in as many years and spawn a child on every occasion. Do we know why? No. But time and mental state *do* matter. You had a traumatic experience last year. This year you moved house, moved to a different country. Psychically, these things still disturb you. When you lose that burden, you will, I assure you, be more likely to conceive. I could always arrange for more thera –'

'Don't need it,' she spat at him quickly.

He smiled. 'Good. That *is* a healthy reaction. But you don't need clinical intervention either. Not yet anyway. Not until we see that the process is still failing when it gets a fair crack of the whip, so to speak. Have you thought of trying another partner?'

She couldn't believe her ears. *'What?'*

'Only a suggestion. We have a taboo that says we shouldn't talk about these things, but surrogate fathers have been used for centuries. For good reason too, and often at the suggestion of the man. If you need an heir, your wife seems healthy, and you suspect the problem lies in your own scrotum, why not bring in a friend to crank the starting handle?'

'I thought,' she intoned very slowly, 'you said that Miles was in perfect working order.' There was a point, she thought, at which she would tell this oddball doctor where to stick his advice.

'Yes,' he sighed, as if she were being thick. 'You're both in perfect working order. But something – the stars, the timing, whatever – didn't work for you. That's not to say it won't if you try someone else. You should talk to Miles about it. He seems a practical man. You may find him more receptive than you expect.'

Alison stared at him, astonished. 'The stars? I thought I was in a GP's surgery. Not Madame Foo Foo's freaking astrology parlour.'

'A closed mind is not an attractive accessory for a beautiful woman, Mrs Fenway. More things in Heaven and Earth etc . . . You really shouldn't put too much faith in modern medicine. We're just the same old quacks with a few new potions. The only reason life expectancy has risen at all is because we now know how to make people die more slowly. Curing things . . . that's still the absolute bugger it always was. There's more than meets the eye in some of the old ways, if you want my opinion. Take the belief that Burning Man, for example, is a particularly fecund time of the year.'

First Sara, now Tyler. Beulah seemed obsessed with the power that lay in a simple point on the calendar. 'But why should that be?'

He picked up a notepad on the desk and started to draw on it. 'Just superstition, of course. But sometimes superstition and science walk the same path. It's just that we haven't learned how to teach them to recognise one another. You're in the country now. It's time to start learning our native rites.'

Tyler tore a sheet of paper off the pad and passed it across the table.

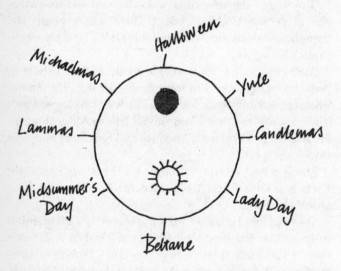

'One way or another, although most of us don't appreciate it, just about everything society believes about the annual cycle of life comes down to this. Does it mean the slightest thing to you?'

She puzzled over the scribbles. '*Nada.*'

'As I thought,' he sighed. 'This is a map of the year.

The same map we've had since pre-Celtic times, in all probability. It's based on the seasons. There are four major points. Halloween is important because it's the beginning of winter, the time when darkness comes to rule the northern hemisphere. It's the exact opposite to Beltane, or May Day if you like. The start of summer, when light is the primary power. The other two important holidays are Candlemas, the birth of spring, and Lammas, the end of summer. In between all these you see the lesser feasts – Yule, which is Christmas, of course. Lady Day was based on the vernal equinox, although the Church just hated the idea of another moveable feast so it fixed the date as March the twenty-fifth, when most years it comes in around March the twenty-first. There is some astronomical calculation behind most of these dates, naturally, which means the Christian calendar cannot always be relied upon. Look at an astronomical one or ask in the village. Then there's Midsummer's Day. Enough said. And the autumnal equinox, which is the basis of Michaelmas, although the dates once again tend to slip a little. That's our night of the Burning Man, or harvest home, as you Americans would have it.'

'Fascinating,' she said blankly. 'What has this got to do with me getting knocked up?'

Tyler harrumphed and continued as if she'd never spoken. 'What I've given you here is a mish-mash of names, of course. The entire Christian church ripped off the pagan heritage mercilessly. So you will find that each of these feasts has an older, less familiar name. Sometimes the connections are quite illuminating. Midsummer Night is also known as St John's Eve, after John the Baptist. Early paintings depict him with marked horns of light above his head. A few even go so far as to show him as a satyr, with an animal's lower torso. The meaning is quite clear, of course. John the Baptist equals Pan, the wild man of the wood, the Oak King, the Green Man. The free spirit of fecundity in nature. Jesus, on the other hand, is identified as the Holly King, born at the winter solstice, sacrificed at the autumnal equinox to the rising power of winter. Like our Burning Man. The Christian thread borrows the tale again. " . . . and the holly wears the crown."'

Alison wondered if he was just plain mad. 'Dr Tyler . . .'

'Yes? You're wondering what this has to do with getting "knocked up"? Perhaps nothing. Perhaps everything. People have believed for centuries that these points in the year have some significance. People still do, they're just a touch more reluctant to admit it. Sometimes the propensity for fertility is stated. Sometimes it isn't. We live in more muted times. Superstition, traditional superstition anyway, is frowned upon. Never mind that every stupid tabloid newspaper is full of so-called astrology columns that would have got their editors burned at the stake not more than three hundred years ago. All I'm suggesting is that you bear these ideas in mind. If they don't work, then you'll have had a jolly nice time trying. If they do, you still won't believe a word of it. Either way, what's there to lose?'

Alison wondered what Sara would have said, listening to this unexpected lesson in country mythology. And she knew. She grabbed his pen from the table. 'Nothing ventured . . . Dates?'

'Halloween you know, and Beltane too, which, as I said, is May Day, though I trust you won't still be waiting by the time that comes round again. There is some dispute about exact dates so I suggest you get rather frisky well before and after. Don't believe everything you find in the Church calendar. And you need to check your cycle, of course. This isn't magic. It can't fertilise Scotch mist. Just offer a little loading of the dice perhaps. Yule ought to be the winter solstice, a few days before December the twenty-fifth to be accurate. Candlemas, let's say February the sixth or so. Lady Day is March the twenty-fifth. May Day when you'd expect it. Midsummer, to be pedantic, should probably be June the twenty-fourth, and Lammas the first of August.'

She scribbled down the dates, wondering which of the two of them was craziest. Tyler looked across at her, satisfied. 'I have to be honest,' he said. 'I'm just a country doctor. I may be spouting dreadful rubbish.'

'I'll try anything.'

'Good. And therapy?'

'Anything except that.'

He nodded. 'Fair enough. I have a devil of a job trying to spend my therapy budget hereabouts. One day they'll just take the damn thing away and you, good lady, will be responsible.'

'I don't need therapy.'

A trace of a smile broke on Tyler's thin-lipped mouth. 'No. Probably not. But you do need to learn to relax a little. Have an open mind. Enjoy yourself. And go at it like rabbits, particularly when you see one of those dates looming. I promise, if you're still in the same boat this time next year, we'll start to look at other options. But believe me, you and Miles will be much happier, and your future children too, if you just let things happen naturally. We are, most of us anyway, blessed with perfectly efficient equipment for reproduction. Start messing around with insemination and all that pseudo-magic and all sorts of nastiness can come out of the woodwork. Guilt. Feelings of inadequacy. Suspicion. Not always, but sometimes. I've seen it. Trust me.'

Alison took his outstretched hand and shook it. She did trust John Tyler, after a fashion. She felt the bone in her pocket. Tyler was making noises that said the appointment was, most definitely, finished.

Over-hastily, she pulled the bone out of her pocket. 'One more thing,' she stuttered.

Tyler was already staring at the small grey object in her hand. 'I don't do *Antiques Roadshow*,' he said.

61

'I . . . I found it. In the ashes of the bonfire. After Burning Man.'

His eyebrows were crawling up his bald forehead like caterpillars squirming sideways. '*You* found it? Yourself?'

'Well, the dog actually.'

'You saw the dog find it?'

'No, I . . . the dog came up to me with it.' She felt deeply uncomfortable and stupid. 'It's burnt. It was covered in ash.'

Tyler took the thing out of her fingers and stared at it.

'Any idea?' she asked.

'They have barbecues on the Minnis. Damned annoying it is too. All that smoke.'

'It looks like . . . a finger?'

He wrinkled his nose. 'A phalange? Possibly. There are 206 bones in the human skeleton. Buggered if I can remember them all. Does look like the sort of thing you get left on the plate after a decent sucking pig though. You can get those from Coopers down in Brabourne, you know.'

He handed it back and she placed it gingerly in her pocket. 'A nice memento of an unusual night,' Tyler said. 'You had this hallucination at the bonfire, I seem to recall. As if it were a rerun of the fire in the office. You can see that link, can't you?'

'Yes,' she stammered. 'But . . .'

'But if there *had* been a body in the bonfire there would have been a lot more left than that little bone. You don't think the crematorium trick is real, do you? An entire human corpse goes in one door and a nice, neat jar of ashes comes out of another?'

'Things could have been swept away,' she said lamely, dimly aware of how stupid she sounded.

'By whom? Why?'

She felt angry. Deservedly so. 'It didn't help, your goddamn wife feeding me pot cakes.'

Tyler sighed, the sound of a man with a burden. 'Ah. There you have me. Bloody woman. Now if someone had put her on the bonfire that might have been understandable. But think about it, my dear. There is a direct line from the trauma you suffered last year to this. You know it's true. Now just take that thing, whatever it is, throw it in the bin and get yourself pregnant.'

He looked purposefully at his watch. Alison muttered something and left. Outside the day was turning grey and chill. She wondered briefly about driving to the top of the Downs, by the White Horse, and throwing the mysterious bone through the misty air, watching it disappear entirely from her life, freeing her to reach for the future. Then she pushed it back into the depths of her pocket and walked to the car.

The next day she was disturbed, at eight thirty in the morning, by a commotion coming down the path. Harry and Mitch Blamire were scrunching over the gravel, Harry pushing a large wheelbarrow with a Rotavator balanced delicately over it. Mitch was behind the handles of a very large and rusty green lawnmower.

'Morning, Mrs Fenway,' Harry bellowed through the drawing room window. His breath made a fog in the morning air. Winter was knocking at autumn's door. The Minnis was beginning to look bare, preparing for the long, slow sleep until spring.

The twins disappeared around the side of Priory House. Alison dashed to the kitchen door, a tiny flame of anger growing in her head. Sara was coming for tea, an important conversation needed to take place. The last thing she wanted was the distraction of the Blamires sniffing around. She put on a pair of sheepskin slippers and went outside onto the patio, only becoming conscious that she was still in her short, silk dressing gown when she felt the chill breeze whipping round her bare legs.

The twins stopped and stared. Never mind the lightning streak, Alison thought. There was one other clear way you could tell the twins apart. Harry always had that insolent smirk on his face while Mitch peered at you unsmiling, trying to look behind your eyes.

'Explanations, boys,' she said, trying to keep some friendliness in her voice. 'What's going on?'

'He didn't tell you then?' Harry asked.

'Who? What?'

'Mr Fenway. Other night in pub. He asked us to look after the garden for you. Said he didn't have the time nor you the inclination.'

Damn you, Miles, she thought. He was spending this Saturday morning in the office. Running the war room, as he put it, and planning to drive back late in the afternoon. 'No. He didn't tell me.'

'Well,' Mitch butted in, 'he told us.' The other twin seemed a mite more reasonable. His voice was less brash than Harry's. One could, she thought, hold out some hope of reasoning with Mitch. 'To be honest, Mrs Fenway, drink was took, on both sides. But Mr Fenway, he was adamant. And a contract's a contract. Even if he was rat-arsed when he made it.'

She sighed and looked at the garden. The grass was now a good four or five inches high. The ornate flower borders were riddled with rampant thistles. Bindweed was twining its way up and over the rose bed. It was true. Miles didn't have the time. And she viewed gardening as a logical extension of architecture; it was all very nice to be involved in the design, but the last thing she wanted to do was start laying the bricks.

Alison looked at the Blamires' battered machinery. 'Miles spent a fortune on a ride-on tractor. I can't believe he's paying you for cutting the grass.'

'Ride-on tractors are made for ride-on wankers, if you ask me,' Harry replied, grinning at his own wit. 'You townies are all the same. Buy one of the things, play with it for three weeks, then stick it in a garage and ask us to do the job. You ever think how much real gardening you could get done for the price of one of them things?'

'Harry,' she answered, and understood there was some defensiveness now in her voice, 'as you may realise, I know nothing of this. Let me call Miles.'

'If you like. We'll just get on anyway. We're not just cutting the grass, you know.'

Mitch came forward with a plastic bag in his hand. It was full of what looked like brown pellets. 'Mr Fenway said you got moles. This 'ere will see off any damn topers, you bet.'

'What is it?'

He opened the bag and a vile, intense stench filled her nostrils. 'Ferret dung. Scares the living daylights out of them. Just sends 'em next door, of course, but since you ain't got no one next door, this place being big and what, that don't really matter. An' if they come back we'll try the strychnine worms.'

'Provided,' Harry added, 'you don't tell no one. They're supposed to be for farms only. Also, you want to be getting out them foreign weeds you got everywhere. Sycamore and balsam and the like. Some Japanese knotweed too unless I'm mistaken. Not native, none of it.'

'Me neither,' Alison noted.

Harry came back in a flash, grinning. 'Ah. But you're too lovely for words, Mrs Fenway. No one would want to uproot you now, would they?'

She silently cursed herself. Harry had been offered that

opportunity on a plate. 'You're too kind, Harry. Hope that gets reflected in the bill.'

He evaded the question. 'Got an entire free day if you like. We can tidy up nice and good.'

She was feeling cold. She wanted to get inside and get dressed. The argument with Miles could wait until he came home. 'How much?'

'Ten quid an hour,' Mitch chipped in. His eyes became remarkably focused when she talked money. Alison felt she was beginning to get an inkling of how the responsibilities were divided in the Blamire clan.

'For both of you,' she said.

'Each,' Mitch insisted. 'And that's less than we get for shovelling the meat down Paternoster Farm.'

It was like a flash of electricity in the mind. She had regretted, more than once, failing to pick up the stray rag that had accompanied Yappy's mysterious bone. But she remembered the letters on it well and, until this moment, hadn't a clue what they meant. 'Where?'

Harry glowered at Mitch, who fell into a sullen silence. 'Never you mind my daft brother. Ten quid an hour it is.'

'I could get a landscape designer for that.'

'Yeah,' Harry replied. 'But he'd only be some poof who'd baffle you with science then leave the likes of us to do the job anyway. Not that many decent labouring gardeners hereabouts, you know.'

'The basis of all commercial pricing,' Mitch interrupted. 'If the punters aren't whingeing, they're paying too little. Ask your husband.'

'Shit.' It was cold. 'Will you take a cheque?'

The twins looked at each other and didn't say a word.

'I don't carry that kind of cash around with me, guys. Nobody does.'

'Let us have it when you do,' Mitch said grudgingly. 'You want us to start on the lawn? Or the flower beds?'

Her teeth were chattering. 'You decide. I am not involved in this. Understood?'

She couldn't wait to get inside into the warm and listen to the radio.

Harry doffed an imaginary cap. 'Right you are, ma'am. Servants going out to the fields now, if it be all right with you.'

She notched her accent up a peg or two. 'That will be absolutely spiffing, my man. On with it now! The meter's not running yet.'

The two bull terriers made their way up the garden, grumbling indecipherably. Alison went back into the house, put on warm clothes, made a hot chocolate and immersed herself in the pages of *The Times*. When she looked out at the back garden again she felt lost for words. The work the Blamires had achieved in the space of ninety minutes was astonishing. Most of the lawn was now a trim, tidy, level green. Thistles and burdock were fast disappearing from the flower borders. In the far corner of the plot, by the stand of young silver birches that broke the prevailing breeze that came all the way up the hill from Romney Marsh, Harry was uprooting a three-foot-tall sycamore sapling using his bare hands. It came out in an instant. She wondered if occasionally he didn't do the job with his teeth, just to relieve the tedium.

Ten minutes later, as arranged, Sara arrived. Over tea, Alison held the bone out in front of her face and let her examine it. 'No clues,' she said. 'I just want you to guess what it is.'

Sara looked puzzled. 'A bone. Obviously. And it looks as if it's been burned somehow.'

She waited. 'And?'

Sara sighed and sipped at her tea. 'I don't know what this game's about, Alison. What do you want me to say?'

'Just tell me what you think it looks like.'

'I'm no doctor. A neck vertebra from a small animal perhaps. Or . . .' Sara stared at it again. 'A finger bone. Possibly. I don't know. Ask someone who does.'

Alison put the bone back in its matchbox. 'I did. I asked Tyler and he said it might be the aftermath of a barbecue. Or part of a finger. Helpful or what?'

'Oh dear.' Sara sounded concerned. 'This is the bonfire thing again, isn't it?'

Alison didn't like the way that came out. She was not behaving irrationally. 'Yappy found that, the day after Burning Man. The day after I saw something inside the fire.'

'Did you see him find it?'

'You sound like Tyler. No. He just came up to me with it. But his face was covered in ash. So was the bone. It was obvious where it was from.'

Sara looked terribly worried. Alison started to curse herself for bringing up the subject. There were better things to be occupying the mind of a newly pregnant woman.

'It could have come from anywhere, Alison. Yappy picks up all sorts of stuff. Buries it. Retrieves it later. I had the corpse of a decomposing rabbit on the back doorstep the other day. How do you know it isn't a rabbit bone?'

'Does it look like a rabbit bone?'

'I don't know,' Sara said curtly. 'And neither do you. I don't like the sound of this. At all.'

Alison took her by the hand. 'Neither do I. But think about it. I see something strange inside the bonfire. The next morning there's this bone. Covered in ash. And Tyler had been talking about sacrifice the night before. What if there really was something inside the straw man? You helped make it. There was room, wasn't there?'

'Of course there was room.' Sara sounded exasperated. 'The thing is hollow. But think about what you're saying. I didn't see anything in the bonfire. Nobody else mentioned seeing anything. If you're right, we're either blind or all part

68

of some conspiracy. Do you think the entire village turned out to watch some poor soul being burned alive? Oh, Alison, I know why you might get obsessed about this . . .'

She had told Sara about the fire weeks before. This miserable episode did shape her life still, she knew that. Sometimes there were nightmares too. But this was different. 'It's not that, Sara. I was not hallucinating. And I saw it all from a different side to you, where there weren't any flames to begin with.'

'What about before the bonfire? What did they do with him then?'

'Thought of that too. The effigy only went on at the last moment. It was behind the pub. Some men took it out, put it on the top, and before you knew it they were splashing petrol around all over the place. It was dark, you couldn't see a thing. And then it was just pure fire.'

'All the same . . .' Sara was thinking about it. Alison felt pleased. She wasn't crazy. She might have got some of the details wrong, but something macabre had occurred on the Minnis that night.

'Remember what happened immediately before that?' Alison continued. 'There was a fight. Or what looked like one. Between who? Not the antis. They were never there. We never found out. What if that's when they were putting whoever it was into the straw man? Binding him, gagging him so he couldn't shout for help?'

'But who would do such a thing? And why?'

'I don't have any answers right now,' Alison admitted. 'It could have been just a couple of people. After the fight. They could have bound and gagged someone, knocked him unconscious maybe. Then, in the darkness, they could have carried the effigy out, put it quickly on the fire, and the rest of you wouldn't have noticed.'

Sara didn't look convinced. 'But if they wanted to do

someone in, there must be easier ways than in front of a crowd of fifty people.'

'I said I don't know. But, if you remember, it did turn dark around then. I distinctly remember there being a bright moon earlier in the evening. It wasn't there when I saw the Burning Man. It was dark. Pitch black by that stage.'

Sara thought about it. 'That's true,' she conceded. 'But still ... it's a hell of a conspiracy to build out of one unidentified piece of burnt bone.'

'And what I saw. What I *saw.*'

Sara folded her arms across her stomach. 'Hmmm.'

Alison felt breathless. Sara was hovering on the edge of belief.

'I still don't understand why anyone would want to incinerate a complete stranger at a public bonfire on our village green.' Sara shivered again and screwed up her face in disgust.

Alison shrugged. 'I don't pretend to know everything. Just that something weird went on.'

Sara fixed her with an intent gaze. 'Perhaps. Perhaps not. But, seriously, Alison. Even if you're right, even if persons unknown did immolate some other person unknown during Burning Man, what business is it of ours?'

'I can't believe you said that. If I'm right, Sara, *someone has been murdered.* Here. On the Minnis. Right in front of our eyes.'

Sara glowered at the mysterious bone, sitting in its nest of cotton wool in the matchbox on the table. 'It seems an awful lot to glean from that one little piece of burnt *stuff.*'

But that wasn't right, and Alison knew it. She thought about the sash around her wrist the following morning, the gag mark on her mouth, and the utter lack of any memory whatsoever on her part about what occurred in the bedroom of Priory House after she was carried home.

Sara stared glumly at her. 'I'm not going to shake you out

of this, am I? This may be just some odd hallucinatory by-product of the accident. God knows, if that happened to me I'd be having them three times a day, in between meals.'

Alison picked up the bone. 'This is *not* a hallucination.'

'Bugger,' Sara groaned. 'So what are you going to do?'

'Talk to the police. You may be right. There's no harm in checking. And also . . .'

Their friendship had reached some kind of crossroads, unnaturally, and solely through her own pushiness.

'Tell me about Paternoster Farm,' she said, and felt instantly ashamed. Sara didn't want to talk about this, *any* of it. And most of all, she realised instantly from the pained expression on Sara's face, Paternoster Farm.

'Why do you want to know about that place, Ali?'

She thought of the way Harry had glowered at Mitch and the rag that Yappy had found, wrapped around the bone. The missing rag was best kept secret, since even with evidence it was hard to sound credible. 'Just curious.'

'It's in Sterning Wood,' Sara said. 'There's a path runs from the top horn of the White Horse. Not easy to find without it. I'm surprised you haven't noticed the stench from time to time. They render meat or something. The Blamires work there part time.'

'Rendering? Isn't that dirty, town business or something?'

'Dirty all right,' Sara said sourly. 'And money in it too. Why do you think the boys are involved?'

'But . . .' It wasn't something you killed someone for. That was what she was thinking, though she didn't dare voice the words. They seemed too crazy.

'There's more to it, of course,' Sara continued. 'And don't ask me, I don't know. This is a village, Alison, and a village is like a family. It has its secrets and you don't profit from picking at them.'

'What . . . ?'

'Shush.' Sara was staring out of the big, wide kitchen

window, out at the garden where the Blamire boys were toiling away around the fruit trees. 'That's enough,' she said, firmly, and turned to face Alison. There was no mistaking: her eyes were moist. 'I don't like this. Not one little bit. You're getting obsessed with something, something that's probably nothing if you want my honest opinion. But nothings, *bad* nothings, can hurt you if you let them. *Please* drop this. It may be my stupid hormones kicking in but I have a nasty feeling about the whole thing. *Please.*'

Alison took her hand. It was cold. Sara was scared. And all the time she'd just carried on, hunting, probing, looking, not thinking about what effect any of this had on Sara. She touched her softly on the cheek. It was damp. 'I'm sorry. I'm a jerk.'

'Yes,' Sara clung to her now and her voice was cracked. 'You bloody well are. But listen to me. None of what you think you see here is true. There was no one in the Burning Man that night. *No one!* This is madness. Drop it now.'

Alison nodded. 'But maybe I'll take a look at this Paternoster Farm place just once . . .'

'*Buggeration!*' Sara was instantly furious, so mad that Alison, for a moment, could scarcely recognise her. In a flurry of swirling clothes she stood up, swearing like a trooper, then took a badly aimed kick at the table. 'Leave it, Alison. *For God's sake, leave it!*'

Alison watched her storm out of the kitchen, slamming the door behind her. The guilt was, for a short while, all-consuming. And the practical implications too. She had one true friend in the village, and now she was watching her leave, in a bitter rage, over nothing more than a handful of ridiculous suspicions and a single piece of unidentified bone.

Alison sat in misery for a while, then rose and stood by the window. To her surprise, Sara was still there, talking to the Blamire brothers by the jumble of low apple trees in the back garden. It didn't look like a friendly conversation. She heard raised voices, and then Sara was off again, marching down the path to the gate.

Alison Fenway could barely remember a time when she had felt so wretched. Except the *one* time.

When she was sure Sara was well and truly gone, she ventured out into the cold day. The Blamires were on her in a moment, eyes blazing.

''Ere,' Harry bellowed. 'What's that friend of yours up to?'

'Excuse me?'

'Asking questions. Sticking her sharp little nose into things that don't concern her.'

'I don't know what . . .'

'Paternoster Farm's what I mean. We got good casual work there. Don't need the likes of her poking around asking stupid questions.'

But, she was about to say, it wasn't Sara who was being over-inquisitive, it was me. Why did Sara want to protect her? And from what?

Mitch Blamire stuck his broad, red face in front of her. 'Farm's got a job to do, Mrs Fenway,' he grunted. 'Not a pretty one nor a nice one. But someone's got to do it. You tell her to leave us alone and get on with it. She's not country and nor's you. Some things you don't understand.'

'Yes,' she answered lamely. Then dashed for the house, trying not to burst into tears. She stood in the kitchen, listening to the Aga grumble like a cantankerous metal beast, her mind a blank. The light was flashing on the answering machine. She pressed the button and Miles's voice boomed out of the tinny speaker.

'A million apologies, Ali, but this is all going pear-shaped. We're having to work through the weekend on some data in from Hamburg. Back Sunday, hopefully. You can get me after five. Meetings till then.'

Goddamn meetings, she swore. Goddamn Miles. The entire day stood empty in front of her, no husband, no friends. Alison took down the bottle of Glenfiddich, poured herself a large one, and curled into a tight, foetal ball in the big leather armchair in the living room, staring out of the huge Georgian windows onto the mist-strewn front garden where the brothers were now at work. An odd cocktail of misery and anger rippled through her bloodstream. She closed her eyes and fell into a dead, dreamless sleep. When she woke it was towards the end of the afternoon. The garden was empty.

The phone was ringing.

'Mrs Fenway?' a remote female voice asked.

'Yes.'

'It's the William Harvey Hospital here. Now there's no real need to be worried . . .'

'Bastard four by fours.' Sara sat upright in the hospital bed and released a stream of vivid epithets that made the elderly woman in the next bed cover her ears. '*Bastard* four by fours. Think they own the sodding place. Come up tailgating you. And don't even stop when they drive you off the bloody road.'

She had a large, purple bruise on her forehead and a black eye. The police said the old 2CV was a write-off. If it hadn't been for a passer-by who came upon the car, upside down in a ditch on the narrow rat run to the A20, Sara might have been in the same state. The nurse had taken Alison to one side when she arrived at the hospital and tried to be as comforting as she could. Minor injuries and concussion, she said. But Sara had been unconscious when they found her, only saved from tumbling through the windscreen by her seat

74

belt. She was upside down, for how long no one knew since the other car never stopped, and there was some abdominal bruising. Alison asked immediately about the baby, and the nurse just shrugged. 'You'll have to talk to the doctor. He'll be round in a minute.'

Sara stared at her now with big, shocked eyes and said, 'I'm bleeding. Not a lot, but they seem worried all the same.'

Alison held her hand and was glad that Sara had given her name and number when they asked for someone to contact. The brief, painful breach between them was irrelevant now. 'Don't worry. That's not unusual and it doesn't mean you've lost anything. At least you're here. They know what to do.'

She would keep the child. Alison felt certain of that. Sara had such determination, such solidity. Still the questions kept on coming. 'Who was it? Tailgating you?'

'I don't know. I wasn't taking much notice. One moment there was nothing behind me. The next I just saw this shape. I braked, and the car was going off the road. I loved that car, you know. It's a good job the bastard never stopped. I would have taken a swing at him.'

'Him?'

Sara closed her eyes. 'It had to be a him, didn't it? Not that I saw.'

'Sara,' Alison said carefully, 'what were you talking to the Blamires about? When you left?'

She groaned. 'Paternoster Farm. What do you think? They work there. I thought it might be worth pumping them.'

This was not the time, she knew that. Alison put a hand on her shoulder and said, very firmly, 'Not now.'

'The boys didn't like talking about it, you know. Mucky business.'

They were interrupted by the duty doctor. He looked about eighteen and utterly exhausted.

'And you are?' the doctor asked abruptly.

'A friend,' Sara interjected.

'And your, um, partner? Where is he?'

Sara smiled icily. 'I'm single. But talk down to me anyway. I'll do my best to understand.'

'Hmmm. I'm keeping you in for a day or two. You got a nasty shake-up and concussion. Have you had bleeding before?'

Sara shook her head.

'Well, it's not that unusual in the first twenty weeks, but it can be a sign of threatened miscarriage. I don't think there's anything wrong just now, but let's make sure, shall we? A spot of complete bed rest for the weekend. I'll prescribe some flurazepam. It'll help you sleep and relax the muscles too. There's not a lot you can do at this stage but rest and wait.'

Sara sighed. 'Can it be harmed? In an accident like this?'

He didn't look much concerned. 'Of course. But a foetus is a pretty tough little character. If it was in trouble, we'd know by now. Some sleep, some rest and it will just go back to getting on with the job.'

Alison patted the bedclothes. 'There. I told you it would be OK. Do you want me to stay?'

Sara looked scared. Alison knew the feeling. They both hated hospitals. 'Only if you want to. No, go home. Come back in the morning with some croissants from Tesco's if you like. The food here is bound to be pure cack.'

'Worse than that,' the doctor said, then ambled off. The nurse arrived with a small tray of pills and a glass of water. Sara did as she was told and, in a remarkably short time, was looking drowsy.

'That'll keep her out for seven, eight hours,' the nurse said. 'You might as well take a break.'

'True,' Sara agreed drowsily. 'Go home. Don't do anything silly. Promise.'

Alison got up, feeling old and creaky. 'Promise. What about the police?'

'Still here,' the nurse said. 'Hunky piece of plod. You can catch him in reception.'

The policeman looked like a rugby player, six feet six in his stocking feet, with blond, close-cropped hair and a sparky, almost naïve expression. She strode straight up to him and asked, 'What are you doing about Miss Harrison's accident? I trust you're going to get the bastard responsible.'

He wilted visibly. 'Don't suppose you smoke, do you? Pop outside for a fag?'

Alison stared him in the eye. He seemed so young. And fair. His blond hair was almost yellow. His skin was pale but not bloodless. He looked the picture of health . . . and absolutely not like a policeman. 'Done,' she sighed.

The night was clear, the stars alive. A bright, full moon stood over the world illuminating everything. He gave her a cigarette and lit it, cupping his hands around hers to guard the match. 'Makes a change from chasing trick and treaters,' he said. 'Justin Liddle, by the way. PC. Community plod. Who the devil are you?'

'Alison Fenway. A neighbour of Sara's in Beulah. She called for me.'

He groaned. 'Oh, yes. The Ya – the American lady. I'd been meaning to call, being your part-time village plod and all. Beulah. What a place. I'd rather spend a Saturday night chasing ram raiders down town than get mixed up with you lot. Which is doubtless why they gave me it. Bastards.'

She was genuinely bemused. 'Why do you say that?'

'It's just . . . weird up there. If people break the law, I go for them. In Beulah . . . nothing's that simple. But then you probably know that better than me.'

'Haven't lived there long enough.'

'No.' He had bright, intelligent eyes that were now looking straight into hers. 'So you haven't been assimilated yet? Once they've got you, there's no chance you'd speak to the likes of me. You could carry out blue murder in the middle of the day up there and I'd bet a penny for a pound there'd be no witnesses.'

She filed the comment, and his name, for future reference. Justin Liddle seemed a very odd policeman indeed. '*Are* you going to find the bastard responsible for this?'

'Sherlock Holmes could do that. Maybe. But I'm not him. She's got no description of the car. It didn't touch her little Citroën, so there's no paint. I can't even see any skid marks on the road except hers. Unless he comes into the station and coughs he's clear away with it. Typical country accident if you ask me. Typical *Beulah* accident.'

She felt the anger welling up inside her again. 'And that's it? Someone nearly kills a pregnant woman. *And that's it?*'

He looked at her and there was an unwarranted amount of sympathy in his face. 'You really haven't lived there long, have you? This isn't *The Archers*, you know. Nice little country folk doffing their caps every time their Morris Minors happen to pass each other. Those lanes are made for road rage. Scares the life out of me driving up there and I'm wearing a uniform. We get it all the time. And unless we grab them while it's happening, or get a number plate, we're stuffed. You tell me. No description, no number, no evidence. How are we supposed to find him? Tarot cards?'

'It's an idea,' she mumbled.

'Right. A Toyota Land Cruiser for the Devil. A Range Rover for the Hanged Man. I'll let you know when we've got the pack assembled.'

She rather liked him and he knew it. 'I'll tell you what to look for. A man with a minute dick.'

'What?'

'Primary source of road rage. Male inadequacy. What else could make people behave like that?'

78

'I'll just have to take your word on that. Seriously though, Alison, you see the problem?'

'Seriously though, *Justin*, I see nothing except Sara in a hospital bed, covered in bruises, wondering if she's about to lose her baby.'

'I'm sorry,' he said. 'I'll take another look at the scene in daylight. In the meantime . . .' He held something out in the moonlight. 'Here's my card. You can always get me on that number.'

She stared at it and thought to herself: policemen who hand out business cards, what next? And wondered about the mysterious bone, nestling in a wad of cotton wool in a matchbox hidden above the Aga. If Miles was on one of his long absences, Justin would be pleasant company for afternoon tea and a little exploratory chat.

'Thanks,' she said, and stomped back into the hospital.

She got home at close to midnight. The lights were still on in the Green Man, where the closing hour seemed entirely dependent upon Norman's mood. She could hear loud, drunken voices drifting across the common. Miles should have been among them. They could have caught up on matters that were falling behind. After Tyler's little lecture about the efficacy of the seasons she'd checked her cycle. That looked good too. She tried not to let the thought get into her head (if Sara loses hers, I can make it up, I can even the balance). But it was useless anyway. Miles was in London somewhere, and there wasn't so much as a single message on the answering machine.

After a couple of drinks she slept late. Then she bought some croissants and flowers at the supermarket and went back to the hospital, a thick, cold clump of dread sitting in the pit of her stomach. It lifted the moment she walked into the ward. Sara was upright in bed looking the very picture of health, and mightily bored too. She wolfed down two croissants in an instant.

'The idiots won't let me out until tomorrow,' she mumbled, her mouth full of crumbs. 'Ridiculous. Not a sign of anything since the accident. Little Horatio or Henrietta, whichever it is in there, is doing very nicely, thank you. And so am I.'

Alison grinned at her. 'You have the mother of all black eyes.' It was more purple than black, and it stretched from her high cheekbone to well above the eyebrow.

'Just as well I am pregnant then. Nobody'd want to shag an old tart looking like this.'

'You'll recover. Back to your old self by Friday. Promise.'

'Yes, ma'am.' She waved an exaggerated salute.

'Sara . . . do you remember anything more about the accident?'

Sara shook her head and flakes of croissant flew onto the pillow. 'Nah. That copper says they'll never find him. At least he looks as if he might try if I could remember something. Most of them couldn't even be bothered. Nice-looking fella as well.'

'But do you think . . . ?' Alison's voice faded. She couldn't understand why the notion wouldn't leave her head.

'What?' Sara replied suspiciously.

'Do you think he drove you off the road deliberately? I mean, it wasn't just the usual road rage thing. He *meant* to do it?'

'No,' Sara said in a monotone. Alison knew she was lying. Sara was just so bad at it.

'Sorry, love,' she said, smiling. 'I'm just being stupid. It was an accident. That's all.'

'You're getting paranoid. Bodies in bonfires. Homicidal

maniacs in our dear, sweet, bucolic paradise.' Sara wasn't smiling when she said that.

'Of course.'

'Now,' Sara said, wagging a finger, 'I will be here for another day, or so the Gestapo with the bum thermometers say. You won't do anything silly, will you?'

'Promise.'

'Hmmm.'

'I mean it.'

And she did too. She kept on meaning it. All the time in the hospital. All through the drive home (and she couldn't help looking at everyone else on the road, wondering how they were driving, couldn't help stopping at the scene of Sara's crash and noticing that the sweet-looking policeman was absolutely right: there was just a single set of skid marks).

By four she was back at Priory House. She walked in the door and yelled, 'Miles!' And cursed herself for being so dumb. In the hallway the green light was winking on the answering machine. She stabbed the button and listened to his apologetic voice. There was a number she could use to phone back. She dialled, got through to an anonymous woman's voice, and then he was on the line.

'Miles. What on earth is going on? When are you coming home?'

'Game's getting dirty. God, I never expected this kind of tactic from the Germans. Trying the same stunts on us we're trying to pull on them. And doing rather a better job too. Major crisis, I'm afraid. No chance of me getting home until Tuesday at the earliest.'

'*What*? Am I supposed to put up with this all the time until Christmas?'

'If you're lucky.' He sounded full of himself. Miles was clearly enjoying the game, and this made it all the more infuriating. 'We're going to have to try to find a white knight, some kind of approved suitor who can keep them from the door. And insert a few poison pills along the way.'

'White knight? Poison pills? What the hell are you talking about?'

'No time to explain now, my love. Just trust me. The short answer is we need to work harder than we've done in our lives, and we'll still lose in all probability. But I'm thinking long. You *do* understand what that means, don't you?'

She understood. 'Yes,' she replied irritably. 'But how long is long?'

'Months. Who knows?'

'Christ! Do I get to see my husband during any of this? Or do I have to make an appointment to come and visit you in town?'

'Now there's an idea. Once my timekeeping becomes a touch more regular. Don't sulk. It's hard on me too.'

Sounds like it, she said bitterly to herself. 'Tuesday?'

'Absolutely. Probably.'

'Wonderful,' she groaned.

'So. How are things?'

'Nice of you to ask. Sara's in hospital. Some bastard drove her off the road.'

He was silent for a moment. 'Oh, my God. How is she?'

'Bruised. Shaken up. She'll be OK. And the baby too.'

'*Baby? What baby?*'

'Jesus Christ, Miles. How am I supposed to keep you up to date if you're not even here?'

'But who's the father?' he asked.

'*I don't know!*'

And she thought about the policeman and what he had said about Beulah. It was weird. No mistake. 'Look, just come home when you're ready and I'll fill you in. OK? And by the way, did you really ask the Blamires to do the gardening at ten pounds an hour. Each?'

Another long pause. 'I suppose if that's what they say . . .'

'If you can't outwit the Blamires, Miles, you won't have much chance with your goddamn Germans.'

'I would not,' he said, suddenly stuffy, 'make that assumption at all.'

And then, to her absolute amazement, he put the phone down. Alison tried to remember. In the twelve years she had known Miles, eight of them married, he had not once done this. They had argued. They had once come to something akin to blows. But nothing measured up to this single, outrageous act of out-and-out disrespect. She felt violated.

'Typical,' she yelled down the dead phone, knowing all the time that it wasn't.

She stared at the empty living room. It looked cold and inhospitable. Then, thinking that there must be some odd kind of logic which justified this sort of behaviour, she remembered Sara's earnest, well-meant entreaty.

Don't do anything silly. Why did friends say things like that? What was the point?

She poured herself a drink. Then she went into the kitchen and pulled out the local map from the table drawer. It would soon be getting dark. The big, rechargeable torch sitting in its holster by the back door would be useful. Paternoster Farm wasn't marked on the map. But she could remember Sara's directions. She'd get there all the same.

By the time she left Priory House the light was beginning to fail. A hint of afternoon haze sat over the Minnis like a grey, wispy veil. There was a sharp, wintry nip to the air. At most, Paternoster Farm was three miles from the village green. She could walk there in under an hour and still have time for a short, exterior examination of the place.

Would this solve anything? She doubted it. But it was

Sunday. *Halloween*. The day was empty. She had seen her plans destroyed by Miles's stupid business engagements. She had watched Sara in the hospital bed, clearly afraid of something she didn't want to talk about. And she had thought about what it must have been like, in the old tin can of the 2CV, to have some monster in a giant four by four come up behind you, roaring and pushing, until the road disappeared beneath your wheels and there was nothing but that short, agonised journey through thin air before you bounced, rudely, painfully, back to earth.

Just one quick look at the place from the outside. That was all she needed.

The route took her across the green, through the lazy scrub at its perimeter, on to the ancient chalk outline of the White Horse. The grass was damp and skeined with cobwebs. Fairy rings of unidentifiable toadstools patterned the slumbering cricket pitch. The longer meadow at its edge was trampled in a random, lazy fashion, as if hundreds of eager lovers had lain down in it to couple. *Badgers*, she said to herself. She was gaining a country eye. She'd seen the same effect in the pasture behind Priory House, and once, early in the morning, watched a delightful squat figure with a black and white face capering, like a swaying barrel, across the lawn. She could handle this country life; it wasn't so hard.

Soon the going became heavier. Grass gave way to bracken and muddy tracks churned by the hooves of the occasional horse. The last hawthorn berries stood in the bare bushes like fairy lights that had lost their power. A tangle of high grass and fern closed around her for a moment, then she was free, on the grass plateau at the very peak of the Downs. It was clearer here. Perhaps a light wind dispelled some of the persistent mist. A thin wash of fast-fading blue broke through from the cloud. The air seemed fresher too. At her feet lay the great swath of the other countryside, the other England, seven hundred feet below, wrapped entirely in a deep, impenetrable fog. Somewhere, in the distance, cars were queuing for petrol, lives were passing, in misery, in joy. Standing on top of the Downs she felt as if she were at the very end of some prominent foreland, overlooking a great, unknown stretch of hidden sea. The locals had a word for this other place, down below. They called it, only half jokingly she thought, 'civilisation'.

The path was on the far side of the chalk horse, just as Sara had said. She looked at the figure carved into the hillside. What had struck her as odd, even the first time she saw it, was the primitive cunning of the design. Most chalk figures were meant to be viewed from afar or, just to encourage the UFO cultists, from above. The Beulah White Horse was different. It was a slim, elegant figurative image of a leaping, prancing horse that was immediately identifiable from the ground, and close up too. The horse was a good two hundred feet across and composed entirely of swirls, arcs and curves, not a single straight line among them. Someone had told her it was Palaeolithic in origin. Once a year (and this would, she was sure, fall on one of those special days Tyler seemed so interested in), the locals walked to the hill at sunrise and cut the chalk edges to preserve the figure for the coming twelve months.

Rituals. There were so many in life, most of them unseen, unrecognised.

She looked up the slope to the point where the two horns stood sharply erect. Horses don't have horns, she knew that, of course. And yet they still seemed apposite. Perhaps they were exaggerated ears. Perhaps the entire figure was not a horse at all but some ancient, mythical beast, an over-endowed unicorn, some natural, forceful spirit of fertility.

'To hell with this,' Alison mumbled. She checked the torch and headed off towards the priapic points above the figure's head. It was getting late. She marched past the nearest horn and spotted the narrow entrance into the wood. It looked like a tunnel; what lay beyond was pitch darkness.

Alison took a deep breath and plunged into the coppice. Immediately, she reached for the torch. This was a different world. The sweet chestnut trees that formed the forest around her had shed their coverlet of leaves which lay now as a soft, brown, rotting carpet at her feet. Spiked fruit cases littered the ground. Darkness was falling through the thick, tangled canopy of slender branches that wove above her like a spider's web. From somewhere came a sound: *chak, chak, chak*. She knew this: magpie. Then a harsh, metallic laugh told her a green woodpecker had burst into flight, cackling its warning to the rest of the wood. She thought about the bird: he deserved to be terrified by the sound of a human footfall. This was some of the last forest in the area. The rest had been slashed and burned, replaced by flat farmland, running for miles, without a hedgerow in sight. Or turned into housing estates. Or rendering plants.

Through the darkness, astonishingly close, came a blood-curdling screech and the flapping of giant, airy wings.

'Owl,' she said into the black space in front of her. And, as if in answer, from somewhere behind, came the more familiar hoot, then the sudden, urgent rustling of the hunt. Something squealed, a high-pitched, terrified scream, and was silent. A mouse? A shrew? Nature red in tooth and claw, she thought. You didn't need to ride with the hunt to know how close it all was.

Alison stomped her green wellies hard and cleared her throat noisily. The wood became quiet. They are, she said confidently to herself, just creatures: animals, birds, small things that hold the two-legged beast in awe. A little noise, the odour of man on the breeze, and they fled in horror. Then she walked on and she realised the silence was not solely due to her own clumsy footsteps.

There was a stench in the air. It was growing, like some-thing alive, and it was quite unlike anything she had ever encountered in her life. When the day was over, when she lay in bed alone in Priory House, her head awhirl with images and memories, she would try to remember her first impressions of the smell that Paternoster Farm possessed. It was, first and foremost, nothing whatsoever *farmy*. But then the name was a hoax, a ruse. Paternoster was a clearing deep inside the remote coppice, in an area no one would ever find by accident, close to no bridle paths or public rights of way, a little island of dread in the impenetrable thickets of Sterning Wood. And it stank, of nothing on earth.

To begin with she wasn't at all sure it was unpleasant. There was something of the aroma of scented carbolic soap or the smell that waved in your face if you stood too close to a newly lighted candle. Then, as she got closer, these impressions disappeared to be replaced by a single, all-encompassing notion that stamped itself on her consciousness. It carried with it but a single word: *meat*. Not blood, not sustenance, nothing that could be compared with the familiar process of the kitchen in any sense. Paternoster stood in a miasma that was the very essence of flesh that had been cooked and compressed, cooked and compressed, over and over again, until it tainted everything around it. She gasped and held her breath, hoping this was just a temporary sensation, a bad smell on the breeze. But it wasn't. When she opened her mouth again the stench entered her, became a taste that coated the entire surface of her tongue, snaked its way into her lungs, squeezing out the oxygen, replacing it with a dark, choking foulness that felt as if it would seep into her veins.

It would be so easy to turn back. There were so many reasons. It was late. Her confused stomach rumbled (this was the smell of meat; it triggered some reaction, always, inside the human beast). Then the moon emerged from behind a long, dark cloud, and lit the wood more effectively than an army of rechargeable torches. She stopped breathing. It was impossible to turn back now. Paternoster was so close. It stood no more than fifteen feet in front of her. Or, to be more precise, its outer wall was that close. It rose, as high as the coppice itself, a solid barrier of wood with a picket top, hiding its secret from the world. It reminded her of *Treasure Island* and the fort in the forest. And, said the rational voice, still working away, they probably put up something like this around Dachau too. *With guards.*

Alison thought about that for a moment. It was early evening on a Sunday. The last day of October. *Halloween.* She understood the work ethic hereabouts, and it did not entail any great degree of enthusiasm. There was no sound from beyond the fence, no light either. This was an opportunity that could only be avoided on a single premise: cowardice. Not a quality she cared to affect.

By the light of the moon she worked her way to the perimeter of the fence and put her ear to the damp wood. The place was silent, empty, occupied by nothing but the ghosts of the thousands of carcasses that had passed through its doors over God knew how many years. Dead cows didn't frighten her.

She worked her way around the fence, looking for a gap, a foothold, anything that would let her see inside. But there was nothing, not so much as a loose knot through which she could peer. The enclosure was circular, that much, at least, seemed obvious. It had no corners, just a gentle curve around the perimeter, so gentle she guessed the interior must be vast, like a circular football pitch. If she worked her way around the wooden wall, she would, eventually, come to some kind of entrance, and the inevitable track that led out of the wood, back to the road.

It seemed to take hours. Then the tree line around her thinned. A narrow gravel roadway appeared, glinting silver beneath the moon, deep ruts in its surface, so big they could only be caused by trucks. The solid wall gave way to a pair of double gates, as high as the fence itself and topped by a roll of barbed wire. There was a chain and a padlock threaded through one door, trailing on the ground. She pushed the free side. Silently, on well-oiled hinges, it fell backwards, moving under its own weight.

Far enough, she thought. Then stood in the gateway and tried to make sense of the scene that lay in front of her. There were rough buildings, giant machines, all silent, and that same, ever-present stench. It was sufficient. Tomorrow, when the sun was up and she had washed the smell of Paternoster Farm out of her hair, out of every cell of her body, she could begin to think, begin to look at the random selection of facts she possessed and start to make sense of them.

'Evidence,' she said softly into the stinking night and, without knowing why, took a single step forward into the compound.

From out of nowhere came the sudden sound of laboured breathing. An enormous, powerful hand fell heavily on her right arm. Harry Blamire leaned into her body from behind, pushing himself against her backside, then peered around her shoulder, and said, 'Mrs Fenway. Now to what do we owe *this* pleasure?'

Alison screamed at the bright, uncaring moon. Far off, in the wild, untended coppice, giant wings rose in a sea of shrieks, then disappeared into the vast, engulfing darkness of the wood.

You bluff. It was obvious. It was the only thing to do.

'I got lost, Harry,' she stuttered, facing him, her back to the dark buildings and machines. The smell was worse again now. She could hear the sound of something mechanical working. 'City folk. Don't know north from south.'

'Lost?' he repeated, his voice full of disbelief.

'No sense of direction.'

'Yeah. And that pal of yours asking all them questions. Funny that, ain't it?'

Sara, she thought. Who went off the road not long after the Blamires had packed up gardening at Priory House.

'I do security here off and on, Mrs Fenway. Got to report you being here. Ordinarily.'

He seemed bigger in the night. She wanted to be home, safe and warm in front of the fire. 'Do what you must, Harry. If you don't want people coming in, you shouldn't leave the gates open.'

He grinned. 'We are the clever one now, aren't we? Heard a noise. Went to look. Still, since you're here . . .'

'I'll be going . . .'

'*No.* You get the full tour. Just like Disneyland.'

With his big hand he turned her to face the plant. 'You know what it is, don't you? Rendering?'

'Sort of.'

'That mean no, do it? This is what you townies get us to do behind your backs. Sight unseen. All the dirty work. Not that I'm complaining. You see all them containers?'

There were rectangular shapes in the darkness, at the far corner of the compound.

'Carcasses. Cattle. Sheep. You name it. All the bits and pieces no one else wants.'

He took her arm and they walked forward towards the giant machines that stood next to a pile of wooden pallets. She could see what they were now. Hoists and pulleys to lift the meat into the main building, a huge windowless wooden shed that stood two storeys high in front of them, a rickety staircase running up the outside.

They reached the bottom of the wooden stairs and he leaned forward to touch a button. A dim yellow light came on over the steps. 'Don't suppose you want to look inside, missus. Men's place, ain't it? Men like me.'

Pompous moron, she thought. 'I'm not squeamish,' she replied. After a while the smell just washed over you. If she'd come that far, she might as well see it through.

'Your choice,' Harry said, and waddled up the stairs, with the rolling gait of a badger.

She followed and they went into the interior of the rendering house. He punched the light switch and, just for a moment, she wondered whether to avert her eyes. But that was her imagination working. The vile smell apart, the interior of Paternoster Farm looked just like she imagined any industrial plant would. It was even easy to guess the purpose of some of the machinery. In the far corner was a grinder, some kind of giant mincing machine. It fed into automatic hoppers that were clearly destined for something more obscure, a huge ironclad vat that ran through both floors of the building, steam rising from vents at the side. The clanking network of metallic beasts suddenly coughed and roared. She leapt in fright. The grinder disgorged something, dropped it into a hopper with a semi-liquid plash, and then, like the car on some ghoulish fairground ride, the hopper took it over to the vat. There, some kind of automatic door opened and consumed the load.

'Computers,' Harry grinned. 'Wonderful thing, automation. Ten years ago there would have been a dozen men feeding this bloody great monster. Now they just load the grinder up and go off for a pint. Works twenty-four hours a day, unmanned during the night. Which is why they need the likes of me to pop in from time to time.'

'Fascinating,' she said. 'Can I have a lift home now?'

He moved beneath one of the dim yellow bulbs and grinned at her. 'Don't you have no curiosity? Don't you want to *know* what it all is?'

She sniffed. 'It's obvious, Harry. *Meat.*'

91

'Wrong. Meat's all gone. You or me have eaten it, or else it's off for dog food. You don't think a scrap of what sells is thrown away now, do you?'

The thought had occurred to her, but it was not something she wanted to pursue. Equally, Harry seemed unlikely to let her go until he'd had his fun. 'What then?'

'The bits that are left. After the knackers have taken off what they can get for pet food. After they've sold the hides for leather, the tallow to the drugs people to make that stuff you put on your pretty face. We get what's still there. And that thing' – he pointed over to the grinder – 'minces it nice and fine. Then we stick it in that whopping great fat fryer there, extract what tallow there's still left, and that big old thing squashes what's left down into nice dry pancakes. *Greaves* they're called. That's what they used to feed to animals, when it was allowed. Now they just pay us to dump it.'

It all seemed so mechanical, so out of place in Sterning Wood. There was something she was missing, too. 'Why are you telling me this?'

Harry Blamire looked deadly serious for a moment. ''Cos you ought to know. These things go on all the time and people like you just cover your eyes. You eat your burgers, you want your meat on the table. But you don't want to know what it costs. You don't want to look it in the face now, do you? Take a gander beneath the surface?'

Alison gave him an icy gaze. She'd had enough of Harry Blamire for one day. 'Is that a specific point you're making? Or a more general observation?'

He was laughing at her and he wanted her to know it. 'You people. You come in here. Think you own it all. And you don't own nothing. You don't *see* nothing. Except what you're not supposed to.'

She folded her arms across her chest. 'I'd like to go now, Harry. Do I get a lift? Or do I walk?'

'Yeah,' he grunted. 'Let me get my keys. Just making the point.'

He turned and walked up a narrow set of stairs to a small enclosed office in the corner of the first floor. She followed him inside. The walls were covered with soft pornography. There was a grubby desk with a phone on it and an even scruffier sofa, with yellow foam poking out of the seams. He closed the door behind her and threw off his tatty tweed jacket.

'No rush is there? I can make you a cup of tea. Glass of whisky, if you want it. We could get right nice and cosy on the settee there.'

Alison glowered at him, wondering whether she could really believe her ears. 'I don't think so.'

'Don't fancy a bit o' rough, now and again?'

'No,' she hissed between clenched teeth. 'And even if I did, I doubt it would be quite *that* rough.'

In two strides he was on her, gripping the arm she raised to strike him, forcing it behind her back. Harry was strong. She remembered the garden. His arms felt like steel. He undid the first two buttons on her jacket with his free hand, then gripped her hair, bent forward and kissed her neck savagely.

'Husband away now, ain't he? I heard that happens a lot. You ever wonder what *he's* up to?'

She tried to push him away but it was impossible. 'He'll be up to beating the living crap out of you. That's once the police are done.'

'The police?' His eyes were bright, sparkling. 'What you think they're gonna say? You came in here willingly. I'll tell 'em I've been shagging you for ages anyway. And it was just a tiff. You think they won't believe me? You know anything about "reasonable doubt"?'

He tugged at the jacket violently and the buttons on the front were torn off. She tried to hug her one free arm to her

93

breast. But he was too strong. She fell back towards the desk, felt its hard edge kick into the small of her back.

'And it's true. In a sense, anyway.'

'Harry,' she said, pleading now. 'Just let go. Just walk away. And we'll both forget this ever happened. Promise.'

'Promise?' He was laughing at her, and she didn't understand why. 'Like I said, you people know nothing. You daren't even look under your own noses.'

'Harry!'

He pulled himself to her, with an irresistible force. 'You think I ain't been there already? I don't know your tricks? Those little sashes? That silk gag in your mouth?'

She could, she thought, distance herself from this scene, watch it as a disinterested spectator, a sprite, a spirit, hovering in the corner of the room, observing two mannikins run through some mechanistic play they had been forced to perform by some hidden, inhuman puppet master.

She stared into his leering face, wide-eyed. 'What the hell are you talking about?'

'Burning Man, my girl. You think I never tasted your snatch that night? Did what I wanted while you was laying there, all white and dead to the world. With that husband of yours telling himself it was all right really, 'cos he wasn't giving you what you wanted. And maybe old Harry and the Burning Man could do it. Huh?'

'What the hell . . . ?'

'One more little service from the local yokel, all fine just so long as milady don't see. And you know what I wonder?'

Her head was in a million places all at once. He tugged at the button of her jeans, she felt the zip being drawn down, his hand groping at her groin.

'I wonder what the real thing's like. Dead good, I guess.'

He thrust a hard, calloused hand inside her knickers, pressing, pushing with fat, stiff fingers.

'No!'

Something fell into her free hand as it searched in a frenzy across the surface of the desk. It was long, slim and metallic. She lashed out with it, out to his face, and she felt the calloused, disgusting fingers withdraw. Harry screamed. His meaty fingers covered his eyes, blood streaming between them. She looked at her hand. Tight in her grasp was a pair of scissors, the blades open. Automatically, without thinking, the silver flashed through the air, and Harry screamed again.

'*Bitch!* You cut me! You done it now.'

She pushed past him, made for the door, praying he hadn't locked it. The handle turned, she rushed out onto the landing, and stumbled towards the stairs. Then he was on her again, like a dead weight, trying to roll her in the wrong direction, away from the steps, trying to trip her, force her to fall on the floor.

Alison stabbed backwards once more, felt the blade penetrate something soft and fleshy, no noise this time. Then she stumbled out of his grasp, out towards the clanking, hissing machines in the corner of the building. Harry Blamire was on his knees, between her and the stairs, his face in darkness, in the shade cast by the dim lighting.

'Let me go,' she said. 'Get out of the way and let me go, Harry. Or I swear I'll use this again. I *swear*!'

His face came up from his chest and the light caught it now. It was covered in blood, there were slashes across his cheeks, above his eyes. The gore dripped down into his grinning mouth. Behind her, something was happening. The machines were starting to wake up, cogs and gears were creaking into life.

'I'll have you, gel,' Harry Blamire croaked, then rose to his feet, like a runner coming off the blocks, started towards her, screaming something she couldn't begin to decipher. 'You can scrap as much as you like, but I'll be fucking you afore long.'

She held the scissors out in front of her face. They glinted in the harsh yellow light. And when he came to her she could see he was badly wounded, was stumbling, this was his last effort. She had fifteen years or more on Harry Blamire. She could defeat him. In one swift movement, she turned to the side, the blade swept through the air, through the passing, falling body. He screamed again, an animal noise, and toppled forward, falling into the iron skeleton of machines that were now in motion, alive, lights winking, innards growling.

The grinder opened, disgorged its load into the hopper, and the huge iron bucket lurched on its tracks, caught the stumbling man in the chest. He yelled, coughed blood into the darkness, and fell forward over the edge, into the wet, disgusting maw of the container.

She wanted to look away but it was impossible. She wanted to stop up her ears, but her hands refused to obey. Harry's bloodied face appeared over the edge of the hopper. He looked stupid. Stupid and terrified.

'The switch, gel,' he yelled. *'For Christ's sake, the switch!'*

She stared back at him, not moving. There was a big red button by the grinder marked 'Emergency Stop'. Alison Fenway watched the hopper grumble across the iron track and carry its contents towards the rendering vat.

An arm came over the side. He could get out, she thought. He could do this under his own steam, without her help. She couldn't move. The will had disappeared from her body.

The hopper lurched again and Harry fell back into its maw. A whirring noise came from the vat. She walked towards the grinder to get a better view. A hatch was appearing in the side of the vast, digesting machine. It revealed an interior that looked like an image from hell, of bubbling fat, fumes, and the unmistakable reek she'd come to know, the stench of Paternoster Farm.

She tried once more. Her arm obeyed. Her hand came

in front of her face. She looked at the bloodied blade, committed the sight of it to her memory, then launched it into the air. It spun, a silver, flashing toy, then fell into the gaping, miasmic mouth of the vat. Harry was screaming again but something, some filter inside her, blocked out the noise, made it unreal, nothing but a background intrusion into a life that was already closing in on itself, confining its existence to one small, discrete set of emotions and experiences, because there was simply no other way to stay sane.

The hopper came to the end of the track and tipped its contents into the bubbling, boiling liquid interior. She watched as a single hand clung onto the lip and wondered, quite rationally, what was happening to the rest of Harry Blamire at that point, what state of chaos had consumed his skin, how quickly flesh would fall from bone. Then the hatch door closed, and so did Alison Fenway's eyes. She was not certain, and she did not want to think about this point, but it was entirely possible that the metal door had severed Harry's desperate hand as it sealed the vat once more.

Not looking at the hissing giant, Alison fastened her jeans, buttoned up her jacket. Then she walked calmly down the steps and stood by the base of the giant vat, listening. The sound of roaring covered everything. A ring of gigantic gas jets had fired up at the base of the metallic container, boiling the contents, starting the process of destruction. She looked at the intricacy of the machine. There was no way Harry could have escaped, even if it hadn't been working. It was tight, enclosed. Until someone came in to remove the contents – what did he call them, *greaves*? – Harry would be left to his fate. And it was impossible to guess what would remain of him then.

She examined the gas burners more closely. They were on adjustable housings that bent them to the base of the vat. She walked over to the nearest and looked at the motors that moved the flame. It took two attempts, but soon she had mastered it. Alison slowly shifted one burner away from the gigantic metal beast and let the housing turn until it reached its horizontal limits. By that stage, the jet of fire was pointing directly at the wooden staircase. Flames were already beginning to lick the steps. They sang and they roared, alive and hungry.

Quite calm, she walked out of the rendering plant, out of Paternoster Farm, back into the night. Halfway through Sterning Wood there was a sound behind her, a deep, booming explosion. She looked back, and the sky was briefly golden with flame. Then she continued, not caring about the bats or the owls, the small, insignificant creatures of the night. Thinking of nothing but Harry Blamire and what he had said.

When she finally made her way back to Priory House, she put everything she was wearing into a black bin liner, double-bagged it inside two more, and deposited the lot in the outside rubbish store. Then she sat in the bath for an hour, shampooed her hair five times, cut her nails, scrubbed at them with a brush, cleaned her teeth, washed her face, over and over again.

When she fell asleep there was nothing of Harry Blamire or Paternoster Farm upon her, not a single atom, a vile, stray molecule. Only the words and the images inside her head.

Ten hours later Alison Fenway awoke and felt oddly rational, determined almost. There was a noise outside. She got up, pulled on a dressing gown, and looked out of the window at the green. Mitch Blamire was on the ancient tractor, pulling the even more ancient mowing machine. The grass was already bare and thin. He was driving round and round in a single, constant circle, over the bald, damp turf that now bore the brown, muddy marks of the vehicle's tyres. Through the glass, damp with the breath she had exhaled during the night, came the sound of Mitch's voice, a high-pitched, unintelligible keening.

YULE

Autumn ran into winter. The days grew desperately short. Thin morning mist gave way to thick hill fog. The earth became a carpet of dank, rotting leaves. The apple trees in the garden were now bare, skeletal black figures in a drab, wet landscape, long, unruly grass at their ankles.

For the first few days after Halloween, Alison spent her energies on the house, keeping it spotless, perfect in every way, trying not to think about Paternoster Farm or wait for the doorbell to ring. The call never came. As far as Beulah knew, Harry Blamire was no more through some tragic, explosive accident.

Even so, for one brief period she actually thought she might give herself up. Might phone the handsome plod, Justin, ask him round for a cup of tea and forgiveness, tell him about Harry's fumbling fingers down the front of her jeans, and how there really was no other choice. The brief, playful meeting at the hospital told her he ought to understand. For all the tentative flirting, Justin Liddle had made some kind of impression upon her. What Alison found difficult was separating how much of it was real and how much a reaction to this sudden, shocking discovery about Miles and his apparent behaviour at Burning Man. Why shouldn't she be able to trust a man? What, if Harry Blamire had been telling the truth, was Miles's real intention? Was it just the drink and Marjorie's dope? And what kind of excuse was that anyway? Miles, drunk or sober, had been party to some vile act of trespass upon her body. One side of her wanted to throw this in his face, demand an answer, then head for the door. But she would have damned herself in the act, and for a deed far worse than a touch of drunken debauchery.

This thought made the image of Justin, reliable Justin, someone who might sympathise, both more alluring and more dangerous. She could imagine sitting him down in the kitchen and laying out the facts, calmly, coolly, over a coffee. And then, she knew, the imaginary Justin would take an imaginary swig from his imaginary mug and ask, 'So why didn't you run from Harry? When he was hurt? Why didn't you stop him going into the furnace? And why, most of all, did you set the place on fire instead of calling us like you should have done, *Alison*?'

'Because,' this imaginary self said, getting impatient, '*it was in the middle of the wood.*'

'And he was injured. Badly, from what you say.'

At which point she would tell him about Miles and the sashes and the little marks the gag left on the morning after Burning Man. And Justin would say, 'Ah, now I understand. The bastard. You'll hear no more of it. In fact, if you want to top your husband too, put him down the waste disposal unit, no problem. Justice is a many-splendoured thing, it moves in mysterious ways. *Tant pis.* What the hell. I'll be getting along now, if you don't mind, Mrs Fenway, and ta very much for the cuppa.'

Oh yes. And after that he'd go outside, climb on his bike, and pedal off into a glorious sunset to a chorus of chirruping skylarks.

There was only one option. Silence. And the search for something to relieve the pain.

Miles finally came home three days later. He wore that strained, ill-tempered look that always followed trouble in the office. Unable to divulge the real source of her grief, Alison had picked an argument about the work and his absence from home, two subjects about which she cared nothing. It was short, loud and painful. When it was done, she thought of making the theatrical gesture and walking out of Priory House for good, a small bag in her hand. But to go where? Crabtree Lodge on the other side of the Minnis? That would have solved nothing, and there was nowhere else to run, on either side of the Atlantic. Miles was not the problem; he was a symptom. Besides, this was her home.

Miles appeared genuinely hurt by her accusations of neglect. He sensed this was something new, something disturbing. But the true core of their dispute remained hidden, unspoken. The double bed in the big room overlooking the green became a cold, still place. Two bodies occupied it, fighting not to touch. The memories were fine when she was alone. She could control them, send them to a place where they did as they were told. But when Miles's big, strong body slipped under the duvet beside her the natural order she had so carefully cultured was displaced.

After two nights of restless tossing and turning, some black, unnatural thing rolling between their silent bodies like an unseen wave of hatred, she made up the bed in the spare room. The mattress was hard there, the sheets chilly and a little damp. But she slept. They never spoke of this distance between them. She out of fear: to admit to hearing Harry Blamire let slip the secret was to confess to complicity in his death. And he, she thought, out of nothing more than mere male distraction. The battle was engulfing Miles; the prospect that he might lose, that they might forfeit Priory House and their life in Beulah into the bargain, was horribly real. He could see nothing beyond the bitter, embattled fight which now gripped Mersons. The war had become something personal, all-consuming.

Sara stayed in hospital for a week. Everything looked . . .

fine, the doctors said. Three days after the incident at Paternoster Farm, when she finally found the strength to return to the William Harvey, Sara had stared at her like a child, full of gratitude and relief. But her eyes were scared too. The hospital wanted her to come back, keep getting monitored. And to take it easy, most of all. Plenty of rest, no strenuous exercise. The two of them hugged and Alison knew exactly what this prescription was: a demand that Sara become some kind of invalid for the next seven months, until the baby was born. The possibility of failure, of that dreadful loss just happening out of the blue, would always be there.

Alison could remember it so well: all the tentative questions, the worries, the simple, open joy that confirmation brought. For all their friendship, she felt deeply, deeply jealous. Sara was pregnant while she was sleeping apart from a husband who rarely came home, and was usually in an introverted, uncommunicative mood when he did. It was unfair. Undeserved.

Inevitably, she thought over and over again of Harry Blamire's parting words. The sashes and the gag. What may – or may not – have occurred on one distant night in September, when the world was warm and the air full of the dust of harvested barley. Was it possible Harry was lying? She tried hard to convince herself and failed. The memory of his face, full of lust and fury in the foul, overheated interior of Paternoster Farm, was not something she was likely to forget till her dying day. Harry had no reason to lie. He had told her, not as a boast, but almost as an explanation, an excuse, for his behaviour. Some unexpected fault line in the way rational human beings treated each other had occurred on the night of Burning Man. All of them – Miles, Harry and herself, and whoever had been inside the straw effigy – lay unwittingly in its path.

For days, while Miles worked distantly in the City, she racked her brain for an explanation. Then, in a sudden revelation, abandoned the effort. That dreadful phrase from the TV – 'moving on' – came to her. It was shockingly apposite. Alison had, she knew, just two choices. Either she could allow Harry's death, and his revelation about what happened on that summer night, to destroy their lives together, and their potential happiness in Priory House. Or she could count it as history and try to get on with the difficult, daily business of being.

Forgiveness was another matter. Forgiveness presupposed comprehension, some understanding of the agreement Miles had entered into with whatever devil he had encountered that night. Nevertheless, there was one indelible truth that never left her thoughts. If she lost her head and confessed all to the likable Justin, she would be the one who was in the dock. Allowing one's wife to be serviced by the village yokel while unconscious may have been bad manners. Unlike murder – and the image of Harry disappearing into the maw of boiling liquid could come back to her so easily when it wanted – it was not yet, she judged, a matter for the law.

Christmas approached, and with it welcome practicalities: shopping and planning, cards for distant relatives, presents for all. The complexities made full employment of her time, and that pleased her. When she pored over the postage charts for New Zealand, or flicked through her diaries to remember the name of some far-off child in Massachusetts, the real concerns that lay deep inside her head could be regarded as dormant. Not dead, not yet. For a while she continued to dread some spontaneous, unstoppable outburst with Miles in which she would rain a flurry of blows on his dark, unyielding chest, empty completely her long treasury of vile epithets, and ask him: *why?* And the answer, she suspected already: *because you wanted it so badly. And someone in the village –* the country medic, of course, who had broached the subject once before – *thought they knew the way, just this once*.

The storm never came. At the very end of November,

when Miles was down for two nights, not the customary one, she had drunk too much Scotch, gone back into the old bedroom, and – the term, when she came to think about it, needed to be very accurate – *let him make love to her*. While Miles grunted about his business, she thought about Christmas, considered the relative merits of beef, goose, lamb and guinea fowl, and whether the bedroom ceiling needed repainting. When it was done, and she lay on the old, familiar dampness, he burst into tears and threw his head on her shoulder, apologising all the while. For the work. For his constant absence.

Normality was returning; some mute form of acceptance would follow. Had she never known, she never would have suspected. It was a one-off aberration, a temporary flaw in an otherwise benign, caring personality. Miles had saved her. She could not forget that. Without him she would be a mess, drifting from job to job, half starving in Manhattan. She had always told herself she could forgive a brief, pointless affair. Was this really any different?

Sara thrived, and ultimately offered Alison the finest, most apposite, of Christmas presents: an occupation. She had come out of hospital looking pale and scared. Within a week the colour was back in her cheeks and she was giggling over how a new consignment of Turkish rugs had just made her a fortune in Brussels. A ritual was born: morning tea at Priory House on Mondays, Wednesdays and Fridays, and a reciprocal engagement at Crabtree Lodge on alternative days, Sunday excepted. Burning Man was never mentioned. The tragedy at Paternoster Farm slipped in and out of the conversation in the space of ten minutes. Sara showed no interest in either subject. To her there was nothing in the world now but the future and the baby.

One day, at the beginning of December, Alison found herself ensnared by the work. Sara had lost her voice and needed her to make some calls. So she took over and spoke with a rug dealer in Kabul and a fabric supplier in Marrakesh. She checked the contents of the warehouse in Hounslow, and became engaged in a long, and ultimately successful, negotiation with a bitch of a buyer for Debenhams. Sara had listened to that one in admiration, touched with more than a little awe.

'Work with me, Alison,' she pleaded. 'I need you. Not just now, but when the baby's born too. We could be partners. I could *never* talk to them like that.'

She was astonished by Sara's naivety. 'You should never let them tell *you* the price, Sara.'

'Why not? If I'm making enough money out of it?'

'It's the principle of the thing.'

'You're tough, Alison. They won't take advantage of you. Just talk to Habitat for me. *Please.*'

Alison picked up the phone, called some snotty buyer in London and announced her precious consignment of Berber wraps was going to Selfridges unless they upped the price by thirty per cent. She listened to the voice on the line: she could almost smell the tobacco in the woman's throat.

'This is ridiculous,' the buyer snarled. 'Put Sara on the line.'

'Sara's out, working out how she's going to afford to run all this and a kid on the money you pay her.'

Madame Silk Cut inhaled. 'Pregnant? *Ahhh.* Fifteen.'

'Twenty-five and a thirty-day turnaround on invoice.'

'Oh, give me a break. Do you think I care about this crap that much?'

Just before Christmas? Alison knew the stuff Sara was supplying them. It was wonderful, and they were getting it for next to nothing, then selling it on at a two-hundred-per-cent mark-up. 'Sara is no spring chicken. *I* care.'

'Shit,' the woman grumbled. 'Well, just this once. I'll end up shoving it into the January sales for less than I paid, you know.'

'I doubt it.'

A smoky laugh came down the line. 'Oh God. You *are* temporary, aren't you?'

''Fraid not.'

'Bugger. These hippie outfits just go one of two ways. Belly up or they discover business. I'm not sure which is worse. Call me when you're in town some time. I'll buy lunch. If Sara has someone serious with her, *and* you can deliver, we might have a lot to talk about.'

She put down the phone and found Sara staring at her from the sofa in a state of shock.

'I can't believe you talked to Nora like that. She's *terrifying*.'

'It's all an act,' Alison said. 'It's just a little ritual we have to go through.'

Three days later they went to a solicitor in Ashford and signed the partnership papers. Sara, Alison soon realised, did need her. The business was at its limits in its present form. She farmed out everything: accounts, stock, VAT, Customs and Excise handling. All she did was buy and sell through a vast, extensive network she'd built up over the years. It was a perfect business model and one Sara, for all her outward appearance of mayhem, managed to control brilliantly. One glimpse at the order book and the accounts also made it absolutely plain that this really was a one-woman business; if Sara fell under a bus, it would collapse instantly.

They talked about the future and it soon became clear what Alison's contribution would be: sales and logistics, keeping the cogs and wheels of the business running smoothly. Sara could do what she thought of as the fun part, calling someone she met years ago in Afghanistan and haggling for a container-load of ethnic oddities. One day, they might get an office. Employees perhaps. But that was a long way ahead. There was a baby to be considered. Perhaps for both of them, now that she and Miles were getting back on track.

They worked hard through December, Alison listening to Sara as she ran the business from the front room of Crabtree Lodge, making notes, underlining points that needed to be ironed out, thinking about ways in which she could ease the workload and cut down on the paper mountain Sara had acquired over the years.

The month flew past. On the morning of 23 December, walking back from the cottage, her head full of VAT forms and the arrangements for bonded warehousing, she realised she was, herself, moving with the seasons. This was the shortest day of the year, the winter solstice. From now on the world moved into light. She could feel some similar change happening inside her too. The recent past was as distant and as dead as Harry Blamire.

Alison turned the corner and saw Marjorie Tyler outside the front of Priory House, standing on tiptoe, peering in through the glass.

Marjorie Tyler stood on the doorstep daring Alison to ask her in. The weather was in two minds about which direction to take. The sky had an ominous, grey underbelly, the wind was starting to die into a scant breeze. Snow was on the way.

'What are you doing tonight? And for the rest of Christmas for that matter?' Marjorie asked. She was wearing a green woollen coat which looked Austrian in origin, and a bright red bobble hat. Her cheeks positively glowed. Alison wondered whether it was fresh air or gin.

'I don't know yet. Miles is away and won't be back until tomorrow. With his father. Plans are pretty open. Arnold is eighty-two. They have to be.'

'Well.' Marjorie folded her arms across her plump chest,

and Alison was grimly aware that the woman was demanding to be allowed in. 'The Tylers customarily hold open house. Christmas Day, three o'clock onwards. Don't feel compelled to bring a bottle, we've got plenty. We thought it might give you a chance to meet more people from the village. And there's the wassailing tonight. Meet a few there too. You mustn't miss that.'

Marjorie stamped her feet. It wasn't that cold. Alison gave in. 'Would you like a coffee?'

'Lovely.' Marjorie beamed, and was through the big front door like a shot, wiping her boots on the mat, examining the furnishings. 'Gorgeous house. You're the envy of every woman within a radius of ten miles, you know.'

'We like it,' Alison replied lamely, and headed off into the kitchen. Marjorie trotted behind her, rolling like an overweight dog following in its master's footsteps. The room was too hot. Marjorie stared at the Aga.

'Ah yes. One of those things. Never did like them. Poncy.'

'We inherited it,' Alison said, trying to smile.

'Of course you did, dear. Lucky old Miles inherited everything, didn't he?'

'We were very . . . fortunate.' It was impossible to work out the reason, but Alison had the distinct impression Marjorie resented the way they had come to own Priory House. 'Wassailing? That's like carol singing?'

'Same sort of thing. Meet outside the pub at six thirty. You need to mingle, you know, meet some new people.'

New people? The village was so small. 'I thought we'd met just about everybody already.'

'I shouldn't think so. Beulah's bigger than you think. It's not just the green. Quite a lot of houses tucked away in the Minnis, in places you wouldn't dream of. Odd bunch out there in the wilds.'

Alison was aware of a stray, rising eyebrow that she was unable to control.

'Oh yes,' Marjorie continued. 'Much odder than us. We greenies are merely Gothic. Out on the Minnis they're downright pagan. Either shagging each other or sharpening the axe for a spot of domestic carnage. In-bred mainly, but middle class in-bred, otherwise we wouldn't be mixing, naturally.'

Alison smiled blankly.

'Just joking, of course,' Marjorie declared. 'In the main they're bloody solicitors with wives who think curing red mite on their blasted chickens is the most important thing on earth. You *have* seen some of these places, surely? On your walks?'

'My walks?'

'Yes. I see you, dear. Downsview may be an ugly, modern box but it is superbly built for an observation point. Nothing escapes my beady eye. You walk. Don't deny it.'

Alison poured the coffee and handed a mug over to Marjorie. 'Guilty. Shall we sit down?'

They pulled up a couple of chairs at the huge pine table. Thomas the cat wandered over from his basket by the Aga, took one look at Marjorie, then collapsed in a happy, warm bundle at her feet. Marjorie took no notice whatsoever. Her mind was on other things. Alison had the distinct feeling she was being pumped.

'What's your favourite walk?' Marjorie asked.

She shook her head. 'Impossible to say.'

'The White Horse? Wait till May Day and the cutting. You'll adore that.'

'I'm sure.'

Marjorie gazed into her face. 'You have *been* to the White Horse, haven't you?'

'Of course,' she replied.

'And beyond? Into the woods?'

'Never,' Alison lied. 'Too far for me. Too muddy. And too dark.'

'Thought so,' Marjorie declared. 'You are a creature of the light. Obvious the first time I saw you. Of course, you do know what's in those woods? Or rather *used* to be?'

Alison took a deep swig of coffee and knew she would not be rattled by this. 'I do read the newspapers, Marjorie. It's where poor Harry died. Am I right?'

'Of course. Did you hear it? They say it was loud enough to deafen the whole village. I was in Canterbury at the time. First I knew was seeing poor old Mitch going bonkers on the green the next day.'

Alison shook her head. 'I didn't hear a thing. What an awful accident.'

'Yes . . .' Marjorie looked conspiratorial. 'If that's what it was. The police are still sniffing around. You know why?'

Alison's breath was short. She didn't want it to show. 'Tell me.'

'No sign of Harry. Ordinarily in fires there's something. A skeleton, I guess. You can't just burn a human body and expect it all to disappear. But they've found bugger all at Paternoster, so I hear. They're struggling over whether to hold an inquest. How do they prove he died?'

Alison gave an involuntary shudder.

'I'm sorry,' Marjorie said. 'I gather you have a thing about fires.'

Alison groaned. 'Doctor-patient privilege really counts for something round here, doesn't it?'

'Oops,' Marjorie said, grinning, and, in an oddly girlish gesture, put a pudgy hand up to her mouth. 'Village life, my dear. Nothing goes on in Beulah without someone knowing.'

'I'll try to bear that in mind. How's Mitch?'

'Gone. For a while anyway. Surely you noticed? Rumour has it he's cashed in the insurance and taken himself off to Bangkok of all places. Now, why would a fifty-year-old man disappear to Bangkok? No. It's a rhetorical question.'

110

Alison thought about it. Even with her brief spell of residency in the village, it was hard to imagine Beulah without a Blamire boy. 'Gone for good?'

'I very much doubt it. The Blamires and Beulah are intertwined. Have been for centuries. Mitch will be back, mark my word. Probably with a horrible dose of the clap, or worse, and expecting my poor sod of a husband to cure him of it. Overnight. With one pill available on the NHS. But that's men all over for you. Is Miles like that?'

Like what exactly? she wondered. 'Miles is . . . very busy,' she said.

'Business,' Marjorie said viciously. 'And they never let slip a blasted thing, do they? John whinges about money all the time. And I wanted a winter holiday in Tobago. Fat chance. I'm not made for cold climates, you know. More a Mediterranean type.'

Alison thought that Marjorie Tyler was probably better designed for gutting seals in an igloo. 'More coffee?'

'Nah. Need to get home. Fit in a stiff drink before the hunter-gatherer comes back from despatching herbivores on the plain. So we'll see you tonight?'

'Perhaps. I don't imagine Sara's going.'

'Hope not. In her condition she should stay at home and put her feet up. We'll probably cover five miles or so, and the weather looks a bit dodgy. Bring wellies, won't you?'

'I'll talk to her anyway.'

Marjorie Tyler sighed. 'You need more than one friend in a village, dear. Otherwise people start to think you're forming a clique.'

She was trying to be helpful in her own odd way, Alison thought. 'I think I'll skip the pot cake tonight, thanks.'

'Oh.' Marjorie's big cheeks went bright pink. 'Sorry. I didn't know whether it was Shrove Tuesday or Sheffield Wednesday that night. Normally I give people a bit of warning. Forgiven?'

Alison said, very slowly, 'Forgiven.'

'Excellent! Now, practical questions. Are you *prepared*?' She gave the word a significance Alison failed to understand.

'Prepared for what?'

'Isolation, my dear. The sudden transportation of our darling little village to Antarctica. Don't listen to the idiot weathermen. They don't know a thing. I'm the honorary village witch, in case you hadn't guessed, and my sources tell me we have snow on the way. In Beulah, that is spelt S-N-O-W. You won't get up or down the hill into Wye, even in a four by four. The last time we had it bad we were cut off for ten days, four of them without power. So. Do you have plenty of oil? Does your generator work? Lots of baked beans? Stuff like that? Come tomorrow it will be a blizzard, and by then it's too late.'

Alison's head reeled. 'Power cuts? Generators?'

Marjorie looked at her. She seemed cross. 'Planning, dear girl. All the men want to do is play with their toys, of course. It's up to you to get the oil in, make sure you have supplies. You won't be able to keep the freezer going, you know, not on any normal generator. If you're lucky, you get lights, a fridge, and enough to keep the boiler pump running. You'll stay warm and you'll eat.'

None of this had occurred to her. 'I'll check.'

'You do,' Marjorie said, rising from the table. 'Getting cut off can be fun, provided you don't starve or die of exposure.'

'Nice thought.'

'Quite. And believe me, it *is* on the way.'

She watched Marjorie waddle across the green, back to her modern house on the far side, then pulled the keys for the outbuildings out of her bag and checked the oil. The tank was two thirds full, thank God. The generator worked on first pull. They had four cans of petrol next to it inherited from the previous owner. She had no idea how long that would drive the thing. And there was food: pulses and cans, dried soups, rice and bacon. They could survive, she guessed, provided the generator held out. Until Marjorie had mentioned it, Alison had never realised how dependent they were on the invisible spark of electricity.

She would go wassailing. It was a shame Miles couldn't join them. Alison felt the need for male company. Beulah seemed terribly like a matriarchy sometimes.

When she reached for her bag to replace the keys, the answer stared her in the face. The cheap white card was still there, face up. She felt an odd, hot flush just taking it out, dialling the number and praying that she'd get an answering machine. No such luck. Justin was at his desk, sounding young and eager and friendly.

'Alison?'

And forward too, she thought.

'I was calling about Sara's accident,' she said, busking. 'Any news?'

'Sara's accident,' he repeated. 'Not something I can discuss with other people. If there was anything to discuss, which there isn't.'

She suspected as much. 'So that's it?'

'Barring a miracle. Are you really calling to ask that?'

'Of course.' Alison hoped she sounded convincing. 'I take it you're policing the big village event tonight, Justin.'

'That being . . . ?'

'Jesus, your village spies are pathetic.'

'Got none, I'm afraid. The job's open if you fancy it.'

Miles would be back tomorrow. He couldn't expect her to stay locked in Priory House, bored to tears, waiting for the warrior's return.

'Wassailing. Tonight. In the Green Man. It's a kind of carolling thing, I think. Half the village will be there apparently.'

'You're on,' Justin said brightly, and she put down the phone. He sounded keen, and not just for the obvious reasons. This kind of impulsive behaviour was a habit she ought to lose. She needed to think things through first. A murder had happened in Beulah. Justin just might be suspicious.

Alison Fenway stood at the window, feeling strangely young. The sky was leaden and pregnant. Marjorie, the village witch, was right. The first fat flakes of snow were beginning to tumble from the sky.

She walked up to the crowded bar of the Green Man and ordered a glass of mulled wine. Justin Liddle was at her side in a flash, out of uniform now, wearing a thick winter jacket and jeans. He smiled pleasantly at her and looked relieved. 'Glad there's someone I know here. Let me buy that.'

She accepted the drink. It was hot and spicy, full of gorgeous exotic flavours. She couldn't help but wonder whether Marjorie Tyler had been involved in the recipe.

'Your friend not coming then? Or hubby?' he asked.

She had phoned Sara before setting out, mainly to get the low-down on whatever wassailing might be. Sara had groaned. 'Oh, *that*. It's nice to do it the once, but no more. And certainly not in my condition. A lot of walking and songs you've never heard of. Plus the drink flows. So what's new?'

'Miles is in London. I think Sara's better off at home,' Alison told him. 'She's done it before. And you?'

Justin shook his head. With his close-cropped blond hair and open face he looked oddly young in the pub. No more than twenty-five, she guessed. 'I'm a virgin too. They only made me community policeman for this area back in July, and that's a part-time thing anyway. But we're supposed to participate. Your friend's OK?'

'On top of the world.'

'That's great. She really scared me after that accident,' he said, and she thought she might have to revise the age estimate: sometimes he seemed barely out of his teens, there was such an air of enthused, intelligent innocence about him. He was so different from Miles. 'I wish I'd caught whoever did it, you know. I tried. There wasn't a thing to go on.'

'All forgotten now,' Alison said. 'Sara has her mind on other things.'

'Glad to hear it.' Justin beamed, and was abruptly jostled at the shoulder by Marjorie Tyler shoving her way through the crowd, a small gaggle of strangers in her wake.

'Ah, PC Plod! You'll never take me alive, copper.' She looked, Alison thought, half cut already. A tumbler full of gin and tonic sloshed in her right hand. Her eyes gawped wildly around the crowded bar, never quite staying on one point long enough to focus.

'Good evening, Mrs Tyler,' Justin replied amiably. 'Festivities always do start early here in Beulah, don't they?'

'Never bloody well stop if I can help it, Justie. You and Mrs Fenway make a nice couple, I must say. Serve that stupid husband of hers right, staying in London all the time.'

Justin blushed and looked at Alison apologetically. She smiled back at him as if to say: *never mind*. Not that she did.

''Nuff prattle and gossip,' Marjorie declared. 'People for you to meet. Frank!'

A distinguished-looking chap who must have been pushing seventy came forward. He was dressed in an old-fashioned knee-length gabardine raincoat and a trilby hat. His face was that of an old army officer, even down to the silver and black moustache. Bright, incisive grey eyes twinkled at Alison from behind horn-rimmed glasses.

'Frank lives in that whacking old pile down the Wye Road. *Sir* Frank Wethered, if you wish to be precise.'

'No need for the honorifics, Marjorie,' the man said in a cracked, upper-class voice. 'Plain Frank will do.'

Marjorie leaned forward, pretending to be conspiratorial. 'You should look him up on your computers, Justie. Frank was an absolute devil in the Cold War. Killed Russkies with his bare hands *and* got a knighthood for it.'

'Balls,' Frank said. 'I was a humble civil servant in the Ministry of Defence, and don't you believe otherwise.'

'Of course, Frank,' Marjorie said and, to Alison's amazement, actually patted the top of his trilby. 'They knight every pen-pusher in Whitehall, don't they, dear?'

'Hmmpph. Mrs Fenway?' Alison took the chilly tan leather glove extended in front of her. 'Welcome to Beulah. Better late than never. And as for *you*, my boy, I have some suggestions about the neighbourhood watch scheme I really would like to discuss.'

'My pleasure, sir,' Justin replied in a precise, polite fashion. 'May I call to make an appointment?'

'Splendid.' Sir Frank radiated pleasure. Alison liked the way Justin dealt with him. She had heard of Frank already: the old diplomat who lived down the hill. Alone now, since his wife died a few years back. She guessed he could be a real pain to the authorities, and Justin doubtless knew that full well. More glasses of steaming wine came across the bar in a waving forest of anonymous hands. She snatched one, leaned close in to Justin's ear and whispered, 'You'll make Chief Constable one day. No doubt about it.'

He smiled at her, and leaned close into her hair, so close she could feel the warmth of his breath. 'I think you need a little more than just good manners for that, Alison.'

'Meaning?' It was odd how the conversation was so private, so intimate in the swaying, noisy crowd of the pub.

'Meaning the modern police force is driven by results. Not who you know. I need . . .'

She put a finger to his lips, quite deliberately, and felt a flush of excitement, something she hadn't known for years. 'You need to solve a *mystery*,' Alison said, and took the finger away instantly, worried she was going too far.

'Precisely,' Justin said. He looked a little pink in the cheeks. The pub was hot, she thought. Of course.

'Welcome to the club,' Alison mumbled.

'Excuse me . . . ?'

But then Marjorie was pushing forward another group of people, some she half knew by sight, others complete strangers. They *were* a mixed bunch, she said to herself, shocked by some sudden, rising snobbishness. There was a middle-aged couple from the tenanted cottages out on the lower Minnis road: a blowsy-looking woman with long dyed blonde hair, too much make-up, overlarge earrings and a downtrodden-looking husband, shorter than her, muscular, like all the farm workers she'd met, but with watery, lost eyes. Too much booze. Too much nagging in all probability. With the couple, and clearly part of the family, though she'd never seen them before, were two youths who looked barely twenty and a girl of about eighteen, again with straggling dyed blonde hair and a face that spelled trouble.

'You've seen Dickie and Angie Cartwright on their rounds, I imagine,' Marjorie said. Hands were proffered to her and Justin. He took the man's and looked embarrassed; Dickie wouldn't look him in the eye. The three children – they could be nothing else – nodded in their direction.

'Pleasetameetcha,' Angie Cartwright chanted, lifting her glass. 'You want cleaning done or anything, Mrs Fenway, you just let me know.'

'Should take a look at her house afore you let her clean yours,' one of the youths said, grinning to show a mouth of ill-formed yellow teeth. 'Mum's a dirty old slag, eh?' Then he planted a slobbery kiss on her cheek.

'Up yours, Gordon,' Angie Cartwright complained. 'That's a nice thing to say in front of Mrs Fenway, I'm sure.'

'Yeah.' The youth gave her a big squeeze. 'But we still love yer, don't we? Come all the way back from Ashford just to see her. Even though the old cow kicked us out the house.'

Angie shook her head. 'Too small for families, these little tenants' cottages, Mrs Fenway. We just couldn't manage with this handful.'

'Need more beer,' Dickie Cartwright grunted. He pushed his way through the crowd to the end of the bar. The three youngsters followed him, but not before the girl gave Alison a long, searching glance. Alison was trying to work out why when Justin leaned down and whispered in her ear.

'If there's one thing I hate it's meeting customers off the job.'

'Him?' she whispered back.

'Both of them. Let's just say, I wouldn't have her in to do the cleaning. You might find you end up with a lot less to clean before long.'

'Now that,' she said softly into his cheek, 'is what I call community policing.'

Justin laughed and said, 'Uh-oh. It's the creepy neighbourhood quack.'

John Tyler came and stood next to them, looking tired. 'So what do you think of Bella?' he asked her.

'Who?'

'Bella. The Cartwrights' girl. She was giving you the once-over.'

Alison didn't know what to say. Tyler didn't seem to miss a thing. 'We never even spoke. I don't know why that should be.'

'Fascinating child,' Tyler continued, and Alison steeled

118

herself for another riveting breach of the General Medical Council's guidelines on patient privacy. 'The conventional diagnosis really ought to be epilepsy. Bella gets the most amazing auras. Sees other dimensions, becomes convinced she knows people she's never met before. Hallucinations. Ringing in the ears. Bizarre tastes and smells. Classic symptoms followed by a classic seizure. And you know what? I spent a fortune on electroencephalography and came up with nothing. The Greeks used to call epilepsy the "sacred disease". Hippocrates said this was all a load of balls, but then what did he know? Small-minded little materialist, which was remarkable for his time, of course. Life's so much more complex than that. Sacred disease . . . I rather like that. Neurologically there's precious little to distinguish between certain kinds of seizure, a sneeze, say, or an orgasm.'

'I know which I'd rather have,' Alison said bluntly.

'Ah,' John Tyler said, waving a finger just to emphasise the point. 'But you have a choice. Or rather you think you have.'

Justin was now distinctly bright pink. There was movement towards the door. Perhaps it could save him. 'Carol singing now, Dr Tyler?' he asked.

Frank Wethered stuck his sharp, foxy face in between them, and Alison was taken aback. He looked quite cross. '*Carol singing*? I should say not. Don't get me wrong, dear boy. We're all good church-goers here. But tonight's Yule. We *wassail*.'

'Of course,' Justin replied, looking blank.

'Luther and Calvin abhorred Christmas,' Tyler said confidently. 'There was a time in Boston, back in the Pilgrim Fathers' days, when they actually banned it. Can you believe that?'

'No,' Alison replied firmly. 'And I come from Boston.'

'Well, it's true, I assure you. Back around the time they were burning your relatives at Salem. The twenty-third is

119

the day that counts, believe me. The winter solstice. The point at which the days cease to get shorter. Light begins to reclaim the world. We start to see an end to the long dark night of our souls. All early societies with an astronomical bent marked the date. The Christians only moved in when they realised it was a feast people were unlikely to leave behind. There was a tradition that Jesus was born on the twenty-fifth of the month, so that was handily transferred to December.'

'It could be true,' Alison said, hackles rising. Tyler seemed such a know-it-all.

'What? The entire Christian tradition? No time for that tonight, but on a practical point the date can't be right, not if the Bible is to be believed. Remember the shepherds. Do they tend their flock by night in December in Palestine, even today? Of course not. Ask any of the locals here. Sheep need tending during one time of the year only. When they are about to lamb. And when do they lamb in the Middle East? Spring. No, Yule is a ceremony with no Christian connotations whatsoever except those that have been tacked onto its hem. And the Church knows this full well. It wasn't even celebrated in England until the seventh century. People had much more interesting things to do.'

Tyler stared knowingly at her. 'Think about it. You know it's true. Mistletoe. Do you imagine that's a Christian tradition? Of course not. The Druidic priests cut it with a golden sickle. It was a symbol of fertility for the entire twelve days of the feast – yes, the Christians stole that too. They didn't *kiss* beneath the mistletoe, my dear. It gave sexual power to anyone who held it over the head of another. It was a fertility ritual, pure and simple.'

Someone passed over a plastic lemonade bottle and thrust it into her hand. She wasn't sure, but it might have been Marjorie Tyler.

'I knew that,' Alison said defensively.

'Good,' John Tyler said. 'Then perhaps there's hope yet. Shall we go?'

She clutched the plastic bottle. It felt warm and comforting. There was probably a half pint of mulled wine inside: spicy and strong. Burning Man wasn't like this, she said. She was more country now, she could cope with these people.

Justin held open the door for her and smiled. 'I hope I'm not making a big mistake here,' he said. There was a smell of paraffin and burnt wood. People were lighting old-fashioned brands made of twigs, like witches' brooms, then holding the burning standards up above their heads. The crowd stood in a small, hot sea of light, then started to move across the green.

'Me too,' she said, and breathed the cold night air. Gently, meaning nothing, merely as a response to the dark, chilly evening, she slipped her arm inside his and they started to follow the throng.

The snow had stopped while they were in the pub. The night was clear now and brilliant with stars. Free of clouds, the sky was working towards delivering a hard, crisp frost. Alison exhaled in a big puff and saw her breath hang in the air. She felt a touch drunk, but there was no mistaking the extraordinary beauty of the evening.

There were probably twenty-five of them in the wassailing gang, and they sang the oddest songs. A long-haired, hippie-looking girl with a fiddle would strike up something like an Irish jig, then everyone would join in, with tunes and lyrics Alison had never heard, odd, folky stuff, all about nature and the seasons, and never once mentioning any element of Christmas, or Christianity for that matter. They sang the first outside the pub, and she tried to hum along (in much the same way she did in church, on the rare occasion a wedding took her there; she was, she remembered, just as heathen as the rest of them). Justin did the same, but tucked his plastic bottle into her pocket. *No drinking on duty.* So perhaps it wasn't a social visit after all. Justin had a touch of ambition about him. Something in Beulah, beyond the everyday routine of being the local community copper, was floating his boat. She didn't want to think what.

After the first song a grinning Norman came out from behind the bar and distributed even more mulled wine. Then the band moved on around the eastern half of the green, taking their plastic cups with them, past the run of modern, detached boxes, stopping at every house to sing, and getting copious amounts of free drink in return. Alison wondered what she was supposed to do about Priory House, which sat silent and in darkness, a huge, imposing pile. Someone had made sure they were well briefed; when they reached the last modern box, everyone turned to march across the cricket pitch and work the western half of the village. She felt relieved. Beulah had its own, precise form of bizarre etiquette and, without Sara to guide her, she had no idea how to follow it.

The hippie girl with the fiddle marched up to them, a broad, pleasant grin on her face. Alison was sure she had never seen her before. A good proportion of the revellers were, she thought, outsiders, and she wondered what their connection with the village could be.

'Star sign?' the girl demanded.

'Cancer,' Justin replied.

'Oh *dear*,' she said, grinning. 'How many Cancers does it take to change a light bulb?'

'Give in.'

'Just the one, provided he brings along his mum. And you?'

Alison hated star signs. 'Scorpio.'

'Oh *double* dear. How many Scorpios does it take to change a light bulb?'

Alison tried to look interested.

'None,' the girl said, not laughing now. 'They prefer the dark.'

'Incisive,' Alison said.

'*I* thought so.'

'And you?' There was a symmetry to this game, Alison thought. She had to play it through.

'I'm a witch.'

'How many witches does it take to change a light bulb?' Justin asked.

'Depends what you want it changed into, silly,' she said, and struck up a fast, racing tune on the fiddle. Marjorie Tyler gave a whoop and, with a surprisingly agile leap, started to dance. Others followed suit. In a matter of moments, the gaggle was a throng of jostling bodies, catching each other under the arms as they wheeled, yelping in glee. To her amazement, old Granny Jukes was propelling herself across the grass in a motorised wheelchair, belting out the tune with gusto.

She stood on the periphery, with Justin, both of them looking amused and more than a shade embarrassed. After the pub, she had unhooked her arm from his. It would be foolish to send out the wrong signals.

'I told you they were all weird,' he said. Justin had very nice, bright eyes, she thought, and they never rested. He was watching every one of the revellers, as if he could commit each face to memory.

'Why are you here?' she asked, taking a swig from the lemonade bottle. 'I mean, *really* here?'

'Community policeman, Alison. Doing my duty.'

'Crap. You're fishing.'

'Damn,' he said, grinning. 'I hope they're not as smart as you.'

'Of course they are. Smarter in most ways.'

She watched the Cartwrights cavorting drunkenly, saw the mother give the eldest boy a long, distinctly sexual kiss, and added, 'Most of them, at least.'

Justin grimaced, took the bottle from her, downed a small mouthful, and handed it back. 'I thought maybe Mitch would turn up. And I really would like to talk to him.'

'Why?'

He shook his head. 'Can't discuss force business.'

'Oh, come on. *Why?*'

'Let's just say, loose ends.' His voice had dropped, almost to a whisper. Justin liked the idea of a touch of undercover investigation, she realised. It was another side to his childlike nature. 'One brother disappears. Dead, says the coroner, though we've got nothing you could call a body. And then the other one's gone, with the insurance money. Thirty thousand quid, and the mortgage paid off. One week after the cheque arrives he's on his toes.'

'It *was* an accident,' she said firmly. 'I thought everyone knew that. And the boys . . . in some way they really loved one another. Mitch would never harm Harry. Ask anyone. Not that I knew them well but there was something creepy about the way they went around together. As if they could communicate without talking. Twins can be like that.'

'Maybe Harry's communicating with Mitch now.'

She shivered and wondered when they'd get a decent drink. The gaggle was stumbling along the poorer periphery of the green. The largesse getting handed out at the door left something to be desired: at one house she had, she felt sure, consumed a small glass of sweet British sherry and the taste was still sticking to her teeth like glue.

'Don't say that. It's too . . . *ugh!*'

'All the same,' Justin continued, 'I would dearly love to have a chat with Mitch Blamire. Both of them are customers of old. And I reckon we've got plenty to talk about.'

The group moved on, and Alison knew where the chaotic rabble was headed now. Someone lifted Granny Jukes's wheelchair over a clump of rye grass obstructing the way. She hoped Sara didn't feel too tired to deal with such a crowd. She should have known better. Once they had roared through a long and distinctly atonal tune outside the front door of Crabtree Lodge Sara appeared in a long flowing white dress, beaming in spite of the cold. She carried a tray that bore a couple of bottles of decent Scotch and several plates of hot mince pies.

Alison caught up with the gaggle, descended on the food and drink like a shot and gave Sara an affectionate peck on the cheek. 'You get my vote as Beulah hostess of the year,' she said. 'Also, as the wisest woman in the village. Why am I here? These people seem lunatics.'

'Yes,' Sara said, shivering a little now. 'But it *is* Yule.'

'Of course. That excuses everything. You're cold, my girl. I don't want you standing outside.'

'No.' Sara took a flurry of proffered hands as the gang thanked her for the food and drink. 'But next year I'll be back. Provided I can get a babysitter. Rituals have their attractions.'

'I will babysit and you can scoff the mince pies,' Alison declared. 'That is a promise.'

Sara gave her a hug. 'You're a real brick. Enjoy yourself.' She looked at the back of the crowd. 'Who's the bloke?'

'Justin. The local copper. Don't you remember him from the hospital?'

'Oh, yes,' Sara said coldly. 'I'm afraid I've never really warmed to the police. Bit of a hunk though.'

'He's nice. You'd like him.'

Sara gave her a penetrating look. 'Really?'

'Don't be ridiculous,' Alison answered, aware of a sudden heat in her cheeks. 'In you go now, off to bed.'

'And you?'

She sighed. 'Thirty minutes more and then it's back home. To put up the decorations.'

'Don't forget the mistletoe.'

'Ha, ha.'

'But, Alison,' Sara said, wide-eyed and all innocence, 'it worked for me.'

Alison knocked back a spare glass of Scotch and said, 'That'll cost you.'

Then Justin came over, smiled at them both, and asked Sara how she was. 'Fine, thanks,' she replied. 'Even better if you track that bastard down.'

'Country drivers,' he grimaced. 'But if you think of anything else . . .'

The gaggle was getting ready to move. The fiddling witch had struck up another tune now, and Alison rather liked it. The girl could play. The notes writhed their way around a lively jig.

Justin listened approvingly. 'She's good. I gather the next bit is something of a haul.'

'What do you mean "a haul"?' Alison wondered. 'Whose house is it next?'

Sara intervened. 'Not a house. They go to the White Horse, and then on into the woods. For the dance.'

'The *dance*?'

'Oh, yes,' Sara said. 'You should see it. Both of you. Once anyway.'

Alison hoped he wasn't getting the wrong idea. 'You game, Justin?'

'Absolutely, Mrs Fenway.'

Sara gave them both a knowing smile and watched them go. They were halfway along the path to the White Horse when it finally dawned. *The woods*. Alison stopped with a jolt. Justin took her arm.

'Are you all right?' He suddenly looked worried.

'Fine,' she said, and grabbed at the bottle in her pocket.

'You look like you just saw a ghost.'

She listened to the fiddle tune, snaking its way through her head. 'No such thing, Justin.'

The White Horse was the colour of the moon, a pale, silvery shape on the curving downland hillside. In the clear, starlit night it had a magical luminescence, as if it glowed in response to their presence, and the music and the laughter they supplied.

Alison felt fine. Justin was there; they were standing at the back of the crowd. She'd be OK. And, on a deeper level, she didn't want to arouse his suspicions. He was there to watch, to *detect*. There were plenty in that crowd who deserved his attention, she thought, and one day, perhaps not so far away, he'd find out who they were. She wasn't the only murderer Beulah had ever seen. Alison knew that instinctively; it sat like a piece of undigested meat in her stomach.

She watched them dance around the figure cut into the chalk, her arm looped through Justin's, trying to think through the boozy fug that sat between her ears. It was hard. The night and the presence of the nearby wood were too real, too large inside her head. She felt scared on one level, but oddly elated too. There was a wildness to the gathering she found stimulating, exciting. Sometimes it was good to be scared.

The nature of the evening seemed to change when they reached the White Horse. The village was a good half-mile distant now, a faint glow behind them. To the east, miles away in the clear night sky, she could see the electric expanse of Canterbury, with the great cathedral at its heart, illuminated by floodlights. From this distance it could have been any ancient, primitive monument: a misshapen pyramid from Egypt, some primeval stone temple from Atlantis. It had a power and a dignity that were missing during the day, when it was hemmed in by tourists and traffic.

Justin followed her gaze. 'It's beautiful up here,' he said.

'Yes.' She clung to his arm. So many feelings, so many conflicting emotions welling up inside her. Then he sniffed the air, a conscious, exploratory gesture, she thought, one very like a policeman.

'Oh, no,' he groaned. 'How can they do this to me?'

'What?' she asked puzzled, and took a deep breath through her nose. 'Ooh!'

Someone in the throng had lit a joint. No, more than one. Alison took a good look at them, Marjorie Tyler first of all, of course, and the roll-ups were appearing everywhere. The spicy exotic smell of marijuana began to percolate the sharp, chill night. People were starting to move from the booze-fuelled thrum of the wassailing into a new, more relaxed, more – hypnotic? perhaps that was the word – phase.

'Tell me it's just the one individual,' Justin pleaded. 'Personal use or something.'

Alison stared at them and stifled a laugh. The music and dancing had stopped, temporarily no doubt, to make way for the dope course. Marjorie and John Tyler were toking away on big ones. The Cartwrights were huddled around each other, trying to roll something in the draught-free space created by their bodies. Even Frank Wethered was smoking. The end of the joint stood like a small red traffic light beneath his moustache. The only individual who didn't seem to be joining in was Granny Jukes, still in her wheelchair, cackling away, a bottle on her lap.

'Sorry. This is a drug den, I'm afraid. Have you got undercover men disguised as sheep? Or are you going to arrest the lot of them all on your own?'

'Sod it, Alison. This isn't funny.'

She clapped him on the arm, harder than she intended.

'Oh, don't be so stuffy. How old are you? Twenty-four? Twenty-five?'

'Twenty-six actually,' he objected.

'Hell, Justin, loosen up a little. Next thing you know you'll be sitting in a wheelchair, checking your birthday cards and discovering you're eighty-five and about to croak. And you know something? You won't be kicking yourself for the things you've done in life. You'll be apoplectic over the things you *haven't* done.'

That sounded rather good, Alison thought. And wondered who it was really aimed at.

Justin was unmoved. 'Of course I don't want to nick anyone. I'd just rather not be here. I am a policeman. It is *illegal.*'

'And that counts for a lot. I don't think. What about Sara's road rage moron?'

'I'd nick him. Like a shot. If he exists.'

'What *do* you mean?'

He looked shamefaced. 'I couldn't find any tracks. It's the first thing women say when they go off the road: a man made me do it.'

She was outraged. 'Sara nearly died in that accident. She nearly lost her child. You think she was in any state of mind to make up ridiculous stories like that?'

'It's possible . . .'

'Forfeit, Justin,' she said, prodding him hard in the chest. 'You owe me a forfeit for that.'

'OK. I'm sorry.'

'To hell with sorry.' Alison stomped over to Marjorie Tyler who was doling out joints now as if they were meals on wheels. 'Two please. Don't hold back on the sauce.'

'Oh,' Marjorie said, beaming, 'Lily Law wants one too, does she?'

'No, but he's damn well going to smoke it.'

'That's the spirit . . .'

She took them back, put them both in her mouth, inhaled deeply. When they were well alight – and the thick, black narcotic smoke was already working its way down her throat – she gently took one out and placed it in Justin's lips.

He took it out instantly. 'This is rapidly turning into one of the worst nights of my life.'

'Patience, honey. It might improve,' she said, then swayed, not too noticeably she hoped, as the drink and the dope said hello to each other somewhere at the back of her head. She looked at Justin. He was pale and unhappy, toying with the joint. 'Inhale, Justin. No cheating. You don't need to make President of the United States.'

He obeyed. Justin rather liked being told what to do, Alison thought. There was the sound of something whirring at their side and Granny Jukes appeared, working the wheelchair like a frantic elf.

She winked and gave them a toothless grin. 'You're a lovely couple, and there's no mistaking.'

'Thanks, Granny,' Alison said, with a smile. The old woman was utterly charming in a batty sort of way. 'But we're not a couple, actually.'

'And that's a load of doo-dah, I must say,' the old woman barked back. 'Plain as anything. Young man here *won* you, fair and square.'

She couldn't help laughing. 'Won me? And when exactly did that happen, Granny?'

'May Day, most like.'

Justin gave her his sweetest smile, which was, Alison thought, very sweet indeed, and said, 'Memory must be playing tricks, Gran. I wasn't here on May Day. Hadn't even met Mrs Fenway or the rest of you lot then.'

'Ah!' she clucked. 'There you go, thinking in straight lines again. Young 'uns today.'

'Right,' he said pleasantly and, behind the wheelchair, made a turning gesture against his ear as if to say: *barmy*.

'You'll see,' she said, and hit the button by her hand. The wheelchair lurched over the grass, back to the gaggle. Then the group was moving again, beyond the White Horse, and into the wood. Not, Alison was deeply grateful to note, by the narrow path that led, eventually, to Paternoster Farm. They went further along the ridge, towards Canterbury, still glowing in the night, and then turned right, onto a broad bridleway, now crunchy with frost.

'Mad as hell,' Justin said, shaking his head.

They marched for a good ten minutes, in silence, in tune with the new, more reflective mood of the night. Then another bridleway appeared to their left. They followed it for ten yards, stumbled up a shallow, grassy bank, through a narrow path surrounded by trees, and stopped.

Alison was, for the moment, speechless. They had found a perfect circle in the woods, very like fresh coppice at first glance. Then she noticed there were no stumpy boles where the stools of the felled sweet chestnut ought to be. The clearing was permanent, a hidden ring in the dense, thriving forest that could only be maintained by constant attention.

'More secrets,' she said, as much to herself as the silent, pale Justin by her side. The words were too loud. Someone shushed her. The wassailers stood at the perimeter of the circle. Frank Wethered walked to the centre. He had discarded the joint now. He took off his trilby hat to disclose a long mane of silver hair that tumbled out from beneath it, fell down below his ears, and onto the collar of his gabardine coat. It made him look, she thought, like a defrocked priest.

'Sermon time,' Alison whispered, nudging Justin, and only just managing to stifle a dope-driven giggle. Someone said 'shush' very loudly nearby.

The curious knight cleared his throat and began to speak. 'Friends, old and new,' he said, in a cracked, wavering voice. 'We celebrate Yule as the turn of the year. When darkness starts to turn to light. When the Mother gives birth to the Child. And we remember what the law states too – for each coming, there must be a going. For each birth, a death. May the circle be unbroken.'

The crowd repeated after him, 'For each birth, a death.'

Alison looked at Justin. He was following their every move. She wondered how far it was from this queer little clearing to Paternoster Farm. A mile at the most, probably. Somewhere in the mud there, beneath the thin covering of snow, were the scattered ashes of Harry Blamire, dust in the dirt, tiny nuggets of carbon indistinguishable from any other flesh that passed through the place's portals. Some drunken, druggy thread of reasoning rose within her consciousness: *For each birth, a death.* Then surely the converse applied too? Otherwise the circle would most surely be broken.

The witch with the fiddle struck up a slow tune, not quite a dirge, but not a merry jig either. Marjorie Tyler appeared from behind a chestnut stand and danced into the middle of the circle. Alison felt the breath disappear completely from her lungs in a single exhalation.

Marjorie was stark naked, a fat, flouncing figure the colour of the moon. Her face wore a rictus of ecstasy, her dark hair had been released from its customary captive bun and now flowed free over her pale, fleshy shoulders. She appeared to be dancing some odd kind of pas de deux with an invisible partner. Marjorie smiled at him, blew kisses, took his arms, pranced around the ring, flew through the air, legs scissoring akimbo. Frank Wethered stood at the centre of the circle, rigid, staring up at the sky, holding his walking stick up to the stars, eyes on stalks.

Alison clutched Justin's arm and the two of them leaned on each other for support. There was some extraordinary beauty, some bizarre poignancy to Marjorie's performance. It reminded her of the prancing hippos in *Fantasia*, although Disney had thoughtfully seen fit to dress them in tutus.

Marjorie had the same large-limbed grace as she slipped naked through the velvet December night with a speed and ease that seemed to defy the laws of physics.

Someone in the ring started to clap. The rest of the mass soon took it up, and began to sing, a slow, harmonious tune that, to Alison, sounded vaguely familiar. Then she remembered. This was 'The Holly and the Ivy', but the cadences, the meter were different. And the words too. They slipped through her head, eluding her, although she found herself trying to sing along with the rest of them, like an awkward, novice mummer.

Justin nudged her and, discreetly, pointed to the far side of the ring. A couple had detached themselves from the circle and were now removing their clothes by a sprawling yew tree at the edge of the clearing. She recognised Angie Cartwright. It was too dark to be sure, but it looked as if her partner was her eldest son. Angie took off her bra and knickers, and walked backwards to lean against the trunk. The youth – and it was the son, she was sure now – marched slowly towards her, a huge erection waving in front of him. Then they melted together, a writhing marriage of pale flesh against the dark bark, and a taut white bottom began to oscillate to and fro.

Justin groaned again, stared at her and mouthed, 'How can they do this to me?'

She emptied the lemonade bottle, remembered the other one in her pocket and opened it. 'Goddamn prude,' Alison mumbled. She half expected the entire circle to break down into some kind of orgy. And half hoped it would too. If this was the sum of Beulah's mysteries – some odd seasonal cavortings in the night – she could live with it, quite happily, even if she was not about to join in.

But that wasn't the nature of the evening. The couple making love against the ancient yew were alone, an emblem, a symbol somehow. Just like Marjorie Tyler, whirling like a dervish around the circle, beneath the bright, cold light of the moon. This was not an orgy, it was a *ceremony*. She nodded. The word was right, even though she had no idea what the ceremony might be, or how she might interpret this long, strange descant they kept repeating endlessly, as if waiting for something to happen.

With a startling abruptness, the song ended. She watched the circle, waiting for what came next. Marjorie had slumped, exhausted, to the chill ground. Beyond, at the yew tree, Angie Cartwright and her son were coming noisily to a climax, Angie moaning like a woman in some cheap porn movie, a rhythmic, anguished cry, not the sort real people uttered, Alison thought. Not in her world anyway.

Someone screamed. No, she corrected herself. *Three* voices screamed: Angie and her mate, and someone inside the circle. She searched the sea of faces and finally saw. Bella Cartwright was rolling her head from side to side, tongue lolling out of her mouth, eyes staring wildly at the sky. Drool fell from her lips; peculiar guttural noises, like the grunts of an unknown animal, issued from her throat. Alison scanned the wassailers for John Tyler immediately. *Goddamn doctors*, she thought. He was no more than four or five places away from Bella in the circle and, instead of trying to work out how to deal with this obvious epileptic seizure, watched the stricken girl with undisguised fascination.

'For Christ's sake . . .' Alison mumbled, and tried to move forward.

Justin held her back, with a single firm, strong arm. 'Don't get involved. Trust me. If it gets out of hand, I'll deal with it. If you go marching in, they'll never forgive you.'

Damned if I do, damned if I don't, she thought. Bella moaned, her eyes rolled back into her head, and she slumped forward onto all fours and began howling and babbling, gibberish to begin with, although it wasn't long before words, real words, appeared, and they sent a chill up Alison's spine.

'Let's go,' she said, tugging at Justin's sleeve. The night temperature had suddenly dropped several degrees. Alison felt alone and exposed in the middle of these people.

Justin put a huge, protective arm around her and whispered, 'It's OK.'

The moon seemed brighter somehow. It illuminated the scene in the circle like some ancient, icy floodlight, exposing the detail, making the shadows hard and black and depthless. Bella rolled on her back, rolled again, gibbering, and the words were becoming half intelligible. *'Muddah, muddah, muddah, bury me, bury me, BURY ME!'*

'She's sick, Justin,' Alison muttered through gritted teeth, knowing it was pointless. And closed her eyes. Harry was there. *There.* She could feel his presence in the circle, dark and evil, everywhere.

She opened her eyes, about to go crazy (Harry is *dead*, her inner voice bellowed). Bella was howling, silver spittle flying in the night air, *'Muddah, mudda, murdah, MURDER.'*

The girl rose up from the snow like a harpy, fists flying, eyes rolling, a savage mask of primal fury, screaming a torrent of abuse, hands windmilling, nails fighting to scratch.

She was no more than three feet from them now and something silver flashed in the moonlight. Justin took one look at it, stepped in front of Alison, raised his arm with a sudden, athletic swiftness, turned the girl and disarmed her in a rapid, twisting movement. Abruptly, she was tight in his arms, gasping for air, staring back at the circle as if she had no idea how she had got there. Alison looked up. In Justin's hand, unmistakable against the moon, was a long kitchen knife. The blade reflected the sky, glinting silver back at the stars.

A short, squat figure moved across the circle, came up to them.

'She's ours,' Dickie Cartwright yelled. 'You don't have nothing to do with her.'

He held out his arms and the sobbing girl fell into them, buried her face in his neck.

Justin extended his arm and showed him the knife. 'You shouldn't be letting her out with knives, Dickie. We'll be getting a nasty accident one of these days.'

Alison watched the rest of the circle. They were all still, silent, but not missing a word.

'She didn't have it,' Cartwright cried, holding her head. 'We don't ever let her out of the house with something like that.'

Alison looked at the knife. It was a Sabatier, or something similar. Something expensive. The Cartwrights wouldn't have a knife like that, not unless they stole it.

'Mr Cartwright,' she said, trying to calm things. 'It's all right. It's not Bella's fault.' She glared at John Tyler. 'She just had a turn, that's all.'

'Some turn,' Cartwright grumbled. 'You know what that was about?' His weasel face glowered at her in the dark.

'No,' she said flatly. 'I don't.'

'Harry, that's what. Harry being dead *and not buried*. How you expect him to rest like that? He's haunting her, that's what.'

'First time I ever heard it called that,' Justin blurted out.

'Damn you!' Dickie Cartwright screamed, and for one moment Alison thought the little man had lost it, he really would come at Justin, fists flying. Instead he shook with rage, holding Bella to him, tighter and tighter, shook like a man about to lose touch with the world.

A large, dark figure came over to them. It was Marjorie Tyler, her nakedness covered by a huge, ankle-length coat. She looked sober and miserable.

'I'm sorry,' she said to both of them. 'Bella's not well. People are still upset by Harry's loss. These things come out on nights like this. It might be best if you went now. It's not a police matter really, is it, Justin?'

''Course not, Mrs Tyler,' he said. 'You get her looked after, Dickie. We'll leave you to it.'

They withdrew from the circle and went back to the narrow bridleway, silent, each waiting for the other to speak. By the time they got to the crest of the ridge and Canterbury was once again visible, its vast orange glow polluting the sky, the lone wail of a violin was wafting over Sterning Wood again. Voices drifted out of the distant trees.

'What the hell was going on there?' Alison asked eventually.

'Dunno,' Justin replied. 'Was it for my benefit, do you think?'

Alison felt as if she were walking over a treacherous bog. One false step could lead to her downfall. 'In what way?'

'They want me to think he's dead. They even seem to want me to think he was murdered. Thick as thieves these village people.'

'Occam's Razor, Justin.'

''Scuse me?'

'The ancient principle which says the simplest answer is usually the best. Dope, drink, drugs and epilepsy do not mix.'

'I thought Tyler said she wasn't epileptic?'

'He said he couldn't detect it.'

'All the same,' Justin insisted. 'Remember what I said when we first met? This place is weird. Weirder than anywhere else I've ever known.'

'I wouldn't argue with that.'

She wished the nagging rhyme would go away. *For each birth, a death.* Sara had become pregnant on the night of the Burning Man. When, unless she was mistaken, someone had died inside the fire. So what evened the balance when Harry slipped inside the rendering vat of Paternoster Farm? Was this some universal rule? People were dying and being born all the time. Did the cry of a new-born child in Argentina equate with the last gasp of some peasant in China? The maths were all wrong.

'Don't be so literal,' Alison muttered to herself.

'Pardon?'

They were almost at the green now, passing Crabtree Lodge where, she was glad to see, the lights were out. Sara was sensibly growing the tiny tangle of cells in her womb, not dancing naked in the snow and wondering whether there really could be such things as ghosts.

'Nothing. Musing to myself.'

Priory House stood huge and dark on the other side of the green. She thought it looked cold and lonely. These moments were always awkward; she remembered that, even though it was a decade or more since one had occurred. They came to a halt in the middle of what was, and would be again, the Beulah village cricket club wicket: hard, taut grass now slumbering beneath a thin covering of white. The sky was starting to lose some of its luminescence. She looked up. Clouds that seemed suspiciously pregnant with heavy snow were scuttering towards the moon.

'My car's over by the Green Man,' Justin said, a touch of nerves ringing unmistakably through his words.

'You'll come in for a coffee first,' she declared, and it wasn't a question.

They sat in the kitchen, opposite each other at the massive pine table, the Aga pumping out so much heat their voices seemed to hang ponderously in the air. She had made Irish coffee, black and thick with whisky. Justin didn't object. It struck her again: in some ways he was very . . . submissive. And she wondered about the tiny bone in its bed of cotton wool deep within the matchbox by the Aga. In another phase of her Beulah existence – how long ago, how distant? – she had dreamed of showing this to him, watching his eyes light up with interest, initiating the endgame for whatever had begun on the night of Burning Man. But that, she remembered, was when the world had seemed somewhat simpler. Harry Blamire and Paternoster Farm had intervened. Now the piece of bone was more than evidence; it seemed a presentiment, somehow.

'Harry and Bella?' she asked. 'You weren't making up that reference to them then?'

'Nah,' Justin sighed. 'Although it was bloody stupid of me to blurt it out like that. God knows, the Cartwrights went through enough trouble with Harry as it is. They may be a bunch of light-fingered toerags but they didn't deserve him jumping on the girl every time their backs were turned.'

She sniffed the coffee. Neither of them slurred their words or seemed remotely affected by the dope any more. The scene in the clearing had seen to that. She felt awake and nervy, sensing the night and his presence. The evening now had an edgy kind of heightened reality that was a form of intoxication of its own. It was 11.30 and she felt she could sit up until morning, constantly alert, if she wanted. 'What happened exactly?'

He groaned. 'Why do I keep telling you things I shouldn't?'

'Because you like me.' Alison smiled, knowing this was a tease.

'Hmmm. This was four years ago, when I first came to Ashford. There was an investigation into Harry for under-age sex. Bella was fifteen. He was forty-five. Nice one, eh?'

'Very Beulah,' she said, nodding.

'You bet.'

'Are you sure it was true?'

He snorted. 'Of course it was. Harry didn't even try to hide it much. He had a lot worse than that he didn't want us to know about.'

'Such as?'

'Such as pretty much anything you care to think of. The one we always got calls about was sneaking around. Seems the Blamires don't go much on the idea of private property. They're always popping into people's gardens, peering in through windows. Peeping Tom stuff, maybe. Beulah seems to put up with it. Then one night Harry tried it down in Wye and we had a real ruckus on our hands.'

Alison puzzled over this one. 'You mean they just walked into people's gardens? Stared into their homes?'

'Whenever they felt like it. And that's only the half of it. We only ever got the boys once and that was for some minor handling offence that didn't even put them inside. But the whisper was they were pretty much game for anything. Nicking. Fencing. Beating up someone you didn't like. There was even word they were doing something with drugs at one stage, not that we ever got to the bottom of that. They were a smart pair, believe me. Which is why I still don't get Harry's disappearance. It just doesn't fit. Maybe Mitch bumped him off. Maybe they offended one of the big fish, which wouldn't be hard if they were messing with drugs. I just don't have a clue.'

She didn't understand. 'Why did that stop you from nicking him for under-age sex? That's like rape, isn't it?'

'That's the point. Not with Bella it wasn't. She was – how do I put this? – not exactly inexperienced. Been at it long before Harry came sniffing around.'

Men, Alison swore inwardly. 'What the hell difference does that make?'

He looked depressed. 'Oh dear. I'm going to get the lecture, aren't I? Well, a big difference actually. Bella was a sexually active, sexually mature fifteen-year-old. Strictly speaking, that made it illegal. But it's like everything with Beulah. You have to use your discretion. We can't just come up here nicking everybody for every breach of the law we see.

If I did that I'd never sleep. There's planning regulations, uninsured cars, waste disposal issues and worse. Incest. The ancient rural tradition of sheep shagging. I can't pull the book out every time I come across something like that. What good would it do? There's a consensus here that things are all right provided they stay inside the village. If everything else goes smoothly – and the big issues, people killing other people, little kids getting beaten up, major-league nicking stay away – should we really be that bothered?'

'Bella Cartwright isn't a sheep,' she said coldly.

'No. But I ask again. What good would it have done if we'd gone ahead? Harry would have got off with six months at the most. By the time he was out she'd have been sixteen anyway.'

'So you did nothing?'

'We talked to him. Had Harry into the station and read the riot act. Wasn't my decision, by the way, it was the chief super's. I wasn't on the Beulah beat then. For what it's worth I thought we ought to throw the book at him.'

'Good for you.'

'I was naïve back then,' he replied. 'Don't you see? What was going to happen did anyway? When she got older, she grew up a bit, realised what a nasty catch Harry was and gave him the elbow. End of story, until halfwit here blurted it out just now. And what do you think would have happened if we'd locked him up? Bella would have got some unrequited love thing about him, visited him in the nick, and taken a lot longer to work out that Harry was no good. She would have blamed herself for what happened. Worse for everyone all round.'

He had a point, she thought.

'What you've got to remember, Alison, is that nothing's ever black and white. Particularly in a place like this. I'm not Judge Dredd, riding in to punish everyone who steps over the line. I'm just the neighbourhood plod trying to make sure nothing gets too out of hand, and calm folks down when it looks like it might. To be honest, if most of the things that go on here end up in court I've probably failed. Because six months later, it'll start all over again, ten times worse in all probability.'

Was this really how Justin saw himself? As some kind of social worker in a uniform? Perhaps, she thought. But there was some ambition there too. Which must have made being lumbered with the Beulah beat doubly worse. Maybe he was just focusing on priorities. There was a lot to be said for that, she thought. *For each birth, a death.* It was Yule, the winter solstice. Half the village seemed to think there was magic in the air. Why should she be the odd one out? Priorities made a difference. Harry and the hidden finger bone, Paternoster Farm and Burning Man, all these things were, to some extent, the creation of her own emptiness, kept alive by this nagging, gaping hole inside her. If she were pregnant, if the warmth of a new life lay nestled deep inside her belly, all these ugly, winged creatures flitting in the shadows would disappear for ever.

She leaned over the table, laid her palm over the back of his hand, smiled and asked if he wanted more coffee. Justin was very pleasant-looking. The spiky haircut was a mistake. He ought to grow it longer to soften the angularity of his face. Nevertheless, he was handsome. He was young and fit and athletic. And he was *good*. Not a shred of malice or deceit in his soul. There was a time when she would have said the same about Miles, but even then there was a difference. She needed Miles; the relationship was based upon that fact. With Justin the dependence might work the other way round. The idea had a sharp, enticing attraction to it.

These were fanciful thoughts. He was looking at his watch, shaking his head.

'So tell me about being a plod,' she demanded, almost too anxiously. 'Do you still get to carry whistles? Don't you have one of those nice old-fashioned helmets somewhere in the closet?'

He looked sheepish. 'They went out years ago.'

'So . . . ?' There was something he was hiding. Justin looked at her and realised this was not going to go away. He reached into his pocket, pulled out a regulation police whistle and held it in his palm.

'Cool!'

Alison picked it up and blew it. A harsh, sharp sound resonated through the huge kitchen.

He winced. 'Embarrassing, eh? It's a lucky charm. They don't issue them any more but my dad gave me it. As a joke. And because he was worried too. He thinks this is a dangerous job.'

Alison gave him back the whistle and watched, with amusement, the care with which he put it back in his jacket. 'He doesn't know Beulah, then? You take that thing everywhere?'

'Like I said. It's a lucky charm. We all need a touch of luck.'

'What about the girlfriend? Does she come when you blow it?'

His shoulders bobbed up and down. 'Not any more. Packed me in a couple of months back.'

'She couldn't take the rigours of a copper's life, I suppose. All the odd hours and that.'

'Nah. She just thought I was a bit boring.'

She laughed. 'And are you?'

'Depends on the company.' He was staring at his empty coffee mug. 'Thing is, she was two years younger than me. She knew even less about what was going on than I did. I never learned anything.'

'Like what?'

'Like anything.' He took his eyes off the dregs in the mug and stared her in the face. 'And she hated the fact I knew that. She always accused me of fancying older women.'

Alison nodded. 'And do you?'

'Yeah. But not for the reason she thought. Not the sex thing at all. It's because they just . . . *know* more.'

'Hell of an assumption, Justin.'

'No, it isn't,' he said firmly. 'When you get older, most people go out into the world and pick things up. Even if you don't know it yourself. I just came out of school, went through college and then put on a uniform. The moment you do that, you put on a shell and lock out a lot of what's out there. Half the people I nick have seen more of the world than I have. And I'm not talking about where they've been. Look at you. American, living here. Furthest I've ever been is Fuengirola.'

'You make me sound a lot more exotic than I really am.'

He stared at her, blushing gently. 'I wouldn't say that. Change of subject. What does your husband do?'

'Works in the City. A lot. As you've probably gathered, he won't be back tonight. He's not around much at the moment.'

Justin didn't look as if he was about to leave, not straight away. 'Does that bother you?'

'Not very much,' she replied in an instant, a touch shocked by her own honesty. However much she hoped to hide it from herself, something had snapped invisibly between her and Miles on the night Harry Blamire blurted out his secret. She couldn't tell Miles what it was. She certainly couldn't tell Justin. There were practical considerations that made it sensible to give Miles a second chance. But they did not diminish the emotional ones. 'Marriages go up and down. I guess we're in a down patch right now. Does it bother you?'

Justin took in a deep breath. She marvelled at her ability to make a man look miserable. 'Alison, I've got to be honest. I don't like where this is going. I fancy you like mad. I did from the moment I first saw you. But' – he looked around the vast, sparkling kitchen – 'all this. It's way out of my league. And you're hitched too. I just get this horrible feeling it's going to turn out bad.'

She was puzzled. 'You don't want to go to bed with me because of my *furnishings*, Justin? Isn't that a little harsh? What about me?'

He kept his hands palm down on the table and stared at the flat pine surface. 'You are . . . amazing.'

'Then be a good boy and run upstairs. Let's have ourselves an early Christmas.'

He did look at her then. His eyes grew wide, like those of a child. *'No.'*

'Why not? You want to. I want to.'

'I didn't imagine it like this.'

'Imagination is a waste of time, Justin.' She got up from the table, walked round to the back of his chair, and started to knead his powerful, tense shoulders through the thin cotton of his shirt. 'God, you're tense. Am I doing this to you?'

'Yes,' he said curtly.

'Much else besides?'

A little hesitation. Then, 'Yes . . .'

'Well.' She took her hands away, and went into the corner, started sorting through a big box of Christmas things Sainsbury's had delivered that morning. 'If it's not to bed . . .'

Alison took out the bunch of mistletoe, clasped it in her teeth, then walked back to the table. In one sudden, swift movement she cleared it of everything, sweeping mugs, tablemats, some spare cutlery and a wicker bowl with fruit in it clean onto the floor. Justin looked at her, terrified. She kicked off her shoes, pulled the mohair sweater over her head, undid her jeans and wriggled out of them. Then, wearing just a plain silk blouse and white, skimpy knickers, she climbed onto the table, reached up and carefully fastened the mistletoe to the fake chandelier with its candle bulbs and dusty wooden frame. She looked at the green cluster of leaves and milky white berries, nodded and said, 'That'll do the trick.'

She fell onto her bare knees on the table and pulled his face towards her, with firm, clawing hands at the nape of his neck. He came, not unwillingly, and for the first time in her married life, Alison Fenway kissed another man in passion, kissed him in a hard, hungry way that she'd never embraced Miles. *Mistletoe and Yule, for each birth a death.* Her tongue went deep into Justin's throat, one hand was scrabbling at the front of his shirt, the other pulling at her knickers, fighting to get her own clothes off. She made room on the table, reached down, tugged at Justin's belt, hoping he'd get the idea. He did too, just. He was up from his chair, finally taking off his shirt, dropping his trousers, letting her see something there that made her breathless.

She shrugged off her blouse, then removed her bra and found herself sweating already, for some reason acutely conscious of the way her breasts hung as she looked down at him. The kitchen was incredibly hot. *Goddamn Aga.*

'On the table,' Alison ordered. 'Lie down and be a good boy.'

Justin slid onto the pine surface and lay there, putting his hands behind his head. His mouth was slightly open, short gasps of breath touched her skin when she leaned over to mount him. And his eyes . . . he was scared somehow, she thought. *Poor boy . . .*

It wasn't right. 'You look as if you're in for a massage, Justin,' she complained.

His hands waved awkwardly off the end of the table. 'Sorry. Where am I supposed to put them?'

Alison thought for a moment then reached over the edge of the table, opened the big built-in drawer, felt inside and pulled out a handful of napkins. She slid onto the floor and moved quickly towards his top half, snatched at one hand, and tied it securely to the table leg. Then she pulled back behind his head, bent down, gave him a brief, tender, upside-down kiss on the lips, and swiftly moved to his other hand, tethering it just as tightly.

'Bloody hell, Alison,' Justin moaned.

'You wanted experience, sweetie.'

'All the same, what if . . .'

She looked at the napkins in her hand. They were fine white linen. A wedding present from Miles's late mother if she recalled correctly. There were three left.

'Oh, shut up, Justin,' she said, more to herself than him, leaned down and, as gently as she could, tied the napkin into a gag over his gaping, protesting mouth. 'What if what?'

He looked sweet, she thought. His bright-green eyes were a little scared. But his lithe, powerful arms had relaxed into the game. Justin liked this, in spite of himself.

Then she walked the length of the table, noted his condition and gave it an affectionate stroke. 'You, I'll deal with later,' she said. With a rapid efficiency, she used the two remaining napkins to tie his ankles to the table legs, and pulled herself back onto the surface to survey her work. Something was still missing.

She walked over to the carrier bag of Christmas junk she had picked up at a stationer's in Wye. There were three sets of miniature felt deer antlers, a party joke for lunch the following day. She had pictured Miles and Arnold slipping them over their heads when the wine was starting to work. Alison took one and gently pushed it over Justin's spiky hair. He mumbled some protest through the gag but she couldn't comprehend it. Horizontal on the table, naked except for the bindings, the gag and the miniature antlers bobbing with the urgent movements of his head, Justin looked perfect.

Spatchcocked. That was the word. Justin was trussed as tightly and as securely as a piece of meat waiting for the oven. He had, too, the same look of mute, fated acceptance one might see in animals heading for the slaughterhouse. What was going to happen would happen and Justin was relaxed and ready for the ride. She looked at the long, arcing shape of his penis. It had an extraordinary natural elegance to it, like the curvature of the earth or some uninvented form of organic sculpture. It was anything but relaxed. It stood rigid, demanding her attention, pleading.

Alison wiped the sweat from her forehead, lifted her legs, felt down for his hardness, found it, then placed herself correctly, let the muscular apex sit there while she edged and angled herself over him. She didn't need to see Justin right then. She closed her eyes and thought of herself, of this meeting of parts. It was so important that this ancient rite be performed properly, with the right degree of ardour, all the right noises. Then, not knowing why, she looked up. The mistletoe sat over them like a green crown, full of pearls that looked like dainty drops of semen, poised in the air, ready to fall from the ceiling, seep through the pores of her skin and spark life in the depths of her womb. She opened her legs a little more, held onto his chest, and thrust down. Justin's maleness rose inside her in a delicious, anxious progress that went on and on, deeper and deeper.

There was, Alison thought later, when she replayed this scene in her head out of pure pleasure, a specific, precise point where this ceased to be a simple, physical act and became, instead, something elemental, something that rang like the rhythm of some ancient verse, like the songs they had listened to on the Minnis that night. The change happened just after that first thrust, a moment after he parried with a rotating, pelvic gyration of his own. She had yelled (screamed?) for him to stop, and slapped down instantly, with a firm, hard blow across his cheek. Justin had to understand, if he could, that this was *her* ritual, *her* performance. *She* would milk the pearls out of him, *she* would make the universe alive in their heads. This was, some distant voice inside her said, her night. *Yule*.

Justin became still again, she came down upon him once

more, pushing, exploring the limits, feeling this hot, stiff, alien part of him become consumed by her inner, liquid warmth. Then, almost imperceptible to the fierce, rhythmic fever that was growing in her head, a small speck of his seed escaped, danced in her reddy core, a tiny, life-filled premature promise of the flood to come. It had the heat and fluidity of freshly spilled blood.

At this point her memory became unreliable. All that followed was beyond logic, beyond purpose. She rode him, screaming and screaming, not taking note of the terror in his eyes. Finally – how long? seconds? hours? – she felt a race of warmth inside her and knew – *knew* – the promise had been kept.

Gasping for breath, Alison fell down upon his chest, placed her face next to his, spoke to the wood, to the fabric of the napkin at his lips.

'My sweet boy,' she panted. 'My dear, sweet boy.'

She looked up at the ceiling. A single berry of mistletoe detached itself from the distant green branch and fell, under a ponderous, magical gravity all of its own, down towards them, down onto the exposed part of his stomach where it rolled slowly into the dense hair at his groin.

Alison reached across his sweating skin and gripped it in her fingers. Then she crushed the tiny, milk-white fruit, felt the juice on her skin, and thrust the charmed, pearly flesh inside her.

It snowed that night. The world was enveloped in a vast, soft blanket of white. When the day dawned, so bright it hurt the eyes, Alison realised she had been aware of the blizzard while she slept. The lines of snowflakes danced their way to earth in her dreams. She watched them swirling in the light, icy wind, stuck out her dream tongue and tasted their delicious dream dampness, cold and sharp.

Awake, alone, she looked at the foreign shape Justin had left in the sheets beside her. He'd gone while she slept. All that remained was this strange, long indentation in the white cotton sheets, now rumpled and, if she cared to look closely, she guessed, stained too. The table was only the beginning. How many times? She had no idea. The room smelled of bodies and sex. She shook her head, trying to make it work, and stared at the bedside clock. It was nine. A good three hours before Miles was due to arrive with Arnold. Plenty of time to change the sheets, to throw open the windows, sweep this odd, yet somehow perfectly apposite, episode out of her life.

Alison pulled on a nightgown left stuffed beneath the bed, was aware that she felt sore and slightly stiff, then stood up and looked out of the window. A line of footsteps ran from the side of the house to the gate. The snow, still coming down in a constant, thick sweep, had half filled them. *Hiding the evidence.* A habit that was becoming rather too familiar. A scientist or a detective, she guessed, could have counted the flakes in the hollow of each heel, stuck his finger in the air and estimated, to the precise second, when Justin had passed this way, his big, ploddy feet making soft indentations in the snow. Before daylight too, he was sensible enough for that. As they both knew, in Beulah people talked. By the time Miles arrived home the footsteps would be gone, long buried beneath the deep whiteness that was covering the world.

She placed her hand gently beneath the silk gown and felt the lower part of her stomach. It was warm and pleasant to touch. Once she would have remembered the physical facts. How long between sex and fertilisation? Did the little wrigglers, as Sara called them, hang around for a couple of days, like men waffling at a bar, then decide to do their stuff? Or was it all in place already? A tiny, squirming organism drilling its way through the leathery shell of a minuscule egg. Genesis. Joy. And all through the intervention of a half-stranger. Justin's face and his strong, lithe body rose in her memory, and it provoked a conflicting mix of emotions. Guilt was in there somewhere, but it was muddied with an overwhelming sense of pleasure. Alison enjoyed Justin, physically and emotionally too. If what she expected truly had occurred, she owed him a debt. How that might be repaid was impossible to judge. Events were running under their own momentum. The best she could do was to roll with the punches and keep her secrets tightly wrapped inside. *Like Miles*. The thought came unbidden, and it made her strangely sympathetic towards her distant husband. A single act of transgression was a small event in the lifetime of a marriage. It was only natural that, once committed, the culprit fought to keep it hidden, perhaps even from his or her own consciousness.

She stared at the thickening clouds of snowflakes milling over the flat, white Minnis and realised this was unimportant. Sometimes events followed each other with an incomprehensible, mystic certainty. Night after day. The footsteps of your brief, necessary lover standing like a scarlet letter in front of your house, then filling, mysteriously, with snow. And the transcendental act: fertilisation. Unseen, undetectable at this stage. Yet *she knew*. Justin's seed was working its ancient magic inside her body. Alison had no doubts. If she closed her eyes, tried to imagine the strange, complex workings of flesh and cell and blood beneath the taut skin of her abdomen, she would, she felt sure, be able to pinpoint the exact moment of conception. When sperm penetrated egg and made life. It was uncanny. The beastly Tyler would doubtless have some explanation. A therapist would call it wish fulfilment. And it was real, as real as the snow falling outside the window or the crumpled sheets on the bed with their tell-tale stains screaming at the four walls of the room.

Alison groaned. She felt both elated and depressed. Then something moved in the sea of whiteness outside. A shape, familiar at once, in a dark-red, hooded winter coat, stumbled down the path, arms full of packages.

'Shit,' she mumbled. Sara had picked the wrong moment. She threw open the window, felt the wet blast of snow in her face and yelled down into the blizzard. 'Back door open. Let yourself in!'

The red hood nodded, then was gone, and Alison dashed into the shower, mind racing. In her head the house seemed to have 'infidelity' written all over it. She couldn't begin to remember all the places she and Justin had found themselves during the night. 'Goddamn mistletoe,' she muttered, and shoved her head under the cleansing water.

Five minutes later, as she was pulling on a pair of jeans and an old sweater, there was a knock on the bedroom door and Sara, without waiting, bounced in, all smiles.

'Made you some coffee, love. And toast. Thought you might need it.' She looked at the room, a taut smile fixed on her face. 'Late night?'

Alison pulled her head through the neck of the sweater and tried to grin. Sara was gawping openly at the tangle of sheets on the bed. 'Sort of. Um. Shall we go downstairs?'

'Of course.'

They marched down the broad Georgian staircase. A pile of presents, damp with snow, stood at the bottom. Alison blinked at the mess. There was mistletoe strewn everywhere . . . on the stairs, on the carpet, on the furniture in the hall. Sara daintily stepped around the more obvious piles and made her way into the kitchen. That, at least, wasn't as bad as Alison had feared. The floor was clean and swept now. The things from the table were back in place.

Sara stared at the kitchen and shrugged. 'This is one hell of a house you know, Alison. I envy you like mad. But, sorry, I couldn't reach *that*.' She pointed at the crown of mistletoe still attached to the kitchen light. 'Don't want to be climbing things right now.'

'No. You are sweet,' Alison said, and clutched the precious mug of coffee. Then she took a deep breath, looked Sara in the face and mumbled lamely, 'It's not what it seems. Honest.'

'Things rarely are,' Sara replied, eyes wide open. 'Don't tell me anything. It's none of my business. I just wanted to drop off the presents. I wasn't trying to pry. Do you want any help clearing up?'

'God, you are an angel.' Alison put down the coffee mug, came over, hugged Sara gently and wondered why she suddenly felt like bursting into tears. She did wipe away a tear, not knowing why, then said, 'Sorry. Everything seems to happen at once in my life at the moment.'

'Sure.' Sara stood back and looked at her oddly.

'What's wrong?'

'Nothing, I . . .' Sara stepped forward and they hugged again. Then Sara pulled back and put her hand gently on Alison's stomach.

Alison felt cold all of a sudden. 'What is it?'

'Nothing. I just . . . Oh. This is mad.'

'*What is it?*'

'You're up the spout, aren't you? I felt it. Just like I felt it inside me, that day after Burning Man.'

'I . . .'

'You *are*! Don't deny it. Oh, bloody brilliant.'

Sara performed a brief tap dance on the kitchen floor, the enthusiasm only somewhat tempered by her condition. Then she twirled round twice, threw herself into Alison's arms, squealing like a child.

'You're bloody pregnant. It's so wonderful. And I . . . oh, will it come out with little PC Plod boots on? No. Sorry. None of my business. I shouldn't have asked that. What about Miles?'

'Sara, calm down. I don't know a thing.'

'If you and Miles haven't been at it recently, you'd best hit the rumpy pumpy button tonight, dear girl. Men are useless at most things but they sure as hell can count.'

'I don't . . .'

'So that's what? Three months apart? I'm an equinox girl, and you're a solstice. Who says old Tyler is talking bullshit?'

Alison grabbed her shoulders and made her stop jiggling up and down like a lunatic. 'Sara, *please*! I don't know a thing.'

'Bollocks,' Sara replied, and gave her that look of insight that sometimes came right out of the blue. 'In a few weeks' time you'll be down the hill to Wye Surgery to do the paperwork. Don't fool yourself, Alison. It's happened.'

'Oh . . .' she groaned.

'I'll take that as confirmation. Can I be there? For the birth? You're welcome to mine.'

'Jesus, Sara. I'm trying to think about Christmas and you're talking about what may or may not happen nine months from now.'

'Oh, kindly cut the crap. You know. I know.'

Alison gulped at her coffee.

'Last mug of that you're having this side of September too,' Sara said. 'And you can cut out the booze and fags too.'

'You're starting to make me feel better already.'

'Wait till the upchucking starts. And I haven't even come close to the really painful bit yet. My cousin Rosie said it felt like someone was pulling a red-hot poker out of your . . .'

'*Whoa*! Enough. I'm still acclimatising to the idea it might all be true.'

Sara beamed at her. 'Oh, it's true. It's written all over your guilty face.'

'I thought you weren't prying. That sounds judgemental to me.'

'Apologies. It's hard not to let these things slip out sometimes. Can I ask just one question before we let this go?'

'You can ask. It doesn't mean I'll answer.'

'Fair enough. *Was it fun?*'

Alison thought of the night. Of Marjorie Tyler flying naked through the circle in the wood. Of mistletoe descending magically from the sky. And of Justin, sweet, strong Justin, who always did as he was told.

'Oh yes,' she said, seeing the images of their coupling run through her head. 'It was fun.'

'Then that's all that matters. A child conceived in those circumstances is bound to prosper.'

'It was fun . . . just the once. I don't think philandering is really my scene. I don't have the courage for it.'

'Hell, Alison. Once is all you need.'

'I know.' She wished she could remember more clearly what she'd said to him. 'I may have to convince Justin of that.' Herself too, perhaps.

'He's only a man,' Sara said very seriously. 'You can do it. And talking of men . . .' She looked at her watch. It was crawling towards ten. 'Hadn't we better finish the cleaning up around here?'

Alison gulped the dregs of her coffee, went to the broom cupboard and started to wade between the dusty implements. Within the hour the house was spotless. She could never have done it without Sara's help. Too many thoughts, too many possibilities would have floated to the front of her consciousness. When they were finished, they took a break at the kitchen table. Alison stared at the polished pine surface, grateful that wood couldn't speak.

'Sara?' she asked, wondering. 'What are you doing about Christmas lunch?'

'Nothing much. Some sarnies in front of the fire in all

probability. The forecast is bloody awful, you know. We'll probably be cut off by tomorrow. God knows when the hill will be open again.'

'Come to us. We've got loads of food. It does mean you'll have to meet Miles's old man, who can be the devil incarnate. I apologise for that in advance.'

Sara grinned. She really hadn't been expecting it. 'I don't want to impose.'

'To hell with imposing. You'd be doing me a favour.'

'Are you sure?'

'Absolutely. Otherwise I have listen to them farting all on my own.'

'In that case, I'd love to. Normally I go to the Green Man and get a bit squiffy but not this year, not a great environment in our present state.'

'Point taken. No drinking. No smoking. God knows how I explain it to Miles.'

'A glass of wine won't do any harm, I suppose.'

Alison patted her on the hand. 'I'll join you on that. Tomorrow.'

'Oh bugger, I nearly forgot. Old Mother Tyler wants to invite us all round for drinks too. She told you, I presume?'

Alison's face fell.

'You two fall out or something?' Sara wondered.

'Did she say that?'

Sara shook her head. 'No. I just thought she looked a bit odd.'

'We didn't argue exactly. There was a bit of trouble at the dancing. More Justin than me, really,' she lied.

'So I heard. It was my kitchen knife that nice little Bella Cartwright nicked when she came at you. Right while I was dishing out the mince pies too. That's why the rural middle class are here, you know. To give the lower orders something to thieve.'

'Hell,' Alison muttered.

'Marjorie doubtless wants to make up. I wouldn't worry about it.'

Alison was puzzled. 'But why should she need to make up? It was the Cartwright girl who went bonkers.'

'Good point. Perhaps she feels responsible, embarrassed.'

Some parts of the night were a blur for Alison. It was hard to work out which one of them, she or Marjorie Tyler, deserved to feel the most embarrassment.

'Sara? You've been to that thing before?'

'Yes. Like I said. Interesting once.'

'What's it about?'

Sara shrugged. 'Another little local ritual, my dear. Nothing more. Nothing less. I suspect we all have them, you know. But we just call them love, hate, lust, greed, whatever. Whereas in Beulah they dress it all up in different clothes and make a little game out of it. That's what I think. It's important to these people, love. Don't ever make the mistake of thinking otherwise.'

'Oh no. I am absolutely convinced of that.'

'Good. Because if there's one thing people around here don't like, it's the idea someone is taking the piss out of them.'

'I wouldn't dream of it.' The image of the naked, flabby body flying through the night ran through her head and failed to prompt any inward merriment. 'Why did you call her that? Old Mother Tyler?'

'Like Old Mother Shipton. She's head honcho witch. Leader of the coven.'

'Witch? You mean that?'

Sara looked uncomfortable. 'This isn't that conspiracy thing again, is it? Your finger bone?'

'No,' Alison replied, and tried to convince herself it wasn't a lie. 'I just wondered.'

Sara was too serious all of a sudden. 'Just drop it. Now, please.'

'I have. All I was asking was what function Marjorie Tyler fulfils here. She's the wife of the weirdest GP on the planet. She grows pot in her conservatory. And last night she was leaping through Sterning Wood stark naked, dancing like a creature possessed.'

'Oh, God,' Sara groaned. She toyed with a ball of tinsel on the table, staring into nowhere. Then eventually she said, very slowly, 'If I tell you this, you promise you will never repeat it. To anyone. And that this subject is now dead and buried. Deal?'

'Deal.'

Sara struggled for the words. 'There's some sort of village . . . organisation. I suppose that's what you'd call it.'

'Organisation? You mean a coven?'

'I didn't use the word. I'm not sure it's even the right one.'

'But it's witchcraft? All these ceremonies?'

'No.' She was uncomfortable, Alison could see that. But if this was the one and only chance there would be to get to the bottom of this question, it had to be pursued.

'I think,' Sara said eventually, 'they'd call it the Old Religion. Sort of like Wicca, although I don't think even that's quite right. I've got a couple of pals in Oxfordshire who are Wiccans. Nice but barmy. It's not the same, not at all.'

'What hypocrites. They go to church!'

'Some of them do. That's not the point. It's like a club or something, not a religion exactly. What interests them is continuity. From generation to generation. And they don't stick pins in wax dolls. Mostly I think it's just harmless, like making corn dollies and stuff.'

'And Marjorie?'

Sara sighed. This was clearly getting more involved than she'd planned. 'Marjorie – and she told me this herself, when she was pissed once – is the Mother. With a capital M. Don't ask me the significance, I don't know. I'm an outsider, like you. Remember?'

'Nice work. Dancing stark naked in the middle of December. How do you get it?'

'You mean how was she chosen?' Sara was starting to look thoroughly miserable.

'Yes. Who was it before?'

'She was pissed when she told me this, love. Maybe it doesn't mean a thing.'

'We made a deal.'

Sara continued with obvious reluctance. 'The Mother before Marjorie was Frank Wethered's wife. Who was, as you may imagine, old.'

'So it's just handed on at death?'

'Not exactly. As I understand it, there are two ways. The outgoing Mother can arrange a successor. It has to be someone who's been initiated, even if the poor cow doesn't know it yet. Meaning shagged, of course. After that, she's gradually introduced into the Beulah ways.'

Alison felt chill and baffled. She wondered why she kept pulling at this particular thread. 'And the other?'

'It's something like natural selection,' Sara said flatly. 'By which I mean brutally efficient. The Mother can be challenged. Overturned, by someone who's stronger or smarter than her. And that's the part that scares me.'

She had to ask. Somehow Sara expected it. 'Why?'

'Five years ago the Wethereds and the Tylers went on holiday together to Madeira. Mary Wethered never came back. She fell down a cliff. Stone dead. And Beulah got a new Mother. Marjorie. Just like that.'

Alison tried to take this in. 'You're not saying . . . ?'

'That Marjorie pushed her? I don't know. The gossip was Mary wouldn't let go, even though she'd been passed the mantle peacefully by no less than Granny Jukes. If I read the rules correctly, that gave Marjorie the right to intervene.

I may be just mad, of course. Frank and Marjorie seem to get along fine. On the other hand . . .'

Sara fell silent.

'On the other hand what?' Alison pressed her.

'It's all for Beulah, love. We're all smaller than the whole. That's part of what they believe, I think. In those circumstances, Frank would have to go along with it, wouldn't he? The greater good and all that?'

Alison wondered, for a moment, if she might faint. The implications of what Sara was saying seemed vast, seemed to spread their icy fingers everywhere.

Sara reached over, took her hand, and stared, very seriously, into her eyes. 'These are just my suspicions, love. No, not even that. Idle bar gossip. Don't read anything into them. But it doesn't make sense to upturn too many stones. This is a wonderful place. These are, by and large, wonderful, if slightly weird, people. But things happen in Beulah. Only to those involved, usually, though I'm not convinced that's a fixed rule in whatever passes for their Bible. All I know is that if you look the other way and don't start to pry, they'll leave you alone. Your little finger bone. Paternoster Farm. All that stuff. It scares me. You're asking questions, and that is *not* a good idea. We're all just supposed to wait until they think we're ready to be told.'

Alison nodded, her head awhirl with a tangle of ideas. There was a noise above their heads. The mistletoe rustled for no apparent reason, and a delicate shower of pearly berries fell on the table, dropped gently onto their hair.

'You've got what you wanted, Alison. How doesn't matter. Just think about the future, and let the past go.'

'Done,' she said. 'It's dead and buried. As dead and buried as Harry Blamire.'

Sara peered at her. 'I didn't realise anyone was sure Harry *was* dead. Justin talking between bouts, I suppose.'

Alison blushed and put a finger to her lips. 'Oops.'

'Hmmm. So no more pursuit of the mysteries?'

'Cross my heart and hope to die,' Alison said and tried to smile.

It was almost one when the Range Rover pulled into the drive. The snow was now almost eighteen inches deep and still falling. The canopy of tumbling flakes was so dense the world seemed to end twenty feet above the ground. Alison watched from the front windows as the two men clambered out into the cold. The weather precluded her going out to greet them. Or was it more than that? Butterflies danced around the empty acres of her stomach. Was guilt visible, something that could hang in the air like a fragrance? Thomas, the ginger cat, watched her accusingly from the fireside carpet.

'Don't be so damn stupid,' she said, to herself and the cat, then walked into the kitchen and waited. The house was fine now, clean and warm, with a neatly decorated tree in the hall and some suitably low-key tinsel around the walls. All three joke antlers, two pristine, one used, had been despatched to the bin, lest fate be tempted. Sara had done most of the work. She had a keen, intelligent eye for design, always knowing how far to go with the tinsel and the fake holly.

The men stumbled into the back porch, and shook themselves half dry amid a sea of grumbling. Then Miles was through the door, beaming, hugging her. It was three days since he'd stayed at Priory House, and when he'd left for London he looked thoroughly miserable. The take-over seemed destined to drag on for ever, with no prospect of a successful resolution in sight. Now he was transformed. He looked younger, brighter than he had in ages. She pecked him on the cheek, in a restrained, wifely fashion.

He looked above her, saw the mistletoe still attached to the light, squeezed her tight, and kissed her hard on the lips.

'Merry Christmas, my darling.' He looked like the old Miles, the one she fell in love with a lifetime ago.

'You seem cheery,' she replied, trying not to force the smile too much. 'Good news?'

'Nope. But it's Christmas. I'm here. I don't need to be back in London for four whole days. And more than anything I don't need to think about bloody Mersons. If they phone, I'm out. Agreed?'

'Agreed,' she nodded. 'Dad?'

Arnold was struggling with his clothes. He was seventy-five, a big man with a shaggy crop of white hair, red, rheumy eyes and a permanent sag down the left side of his face where a minor stroke had taken its toll three years before. She could remember Arnold as a handsome, upright man, just briefly, when she first met Miles. Then, with a silent, relentless cruelty, age had begun to bear down upon him. The stroke was the harshest blow because of the physical blemish it left. Arnold Fenway was vain. He had seen four wives leave him over the years. It amazed her that Miles was the only legitimate offspring of what must have been a very active life. Miles sprang from Arnold's second marriage; his mother had died, broken and semi-alcoholic, in a nursing home outside Maidenhead almost six years before.

'Don't bother about me,' Arnold grumped, tugging at a grey cashmere jacket. 'It's a bloody wonder I'm still alive after that drive up here. Are you both insane?'

She came over, helped him with the jacket, brushed his good cheek gently with her lips. 'It's the new us, Arnold. Country landowners. Merry Christmas by the way.'

'Bugger the country. What's wrong with Godalming? Did you see what it's like out there? The sodding Antarctic! Just because cousin Emily left you the place doesn't mean you had to move in. Why didn't you do the sensible thing and sell it?'

'Because we like it here. And it's snowing in Godalming too,' Miles said pleasantly. 'If you've got to have a blizzard on your doorstep, I know where I'd rather be.'

'Huh. *You!*' Alison listened in patience and smiled at him. The disfigurement was getting worse. The loose flesh hung down below his face like a deformed turkey wattle. It didn't help his temper. Yet this was, she knew, only the outer, tetchier side of Arnold. Sometimes the old man could be incredibly sweet and thoughtful. It was merely age that brought out the grumps. 'What about me?'

'You look wonderful,' she lied.

'What utter pisshh,' he hissed. Poor Arnold, she thought. Even his dentures were starting to let him down. Then he tried to grin meekly. 'But it's nice of you to indulge an old fart. Merry Christmas, old girl.'

She hugged him and felt the brush of stiff bristle on her cheek. 'Come on,' she said, then took his jacket and led him through to the hall. 'I've made you up a bed in the study downstairs so you don't need to worry about getting anywhere. I've got in your favourite whisky. The chairs here are marvellous. I've even ordered a special Christmas dinner.'

Arnold cast her a sly look. 'Oh please God, not some awful bloody Mediterranean crap again. If you put me anywhere near a plate of couscous I swear I'll walk home, whatever the weather. Buggered if I'm eating birdseed for my few remaining months on earth.' He marched into the living room, fell loosely into one of the big armchairs and held out his hand. 'Drink. No water.'

Thus did Christmas begin. Arnold happier with a Scotch and a book than she had seen him in years. Miles utterly charming. And the snow falling from the sky in a constant, smothering blanket. By midnight, when she opened the curtains in the living room, the world outside was utterly featureless. Arnold had shuffled off to bed around eleven.

Miles had stayed up with her, reading, drinking a little too much, so unusually relaxed she couldn't complain. He came up to her at the window and kissed the back of her neck.

'Will you look at that?' Miles said, his voice rich in wonder. 'I doubt even the Range Rover could get us out of here now.'

'No.' She couldn't work out how that made her feel. 'Do you *still* like it here?'

He came to stand by her side and didn't answer immediately. Together they watched the white cloud tumbling to the strange, misshapen earth. 'Love it,' he said finally. 'I realised as much, when I drove Dad up the hill today. Through all the snow, him moaning every inch of the way. I *love* it here. I don't care what happens anywhere else. Not even with Mersons. We're staying put. Agreed?'

'Yes,' she said gently, fearful of the doubt in her voice.

'Alison?' She could smell the strong aroma of whisky. 'I know I've been awful these last few weeks. A real shit. And I apologise. It's nothing to do with you. It's all me. And the company.'

She closed her eyes and prayed he would change the subject. 'You don't need to apologise. You keep me, Miles. Not just financially. In every way. If it wasn't for you I'd be dead now.'

'No, you wouldn't,' he said, and stroked her hair gently. 'You had an awful experience. Anyone would be affected by that. All I did was what I was supposed to do. I'm your husband. I love you. I need you to be happy, and that's for the most selfish reason in the world. If you're not happy, I'm not either.'

She put her hand to his cheek. It was a touch red from the whisky and he needed a shave. 'Sometimes I don't think you know me, Miles. Not at all.'

'And you know me?'

She would have answered that question so swiftly once,

before Burning Man and Paternoster Farm came along to muddy the waters. Miles, the Beulah Miles, was changing too, of course. Just as much as her.

'You're a winner, aren't you, Miles? You want things. You want to make them yours. I think that perhaps I never understood that before.'

Miles took a sharp intake of breath between his teeth, thinking. 'I suppose that's right. The odds are the Germans will get us. Six to eight weeks at the most. When that happens they either give the top job to me or Andy Moorside. Whoever doesn't get it is out, and I suspect with bugger all of a pay-off.'

'Scary,' she said, half amused, half disappointed that he assumed automatically she was talking about work.

'No, it isn't. Not any more. It's just money and work. We're more important than that. This place is more important. I've thought about my priorities. You're at the top of the list. Making you happy. Giving you a child. Though' – one eyebrow rose in amusement – 'we have to do the necessary, of course.'

She said, very carefully, not wishing to offend. 'Not now. I'm wiped out. Sorry.'

'Oh.' The old Miles, the understanding one, gave her a fond grin. A touch smug too, and she had never really noticed that before. She admired Miles. She loved him, perhaps. But Justin Liddle was different. There was something bright and shining and undamaged inside him that Miles had never possessed. A part of her was privately glad that it was Justin's child growing within her body. She stifled the thought on the instant. This was a terrifying, complex game, largely of her own making.

'Are you OK?' Miles asked, concerned.

'Fine,' she said, and picked up an errant mistletoe berry that had detached itself from the sprig attached to the great, gilt mirror on the wall.

Christmas Day in Beulah was magical, like a childhood dream, full of mystery and wonder. The outside world had receded altogether, as if there were nothing in the universe beyond the soft, rolling whiteness that now held the Minnis in its gentle folds.

The snow had stopped just as the occupants of Priory House were beginning to stir for breakfast. By the time the coffee and croissants were cleared from the big pine table, a bright, cheerful sun had risen and the sky was utterly cloudless, a pale, pure cerulean translucence that sat above the hilltop village, unsullied even by the contrail of a passing airliner.

The snow was so thick it was hard to recognise any individual part of the vast, sprawling common. The cricket pavilion looked like a confection in sugar, perched on a birthday cake cooked for the offspring of a giant. The tall, sprawling hawthorn bushes at the edge of the pitch now resembled small, glistening peaks from a surrealist landscape. On the far side of the common, one of the local horsy types had dragged out a dark, muscular mount, tethered an ancient sledge to its rear, and was slowly parading over the pitch with three squealing children clinging loosely to the contraption. They made slow progress. The snow was deep and thick and very, very soft. Alison briefly wondered how Sara would ever make it the half-mile from Crabtree Lodge, across this plashy sea of white. Miles, solid, reliable Miles, would find a way.

The Beulah snow was quite unlike any she had ever seen. In the house in Boston's Back Bay, when she was a child, snow possessed a fleeting, pristine beauty, before the pressing population ruined it with muddy footprints and motor vehicles that turned everything, all too soon, to mucky, vile slush. In Manhattan, the transformation occurred even before the flakes hit the ground. Blackness and dirt were everywhere in the city, ingrained deep in the snow as it fell. What charm a blizzard had in the city was gone by six in the morning when the commuter flood began to trickle out onto the streets.

Beulah was altogether different. The snow fell pure white and remained that way, a virgin blanket on the ground, save for the tell-tale marks that told of another population, of fur and feather, unseen for the most part, but always active. Sparrow tracks skittered across the flat, perfect alabaster plain in front of the window. Blackbirds had brushed through the powdery surface making long, random lines. There were bigger footprints too – a badger, perhaps, or a fox. And a curious, geometric trail that might have marked the loping gait of a hare.

They lost track of the time as they stood together at the window, rapt in this scene. Then she shivered, and Miles walked over to the slumbering embers of the big log fire, rattled them with a poker, and threw on another piece of wood. Sparks rose out of the ashes, followed by flames. A soft, living heat worked its way out from the Adam fireplace into the room, and with it a delicious organic log fire smell. Miles tentatively stroked her hair. Some kind of peace was being made, on both sides, she thought. And it felt right, for the moment. This was no time for war, above or below ground.

Arnold, dressed in a somewhat ridiculous purple cardigan and loud green trousers, shuffled into the room, was about to speak, and, with a rapidity which, for him, was surprising, took in what was happening. He gave them a sly, foxy look then joined them at the window.

'Missing Godalming, Dad?' she asked.

Arnold grunted, not unpleasantly, and stared at the tracks outside the window. 'Not at all, me dear. But please no carols yet. I am still adapting. We never did come here when Emily was alive, you know.'

'What was she like?'

'Emily?' Arnold grimaced. 'Wish I could answer that question. Daughter of my uncle Bernard, one of many Fenway family strands, none of them interlinked, sadly. Family battles. Saw her once, when she was fifteen or so. Gangly thing but not unattractive. She never married and she was Bernard's only child. I imagine she had no one else to turn to with this place.'

'Yes.'

'Still,' Arnold said, 'you deserved some luck.' He peered out of the window at the filigree of tiny footmarks in the snow. 'Goodness me. A stoat.'

Alison blinked at him. 'You're kidding me. Mr Suburbia knows about animal tracks?'

He gave her a frank look and she realised that, even after all these years, there were things she had not begun to know or understand about Miles's father. 'I recognise a stoat trail when I see one. Lovely creatures. Keep down the mice and rats. And why shouldn't I? They sent me to a farm, during the war. Evacuation. Down near Cirencester.'

Miles looked as surprised as she did. 'You never mentioned that, Dad.'

'No,' he replied, trying not to make it sound sour. 'Some things you don't talk about, do you?'

Alison could feel some turning point in the relationship between the three of them. It hung in the air, like the smell from the log fire that was now roaring in the hearth.

'I liked it there,' he said. 'I had a girl . . .'

Alison blurted it out, before she could think. 'Where didn't you, Dad?'

For once, Arnold did look offended. 'She was the first, dear. The first one I ever loved. That does matter, you know.

168

Even for someone like me. Although,' he added dreamily, 'I suppose I wasn't that me back then.'

'And?' she asked, knowing he expected it.

Arnold gazed at her with those big, rheumy eyes, and she realised, with a sudden chilly grief, how much he hated being old. 'When the war was over, so were we. I hated the country after that. Never went back. Not if I could help it.'

'Well, you're back now,' she said.

'Yes.' He appraised them frankly. 'And seeing you here together, I realise what a stupid old man I've been. It's home, isn't it?'

She put an arm around his shoulder. The old man nearly jumped out of his skin. 'We all do stupid things, Dad,' Alison said. 'We're only human.'

'I know,' Arnold replied quietly. Then hugged her, quite tightly too. 'You're a hell of a girl, you know. Miles is a bloody lucky man. I never told you that before. I should have done.'

She blushed.

'And after *that*,' Arnold said, taking hold of her arm, 'I would care to be introduced to your vintage port.'

Drinks followed – for her, a little red wine with Badoit – and then the Fenways' first Christmas in Beulah began in earnest. Miles was transformed into a man of action. He brought out the little tractor from the old barn at the back of the garden and, finally, Alison realised its worth. A small tow-truck went on the back in place of the grass-cutting gear. Methodically, he transferred logs from the wood store into the truck and ferried them through the snow to the back door. Then he fired up the generator, checked the system was working, measured the fuel in the storage tank and worked out they could spend a good four days in comfortable isolation, even if the power from the outside world disappeared entirely.

After that, there was another change of gear on the back of

the machine. The tractor swept the drive clear of snow, right down to the public road that ran by the side of the green. Miles even made a space in front of the house, though quite why Alison didn't know. Not a car moved in Beulah that day, and it wasn't just because of the snow, which had already blocked the hill down to Wye to everything but the most serious of four by fours. The village had become a world of its own. If you walked too far from the gigantic white prairie of the Minnis, Alison mused, you might just fall off the edge.

Then Miles ventured across the green on the tractor and fetched Sara back in the re-attached tow-truck. The two women clucked and fussed in the kitchen, with Arnold watching them. Miles, with no protests, made an excuse, put on a pair of wellies and disappeared to the Green Man where, legend had it, Norman would stand a single free drink for every regular who made an appearance.

Arnold watched him go – a little wistfully, Alison thought. 'We can get you there if you want,' she offered. 'It's a tough couple of hundred yards on foot. Or, if you can stand the shame, I'll drive you there on the back of the tractor.'

The old man burst out laughing, and Alison was astonished. This was a sound she had never truly heard in the twelve or more years she had known him.

'What would an old sod like me want with a pub?'

Sara wielded a professional-looking knife at some parsnips. 'Oh come, Mr Fenway. Male companionship. Ribald chatter. The freedom to fart at will.'

Arnold chuckled again. 'Hah! You think I haven't had enough of that for one lifetime? And it's Arnold, by the way. You must always follow the general convention of addressing the very old in the same way you speak to the very young.'

'Quite so,' Sara said, and actually patted him on the head. The mass of white shaggy hair shook with mirth. 'Now can we get you anything, Arnold? Or do you need a nap?'

The old man positively roared and Sara followed suit.

Alison quartered a potato while watching them. 'I can see you two are going to get on like a house on fire.'

'God,' Arnold exclaimed. 'Women today. You know what I hate most about being old? It's not being able to chase you lot around. The percentage of interesting women in the world has increased *parabolically* since I was a lad. Most of them then were just . . . plain boring, I'm afraid.'

'Is that why you needed so many of them, Arnold?' Alison wondered aloud.

He shrugged, taking it in his stride. 'Not really. I can't blame them. It was me entirely.'

He watched her finish the last of the potatoes and throw them into the pan, then asked, 'You don't mind me saying something, do you?'

Alison stared at the chopped vegetables in front of her, wondering what to do next. The beef was settling into a nice cruise in the Aga. The smell wafting out of the oven was wonderful. 'Of course not.'

He stood up, and made his way over to the table. 'You really shouldn't roast potatoes in corn oil, Alison. It's nasty stuff only fit for pigs.'

'So,' she asked, 'what would you suggest? I am not aware of seeing you cook anything except frozen Waitrose dinners this last decade?'

'Nobody cooks for themselves, dear. One day you may find that out. But there was a time when I cooked for others, and very successfully too.'

'I'll bet,' Sara grinned.

'When I was in the Périgord I preferred to roast potatoes in duck or goose fat,' Arnold continued.

'Shit,' Alison said icily. 'I knew there was something I forgot in Sainsbury's.'

'Well . . .' He glanced around the kitchen. It was remarkably well equipped and provisioned. 'Good beef lard – and I mean good – or a decent virgin olive oil.'

Alison opened a cupboard and pulled out a litre of super-market finest. Arnold opened the bottle, sniffed, then poured a smear onto a wrinkled finger and tasted it.

'Hmmm. Surprisingly good. Italian, of course, but it'll do.'

'Pleased to hear it,' Alison said with a forced smile. 'Any-thing else?'

'Yes, the parsnips. What do you propose?'

She gave him a cold look. 'An ancient technique I learned from the English. You boil them in water until the buggers become edible.'

Alison could not believe it. Arnold and Sara quite clearly exchanged a look of concern right in front of her eyes.

'Seems a waste of a parsnip,' Sara noted.

'I do apologise. I wasn't aware I was feeding two leading lights from the Royal Society for the Prevention of Cruelty to Root Vegetables.'

'Waste of an Aga, too,' Arnold added, ignoring the sar-casm. 'Boiling is an English culinary vice, best used sparingly. I'd just spread them with butter, sling them in to roast fifteen minutes after the potatoes. They should toffee up quite nicely.'

'Sounds good to me,' Sara concurred.

'Whose side are you on?' Alison murmured between grit-ted teeth.

'And . . .' Now there was a true note of concern in Arnold's face. 'What, pray tell, is that?'

He pointed a long, wizened finger at the offending object. It stood immobile on the work surface next to the Aga. Alison swore inwardly. She had meant to hide the thing. 'Red wine gravy. In a packet.'

Arnold actually shivered.

'Dad,' she said, 'I cannot, for the life of me, make gra –'

'Don't even use that word,' he interrupted. 'It has such . . . *connotations.*'

Arnold rifled through the contents of the spice shelf. In under a minute he had found some herbs and a packet of dried Italian mushrooms. 'Shallots?' he asked.

'Those I do have,' Alison said, and quietly dumped the offending plastic pack of gravy in the bin.

'Good.' He gave her the mushrooms and ordered her to soak them in boiling water. 'Leave the sauce – note that word, daughter-in-law – to me, please. An old man must make some contribution.'

'Some contribution?' Alison answered back. 'You've just about commandeered the entire meal.'

Arnold kissed her sloppily on the cheek and grinned.

'Oh dear.' She could only laugh. 'You're still just an old rake at heart. Winning women through their stomachs. Where did all this sudden charm come from?'

'You lot,' Arnold announced. 'And thank you kindly. I could take a sherry by now. Will you join me?'

Alison shook her head and caught his canny eyes.

'I'll get your drink, Arnold,' Sara said. 'And put on some tea for us.'

She went out to hunt for the drinks cabinet.

Arnold watched her go. Eventually, when Sara was out of earshot, he asked Alison the inevitable. 'You haven't told Miles? He ought to know.'

She shook her head. 'What a cunning old rake you are. Just because I don't drink, it doesn't mean . . .'

He looked faintly insulted.

'There's nothing to know, Dad. Really. It's just female intuition. And after the last disaster I want to be so certain. For both our sakes.'

'For *all* our sakes,' he corrected her.

'Quite. So not a word.'

Arnold beamed. 'Of course.'

Sara returned with the sherry.

'To motherhood,' Arnold said, and shakily raised his drink.

Miles returned at one, commendably sober and upright, took one look at them and burst out laughing.

'What's the matter?' Alison asked, affronted.

'You look like something out of *A Christmas Carol*. The Fenway clan assembled for the traditional repast. Even you, Sara.'

'Thank you, Miles,' Sara said, and bestowed a genteel kiss on him.

'We need,' he continued, 'crackers and silly hats.'

'Well, we haven't got them,' Alison muttered, glad the tell-tale antlers were at the bottom of the bin. 'Just this.'

They looked at the table. The rib of beef, the product of some secret location of Sara's on Romney Marsh, was Dickensian too: a big slab of meat with four caveman-size bones jutting out the top, sitting in a puddle of its own bloody juice. The vegetables had worked wonderfully under Arnold's tutelage. The red wine, shallot and ceps sauce was rich and earthy. They sat around the table and gorged themselves for more than two hours, chattering in a raucous, random fashion about nothing in particular. Miles and Arnold disposed of a couple of bottles of best Bordeaux, the women drank Badoit. Then came Christmas pudding, from another of Sara's secret locations, followed by coffee and, for the men, vintage Armagnac. By three thirty, when the last of the plates were cleared away, the dining room had a pleasant, slightly overheated fug about it, of food and drink and indolent chatter. Alison felt full, but not over-stuffed. The notion of a roast beef sandwich around nine in the evening, nicely rare, with horseradish on it, was firmly lodged somewhere at the back of her nutritional consciousness.

Alison watched the men empty their cups then went into

the kitchen to make some more coffee. Sara, purposefully, followed her.

'Um . . .' Sara said hesitantly.

For a moment, Alison didn't understand. 'Oh hell. I said we'd go to the Tylers, didn't I?'

''Fraid so.'

'Do we have to? Frankly I feel wiped out. And your little tale yesterday about Marjorie and her holiday in Madeira doesn't exactly fire my enthusiasm either.'

Sara winced. 'Just for half an hour, love, then you can drop me off home. I know they're odd people, but they won't be unpleasant. And I was probably talking bollocks yesterday anyway. Village gossip. Just think of this as diplomacy.'

'Perhaps we should leave Arnold here. He's half pissed as it is.'

'I don't think you'll find him amenable to that idea, actually. Seems to me Arnold is having the time of his life.'

Alison pushed away the full cafetière on the table. 'You're right. As usual. Let's stir the men then.'

Fifteen minutes later, after much semi-drunken shuffling on of clothes and wellies, Miles Fenway's red mini-tractor set off across the flat, white expanse of the Minnis. The daylight was almost gone. The snow was crisp beneath them, close to freezing in the icy conditions. The moon was big and luminous in the night sky already, clearly horned, a chill white shape in the fast darkening sky. The lights of a solitary airliner flickered red and green a little to the left of the unmistakable outline of the Great Bear.

Miles drove while the rest of them sat in the back of the tow-truck, feeling like children, grinning stupidly at one another. The tractor bounced awkwardly somewhere near the north wicket of the submerged cricket pitch.

'Owzat!' Alison yelled and listened to the odd sound her voice made in the chill, thin air. 'You all right, Arnold?'

'Never better, dear girl,' the old man replied. 'You know, for a Yank, you make a damn good English gel sometimes.' He sat opposite her, next to Sara. The two of them were scrunched up together, their arms entwined, giggling like youngsters. *Generations*, Alison thought. Such a strange concept. Had Arnold been – what? – twenty years younger, he would have been making a pass at Sara now. Perhaps, in his own way, he was. In another alignment of time, with a different shuffling of the cards, he could have walked out of the icy darkness, looked at her condition, and provided some kind of stability, the solid, occasionally awkward rock of fatherhood. Kids did need that. Alison felt absolutely sure of this fact. Arnold, for all his faults, understood this too and doubtless did his best. Miles had turned into an adult with precious few neuroses; it was one of the reasons she picked him. Alison felt she had enough to bring to the party herself.

There was a sudden scraping noise from the front, and they were abruptly thrown to a halt. Sara fell on Arnold in a giggling heap.

'Shit,' said a bemused Miles from the driving seat. 'I think I hit old quacky's gatepost.'

'*Please*,' Alison hissed. 'Don't call him that. He might hear.'

Lights were blazing inside the Tylers' big, modern box. A battered Daihatsu four by four was parked in the drive, new tyre tracks announcing its recent arrival. The tractor lurched into gear again and then went into reverse. The three of them fell upon each other for a final time, and Alison let loose a stream of invective that seemed loud enough to wake the slumbering village.

'You're a fine one,' Miles bellowed when they came to a halt. 'Most people around here haven't heard toilet talk like that since Harry Blamire went walkabout.'

They all climbed down from the tractor and stared at

the entrance to the Tylers' drive. A large concrete gate-post, previously covered in snow, lay in shattered chunks. The front door opened to reveal the unmistakable shape of Marjorie.

'Buggeration,' Miles exclaimed. 'Knocked your post down. Send us the bill, eh?'

'Sod it,' Marjorie yelled, and jerked a thumb back inside the house. '*He* can pay. I hated those bloody things anyway. Do come in by the way. I'm freezing my arse off on the porch.'

The three of them shuffled through the snow to the door. Alison caught up with Miles and hissed, 'Thirty minutes and we're out of here.'

'Done.' Miles nodded.

The large, inelegant living room was hot and smoky. Frank Wethered was slumped in one corner, puffing on a pipe. Granny Jukes was by his side in an armchair, fast asleep, with a fag in her hand. John Tyler was holding forth loudly to a red-faced farmer type whose nose was deep in a half-pint glass of whisky. A good dozen vaguely familiar faces lounged against walls, gossiping nonchalantly. Alison sized up the room and smiled: there'd be no problem sneaking off without causing a commotion. Then she felt someone take her arm gently, secretly, turned and stared straight into the smiling, open face of Justin Liddle. He was wearing a light, cheap jacket, white open-necked shirt and jeans. A glass of orange juice sat very visibly in his right hand. Justin gave her hand a squeeze then let go.

'Mr and Mrs Fenway. Miss Harrison. And you, sir?'

'Arnold is Miles's father,' Alison said, thoughts whirling. 'Down with us for the holiday.'

The two shook hands, Arnold wearing his suspicious face.

'I'm the village plod,' Justin said amiably. 'And bloody awful at it too, judging by the amount of licentious behaviour going unpunished hereabouts.'

'I didn't realise licentiousness was illegal,' Arnold replied coldly.

'Only a joke, sir.'

'I didn't realise policemen joked.'

Justin burst out laughing. 'Ha, *ha*! Drinks now? Mrs Tyler is kindly allowing me to wait on her guests before I go on duty this evening. Perhaps you could give me a hand, Mrs Fenway?'

Damn, Alison thought, and followed him mutely into the empty kitchen. It was decorated with a minimum of taste and much Formica.

Justin gave her a glass of champagne, grinning inanely, took one himself, and said, 'Here's to us.'

'What do you mean?' Alison replied instantly, putting the glass down.

He did a double take. 'What do I *mean*? Did I dream the other night or something?'

'Justin,' she said, glancing at the door. Miles and Arnold were now deep in conversation with Marjorie Tyler. Sara was with them, but her attention was wandering. She looked into the kitchen, worried. Alison took a deep breath and stared Justin in the face. 'This is not the time or the place.'

'So when is?' he asked, over-anxiously.

She closed her eyes and wished herself elsewhere. 'Don't push me, Justin. We were both somewhat drunk the other night.'

'I know that. But it was more than the drink, wasn't it? You felt that too?'

She cursed herself for agreeing to make the journey across the Minnis. It would have been so easy to have spent a drowsy afternoon in Priory House.

'Alison? Say something please. Even if it's just to tell me I'm being stupid.'

She looked back into the living room. Arnold was in full

spate. Miles watched him, amused, in control, charming as usual. Better to have no men in your life than two, she thought.

'It's too soon,' she said. 'I don't know what to think. Don't rush me.'

'Right. All part of the service, I suppose. God, I bloody hate this place.'

'You don't mean that, Justin. I'm sorry,' she said without looking at him, then quickly scooped up two glasses of sparkling water and went back into the room.

Sara stared at her balefully and asked, 'Are you OK?'

'Fine. Just passing the time of day with our friendly neighbourhood copper.'

'Never liked 'em,' Arnold said. 'Rotten job, for sure. But what sort of person would want to do it? Answer me that.'

'He's all right,' Alison said. 'Don't be so judgemental.'

'Life is judgemental,' Arnold droned, a touch of his old self coming to the surface. Then added promptly. 'Sorry, did that sound pompous?'

'Not at all.' John Tyler had crept up on them stealthily. He stood, swaying gently, face ruddy and sweating. Alison thought: *you could squeeze a cheap bottle of Scotch out of those cheeks*. At least Tyler behaved to type for a GP now and again. 'Humanity *is* judgemental. And why not? It separates us from the animals.'

'I thought it was our rationality that did that,' Alison said quietly.

'Depends what you mean by rational,' Tyler replied in an instant. 'Is love rational? Or faith? What's a stick of incense and some ancient stories got to do with reason?'

Arnold dangled a long, ancient finger in the air. 'Bugger all. Mumbo jumbo, the lot of it.'

'Ah,' Tyler observed, watching the waving digit as if it were some magic wand. 'The wagging finger, having wagged, wags on. Nor all thy piety nor wit shall lure it back. Powerful mumbo jumbo. Half the world revolves around that.'

'More fool them,' Arnold observed. 'Are you pissed, old boy? No offence.'

'Dad,' Alison whispered through clenched teeth.

'Drink has been taken,' Tyler replied. 'And why not?'

'It is Christmas,' Miles said, trying to be helpful.

'Oh yes,' the unsteady doctor bleated. 'That too. The point is . . .'

'Mumbo jumbo,' Arnold interjected, and gave Alison a look of absolute mischief that would not have been out of place in a ten-year-old.

'The point,' Tyler continued unabashed, 'is that you, sir, are old. You should be thinking about these things. How many years, months, left on this earth? Any idea?'

Arnold seemed to go a shade paler. 'I was planning on being dragged out kicking and screaming around a hundred and two.'

Tyler gave him a professional once-over, up and down. 'I wouldn't take bets on it, dear chap. One stroke already, by the looks of you. Actuarially, that puts you well along the down escalator already. There's so much that can go wrong. Prostate. Heart. Lungs. And it's just not worth fixing. Like patching up an old banger you know will peg it again ten yards down the road.'

Alison stared at the white, matt ceiling of the anonymous, modern dining room and wondered whether, one day, she would follow her instincts and disembowel John Tyler, very slowly, asking for his observations along the way. 'I think,' she said finally, 'it is the height of rudeness, even for you, Dr Tyler, to go around reminding any pensioner in earshot how mortal they happen to be.'

'But if I don't tell them, who on earth will?' Tyler drained his glass, and picked up a half full one, which could have been anybody's, from the mantelpiece.

'Why do they need to be told?' she asked, exasperated. 'They know. We *all* know.'

Tyler tried to nod his head sagely. 'Ah yes. They *know*. But they won't recognise it. Like our friend here, who thinks he'll sail through to a hundred and two, when the truth, as any bookie will confirm, is he'll doubtless be pushing up the daisies, or, more likely, be getting poured into an urn, before the year is out.'

Arnold drained his glass, eyed Tyler beadily, and said, very slowly, 'Care to place a bet on that?'

The doctor's eyes rolled in disbelief. 'A bet?'

'A hundred quid,' Arnold continued. 'I'll pick it up here, next Christmas. Personally.'

'Done,' Tyler said. 'And where do I pick up *my* money when you lose? I'm not going to the funeral. They're so boring.'

'I'll stand bail, not that it'll be needed,' Alison said quietly, and then was pushed, quite forcefully, by Marjorie barging her way into the conversation.

'John!' she barked loudly. 'You're not bloody betting on patients again, are you?'

'He's not a patient, dear,' Tyler replied flatly.

'All the same. You'll end up in front of the General Medical Council one day.'

'I'm sure,' Alison said sweetly, 'they'll have much more interesting things than that to look at.'

'He bet on someone's sodding brain tumour last year,' Marjorie continued, unaware of the jibe. 'That was fifty quid down the tubes. It's an act. He always loses, you know. It's his way of encouraging them.'

'Not at all,' Tyler said, looking hurt. 'Just a harmless wager.'

Life or death, Alison thought. Very harmless.

'And,' the doctor continued, eyeing Alison all the time, 'if

181

it makes our ancient friend here, and a few of those around him, think a little more about our joint mortality, all the better.'

'You're a public benefactor, Dr Tyler,' Alison said carefully. 'A saint.'

'Saint Nicholas, perhaps,' Tyler added gleefully. '*Old Nick*. I am the true spirit of Christmas. Or Yule, to be precise. Will you join me under the mistletoe, Mrs Fenway?'

She looked at Miles, who was quite baffled by all this. 'I shall save the mistletoe for later, Dr Tyler. And for home, I think.'

'Excellent,' Tyler beamed, and gave her an unwanted, fleshy kiss on the cheek. Tyler kept his head close to hers, leaned forward, whispered his hot, whisky breath into her ear. 'Remember the season, dear girl. This could be your lucky night. If you're not there already.'

Ten minutes later, although it seemed like a lifetime to her, they were outside. Sara and Alison sat next to each other in the tow-truck while Miles drove, very carefully, through the snow to Crabtree Lodge.

Sara looked at the gorgeous night sky. 'I should tell you, Arnold, that Dr Tyler is a weird bird.'

'You don't say,' Arnold replied from the far side of the tow-truck. 'I'll take his money though. You watch me.'

'You bet, Dad,' Alison added, and gave him a supportive punch on the knee. 'And next year we make it double or quits.'

'Quite,' Arnold said quietly. 'Although he has a point, I suppose. We don't talk about dying, do we?'

'Why the hell should we?' Alison asked.

'I would have thought that was obvious,' Sara said. 'Because if you leave it to the last possible moment, the people you love most, the ones you most want to talk to, might not be there to hear you.'

Miles bent backwards from the driving seat and yelled,

'What a bloody morbid conversation. Newsflash, people. It's Christmas.'

'Hear, hear,' Alison said, and was suddenly filled with an urge to be home, in their warm, comfortable bedroom. Underneath the mistletoe.

'Suppose you're right,' Arnold agreed as they pulled up outside Sara's cottage. 'In fact, come to think of it, that bloody doctor may well have been the most ignorant human being I've ever met. Stupid quack was probably wrong on everything.'

'Everything,' Alison repeated. They said goodbye to Sara, who walked, slowly, looking exhausted, down her snowy path. Then the little tractor headed back over the green, back towards the bright, glowing lights of Priory House. By the time they arrived, the sky had changed. Broad, black clouds, with silver underbellies illuminated by the moon, were sweeping in, obscuring the stars. The first flakes, soft and huge, were beginning to float out of the sky.

'Loads more snow on the way,' Miles said, dropping Alison and Arnold off by the back door.

Alison shivered, and raced inside, into the warm, bright interior of home.

'Miles.' She sat at the dressing table in her underwear, staring at her face in the mirror, toying with the antique wedding ring on her finger. Outside the window the snow was falling as a steady, dense cloud.

He was already underneath the sheets, expectant. Gingerly, he patted the pillow and said, 'Come and tell me about it here.'

She took off the ring, put it on the jewellery tray, walked to the bed and sat upright on it, her back against the headrest. 'Have you ever wondered what it would really be like to have a child?'

He shook his head, puzzled. The drink and the day had taken its toll. He looked sleepy. But determined. 'What do you mean? Of course I have.'

'But really? I'll get fat and stupid and talk about nothing but schools and clothes. You'll get bored with me. We'll become like the people we used to laugh at. Like our parents.'

'I don't think I'll turn into Dad,' Miles replied, very seriously, shaking his head.

'Don't be so picky. You get my point?'

'No, I don't! Of course kids would change us. They're supposed to, aren't they? But you seem to assume it would be for the worse?'

'It's just . . . it frightens me. Everything is so irreversible. What if your job doesn't work? What if Beulah doesn't work?'

'I thought you loved it here. You seem so well, Alison. Have you taken a good look at yourself in the mirror recently?'

She had, and she knew what he meant. She had a colour to her cheeks that had never been there before. She felt strong and vigorous. And happy most of the time. But there was more to it than this. There was the question of behaviour. Of stability.

'I am happy here. Now. But that doesn't mean it will last. Miles. What if *we* don't work?'

The question took the wind out of him. He visibly deflated on the pillow, and she felt terribly guilty on the instant.

'I didn't mean now,' she said quickly, stroking his face. 'I meant some time in the future.'

He turned towards her and put his hands together in an odd little gesture, as if praying. 'Listen, Alison. I'll say I'm sorry as much as you want me to. I know I've neglected you recently. I plead guilty.'

She reached out and put her fingers to his lips. 'No. I wasn't asking for that.'

'In that case,' he replied, 'I don't understand. At all.'

And that was true, it was so obvious. Miles was utterly guileless, she knew as much all along. 'What happened on the night of the Burning Man, Miles? What *really* happened?'

His dark face looked guilty for a moment. 'Do we have to go through that again? Something stupid. Something I'd like to forget. I'd had too much to drink. Bloody Marjorie was handing around her pot cakes like they were bonfire toffee. And . . .' He struggled for the words. 'There was something in the air that night. You felt it too. If you recall.'

Oh, Alison thought, *I recall*. And not just Burning Man either. The fiery furnace inside Paternoster Farm and the way it devoured Harry Blamire were always there too.

'But, love,' he continued, 'that's in the past. We all have skeletons in our cupboards.'

'I know,' she said plaintively, and knew she was lying. Nothing would please her more than to tell him about Harry Blamire and his fiery end. Yet, she had to ask herself, wasn't that because she could pass on some of the blame to Miles himself? And Harry was just one secret. There was the night with Justin. The possibility – no, she *knew* this now – the certainty that he, not Miles, would be the father of her child. Nothing could steal that from her lips.

'Then,' Miles whispered, bringing his face to hers, 'let's bury all that here and start afresh. This has been a wonderful day, love. I feel closer to Dad than I've ever been. Closer to you too. Forget the job, forget the past. We have each other, Alison, and I love you now, more than ever.'

'Yes. Ditto,' she said automatically.

He laughed. 'Don't lay it on too thick.'

'Oops,' she giggled. 'I am a cow sometimes, aren't I?' That

was another thing about Miles. He indulged her, and asked so little in return.

'No. I mean, yes.' He was serious again. 'Oh God, Alison. Why do we always have to pretend we're perfect? I'm not. You're not. What does it matter? When you were sick, I thought I might lose you. It takes some time to come back from all that. There was the move. There was you, and you've changed.'

'Yes.'

'And I know you won't go back. To those bad things.'

'You mean being clinically depressed, Miles. I suffered a nervous breakdown, love. You don't have to couch it in awkward phrases. I was crazy. Deranged. Out of it . . .'

'Shush.'

'All the usual words. They'll do,' she finished. 'And no, I won't go back to those things. I might choose something new, something similar. But not the same. Can you accept that? Can you believe I might not be the tame little wife waiting at home for you?'

'If I'd wanted a tame little wife I would have looked elsewhere,' he said firmly. 'And you're not going back to anything. You're brighter, stronger, *better* than I've ever known, and this house, this place, they have some part in that. Me too, I hope.'

Not just you, Miles, she thought. There was infidelity to conceal, a murder to hide. It was amazing how a few logistical problems could stave off boredom. But he was right. In some ways she was more in control of herself than she could ever remember.

'And we will have that child,' he said. 'Promise.'

'Yes,' she answered, and sat still, patient, as he fumbled with the fastening of her bra. The little clip fell away. He kissed her breasts, slowly, each in turn. Alison felt her nipples perform their primitive response, growing until there was enough for Miles to work with. She pushed her thumbs

186

down the sides of her knickers and eased them off, then, with Miles still suckling away like a desperate brat, slid under the bedclothes.

He stopped, and his big, enthusiastic face came up to hers. 'Toy box?' he said, with a hopeful glance at the cupboard.

'No more toy box,' she replied solemnly. 'We are past the toy box stage, Miles. For ever. We have to find our own magic.'

Alison kicked at the duvet until it fell from the bed and leaned over him. Miles reclined in his nakedness. Still a good body for thirty-five. Taut and muscular, with a dark, natural tan. And ever ready for action. She stroked him gently and Miles emitted a long, slightly theatrical sigh.

'There are,' she said, 'so many things you can do without toys. For instance . . .'

Some moments later, Miles Fenway moaned long and loud, nothing theatrical inside the sound at all, just joy and the promise of a sweet, sharp ecstasy around the corner. Arched over him, with her mind somewhere else altogether, Alison was briefly aware of two things. From downstairs a sound, like the kitchen door opening and closing. And, deep inside her, already dancing to some primeval beat, the faint stirring of a new life.

What Arnold found odd was that after Miles and Alison went to bed, leaving him in the study, and the time still only ten o'clock, the grumpiness had returned. It was as if the long, joyful thaw that had made this Christmas Day so memorable had suddenly stopped, reversed itself, and the ice age had returned in its place. Lying on the makeshift mattress on the sofa, wondering why he didn't deserve a real bed like everyone else, Arnold was acutely aware of the cruel injustice of old age.

In his own mind, he was still the Arnold Fenway of his youth: bright, quick, eager, if a little too willing to slip into snideness and cynicism when the opportunity arose. What failed him were the ephemeral things: the flesh, the curious internal plumbing that kept the human beast alive and then, for no reason he could understand, decided one day to go into decline. He brooded on this for a while, then got up, threw on the old dressing gown and slippers he had brought with him, shuffled through to the kitchen for a glass and the bottle of malt and returned with both to the sofa, quietly cursing the world in his head. Arnold liked the booze, too much for his good health, he knew that. But there was drinking and drinking. The way he sank the malt, seated bolt upright in the study of Priory House, was not like him. It had the steady, deliberate rhythm of the binge, with its ritualistic deadening of the senses. Two good tumblerfuls and then he'd be out of it, dead in some dark, dreamless sleep, only to wake up the following morning with a filthy head and a vile temper. *Normality returns*, Arnold thought sourly, and couldn't work out why the prospect seemed somehow appealing.

He stared out of the window. The blizzard was in its stride by now. The snow came a good two feet up the narrow full-length windows that opened onto the back lawn. It was just possible to make out the skeletal outlines of a rose bush behind the pane. Beyond that the night was a thick, shifting snowstorm. Arnold suddenly gripped the whisky glass more tightly. Something outside moved. He was sure of it. Something large and upright.

'Bloody yokels,' he swore quietly. Arnold had theories about intruders. Briefly, when he was young, he had lived in Kenya, during the Mau Mau emergency, and those were formative years. People in your garden were bad news. You either locked the doors and sat tight, waiting for the petrol bombs to come. Or you got your gun, went outside and fired first. It was simple yet, in those rudimentary times, effective, and it coloured for good Arnold's attitudes towards dealing with trespassers.

But you are old.

He grunted, forced himself to his feet, opened the door and went to the foot of the stairs. Miles could deal with this. It was his house. Arnold paused at the bottom of the staircase. There he heard noises which filled him with utter despair. Upstairs, in the quiet, private quarters of the bedroom, Miles and Alison were making love. That lost cocktail of sounds – the squeaking of bed springs, the low, throaty moans of physical pleasure – fell down the stairs like rain.

Arnold listened and tried to understand the complex flood of thoughts and emotions running through his head. There was guilt, shame almost, for sure. And puzzlement too, that time should wreak this cruel trick on him. In his head it was only yesterday that Miles was a small, bright-eyed child, sitting on his father's lap, demanding stories, demanding attention. Then, in the blink of an eye, he was grown, a man, performing this grunting ritual, with a beautiful, complex wife of his own. It made Arnold wonder what had happened in the intervening years. What line led from there to here? And how much laughter, how many tears, did it pass along the way?

Alison cried out, a long, insensate howl, and Arnold, in his still young and vivid imagination, saw her, naked, beneath Miles, both of them locked together in that distant place that lay beyond the earthly senses where the ritual, at its elusive best, always led. Arnold shook his head and, unsteadily, worked his way back to the sofa. The sounds produced such memories, and in these lay time's cruellest trick of all. He closed his eyes and saw, so clearly it was real, a night, long ago in Cirencester, two bodies, naked in the straw of the old barn, huddling against each other because of the cold. Arnold could smell the place, smell her, the cheap, sweet fragrance of eau de cologne. It had been a long, desperate admiration on his part. She was older, the other boys said things he didn't understand, and she was beautiful. So beautiful it made him speechless when she was around. She was kind, she didn't treat him as an oddity like the others. He was from the city, that made him unusual to her. And one night, when the rest were elsewhere, she had taken him – it was her choice, he would have stayed tongue-tied for ever – to the barn, and undressed him slowly, kissing his hair, kissing his eyes.

There was no God, of that Arnold had become sure over the years, when the memory had refused to fade from his head. A benign deity would have erased it, prevented this stain inside him spreading, poisoning every future relationship he would have in a long, full life. Instead it stayed alive, for ever, even now, more than sixty years after the event. He could almost touch her pale, warm skin, feel the rosy hardness of her nipples. And he could remember, too, his own feelings at that pivotal moment: that, after this long period of distant admiration, this was now the beginning of his life. He had found love, a joyous, mutual sharing. From this point on there could be only sweet goodness in the world. He had finally found a purpose, and it came in the shape of someone else.

Shaking with fear and fury on the sofa, the malt whisky spilling over the edge of the glass, Arnold recalled the innocent delight he felt when they went beneath the straw together. This was the beginning of a lifetime of devotion. There was no need to rush a thing. The physical side was something they could grow into, over the months, over the years, slowly, delightfully, subsuming their identities into a single, shared oneness. So when she touched him, when she moved too close, he did nothing, smiled, kissed her, whispered his love, in words so fulsome and flowing he wondered, at times, whether she understood.

After some hours they dressed and returned to their separate homes. The young Arnold spent the next day in a dreaming paradise, desperate for their next tryst. But it never occurred. A month later, when she had been noticeably avoiding him, they met and she hardly spoke. Arnold had talked, though, to others, and it was like a jigsaw that suddenly fell into place with an awesome, terrible certainty. There were words he only dimly understood, words like 'slag' and 'mucky'. He spent weeks living through a nightmare of doubt until, finally, he saw her again, alone in the barn, and told her all the thoughts that had been running through his head, all his dreams of love, his hopes.

She had grinned, a little stupidly his adult memory now recalled. And said, in a broad country accent, 'You're just like the others. You just wanna tup me, don't yer?'

Arnold lost his virginity that night. With it, he realised soon after, when she had disappeared entirely from his world, went some basic function of human trust too.

The present Arnold Fenway saw all this in his head, heard her voice, smelled her fragrance, felt the sharp prickling of ancient straw on flesh that was now old and wrinkled and dying. The memory filled him with a black, all-consuming fury. From upstairs now, louder than ever, came the sound of climax, a long, mutual bellow that, for Arnold, was as much terror as rapture, as much animal as human.

He stared out of the window, out at the snow, feeling murderous, and saw there something that made his blood boil. There *was* an intruder. A face briefly stared back at him disfigured by snow, but with something odd about it that Arnold's mind could not at that moment, filled as it was with memories, begin to decipher.

He waved an ancient, bony fist at the figure. It withdrew into the whiteness. Arnold let out a long, low howl of anger.

There were intruders in the grounds, and all Miles could do was fornicate.

He stumbled to his feet, feeling suddenly alive and active, went to the kitchen, opened the back door, and, in his long dressing gown and slippers, stepped into the outside world. It was cold, Arnold knew that, but this was somehow important. Miles and Alison had found some island of happiness in their lives. It had even, briefly, touched him. And now someone was violating this, like a Peeping Tom, crawling through the night-time blizzard to peer through windows.

Furious, yelling words that meant nothing, Arnold stepped out into the garden and walked into the teeth of the gale. The snow entered his eyes and ears, he felt its clean, icy coldness in his mouth. His feet went first damp, then cold, and finally numb. He walked, screaming nonsense at the top of his voice, out into the darkness, away from the lighted kitchen of Priory House, out to the back of the big, sprawling, snow-covered garden.

It was a while before Arnold asked himself why. By that time he was lost. There were no lights anywhere, nothing but the hazy illumination of the moon through the torrent of snowflakes falling on his head. Nor was there anyone to be seen. Arnold cursed and fell to his knees. Suddenly, he was cold, cold in a way he had never known before. The ice seemed to have penetrated his body, eaten its way straight into the blood and bone. He could no longer feel his fingers.

Arnold Fenway closed his eyes for the last time. Still there, laughing at him from his dimming consciousness, was the ancient image: naked bodies against straw. And more too. With his final shred of consciousness, he recalled something else. The face against the window, odd against the blizzard. Arnold's fading brain decoded the picture. This was no ordinary face. Down one cheek, livid and visible, as white as the snow itself, was a scar. Like a lightning bolt. It zigzagged once in the image running through his head then faded into the swelling, enfolding darkness.

The phone rang in the small, neat Ashford flat at seven. It took three hours for the search team's Range Rover to fight its way up Vipers Hill through the blizzard. Justin Liddle's head ached all the while, and not just from the excess of whisky in which he had sought consolation the previous night. It was, he found, impossible to erase Alison from his thoughts. Her memory filled his imagination to the brim, excluding all else. He felt a palpable, physical ache, as if only her presence could validate his existence. And yet he feared meeting her again too. Rarely had he felt so miserable.

All the village turned out for the search. Miles remained in the kitchen, overwrought, as if he knew the inevitable result. Justin had spoken to him briefly, his head full of whirling emotions, and found Alison's husband to be as he expected: good, decent, handsome, and perhaps a little dull. In the end, it was John Tyler who came across the body, beneath a mound of snow, close to the perimeter of the garden, where it met the Minnis. Justin watched as Tyler performed the unnecessary test for life. Silently, Alison, in tears he hated to witness, joined them. Tyler seemed genuinely overcome by Arnold's death, more than Justin had expected. Beulah was never predictable.

Tyler was a different man, seemingly unrelated to the loud-mouthed boor at the party. He stared at Justin with resentful eyes. 'I hate this part of the job, you know. Arnold was such a spunky old man. He looked pretty croaky, to be honest, which is why I went along with that joke about a bet. But . . . why on earth did he go outside?'

'We've no idea,' Alison replied. 'I can't think of any explanation whatsoever.'

'I have to ask this,' Tyler said tentatively. 'Had he ever talked of suicide?'

'No,' Alison answered, and didn't bother to hide the testiness in her voice. 'He could be a miserable old bugger. Usually he *was*. But yesterday . . .' She remembered the playful arguments in the kitchen, the way the old man had loved being around her and Sara. 'Yesterday was probably the best I've seen Arnold as long as I've known him.'

'Then remember him like that, Alison. It's the best you can do for him.'

'I will,' she answered quietly.

'So what you're saying,' Justin broke in, 'is that you've no idea what happened. I don't need to know about the personal parts.'

'Why?' she wondered.

Justin and Tyler exchanged glances. 'Sometimes it happens that people near the end of their lives feel something has been completed,' Justin explained. 'Like the end of the record, I don't know. If you realise death's just around the corner, maybe it makes sense – to *some* people – to embrace it smiling instead of cowering in the corner. Is that right, doctor?'

'Not my field,' Tyler said. 'Or yours.'

'If there's a hint of suicide,' Justin continued, 'you're into all the fuss of a full coroner's inquest. Which no one wants. Unless you and Mr Fenway feel differently.'

The ambulance men arrived and started to lift the frozen shape onto a stretcher.

'He's dead,' she said. 'That's all there is to say.'

An hour later Justin found her standing by the kitchen door, looking at the sea of footsteps in the snow. There seemed to be so many. They must have felt like a violation of the precious, private space she had built around herself. Miles was inside on the phone, looking devastated.

'I'm so sorry,' Justin muttered. 'How are you feeling?'

'How do you think?'

Justin grimaced. 'Stupid question. Sorry. That's the trouble with death. Everything about it is so deeply, irrevocably stupid.'

He kicked his boots on the ground to shake off the snow and looked at the sky. It was clearing. The blizzard would not return. Beulah was making another of its strange, sudden transitions, to some new, altered state. In the distance, Sara was wandering across the snow-covered Minnis, struggling back to her cottage before the light failed altogether.

'I need to see you.'

'Jesus Christ, Justin. Now, of all times?'

'You're not listening.' His face was taut with anxiety. 'I *need* to see you. I can't stop thinking about you, seeing you. It's like there's a picture of everything we did together, running through my head. All the time. I have to . . .'

She clamped her hands over her ears, screwed her eyes tightly shut. Justin looked through the window into the kitchen. Miles, still on the phone but halfway to maudlin drunk judging by appearances, was peering back at them.

'Go away,' she hissed.

'I can't. You won't leave me. I can taste you in my mouth. I can hear the sound of your voice when we were there together, there . . .'

Alison began to sob. There was no precedent, he thought, for feeling so wretched. This kind of despair, so insistent, so mindless, was quite beyond his experience.

She stumbled for the door.

'Funny old world,' he observed, with a sudden, easy cruelty he found loathsome. 'As someone was saying only the other day, "For each birth a death".'

LADY DAY

The beginning of the year was a time of extremes: swells of joy, pits of anguish. On a wet, cold Wednesday in Godalming they sat in silence as Arnold slipped behind the curtains of the municipal crematorium and became just a picture in the head, a memory, fading with the passing of time, like a painting made of unsatisfactory pigments. Seven weeks later Alison sat in John Tyler's surgery listening to the words she thought she would never hear again: she was pregnant. There were no apparent problems, and she would probably run full term by the middle of September. Around the time, she thought immediately, of Burning Man.

All the while the weather stood locked in a stubborn idyll that left the soft, thin winter sun playing over a scrunchy scattering of frost for days on end. Sometimes she would look out of the front windows of Priory House and stare at the Minnis, enraptured by its beauty. It seemed an enchanted place, a fairytale landscape in which the people were mere players, a small part of a larger story. The few dog walkers and stray ramblers who traversed it in the short, bright days would leave soft, dirty footprints in the firm hoar frost. Then the temporary thaw would come and the Minnis would take on a different complexion. It reminded her of some slumbering giant half waking from hibernation, brought to life by the random activity on its surface. Jackdaws chased skinny mice and voles in the long, frozen grass on its outskirts, screaming chak-chak-chak all the while. Stray badgers lolloped over the hidden wicket, waddling like Marjorie Tyler rolling towards the next drink.

She put food out in the garden for the birds and watched as they swooped out of nowhere, a sudden, life-filled blaze of colour against the flat, dormant pigments of winter. Bullfinches fought over peanuts, their chests blood red, heaving with effort. Robins darted alone at the edge of the proceedings, like solitary robbers stalking their victims. Tits fell through the air with the aimless, lazy progress of dandelion seeds caught on the breeze. Blue and long-tailed, great and coal, willow and marsh, they flew in a scatter through the garden, bickering on the wing over a scrap of bacon fat, a sliver of sunflower husk. Then, on the day she was due to meet Tyler to hear the news, just before she got in the car, she looked out of the window and saw the broad, majestic shape of a spotted woodpecker swoop down from the naked coppice at the back of the garden, grip the seed holder in a tight, avaricious embrace, and flash its handsome head and beady eye at her. The long, powerful beak stabbed at the food in the container, stabbed at anything else that came within pecking distance. Far away, at the rear of the garden, a fox trotted across the frosty ground, its vivid red brush proudly erect. Something dark and feathered struggled in its mouth, a blackbird she guessed. The pheasant had returned too, looking bedraggled and desperately hungry, gambolling frantically towards her across the grass every time they met. The Beulah year had begun anew.

In the blink of a delighted, anxious eye the close of February approached. She had been certifiably pregnant for an entire week, and now dutifully measured each precious breath to make sure it was perfect, would keep her alive and healthy until this fragile cycle was complete. And the rains began; on a damp, dark Friday, Miles came home in a driving storm from the fast-closing negotiations with Farber, threw his briefcase on the kitchen table, walked over to her, kissed her once on the forehead and looked at her in silence.

She gazed beyond his shoulder into the back garden. The rain was coming down in powerful, diagonal streaks, flattening the grass and the ragged perennials. The earth had turned to mud.

'Oh shit,' Alison murmured softly into his ear. 'What is it?'

He walked over to the fridge, opened it and pulled out a bottle of vintage Krug that had sat there since Christmas. 'You'll have just a little glass with me?'

She shook her head. 'No, Miles. Not until this child is happily squealing away in a Moses basket upstairs.'

'Well,' he said, with no bitterness in his voice, 'in that case I shall get steadily pissed on my own. Sod's law, you know. The moment fatherhood approaches, redundancy cannot be far behind.'

He poured himself a tumbler and sat at the table. Alison half expected him to burst into tears. She went over, put an arm round him and patted his dark head. 'What the hell happened, Miles? You've been working your tail off these last few months.'

'Ah,' he said, smiling at her, 'how true. Not that that means a thing. You know I've learned so much since this all began. It's been like a complete education, cradle to professional grave. I wish Dad were still around. He'd have some neat, cynical explanation about how I should have seen it coming all along.'

'Seen what?'

He finished off the glass and poured himself another one. 'There I was trying to stiff Andy Moorside for the top job, while all the time some bloody little whippersnapper from Forex was busy stiffing us both. Nasty little oik called Ron Atkins. *Ron?* I ask you. Comes from Basildon of all places, started work as a messenger. The Germans liked that apparently. They think Mersons has been ruined by the old school tie. So they go out and get an Essex shell suit instead.'

She tried to take it all in. 'But you know the business inside out. You've been negotiating with them for months.'

'Yes. But Atkins got roped in to run some due diligence information or something. It got him a line into Frankfurt and, boy, did he play it well. I went into the last meeting today, the one where we threw in the towel, and old Andy and I shook hands before we went in. It was obvious one of us was going to get the job. We get through the door and there is bloody Basildon Man smirking away next to the Farber top brass. It's three months to see through the handover then we're both out on our ears.'

She felt her blood begin to boil, and tried, desperately, to stem the rising anger. 'But does this . . . Atkins *know* anything about Mersons?'

'Bugger all. That's the worst part of all. He's an adequate barrow boy for Forex, don't get me wrong. But he hasn't a clue about the bigger picture. Won't last five minutes in the job. Unless . . .'

She followed his line of thought. 'That's what the Germans want? Is it?'

He put the glass down. It was a sensible question. 'No. I don't think so. I reckon he's just done a good number on them.'

'Then *fight*, Miles. God knows, you've been doing that well enough since this nonsense began.'

'But,' he replied, trying not to sound condescending, 'then I'd be fighting for my own skin, wouldn't I? They can't possibly fall for that.'

Miles looked trapped, lost for a solution. It was a new experience, for both of them.

'Oh, darling,' she said. 'It'll work out.'

'Things get worse,' he said quietly. 'I've got three months' paid work but they're reviewing some of the compensation clauses. I won't be leaving with much more than a token pay-off and the state minimum redundancy. I've got till the end of the year at the latest to find some alternative work that pays the same sort of income. Or we have real problems.'

'The end of the year?' She always knew when he was being shifty.

'Maybe a little sooner than that.'

'Such as . . . September. We could have to sell the house around the time the baby comes, Miles?'

He nodded. 'I can't lie to you about this, love. That's about the sum of it. I can squeeze things a bit with loans. We have a decent chunk of equity in this place. But if I'm not earning a decent slab come September, we'll have to put it on the market and hope to get a buyer completing before Christmas.'

'*Shit!*' Angry tears welled in her eyes. 'It's all so unfair.'

He let the fury subside a touch. 'Hey. Don't give up. I'm putting calls out all the time. Something will work out.'

'I thought,' she said, and disliked intensely the coldness in her voice, 'you didn't know anyone outside Mersons? I thought the fact you'd only worked in the one place mitigated against you?'

Miles nodded wryly. 'What a memory you have. It's not going to be easy, I admit. But I'll do my damnedest.'

She sat rigid in silent fury. Miles leaned forward and took her hands in his. 'Alison. Don't lose sight of a few things.'

'Such as what? For once we find a decent place to live. I'm pregnant. I'm settling down for the first time in my life. And now you tell me it could all disappear from underneath me.'

'Us,' he corrected her.

'Sorry. *Us*. There I go being a cow again.'

Miles sighed patiently. 'Listen. This is just about bricks and mortar. Numbers on a piece of paper. Even if we have to move out of here in October or so we won't be broke. That's why I won't leave it too late. We'll have equity. We'll have each other.' He patted her stomach lightly. 'We'll have thingie in there too. What's all that against some stupid little career hiccup? Nothing. In fact . . .' He put his hand gently on her tummy again. 'If you told me the price of this was losing everything I had at Mersons – going out and driving a milk float or whatever – I'd pay it. I wouldn't even think twice.'

Alison gazed at him through a flood of hot, resentful tears. Then wrapped her arms around his neck and pressed her wet face against the bristle of his chin. 'Oh, Miles,' she blubbered. 'I really am a complete bitch, aren't I? There you are, losing your job to some talentless shit. And all I can think about is me, me, me.'

'Hey.' He pushed her gently away and stared into her eyes. 'You're just doing what comes naturally in the circumstances. I wouldn't expect anything else.'

Poor Miles, she thought. So naïve. He was, in a sense, right. Being pregnant made her fearful, made her crave security. But there was more to it than that.

'We could go somewhere else in the village,' she said.

'I'll keep my eyes open, just in case. There's the Blamires' cottage for one thing. With Harry dead and Mitch disappeared to Bangkok or somewhere to catch strange diseases, my bet is that'll be on the market before long.'

The vivid images from Paternoster Farm rose furiously from the depths of her memory. She pulled the sleeves of her cardigan around her for warmth. 'I don't want to live there.'

'No.' For an instant Miles was looking at her oddly. Then he grinned, the stupid, affecting Miles grin she recognised. 'Friday night, dear. You mind if I pop over to the Green Man for a while and drown my sorrows?'

'No. In fact I'll be furious if you don't. You need your mates, not some hormone-raddled, nagging wife.'

Miles leaned over and kissed her forehead. 'Sometimes, my dear, you sell yourself terribly short.'

The Monday after Miles broke the news, and had returned to London for even more long days and nights finalising the merger, Alison tried, very deliberately, to blank it out of her head. What would be would be. Just thinking about the treachery at Mersons made her furious. So furious that she seemed able to spread that rage to those around her too, which was deeply inhospitable. She did not believe in tree-hugging theories, or the notion that a child in the womb would be improved by sweet thoughts and nursery rhymes. But Miles's plight – not simply her own – filled her with such disgust for London that she feared it could one day damage her well-being. And so, she hoped, the subject would be closed, until events would make it impossible to hide one way or another.

Sara was the very picture of impending motherhood. She wore the same loose, flowing clothes she favoured when Alison first met her. The bulge at her stomach was noticeable but still unobtrusive, more a natural extension of her own body than the added physical burden Alison had witnessed, with horror, in other women. Her complexion, once pale, was rosy, almost to the point of exaggeration. There were times when, Alison could see, she was exhausted. But between these she had a vibrant, effusive enthusiasm about her that brought almost every room, every conversation to life.

She had brought a notebook computer with her for the business.

Alison glowered at the thing. 'We can afford this, I imagine?'

Sara beamed brightly. 'Of course we can. You're the money wizard. Haven't you been reading your own figures? Turnover's up. Profitability's up. Time to invest for the future.'

'I suppose so.'

Sara sighed, somewhat impatiently. 'I mean this, Alison. We are both about to undergo a painful, mind-numbing process. You help me through my wild patch, I'll help you through yours. As best I can. And in any case we may still have to go out and get some help. There's a lot of business coming in. Particularly those Moroccan fabrics. And don't think the dragons at Debenhams will give us any leeway for mistakes just because we're up the duff.'

'True. I'll work at it. God knows, the money might come in useful.'

As partners they might hope to clear £35,000 gross each the way things were going, Alison guessed. On paper it sounded a lot of money. Compared to the wad Miles was bringing home each year, it was small change.

Sara watched her, wondering, and finally asked, 'What, precisely, does that mean?'

'I think,' Alison said very slowly, 'we may be in for a little belt-tightening. Or about to go a touch bust.'

She told the story as flatly and unemotionally as she could. In spite of this, Sara listened in a state of mounting fury, her face reddening all the time. When it was done, Sara rattled off a number of quick-fire questions about timing and mortgages and insurance. Alison did her best to answer them, which wasn't easy. These were things she left to Miles entirely. Then Sara folded her arms, her face like thunder, and embarked on a long rant, rich with curses, about the treachery of men. Alison listened with growing amusement. Sara seemed more incensed by the tale than she.

203

'I know what you should do,' Sara concluded. 'Get on the next train to Cannon Street, walk into that little sod's office and cut his balls off. If he has any. Which I doubt.'

'Now there's a practical solution,' Alison said, trying to stifle a brief bout of hysterical laughter. 'Why didn't I think of that?'

'Make you feel a sight better. That's what counts. I can't *believe* it, love. You and Miles belong to this house. It's you. No jumped-up little Essex squirt should be allowed to come along and try to take it away. Just when everything's going so beautifully.'

Alison felt like Miles must have done when he was lecturing her. 'It hasn't happened yet. Miles should pick up another job. We've got time to sort things out.'

Sara banged her empty mug on the table. 'That is not the bloody point. I know the City's just a bunch of sharks in suits, and Miles just happens to be one of the nicer ones. But even sharks have some sort of code. This kind of thing makes me absolutely livid. We might as well be animals. Except that's being unfair on them.'

It was a wonderful act, Alison thought, and it was having the desired effect. She could feel her mood lightening. 'Calm down, Sara. I don't think I've ever seen you this mad.'

'You don't know the half of it,' Sara replied through gritted teeth.

'There are,' Alison continued, 'lots and lots of solutions. We could come down in the world. Find a smaller house, a smaller mortgage. We've got some money. Perhaps we could even work things out so that I kept Miles for a change. He could do the books for us.'

'*This*,' Sara said crossly, 'is your house. Can't you feel it? It's beautiful. It's been in the Fenway line for years. And it fits, doesn't it? Don't you know how rare that is? It's a sin to take that for granted, Alison. When you get something that feels just right you have to fight for it, make sure no one takes it away from you.'

Sara could be so odd sometimes. Perhaps it was the hormones, Alison wondered, and immediately felt foolish. All lives had hidden baggage somewhere behind the scenes.

'I love this house,' Alison said. 'I love this village somehow as well, for all its peculiarities. But bricks and mortar don't come before blood, Sara. If we have to move, we will. Somewhere nearby, and we'll be happy there.'

'Don't count on it,' Sara replied with a sudden, icy bitterness. 'Happiness doesn't fall from the sky. You find it, you keep it, you make damned sure no one ever takes it away from you. And it's rare, Alison. Most people just pray for deadness, pray they can get through the day. The likes of us, we're special. We *crave* happiness. And we're not alone, which is why, though you probably don't understand it, you feel at home here. Beulah's special too. Old Mother Tyler with her pot in the conservatory and her little ceremonies. Frank Wethered baying at the moon. Granny Jukes spouting nonsense in between fags. They're chasing the stars, Alison. We all are. We're not like the rest of them. You included.'

Alison listened to the gentle tick-tock of the grandfather clock in the dining room. Outside a jay squawked happily. A blur of brightly coloured feathers flew past the kitchen window and the bird alighted on the rotting husk of a Bramley that had somehow managed to cling to the bare branches of an apple tree in the garden.

'Sometimes,' Alison said eventually, 'I wonder if I know you. If I know anyone here at all.'

'You know us,' Sara replied, a wan smile returning to her face, her colour getting back to normal now. 'You're one of us. I saw that from the start. So did Mother Tyler too. You belong here. In this house. And you should damn well make sure you stay here.'

Alison made a mock salute. 'I'll do my best, cap'n. What

is it they say back home? "When I lead, follow me. When I retreat, shoot me. When I die, avenge me."'

Sara gave her a playful punch on the arm. 'That's the spirit, soldier.'

Alison laughed. 'You'll never guess what Miles said. If we needed to cut the mortgage, we could always pitch into the Blamires' cottage now Harry and Mitch are gone.'

Sara went suddenly pale. 'You are joking, I trust?'

'Oh yes.'

'Far too small for you. Besides, Mitch will be back when the money runs out. As soon as the cricket starts, that's my guess. He's addicted to that ancient tractor of his.'

'Just a joke. Really.'

'Mind you,' Sara continued, 'in regard to the Blamires something is afoot, that I *can* tell you.'

Something tiny and alive fluttered inside Alison's stomach. 'What do you mean?'

'Your friend Justin has been sniffing around. Asking questions. Wandering around Paternoster Farm looking very puzzled. I spotted him there the other day when I took Yappy out for a run. Spotted him on the Minnis too, keeping an eye on this place. An ambitious little bugger is our Justin in more ways than one. He doesn't plan on being a village plod all his life, mark my words.'

'Did he say . . . ?' Say what? she wondered. She had tried to keep Justin out of her thoughts, along with Harry Blamire, and had had precious little success with either of them.

'He was onto me like a shot, I can tell you that. Asking about Harry. And also . . .'

Sara suddenly shut up, remembering something.

'Also what?'

She shook her head. 'I don't know, Alison. I can't put my finger on it. But you be careful there. I have a horrible feeling Justin thinks you two aren't quite over yet.'

She went silent, wondering whether to say it. 'You are, aren't you?'

'Of course,' Alison replied instantly.

Justin Liddle's shift began at six the next morning. An hour later he was climbing up Vipers Hill, through wisps of ragged mist. This was the fifth time in seven days he had driven directly to Beulah, wondering if he could pluck up the courage to walk into her life again. The Minnis was so open and busier than he expected. He couldn't bear to embarrass her further by being seen. Equally, he needed to be near to her, to drink in her presence, be close to her torn, fragile beauty. In one sense Christmas now seemed years away in his memory, and her absence over this vast expanse of time left him in constant despair. Yet there was some strange, elemental nearness in his head too; from time to time, unbidden, unsought, the images of them together, naked, writhing on the table, on the floor, in the great bedroom of Priory House, replayed themselves in his imagination with a shocking, vivid accuracy.

He parked the car close to the pub and, to provide an excuse, posted a leaflet about the neighbourhood watch scheme on the village notice board. Miles's car was gone from the drive. One morning Justin had arrived early and seen him reversing out onto the common at six thirty, heading off for the long commute into London.

Today, Justin was able to watch Beulah come slowly to life, at its own measured pace. At just past eight the draymen arrived at the Green Man and lazily began to heave barrels into the cellar at the front of the pub. A couple of minutes later John Tyler came out and walked the few short steps to his Daihatsu. Marjorie watched him from the door, waving as he went, an odd, touching gesture, Justin thought, in such a strange, distant couple. Vic, the local roundsman, delivered newspapers and milk at eight thirty, driving his old white van at a steady fifteen miles per hour everywhere. A solitary horse rider crossed the edge of the green, leaving muddy footprints in the outfield of the cricket pitch.

The day had a sullen, leaden feel to it. The sky was a monotonous grey, the ground damp with overnight dew. There was no wind, nothing on the air but the faint, sweet smell of decay, of rotting leaves and weak vegetation wondering whether to give up the ghost. He could walk up to the door of Priory House, he knew. There were excuses galore. Still something prevented him, and Justin tried hard to analyse exactly what it was. Not fear, that was certain. Over the weeks since Christmas he had come to understand that he and Alison shared some linked destiny, even if she fought hard to reject the idea. They would be one. Some ceremony of fire might have to be negotiated to reach this state of bliss, but that would be welcome. He was about to break up a marriage. He deserved to suffer. Most important of all, she had to be protected from the pain. There was enough of that already in Alison's life, and its effects were, on occasion, all too obvious. The obsession about Sara's mysterious accident. Her nervous, feverish interest in the queer rituals of the village. Alison was a woman on the edge, and he bore much of the blame. It was important for her own sanity to tread with care.

Then there was Priory House too. The place was so grand, so foreign to everything he had known in life. It was like walking into one of the smaller stately homes. And such memories too. When they met – and meet they would – it needed to be on neutral territory.

A shape appeared in the front window of the house on the far side of the green. Justin started the patrol car and drove, very slowly, around the common, parking briefly outside Priory House. Her face, pale and lovely, met his for a moment from the window. Then he drove again, just as slowly, around the common, onto the dead end single track that came to a halt just short of the White Horse, glancing back once to see her upright form in the window following his movements.

He parked on the verge close to the end of the lane. The Downs were deserted. In the distance lay the flat, grey sprawl of Canterbury. Even the magnificent structure of the cathedral seemed pale, drained of splendour, under the drab February sky. Lone crows squawked half-heartedly through the low coppice brush that formed the woodland edge. He remembered the evening before Christmas Eve and the scene in the clearing. The sweet chestnut trees that made up the coppice seemed small and insignificant now, random clumps of timber made to be cropped. Only the occasional standard, tall and majestic, with mature, wrinkled bark and a presence that spoke of age, made any impact on the landscape. The wood seemed to have shrunk into itself for the winter. All that grew out of the ground was the epitome of decay: fungi, the colour of dead flesh, everywhere, the monotony leavened only occasionally by the bright, flecked red skin of the fatal fly agaric, poised at a jaunty angle, as if inviting the nearest goblin to jump on its livid back.

He looked for the path to the circle. Eventually, by following the lines of denuded grass, he came across it. Not more than three feet across, it led, in a meandering line, into the living forest beyond the bare, scalped coppice at the perimeter, with its tree stumps and thick, spent foliage.

Inside, the wood was alive, but in the most infuriating of ways. Small bodies moved through the leaf mould, warned by his footsteps. Elusive birds flitted from tree to tree, making sounds he couldn't begin to recognise. Justin Liddle felt he would never really be at home in the country. In a very short period of time – in the light, he realised, these were not great distances at all – the clearing where Marjorie Tyler had danced naked appeared to his left. Something moved there. On the bare, dormant grass a young roe deer was trying to gain some nourishment from the bark of a small stool of chestnut in the fresh coppice beyond. The animal was aware of his presence, even from twenty feet, with no wind to carry the human smell. Its head jerked from side to side, the beast's slender legs stamped once and it was gone.

He sat on the stump of a felled sycamore and lit a cigarette. This was a cowardly way to proceed, he thought. Wasting time in a forest clearing when he was supposed to be earning his pay. Justin thought about Harry Blamire and his mysterious disappearance. He'd spent hours hanging around Paternoster Farm, wondering about what might have happened. The site of the vile plant could not, he realised, be far away. He pushed on further into the wood. Soon there were the familiar sounds of engines and men and work under way. The site was a mess. A couple of diggers were busying away, flattening the timber walls that once kept out the curious. The big gates, black from the fire, lay on the ground, shattered in most parts, serving as planks to give access over the swamp of mud Paternoster had become.

The workmen, with their helmets and ear protectors, looked up, gave him the sour, cursory glances that went with the job. Nothing would escape the demolition team's attention. Very little of the plant's buildings had been left intact by the explosion. What remained was now either dismantled, and piled in a growing heap at the far side of the clearing, or gone altogether, along with everything mechanical, even the giant furnace itself which was blamed for the catastrophe. The place looked like the aftermath of a gypsy encampment which had upped sticks in the middle of a very damp and muddy night.

He turned to go and found her staring at him from

the track that led from the clearing. She wore a flowing, dark-green coat, big at the front, ready to accommodate the swelling child. Justin had learned about the pregnancy while listening to Marjorie Tyler gossip. He still couldn't pin down his feelings. Without knowing hers, it was probably impossible. He stood in front of her, saw the extra colour in her cheeks, how well she seemed.

'You look great,' he said.

'What are you doing, Justin?'

'Fishing. Hoping. Praying.'

'I don't like it here. Can't we go some place else?'

They walked back to the clearing, back to the sycamore stump, and she watched him smoke another cigarette, both of them avoiding the obvious subject.

'Why are you wasting your time here, Justin?' she asked. 'It's just a building site.'

'I might ask you the same thing. I am the copper, you know.'

'I was invited, wasn't I?'

And she came. That meant something.

He shrugged. 'Terrible at this, aren't I?'

'No.' She looked lost. There was nothing he wanted more in the world than to hold her, to touch her. To rekindle that fire. 'But you needn't have bothered. I heard you'd been hanging round here anyway.'

'It's bloody Harry Blamire, of course. Mitch is still AWOL, though my bet is he's either back here now or likely to be swiftish. I know how much money those boys had in the bank, and it wasn't enough for a lifetime swanning around the world from strumpet to strumpet.'

'And Harry?'

'Harry's dead,' he said flatly. 'OK, OK, I know I said maybe he wasn't. But the coroner was right and I was wrong. Forensic pulled some bits of bone and stuff out of the quagmire there. Quite a lot actually. No proof it's

211

Harry, of course, but who else could it be? Not that they'll waste money on DNA testing to prove it.'

'So,' she said firmly. 'There's your mystery resolved. A nasty industrial accident. And Mitch just took off out of grief or an impulse to spend the contents of their joint account.'

'Yes.' He knew he looked dubious.

'You mean it didn't happen like that?'

'Probably. But there's just weird things about all this, Alison. Like these bits of bone. Forensic couldn't work out what was going on. They weren't just burned, they'd been *cooked* or something. And compressed. And they were all mixed up with bits of animal too. How d'you explain that?'

'It was a big bang, Justin. Everyone in the village heard it.'

'Yeah.' He was still sceptical. 'Except you. But you're not Beulah, are you? Not yet at any rate?'

'I'm me, Justin. You of all people ought to realise that.'

'Oh, I do. Can I show you something? Just between the two of us for now?'

Her response surprised him. This idle, pointless chatter about Harry meant nothing. It was their way of working round to the real subject. Yet there was something close to fear in her face.

'Only if you want me to,' he offered.

She followed him back towards the site of the farm. He pointed to the remains of the plant. 'You live at Priory House, right?'

'Go on.'

'So there must have been a prior or something at some stage. Where's the church? Have you ever wondered?'

'The church is in Elmleigh, Justin. Four miles away. I asked John Tyler that very question. I was curious too. But it makes sense if you think about it. These are big country parishes. The god squad must have had to cover miles. It

212

makes more sense for them to be central rather than stuck next to the church.'

They strode out of the blackened area and into the low brush of the wood.

'Yes,' Justin answered. 'John Tyler told me that as well. Only one problem. Elmleigh already has a rectory. The vicar still lives there. And Elmleigh and Beulah have only been one parish for five hundred years or so.'

'Only?' She sounded amazed. Sometimes he forgot she was American and possessed a different sense of scale about history.

'Yes. Only.'

'Five hundred years is a long period of time.'

'Not for Beulah it isn't. You can find out an awful lot from the history books over in the Canterbury Cathedral library, you know. Spend a few hours over there and five hundred years seems nothing at all.'

They stopped by an ancient oak tree. Rotting acorns, gnawed by squirrels, littered the ground. 'Why,' she asked, 'are you spending your time reading old ecclesiastical records, Justin? What does that tell you about Beulah?'

'That's the point. Bugger all. Your house clearly was religious property at one stage. I looked up the Grade I listing. The foundations go back to the thirteenth century. The Georgian and Victorian parts of the house were added on, obviously. The trouble is most of the records are incomplete or just plain missing, and no one knows why. But it wasn't attached to a church. It was part of a small monastery, the place where the big boss lived, in all probability.'

She looked at him amazed. 'A monastery? Here?'

'Why so surprised? Priory House is where the prior lives. And think of the name of this place. *Paternoster* Farm. It means "Our Father". And Beulah itself. Do you know what the word means?'

He could tell from her face it rang a faint bell. 'It's just an

213

old name. There are places called Beulah back home. One in New England, I think.'

'It means married to God. Favoured and blessed. It means a kind of paradise on earth. So where is the priory? There aren't any records, or much in the way of surviving buildings, but it was here all right. Until around 1525 when there's just a brief reference in the records to it being "abrogated", to use their word.'

She racked her brains. 'Ah! I have it. Just because I'm a Yank you think I don't know history. Henry VIII and the dissolution of the monasteries. Plenty of places got pillaged then.'

'And you,' he said, wagging a gloved finger, 'think that, just because I'm a village plod, *I* don't know history. I've got a 2.1 in medieval history from Warwick as it happens.'

She looked amazed. 'What? *Medieval history*? Why the hell are you a cop, then?'

Justin felt a touch offended. She really had seen him as a complete innocent. 'It was either that or teach. And kids scare the life out of me frankly. Is it that hard to believe?'

Alison seemed lost for words for a moment. 'No. Sorry, that sounded terrible. But why are you doing this, Justin? What's your point?'

He grinned. They were back on track. 'All in good time. I know a little about this period of history and I can say with all confidence you are out by a good decade. Whatever happened here took place in 1525. Henry didn't even break with the Catholic Church until 1533. So it pre-dated the dissolution. Henry was still a good Catholic. Whatever his reason for taking against the Beulah monks, they were good Catholic ones.'

Justin kicked at a spot of earth until it exposed what looked like ancient brickwork. He moved his boot again, and, with the soil out of the way, it was clearer to see.

'Let me show you more,' he said. They walked into the

tangle of coppice, Justin carefully bending back the supple branches so she could get through safely. After a good hundred yards he stopped. There was an excavation here. It had revealed, a good three feet beneath the surface, some kind of foundation work, of a substantial size.

'I started poking around when they found bits of stone and plasterwork after the accident. I'm no archaeologist. If the blast hadn't exposed something in the first place I'd never have got here.'

'I don't understand,' she said. 'Where does all this lead?'

He looked a little lost. 'I don't know. What I *do* know is that this place is not just some thirty-year-old rendering plant in the middle of nondescript woodland. There was an entire medieval community here until 1525 and then, for reasons unknown, it was destroyed.'

'Justin,' she said, '*this is a wood*.'

'Now it is. But all of Sterning Wood is no more than four hundred years old. This is man-made forest, not ancient woodland. I checked that too. And remember something else. *This is where they dance*.'

She remembered the dance, he thought. Perhaps, in her own head, that night was still just as vivid as it remained for him.

'I don't see what this has got to do with Harry Blamire. Or anything else for that matter, except a little local gossip and folklore.'

Justin shrugged. 'Me neither, really. I just get curious sometimes. And when I get curious, I dig. I look for things. Alison . . .'

She wanted to be home, he guessed. It was in her face. She wanted to be comfy in front of the fire, with a cup of tea and some decent music drifting through her head, thinking about anything on earth but some obsessive plod who thought one night of frenzied sex entitled him to a portion of her future.

215

He shuffled, looking uncomfortable. 'I only found one hard piece of evidence about the dissolution of Beulah and that, interestingly enough, was in London, in the British Library, not Canterbury. Maybe the medieval shredders never quite made it there.'

She waited. 'You went to London. For this? For God's sake, why?'

'You tell me. They tried the prior. The man who lived in your house as it was then. They convicted him of a whole string of things . . . murder, licentiousness, heresy, apostasy, treason. They made him out as a real rogue. A kind of pagan Robin Hood, stealing from the Church, keeping a string of mistresses, exercising *droit du seigneur*, which I think translates as screwing whoever he felt like. There was bastard offspring everywhere, if you believe the evidence.'

She didn't seem surprised. 'Sounds like Beulah through and through. What happened to him?'

'Hanged, drawn and quartered on Tower Hill in 1527, along with the squire who shopped him, doubtless under torture of course. They put the heads on a pike at Traitors' Gate. And it was all really queer. I looked at the other executions at the time. Henry wasn't topping the clergy just then. He was definitely a special case.'

Alison looked at her watch, tried to smile, then said, 'This is an interesting fairy tale, Justin. But I have to go.'

'His name was Prior William Fenway. And the squire was one Robert Blamire. Five hundred years ago, Alison. The same line.'

She went pale. 'Coincidence.'

'Perhaps. I don't know.'

Alison came up to him, put her hands on the front of his jacket, looked him directly in the face. 'Why are you telling me this, Justin? To make some bigger mystery out of it all? To make me need you?'

'You do need me, love. Even if you don't realise it yet. You need me because I love you. You need me because there's something queer going on here and I think you know that as well as I do.'

'No,' she said firmly. She'd looked at him the same way that night in the kitchen, he recalled. There was always a moment of refusal before the inevitable happened. 'I'm sorry, Justin. It was a mistake. I was drunk. We both were. I can understand if you hate me. All I can do is apologise.'

He laughed and saw some light of interest and amusement in her eyes. 'I don't hate you, Alison. Whatever made you think that?'

'I led you on. That was wrong.'

'Oh.' He looked back at the clearing, trying to remember something. 'I thought we led each other on. That's how I recall it.'

'Either way. It was a mistake. And . . .'

'It meant nothing?' he suggested.

'It meant something at the time.'

He had to ask. 'And now you're pregnant. What if it's mine?'

She took a deep breath and he knew. 'Trust me, Justin. This is not your child.'

He gave her a copper's look. The one that said: *really*? 'It's funny, you know,' he said. 'If you'd told me before that I could, just for one day, one hour, have something I wanted so badly, and then never touch it again, I'd have leaped at the idea. Like getting one minute in heaven, and being able to survive on that memory for the rest of your life. But it doesn't work like that. You just become aware of what you might lose, and it's *worse* because you know what it is, you *know* that's what was supposed to happen.'

She put a cold, soft hand to his face. 'Believe me, Justin. It isn't. Miles and I are meant to happen.'

'Because you love him?'

It was an unfair question. He had no real experience of

love. And for her, who'd seen so much more of the world, the word possessed such flexible, elusive meanings. You could turn them round to embrace almost anything you liked. 'No. Because it's right. And we're not. Sometimes things fall into place, and not always how you expect them. Or want them even. But they're *right*. Beulah's like that somehow. There are times it feels mad to be there. Yet I wouldn't leave it for all the world. I can't explain it. I can't say sorry enough for making you think it might be otherwise. But that's how it is and you've got to live with it.'

He stared at the bare forest, thinking. Then, purposefully, but with no force, no aggression, bent down, put one hand to the back of her head and kissed her, feeling the tiny mote of resistance disappear the moment their mouths met. In this heightened state, bodies locked together, eyes closed, blood pulsing, the forest seemed part of their embrace. The wings of some giant bird beat close overhead.

Softly, with no real conviction he thought, she pushed him away. 'I can't do this, Justin. I'm pregnant, for God's sake. Life's complex enough as it is.'

He knew from her face that Miles never looked at her like this. He offered something she had never experienced before. He eased his hand beneath her coat, felt the gentle round shape of her stomach, moved upwards and cupped her breast.

'Don't, Justin.'

'I won't,' he said softly, and withdrew his fingers, watching the way her lips opened as he let go, hearing the gentle whisper of her involuntary sigh. 'Not until you ask.'

On the second Monday of March Sara called. She was in a discernibly flustered state. The hospital had been making

218

noises about over-exertion. Nothing too worrying, just a general observation that women in their mid-thirties who were now well into the maternity game ought to be slowing down somewhat. She looked fighting fit, and then Alison checked herself at the thought. Miscarriages didn't just come to the pale and sick. Sometimes the cells rebelled inside the healthiest of women, at the most unexpected of moments. If the doctors were concerned, the only thing to do was nod your head, sit down with a weak cup of tea and watch the world go by.

'I'd go if I could,' Sara said miserably. 'I need to get out of this place some time.' There was an important meeting with the owner of an outlet at Camden Lock. Alison's experience with buyers had largely revolved around negotiating prices and chasing unpaid bills. Perhaps it was time she entered the meet-and-greet business too. 'Maybe you could get together with Miles,' Sara suggested. 'Stay there for the evening. Have a meal. You don't need to give up on London, you know.'

Alison smiled wanly. 'Miles is still fighting a losing rear-guard action to keep his job. Eighteen hours most days. The last thing he wants is me pleading to be led to the trough when he comes back from the battlefront.'

Sara looked cross again. 'I still think you should go up there and take a pair of scissors to that bastard's bollocks. What's he called again?'

'Ron Atkins.'

'Ugh! You can tell he's a little shit just by the name. How can the Germans think someone like that's worth running a fine old thing like Mersons? My dad had an account with them for a while. Didn't do anything spectacular but at least you never had to worry the money would wind up in the Cayman Islands, buying sleazy cocktails for some fugitive lounge lizard from Basildon.'

'Sara. As I said. It is a losing rearguard action.'

'All the same. Whoever turns that lot round is in for a

knighthood at the very least. Maybe even a peerage. Could you imagine it? *Sir* Ron Atkins? Lord Atkins of Clacton?'

She seemed to be getting bigger by the day now, Alison thought. The hormones were really racing at times too. 'We have a thing about Essex, don't we?'

'A thing?' Sara repeated indignantly. Thomas, on cue, wound himself round Sara's legs and started to emit a soft, soothing purr. Sometimes Alison could swear the cat was psychic. 'Essex is . . . unspeakable. Shell suits and cheap cocaine. And they're running half of bloody England.'

'You don't think that might be a somewhat stereotypical exaggeration?'

'No, actually, I don't. I had a boyfriend from Essex once. They could make a film out of it. Call the thing *Nightmare on Dagenham Street*. And here I am, running up to middle age as an impending unmarried mum flogging cheap, Third-World wickerwork for a living.'

'Essex clearly has a lot to answer for. You've convinced me. I'll go to London. I'll be back before Miles is anyway.'

'Oh, you are a sweet.' Sara looked uncharacteristically miserable. She stuffed another biscuit in her mouth and moaned through the crumbs, 'Sorry about this. It happens once in a while.'

'And then goes away. Don't worry. It happens to us all.'

'No, it doesn't.' Sara was back to being awkward again. 'You really don't want anything else, do you? Just a nice house, a nice family . . .' She looked around the kitchen. 'All *this*.'

'It's good enough for me,' Alison nodded, and was glad Sara's normal state of prescience seemed to be on hold at this stage of the pregnancy. The encounter with Justin continued to disturb her, more than anything because she realised, soon afterwards, how much she regretted not taking it further. 'God knows, it's hard enough just trying to keep that all together.'

'Point taken. Oh . . . nearly forgot.' Sara reached into her bag and pulled out a fat brown envelope. 'When you meet Simon at the stall, don't forget to give him his present. He won't really want to talk product much.'

Alison took the envelope and peered inside. It was stuffed with twenty-pound notes, lots and lots of them. 'Er, what, my dear, is this?'

Sara waved her hands in the air. 'A bung, darling. A bribe. Sweetener. Graft. Payola. But bung will do just fine.'

Alison stared at the money. There must have been at least a thousand pounds. 'Do we have to do this? How does it go through the books?'

Sara looked at her, pityingly. 'Oh poor, sweet Alison. You are so naïve sometimes. This is the way of the world. I'll introduce you to it if it's the last thing I do. But not now. You've got a train to catch.'

An hour later, the envelope making a guilty lump in her handbag, she was on the train to London, realising, with a sudden shock, that this was the first time she had entered a city since she left hospital. Even such a short absence had an effect on her. Alison watched the pleasant green landscape of rural Kent float past. Grand oast houses converted into palatial homes, sweeping fields of sheep, the vast deer farm near Maidstone, the lazy Medway, with its tangled collection of houseboats and weekend gin palaces. Then the high cliff face near Brand's Hatch beckoned, the train entered a tunnel, there was a brief glimpse of truly moneyed suburbia posing in artificial, rural surroundings, and the city was upon her. Grubby, overcrowded streets stretched in every direction, nameless, impossible for her to place beyond the hidden, hazy geography in her head that said, in a sniffy tone, 'south London'.

In the distance, glinting against the leaden sky, the tower of Canary Wharf rose to break the monotony. Tower Bridge flashed by and the Thames stole into view, dirty and lethargic. The train disgorged its contents into the empty nothingness of Charing Cross only fifteen minutes late. Alison walked outside and looked at the city. Already it was different from the London that still lived in her memory from earlier visits as a worldly tourist. Some distance had grown between its harsh, over-eager physicality and the quieter, subtler self she had, thanks to Beulah, started to develop. She could watch the locals, obsessed with being first to the front of the taxi queue, bustling through the gates of the Underground, and find some amusement in their anxiety. Before, she would have been alongside them, fighting, fighting, all the time. Now, she took her time, walked to the back of the taxi line wearing a wry smile, thinking, content. It was a pleasant discovery. Perhaps, in time, she could learn to love the city again.

The cab was a luxury for a journey that was just as easily made on the Tube. But she wanted to see these half-familiar streets in this new, curious light she'd found. And so, at a snail's pace in the choking traffic, the black cab worked its way out through the West End, north to Camden and deposited her in the little corner of tourist tat that was the Lock.

She listened to Simon sweet-talking an American into buying some Nepalese raffia work and realised he was not at all what she had imagined. Around thirty, clean shaven, with receding fair hair and a green Burberry wax jacket, he seemed to come from the public school end of the market trade, speaking quietly with a polite, upper-class accent. Little of this supposed background showed in the premises. The outlet, over-optimistically named Coconut Key, was housed inside a wooden shack designed to resemble a Caribbean village store. Trinkets and odd furnishings were everywhere, dangling from the low ceiling, scattered on old barrels and ancient, battered trellis tables. Alison realised with a shock that she was quite unable to recognise which, if any, of the items on sale were theirs. The goods of the trade never appeared in Beulah. They lived inside Sara's head, and found their way around the world thanks to Alison's diligent chasing of consignment numbers and tardy cheques.

She stood by the till. Simon eyed his visitor suspiciously. 'What happened to Sara?'

'Felt sick, Simon. You know what ladies are like when they're expecting.'

'No, I don't, thank God. Enough to worry about without that.'

Alison smiled. 'How touching.'

'So you're the famous American, eh? What a game this is.'

He licked his lips and looked at her expectantly. Alison was determined to make this run as long as possible. A thousand pounds was a lot of money. Finally, after a decent wait, she pulled out the envelope and said, 'Oh yes. Sara said to give you your – what was it now? – *bung*?'

'*For Christ's sake,*' Simon hissed between clenched teeth. 'Why don't you just put an advert in the *Standard*?' He grabbed the envelope, quickly peered inside, then stuffed it into one of the jacket pockets. Now she looked closely, it was a fake in any case. Much like Simon, she suspected.

'Sorry. I thought you were the boss.'

'I am,' he said sourly. 'All the same.'

'Right.' Simon could be quite a handful if he felt like it, she guessed. 'Sorry. Do you want to talk about future orders?'

'Not really. You can tell her the lampshades made out of coconut shells are a heap of shite. Can't even shift 'em at what I paid.'

She stonewalled the obvious invitation to take the goods back. 'Will do, Simon.'

'And keep the Afghan gear coming. If it wasn't for

that I'd be out of business. It's one permanent recession around here.'

'Ah, the joys of retailing.' Shopkeepers were, she had regrettably come to believe, even finer moaners than the average farmer. 'We've got a new catalogue coming soon. I'll let you have one.'

'Yeah.' A gaggle of Japanese tourists had wandered through the door and were examining the pile of discounted coconut lampshades with obvious admiration. 'Are we done now?'

'I believe so.' Alison beamed. Then she stopped by the Tokyo party on her way out and told them, in the finest Home Counties accent she could muster, that Harrods was selling the selfsame coconut lamp for almost £100. She watched at least six of the hideous objects carried lovingly towards the till. Simon gave her a sickly grin and she was out of the door, out into the grimy London air, with its stink of cars and faint, oily soot.

She looked at the grubby tangle of buildings and waterway that was Camden Lock and said, 'Once a year, me dear. And no more.' A piece of her past, the marked, flawed past that had followed her around for ages, would remain in the city, detached and distant the moment she boarded the homeward-bound train at Charing Cross.

She was making her way through the station, glad to be ahead of the early evening homeward rush, when two familiar figures sidled up beside her. Alison's heart sank. John and Marjorie Tyler looked exactly like rurals making a pilgrimage to the city. He was in a dark overcoat of indefinite age, with a patina of ancient cupboard dust at the cuffs. His face was even more bloodless than usual. Marjorie wore a shiny fake Burberry, a vast billowing tent of waxed green that seemed big enough to engulf the whole of platform six. Both carried shopping bags that betrayed an outing to Oxford Street. Alison found herself grateful the contents were out of sight. The taste of Beulah's odd couple was something she preferred to encounter on a dark night, and preferably after a few drinks.

'Bloody hell!' Marjorie bellowed. 'Another one about to make it over the wire.'

Alison grinned weakly. Tyler had a sheaf of magazines under his arm and looked as if he couldn't wait to get his long, pale nose inside them. 'Just up on a little business,' she offered.

'Ah, that nice little gaudy-baubles empire you run with our Miss Harrison.' Marjorie beamed. 'Glad to see a little enterprise in the village. You travelling first or second, dear?'

'Second. Pennies tight at the moment.'

John Tyler gave her a baleful stare. 'Join the club. Never mind, Marjorie will sort it out.'

'Of course I will,' Marjorie said. 'Mark this well. Your first lesson in the art of assertive train travel.'

A lone city type bearing an umbrella and a battered leather case was about to claim a long, empty bench seat, the fabric mended with tape after an obvious slash with a knife. With astonishing speed Marjorie launched her entire shopping pile in front of him and yelled, 'Incoming!'

She pushed her way past the man, collapsed into a good half of the three-person bench opposite her bags, and splayed her legs to get more room. Alison sat next to her. Marjorie ordered her husband to 'park his bum' then said, in a very loud voice, 'Bloody hell, John. Next time I come up for aerobics kindly ensure I remember the anti-pong, will you?' She flapped her vast arms; the movement of the fake Burberry made her look like some giant bat that would never escape the pull of gravity. 'I stink worse than a brickie's

225

arse, thank you very much. Did you get some drinkies by the way?'

The city type fled silently and a group of gossiping women in the adjoining seats upped bags and walked to the end of the carriage. Tyler looked at his wife, reached into his pocket and threw a can of ready-made gin and tonic across to her. He pulled four more out and looked at Alison. 'Fancy one? I've got G and T, whisky and dry ginger, voddie tonnie or a coconut daiquiri.'

She shook her head. 'No alcohol for the duration, thanks.'

'Your decision,' he said in a flat monotone.

Alison could feel her blood begin to boil in that familiar, Tyler-induced way. 'I thought you might approve of that,' she observed.

He looked astonished. 'I'm a village quack, not the guardian of the Pearly Gates. A little alcohol never harmed anyone.'

Marjorie popped her drink with a fizz. Tyler mused over the collection on his lap, chose the coconut daiquiri, and opened it. Then the two of them clinked cans and said, in a very doleful fashion, 'Cheers.' After which Tyler pulled out a magazine and buried his head in it. Alison looked at the cover. It was *Caravan Monthly*. She closed her eyes and wondered whether she really dared get up and sit somewhere else. But it simply wasn't possible. They would doubtless just follow her around like hungry stray dogs.

Marjorie peered inside her bags. One contained clothing of a colour so livid it seemed to radiate beyond the top of the carrier. 'Not a bad haul. And I got to see my sister Lorna in Barnsbury too. Poor cow has got some bloody French kids on a school exchange trip. What an idea. Foreign exchange. They ought to call it "Tadpoles to Go" if you ask me. That's what you get when you start breeding.'

'I imagine I have that to look forward to,' Alison said, trying to sound sweet.

A handful of commuters who had boarded at Waterloo East drifted towards the front of the train. 'Townies!' Marjorie barked vehemently, the froth of the drink on her top lip. 'What do you make of it, eh? No spunk, not one of them. Like little mice. Clambering on the train each morning, clambering back at night. *Squeak, squeak, squeak!*'

They pulled in to London Bridge. An inoffensive-looking pair in city suits came through the nearest door and eyed the shopping. Marjorie glowered back at them and bellowed, 'They're all a bunch of effing wankers if you ask me.'

'Including my husband, presumably,' Alison noted sharply.

'Not at all,' Marjorie replied, unfazed. 'Miles *drives*. He's his own man. Not a creature of Connex Sodding South East. And he's going places. Unlike these drones.'

Alison said nothing. Marjorie gave her a penetrating stare, then a look that said the penny had dropped. 'Oh God, dear. I forgot. Sara told me there was some problem at work. Job going belly up. That right?'

'Just about,' Alison replied, and wondered how she might cure Sara of her penchant for gossip. It was a village trait, true, but not an attractive one.

'What was the bastard's name? Something common. Sara mentioned it.'

'Ron Atkins. Known as the Chelmsford Kid or something.'

Marjorie whistled. 'Ooh. Sounds nasty. Why don't you fix him?'

Alison sighed. The Beulah attitude seemed to be to treat problems like chickens; when the time was right you just had their necks wrung. '*Fix* him?'

'One way or another.' Marjorie shrugged.

John Tyler looked up from the pages of *Caravan Monthly*. 'Just send him to me. I've got a million ways of dealing with awkward buggers. You know, people never think about it, but a GP has a unique role in British life. We can knock off whoever we like, when we like. Fast or slow, it doesn't matter. And you need to be a real nincompoop to get found out. Bloody right anyone who gets caught winds up in front of the General Medical Council. Incompetent shits like that shouldn't be allowed to practise in the first place.'

'Now there's a comforting thought,' Alison replied, trying to smile.

'Oh,' Tyler said wearily. 'I get it. You're offended. Tell me, my dear, do you believe in euthanasia?'

'Of course. Any rational person does. In the right circumstances it's the kindest thing to do.'

'Ah, "kind". Now there's a word. So if it's OK for me to knock off the physically infirm, why shouldn't I delete a few socially infirm ones along the way? God knows, *they're* more annoying by far.'

'But . . .'

'No,' he interrupted. 'Let me guess. *That* would be murder. And "euthanasia" isn't. I'm just a country quack. Too stupid to see the difference.'

Marjorie touched her arm. 'Not a good subject for him, I'm afraid. He hates the whole idea.'

'It's just another way that people expect someone else to make their decisions for them,' Tyler opined, and shook the pages of the magazine as if that somehow hammered home his point. 'And there's the linguistic issue too. Killing people is killing people. It's insulting to dress it up in fancy names.'

Alison watched Bromley go past outside the window and wondered if she would ever second guess one of John Tyler's opinions correctly.

'Subject closed,' Tyler said, and was immediately back inside the covers of the magazine.

'All the same,' Marjorie continued. 'There are little things you can do. Or rather *I* could do. In return for a favour.'

228

Alison's head was in a whirl. 'Do what? A favour?'

Marjorie actually looked around to see if anyone was close enough to listen. Alison wondered what information she might have to impart that required such discretion. If murder by medical practitioners could be discussed at the volume of a Dungeness foghorn it had to be pretty tasty.

'I know we had that funny turn with Bella Cartwright at Yule,' Marjorie confided in something approaching a whisper. 'But you do fit in with us, don't you? You do belong. We all feel that in the village.'

'We're very happy in Beulah,' Alison replied cautiously. 'I hope we can manage to stay there.'

'Of course you will,' Marjorie said quickly. 'The thing is, it would be so much nicer if you were a part of the village. *Everything.* I'm inviting you, if you like.'

'Inviting me to what?'

'Our little get-togethers. It's not just Yule. We have fun all year round. Quietly. Harming no one. It's like a tie that binds us. And most of us plan to live and die in that village, you know. You need bonds like that over the years.'

Alison was both curious and alarmed. This was Marjorie opening up a little, with some kind of offer on the table. And she had no idea what to make of it. 'Marjorie, I don't know what you're talking about. All these things . . . the Burning Man, Yule. It's witchcraft or something?'

'Oh God,' John Tyler groaned. 'I knew that word would come up sooner or later. Yes, dear lady, you're right. We all sit around sticking pins into wax dolls of the people we hate. Marjorie has a broomstick and a pointed hat somewhere too, don't you, my sweet? Let me summon up some pleasurable succubus right now.'

He puffed up his chest and in a loud theatrical voice recited, 'By Bes-na-Maut my breast I beat; By wise Ta-Nech I weave my spell.' Then he pulled the can of whisky and ginger out of his coat pocket, popped it open and threw the spare gin to Marjorie. 'There,' he said with a sudden, bright smile. 'That worked!'

'Shut up, John,' Marjorie snarled. 'You can't expect her to understand. She's only been with us two minutes.'

'I'm not really a joiner,' Alison noted lamely.

Tyler looked up from his magazine. 'It's not about joining. It's about belonging.'

'Well . . . I still don't get it. And I've got plenty else on my plate.'

Marjorie gave her a canny look. 'I was offering a *deal*, dear. You do something for me. I'll do something for you.'

They were, she knew, mad. Crazy as a van full of badgers, to use one of Beulah's favourite phrases. 'I don't have much time, Marjorie.'

'You don't need much time. We just have our little meetings at the important points of the year.'

'Told her all that,' Tyler said behind the pages. 'Even drew her a picture. Don't think it went in.'

Marjorie tried to find the words. 'It's just folklore. A social thing. Hard to explain in words. Why don't you just come along? Suck it and see?'

'When? No promises.'

Tyler put down the magazine. 'March the twenty-first is the vernal equinox. Astronomically, this is the point where day and night are of equal length. From this point on, light begins to reclaim the world. After that, it's straight to Beltane – May Day, as you doubtless know it.'

'And that *is* fun,' Marjorie interjected, a broad grin on her face.

'The mythological point about the vernal equinox,' Tyler continued, 'is this issue of light defeating darkness. The *Mabinogion*, which is Welsh, in case you didn't know, is particularly interesting here. One way of interpreting the yearly ritual is that the god of darkness, in this case Goronwy, kills Llew, the god of light, each year at the autumnal equinox. With a little help from Llew's faithless wife Blodeuwedd, of course, since she is the only one who knows the weakness, the Celtic Achilles heel, by which he may be slain. She betrays her husband in order to expose him to her lover. Then, after a season in hell, the husband returns and wreaks his revenge. There's the same atavistic notion in our night of the Burning Man, as you may recall. And the seasons change. In turn, the god of light is reborn each Yule and rises to murder his brother at the vernal equinox.'

'Brother?' Alison asked, trying to absorb all this.

'Oh yes,' Marjorie said, suddenly very serious. 'The Mother is the Great Goddess. She's above them all. Which is why . . .' She suddenly blushed. Alison was astonished. It made her look unexpectedly vulnerable.

'You're the Mother,' Alison said. 'That's what all that dancing was about?'

Marjorie nodded. 'Symbolically. Nothing actually happens, you understand. All that nonsense with the Cartwrights boffing in the bushes . . . that was just the Cartwrights being themselves.'

Alison thought about all this. 'Isn't March the twenty-first around Easter weekend? I thought it was early this year.'

'A happy coincidence,' Tyler agreed. 'The vernal equinox is an astronomical date. Easter is a moveable feast because of church bureaucracy, nothing more. Incidentally, some of the pre-Christian pagan texts have the god of light descending into the underworld for three days before he rises on the equinox. Now does that sound familiar?'

They were back in the country now. She recognised the deer park outside Maidstone. It felt comforting to be heading home. 'Of course it does,' she replied. 'But where do I fit in all this? I'm just a townie. An outsider myself.'

'No,' Marjorie said and wagged a fat finger in the air. 'You are an extraordinary woman, Alison. You have empathy. You have a sense for these things. I've seen that all along. So has John, not that he'll let on.'

'I'm really not sure this is me.'

'Alison. I need a helpmate. Someone who can watch me. Learn from me. One day, perhaps, take my place. Being Mother isn't easy. Bit like being a football manager. When you're winning, everyone loves you. When you stumble, the hounds are chomping at your throat. And we haven't had many good seasons recently, to be honest.'

'There must be someone better. Someone from Beulah.'

'Who? The village has lost half its population over the last twenty years. Young people move out, go to London, never come back. So what we have left is the likes of Bella Cartwright, a fine girl in her way, but too daffy upstairs to be of use to me.'

'What about Sara?' Alison felt horribly guilty for even suggesting her friend, but she was desperate.

Marjorie gave her an incisive look. 'We never speak about who we invite. It's sort of a rule. But let me just say, I talked to her. It didn't work out.'

'So you want me to be the sorcerer's apprentice?'

'No sorcery,' Tyler said without looking up from the page. 'There's no such thing.'

Marjorie looked close to pleading. 'It's just some old native rites, my dear. They mean nothing to anyone else. We're probably soft in the head even to keep them alive. But they have been around for a long time. Centuries and centuries. And we don't want to lose them.'

'It's like Christianity,' Tyler said, and now he was looking at her. 'It may sound like poppycock now, but when you're facing death's door a spot of insurance might seem very attractive just in case there is someone with a check-in register sitting on the other side. After all, on one level, we know our little rituals do work. The world's still turning, isn't it?'

232

'The world,' Alison said very deliberately, 'is absolute bloody chaos.'

'Not in Beulah it isn't,' Tyler replied. 'We may have our eccentricities. But we're immune to the nonsense out *there*.' He waved at the outskirts of Ashford now coming into view, almost as dirty and as drab as London.

And that much, she knew, was true.

'Is it a deal?' Marjorie asked.

'I'll think about it.'

'Yes!' Marjorie Tyler looked positively beatific.

'I said I'll *think* about it.'

'Of course you will.' John Tyler was expressionless, staring out of the window at the dying day.

'Marjorie?' she asked. 'How did you get the job?'

Marjorie Tyler was staring out of the window, ignoring the question. 'Look,' she exclaimed. 'Wye at last. We could pop into the Tickled Trout for a quickie on the way home if you like.'

The third week of March saw the first tantalising promise of spring. The rains lifted, the sky became a piercing blue coverlet over the slowly waking earth. Then came the heart-stopping phone call. Miles rang from the office one Thursday morning with the news. Ron Atkins was out of the game. The Germans had been forced to reconsider their entire strategy.

The choice of Atkins had been a deliberate attempt to take Mersons out of the world of the old school tie. Now they felt they had made a dreadful mistake. The old order had to take charge anew, but not quite with the same faces at the helm. Andy Moorside, Miles's old boss, was reluctantly persuaded to take early retirement in favour of the ascension of Miles to the helm. Every dream Alison and Miles had ever had about the future seemed to be on the verge of coming true. It seemed uncanny.

'But why?' she asked. 'Why did he quit?'

'It's a mystery to me. He walked into the office this morning with a beaut of a black eye and told them he wanted his old job back. Just cracked, it seems. I've never seen the man look so nervous. Looks like he had some kind of bundle on the way home. It gets to people like that sometimes, you know. One minute they're in control, the next they're blabbing for Mummy.'

'But . . .'

'Darling,' Miles reminded her tactfully. 'Could you sound a little more pleased? I am in. Atkins is out. Entirely. The idea he could just return to Forex was ridiculous, of course. I can't believe he thought it was even possible.'

'But *why*?'

There was now a distinct note of exasperation in his voice. 'Good God, Alison. Who cares?'

Walking on the edge of the Minnis later, Alison was abruptly engulfed in a sea of swirling white. The blackthorn bushes that had been so full of sloes the previous winter were now in blossom. On bare, black branches stood a foaming froth of lovely flowers, alive and flourishing in the post-winter landscape. She looked at the flowers for a while, found the small penknife in the pocket of her jacket, and began to cut a few.

There was a noise behind her. Alison turned and saw, close up for the first time since Christmas, Bella Cartwright. The girl looked younger in daylight. Her skin, pale, without make-up, had a raw winter roughness to it. Her sharp brown eyes shone, half curious, half suspicious.

Bella looked at the branches and said, 'You don't want to be taking them in the house, missus. Bad luck. Everyone knows that.'

234

'Not me, Bella. Just a townie, remember?'

'Yeah.' She was walking a small, scruffy mongrel. Its lead was a piece of old rope. Alison looked at the dog. It seemed harmless enough.

'Why don't you let him run around?'

'It's a bitch,' Bella replied. 'Bleeding thing just goes bonkers if it's off the lead. Digging crap up. No end of trouble.'

'You mean it never gets to run around?'

'Don't know what it might dig up, do you?' Bella said sharply. 'Not around here?'

They were on the village side of the White Horse. The wood, with its mysterious clearing and, beyond, the remains of Paternoster Farm, was only a mile or so away.

'You getting a dog then, missus? With a kid coming along, that would be nice. Have this one if you want.'

'I think a baby's going to be enough to cope with, don't you?'

'No idea,' Bella said somewhat sourly. 'No use asking me.'

'Perhaps one day.'

The girl was examining her, she could see that. And making no attempt to hide the fact. Finally, Bella asked, 'Didn't they say you was loony tunes once? Just like me?'

Alison took a deep breath and found herself smiling; another example of the fine spirit of Beulah frankness. 'I had a breakdown. Before we moved here. It's all over now, thank goodness.'

'A breakdown? You mean like it was here one moment, gone the next?'

'Sort of.'

She seemed disappointed. 'Well, that's not like me at all. My mam says it's 'cos I was born funny. Old quacky Tyler reckons it's a gift.'

Alison found herself feeling sorry for the girl. Whatever the affliction was, it made her stand out, and that was something no one in Beulah wanted. 'What do you think it is, Bella?'

'A pain in the arse!' the girl replied with a grin, and then turned serious again. 'You aren't going to pick them flowers, are you, missus? It's bad luck having 'em in the house. Honest.'

Alison threw the branches down. 'I'll take your word on that. Fancy a walk to the end?'

They ambled off to the escarpment with the bold chalk figure on it. A light breeze rose up the hill as they approached the edge. There was warmth in it, the prospect of summer in a breath of air.

'So,' Alison asked, remembering Christmas, 'what is this illness? Or gift if you like?'

'Seeing things. Or dreaming things more like. It's not like they're true now, is it?'

'I don't know.'

'Oh no? What about that time at Yule when I went barmy? I had this picture of Harry and you together. Shagging. And then worse. And that wasn't true now, was it?'

Don't pick at scabs, she thought, Sara had said this so forcefully. Easy advice to give, hard to follow. 'What was the "worse" part?'

Bella shuddered. 'Blood and things. And fire. It was *horrible*.'

'But what happened?'

'You killed him. In my dream.'

Alison exhaled a brittle laugh, briefly closed her eyes and saw a vast metallic monster, belching fire, devouring bodies.

'You OK, missus?'

'Perfect,' she replied. They stopped at the edge of the Downs and stared at the flat, long sweep of the Stour valley, with its distant hamlets, the busy main road of the A28 cutting through the view and, in the east, the sprawl of Canterbury.

236

'Why do you think you dreamed that, Bella?'

'I asked a couple of people.' Alison felt suddenly chill. 'They said it were obvious. First there was the fire. Then there was Harry gone. And you being a foreigner. New and all. Old Tyler said it was my subconscious putting all them three things together, mixing 'em up and coming out all in one go. He said you could "deconstruct" – or something like that – everybody's dreams, and the only difference with mine was that they happened while I was awake.'

'Who else did you ask?'

Bella cast her a querulous glance. 'Couple. Don't remember exactly. Why's that important?'

Alison took her by the shoulders and stared into her face. 'People misread gossip, Bella. Even when it comes from dreams. People like the police, for example.'

Bella threw back her head and laughed. Her hair splayed out behind her. It was grubby blonde and too long. Shame, Alison thought. She could be a pretty kid. 'You don't think I'd go telling the law, do you? Bloody Nora! My dad'd kill me if he found out I'd been speaking to the likes of them.'

Alison tried not to look too relieved. 'Good.'

'And anyway it's bollocks, isn't it? Your copper wouldn't be interested in tittle-tattle like that. He's looking for evidence. Looking everywhere from what I hear. Looking for that and a few other things too.'

Alison said in a steely voice, 'He isn't *my* copper.'

Bella dug an elbow gently into her ribs. 'Naw, course not. Nothing wrong with a bit on the side though, is there? All *them* get up to it.'

Alison remained silent, conscious she was being judged.

'You're a one, aren't you?' Bella said, looking sly. 'All posh and stuff on the outside. But inside . . . you're just like us, aren't you? You get the dreams too?'

'Just the odd nightmare,' Alison hissed.

'I'll bet. Still waters run deep and all that. Old Mother

Tyler knows, that's why she's got her eye on you. Says you're one of us all right.'

She knew so much, or appeared to. 'Meaning what, Bella?'

'She's after you to join in. She's been doing it all on her own ever since Mary Wethered popped her clogs. That's not supposed to happen for long, and she's not that smart at some things either. Sal won't do it. I'm bonkers and too young anyway. Can't go getting some Ashford slag in, seeing as whoever does it probably gets to take over when Marjorie goes her way. Unless . . .' Bella checked herself.

'Unless what?'

'Unless something . . . untoward happens.'

Alison felt exasperated. 'Please say what you mean, Bella. These mysteries become a little impenetrable after a while.'

Bella looked uncomfortable. 'Can't now, can I? You ain't even joined yet and that's part of the deal. You don't get to read the book before you go into the Masons, do you? Why should we be any different?'

'You mean this is supposed to be like the Masons?'

'Mebbe. Except from what I hear our ceremonies are a bit more interesting. And we can do each other favours from time to time. Which they ain't supposed to any more.'

The conversation on the train reared back into her head and with it a surge of dread and anger. 'Favours?'

'You bet,' Bella replied firmly. 'We're an endangered species out here, missus. All them townies wanting our homes. Building everywhere. Stopping us farming like we want, doing what we want. How d'you expect us to get along without knowing who's a friend and who ain't?'

'And who, in particular, is good at doing "favours" around here?'

Bella shrugged. 'There's the other problem. Mitch and Harry. And neither of them's about now, are they?'

'So in that case . . .'

'*No!*' Bella interrupted crossly. 'I'm not saying no more. Not till you come in. It's not fair you should be asking either. Old Mother Tyler thinks you could be one of us, that's fine. It's her decision. Your choice. But don't get me wrong, missus. I like you. We all do. That's why you got invited. It don't just happen, you know.'

Alison tried to calm down. 'I'm sorry, Bella. It's very flattering, I'm sure. It's just that I would like to know what I'm taking on. And what the price is.'

'Huh.' For a moment the girl looked distinctly unpleasant. 'That's a real townie thing, innit? I bet come Christmas you want to know exactly what's inside that box before you open it. Otherwise you'd be scared to rip the paper off in case you didn't like what was there.'

Alison was silent. It was a remarkably accurate observation.

'You want my advice, missus. You should go and talk this out with Marjorie. Ask her your questions. Not me. She's expecting you Monday, that being the holiday. We got work to do with the year starting up again.'

'What . . . ?'

Bella waved a hand. 'Now I don't wish to be rude. But I've said my piece. One day, who knows? Maybe you'll be making the same invitation to me. Passing things on peaceful like, generation to generation. Or whichever way turns out best.'

'Bella, you can have it now for all I care.'

'Too young. Like I said. And don't you treat this like it's something worthless.'

'I'm sorry,' Alison said. 'I didn't want to offend anyone. But I don't like getting pushed into things without being asked first.'

Bella grinned. 'No problem. You got spunk all right. You'll be good when it comes to the favours. Marjorie was right there. Maybe you did do old Harry in, eh?'

239

'Oh yes,' Alison said without thinking. 'I am one vicious bitch when you get on the wrong side of me, Bella. You'd best make sure everyone understands that.'

The girl blanched. 'I will. Didn't mean to get you going. Honest.'

Alison glowered at her and stomped off back to the Minnis, a tiny worm of ire wriggling through her head.

Ten minutes later, after a futile effort to calm herself seated on a bench overlooking the green, she walked over to the Tylers' house and rang the bell. Marjorie beamed when she opened the door. 'Come in. Tea and biscotti. Nothing narcotic, promise. I know you'll be thinking of the little one.'

Alison stood in the plain modern hall, with its naff paintings and ridiculous bric-a-brac and folded her arms. 'I don't want a goddamn cup of tea, Marjorie. I'm mad. I want an explanation.'

Marjorie blinked. 'Of anything in particular, dear?'

'Of why Miles is now winding up running Mersons instead of getting kicked out with a pay-off. Of how the guy who was supposed to get the job is suddenly too terrified to take it. Favours, Marjorie. Have you been doing a few behind my back?'

Marjorie looked puzzled. 'Good news then, is it?'

'You ought to think about the possible consequences of your little games sometimes. That poor bastard Atkins could go to the police.'

Marjorie looked at her blankly. 'I don't know what you're talking about, Alison.'

'No. Of course not. You scratch my back, I'll scratch yours. Who did you send to do your dirty work now the Blamire boys are gone? And now, I suppose, you think I'm coming along to your little naked Morris dancing festival or whatever it is you're doing on Monday?'

'We don't do "Morris dancing",' Marjorie replied icily.

'But you're welcome, of course, particularly if you think you've got something to give thanks for.'

'Thanks? Are you serious?'

'I said some prayers for you. I wished, fervently, for your problem to go away. That's all. It has. Be grateful. It's not for either of us to ask the who or why of it all.'

Alison was furious. The woman was clearly going to bluff this out with a display of brass-necked innocence. 'Listen, Marjorie, I *know* this was you.'

Marjorie looked intrigued. 'Do you? We go through life knowing so many things that turn out to be poppycock. Back at Yule, Bella Cartwright *knew* you did something wicked to poor Harry Blamire. So much for that.'

'That is *not* the point. I want you to understand this and understand it well. You do not interfere in our lives. You do not work your favours for me again.'

Marjorie looked offended. 'We had a deal, Alison. I don't think you quite understand what you're saying.'

'*We had no goddamn deal!* Don't you ever listen? Miles and I just want a nice, quiet life here. Raising kids. Earning a living. We don't want to join in your games.'

'Too late for that, dear,' Marjorie replied opaquely. Some dim light of anger flared in her eyes. 'And besides. Don't be so stupid. It's because of the child we want you. To an extent. Don't you see?'

Alison couldn't even begin to peer through this. 'What?'

'Beulah is dying on its feet, Alison. They go to the towns, they go to the cities. The only way we can survive is to bring people back. And make them part of us. This year looks so promising. A child for Sara at Midsummer. A child for you at Burning Man. We did play a part, you know. If you hadn't listened to John, you'd still be as barren as Lapland right now.'

'Dammit, Marjorie. This is my child.'

'Of course. What's paternity anyway? Only a beginning.

One day we'll have children at all four points of the star. And then we start to heal again.'

Alison's mind performed cartwheels. She thought of John Tyler and his little drawing, the seasons shifting through their motions like cogs in some great, giant mechanism. 'What are you saying, Marjorie? That all that stupid bullshit your husband gave me is part of some plan?'

Marjorie sighed. 'How do you think it was in the old days? A child at each cycle of the seasons. Harmony with the earth, woman. You don't think we invented this, do you? You can be very dense at times.'

Alison felt her mind focus in on itself, become absorbed entirely on making a single point to this strange, obsessed woman. 'Marjorie, listen to me and listen very carefully. I am telling you now, we are not part of your game. Whatever you thought was agreed, wasn't. And in future you keep your prying fingers out of our business. Understood?'

Marjorie raised herself up on her heels. This brought her almost eye to eye with Alison. There was fury in her florid, shaking face. 'Oh yes. I understand. I marked you wrong, my girl. You really are just another townie out for what you can get. You don't give a damn about us, do you? It's just I give and you take. And to hell with the village. To hell with centuries of tradition. Or is it . . . ?' The red cheeks paled a touch. 'Have you been listening to the gossip, dear? Is this what it's about? Think you can do the job better yourself?'

The woman was mad. There could, she thought, be no other explanation.

Alison Fenway turned on her heel and walked out of the dreary modern house, out onto the green, hearing Marjorie's furious voice rising to a bellow behind her. It was odd, but somehow she felt as if she had chalked up a victory, albeit one that, the more she thought about it, left her feeling somewhat scared.

The wood was a mistake and they both knew it. Yet she could think of nowhere else when she called. Alison now lay cradled in the disfigured arms of an ancient chestnut, Justin still locked over her, moving gently, licking her neck, breathing warmly into her ear. It was a chill spring day and they had made love frantically, without questions, half-clothed in the mid-afternoon. And there were no regrets. For him, this was the true beginning, a genuine, mutual seduction, not the hurried, booze-fuelled frenzy of Yule. Alison was coming round, realising his importance in her life. She was the one who called. She had scarcely resisted when, without a word, he had removed her jacket, bent down on both knees, kissed her stomach, first through the silk of her shirt, then, tearing away at the buttons, moved his tongue over the hardening flesh of her navel.

Afterwards, silence, with nothing to say, no embarrassment there. She waited, relishing his enjoyment as he stirred within her, felt him stiffening again, and put a hand to his damp, spiky hair.

'Wait,' she said.

'I waited long enough.'

His body jerked. She felt the cold metal buttons of his jacket press against her naked breasts.

'Justin!'

She locked her legs around his waist, held him to her, staring into his eyes. There was a wildness there she hadn't seen before. Something dangerous hung in the air.

'I need something from you.'

He paused, still stiffening. 'Ask,' he gasped. 'Ask anything.'

She gripped his hair, felt down through his clothes, down to his groin, fired his arousal.

'Later.'

Beneath them, unseen, something rustled through the dead leaves. The zigzag back curved across the earth, a single reptilian eye aware of the ritual occurring above it. The viper disappeared into the forest. In the wild wood, they screamed.

It had only come to her after John Tyler's lecture on the train. Miles's birthday fell over the holiday. He would be thirty-six this year, on Easter Monday, and firmly set on a rising career. And called away again, with just time for lunch in Beulah before some urgent meeting.

The idea for the present was his own. He had idly dropped into the conversation the news that some of the boys in the Green Man were forming a clay pigeon club. There was talk of banging away at the odd pigeon and rabbit too, perhaps even migrating to the major league of pheasants one day. Miles had never touched a weapon in his life, as far as she knew. The idea had some vague appeal to him because of the blokey clubbishness surrounding it rather than any great conversion to the business of field sports.

He never mentioned it again, but the idea lodged at the back of her head. Justin was able to provide the paperwork – the precious shotgun licence. After that it was just a question of buying the right weapon. She determined to ask the advice of the man in the gun shop, select a price range, then haggle as hard as she could.

That Easter Saturday when she drove into town, the row with Marjorie still bubbling in her memory, she stood in the shop for nearly an hour, talking to the cheery chap behind the counter, weighing up the pros and cons of the arsenal he had on show. The price range had risen considerably after the sudden turnaround in Miles's fortunes. There was such choice: cheap, functional farmers' guns; delicate, light models 'for the ladies' and, at the top of the scale, some exquisitely made weapons that seemed as much examples of an artist's craft as deadly machines for taking flying bundles of feathers out of the sky.

The shopkeeper took a canny look at the way she was lingering over the pricey ones, then went inside and returned with something which, Alison knew on the instant, she just had to possess. He called it a Purdey High Deco. To her it was simply one of the most beautiful articles she had ever seen.

It was a twelve-bore, top-lever gun, double-barrelled, with a stock of polished burr walnut. From the trigger guards to the chambers the metal was covered in fine, filigree engraving, extravagant whorls, patterns of tumbling, encircling leaves and deeply chiselled dragons straight out of a child's fantasy book. She held it in her hands, felt her palms move automatically over the smooth wood, then pointed the barrels at the ceiling of the shop and said, very quietly to herself, 'bang, bang'. It was sufficiently compact and light to be used by man or woman. And if Miles grew tired of shooting, she would put it in a case and hang it over the grand Georgian fireplace. It was that beautiful. The store owner eventually settled for £6,750 including a handsome leather case, charged directly to her credit card. Then he put the weapon inside a discreet cardboard box, threw in a variety of shells, some for clay pigeons, others for live targets, and carefully carried the lot to her car for the journey home.

The weather was mixed on Easter Monday. Squally showers blew in from the east, chilly and vicious, with the hint of ice on their breath. In between the rain the sun shone eagerly on the damp, green landscape that was now slowly coming out of its slumber. She made lunch for Miles and Sara, a brief birthday celebration before he returned to town. As she cooked, a pair of amorous hares danced beneath the apple trees in the garden and then scampered off into the woods. The lone pheasant limped across the vegetable patch, tail feathers half gone, bare skin at its neck, looking exhausted. Libidinous songbirds tumbled across her field of vision from every direction. Tits fought with each other through the branches, on the lawn, small black beaks flashing, wings a blurry haze of energy. Chaffinches hung around in sparky, argumentative pairs, bright, red-chested bullfinches paraded through the garden like brash soldiers home on temporary leave and desperate for a quick one. The cycle had turned again with a shocking rapidity and, thinking back to the episode in the wood, she felt a part of it herself. This was altogether new. In the city the seasons simply ran into each other with few signs to mark the changes. Here the progression of the year was all around her, assaulted her senses with a procession of shifting sights and smells, working its way into her own life too.

As she prepared the meal, Alison became aware that she had adapted her culinary tastes to the Beulah year too. The chaotic farm shop down the hill on the A28 was a treasure-house of winter vegetables straight from the field: fat leeks, misshapen parsnips, potatoes that had a wonderful, earthy taste about them. She bought the farm's home-reared pork and marvelled at how much flavour lay beneath the thick, unfashionable fat. Pheasant and widgeon, teal and woodcock, the cornucopia of the countryside made its way to the table of Priory House. Jugged hare, pigeon breasts simmered slowly in beer, with lettuce to break down the fibrous flesh, pheasant in Kentish cream and cider, a ragout of wild mushrooms – ceps, chanterelles and blewits – picked on the hinterland of the Minnis, from places she was beginning to discover for herself. All these flowed out of Alison's kitchen from the flashing Sabatier she wielded with an ever-increasing skill.

For Miles's birthday she briefly boiled three wild duck to get rid of the fishy taste, then roasted them, each with a spiced pear inside the cavity. The meal was served with roast potatoes, parsnips toffeed as Arnold had shown her, leeks in buttery cream from the farm and chubby winter carrots that made the anorexic supermarket variety seem insipid, watery things. Miles and Sara sat with knives and forks poised expectantly like children on a treat.

'Where,' Miles asked, mouth full, 'did you learn to cook like this, darling? In New York it was all noodles and lemon grass.'

'Christ, yes,' she said, shuddering. 'Lemon grass. Like eating toenail clippings dipped in disinfectant. Why didn't we ever realise that?'

'Conditioning,' Sara said. 'Peer pressure. We don't have that up here. You're allowed to indulge your natural instincts. Which, faced with grub like this, means pigging out. Of course, Miles, *we* have an excuse. Feeding two.'

'I'll just get happily fat then,' he said cheerfully.

After home-made *tarte tatin*, with the last of the winter Bramleys, he opened his present. The gun seemed bigger in Priory House somehow and Alison was uncertain whether she liked it quite as much. The filigree and the chiselled dragons were just as breathtaking as they were in the shop, but, out of its case in the ordinary surroundings of the home, it was more clearly a weapon. Miles grinned and picked up a handful of shells from the box.

'Got to give it a try, haven't I? Down the bottom of the garden.'

'Don't you go killing anything,' Alison warned. 'Particularly not my pal the pheasant. I'm fond of that foolish old bird.'

'More fond of him than me?' Miles asked.

She kissed his cheek. 'About the same.'

The women watched him walk outside, the gun carefully broken over his arm, just as it said in the books.

'He reminds me of the pheasant sometimes,' Alison said, watching him march down the garden. 'The same strutting confidence, the same puffed-out chest.'

'Miles is one good bloke,' Sara observed. 'You're very lucky.'

'I know. But they're all children really.'

Sara had that uncomfortable look. 'Alison?'

'Oh dear. What have I done now?'

'I don't want to cause problems . . .'

She wondered what was coming. The company was running reasonably well. Sara was progressively shifting work across in preparation for the birth. Tyler had decided on the most likely date: June the twenty-first. The summer solstice, as he doubtless pointed out. There was a ruthless mathematical precision about these things if you decided to get pregnant on one of his magical quarter points of the year. The human gestation period determined, complications aside, that to conceive on one significant date would, inevitably, lead to a birth very close to another.

'Fire away,' Alison said.

'It's Marjorie Tyler. I had her round about your argument. Not that she gave any details. I really think you two should make up, you know. It's a small village, love. It doesn't pay to have enemies.'

Alison thought about Old Mother Tyler and her little favours. Making up was not high on her agenda just then.

'Don't get involved, Sara. There's no rule that says you have to like all your neighbours.'

'No. But you still have to live alongside them.'

'More's the pity in Marjorie's case. I'm sorry. She's just . . . beyond the pale. With her secrets and her little favours, just to get me dancing in the fairy ring with her or whatever.'

Sara sighed. 'People take those things very seriously. You shouldn't mock.'

'I didn't mean to. I just don't want Marjorie messing around in my private life, that's all. Jesus Christ! It's so goddamn impertinent.'

'That's the village for you. We have our big secrets. We have some things that don't stay secret at all.'

'Mine do.'

Sara paused before saying it. 'Not as much as you think.'

Alison felt giddy all of a sudden. 'Meaning what, precisely?'

Sara glowered at her miserably. 'Jesus, Alison. Do you think no one else goes in the woods? Do you think you're really going to get away with cheating on Miles like that?'

Alison cleared away the empty plates, an automatic reaction. 'I hadn't realised I was being spied on.'

'*You're not!* God, you can be so *dangerous* sometimes. I saw you walk past the cottage and thought I'd catch up with you for a walk. By the time I found you . . . well. What can I say?'

'I hardly think you're in much of a position to start getting moral on me, love.'

Sara's bright eyes flashed with fury. 'It's nothing to do with morals. I don't give a damn who you screw in your spare time, although I think Miles may have an opinion on that. It's about common sense. You've got everything anyone could want here, Alison. A beautiful home. A loving husband. A child on the way. And it's as if . . . I don't know. You just enjoy putting it all at risk sometimes.'

She could imagine how it might look like that from the outside. Sara couldn't see Harry Blamire's face disappearing into the fiery maw of the machine in Paternoster Farm, or hear his words ringing through the memory, over and over again.

'Don't judge me, Sara. You don't have that right.'

Sara was pleading. It wasn't a comfortable sight. 'I'm not. I'm trying to help you. Ali, you're my best pal. I can't watch you screw things up like this.'

Alison looked through the hall into the open kitchen and out of the back windows. Miles was still playing with the gun but he could come back at any moment. 'I can't talk now. Come back tonight. Please.'

'Why? So you can sweep me up in all this madness too? You don't get it, do you? I don't want explanations. I don't want to be a part of all this. They're already talking about you having something to do with Harry's death, you know. Justin can't be long behind.'

Alison felt her face go bright crimson. 'Did Marjorie say that? I'll kill the bitch, I swear it.'

She took Sara's hand. 'Listen. You told me once that some things are best left dead and buried. You were right. Enough said?'

Sara blinked. 'Whatever you say.' Outside there was the muffled sound of the shotgun, two distant blasts, one after the other.

'If he's killed anything . . .' Alison said slowly. 'Please come tonight.'

Sara looked uncomfortable again. 'Don't take this the wrong way, Alison. But you have to be careful when you go into business with a friend. You have to keep the business and your friendship apart. Otherwise both can go down the pan.'

'Ah,' Alison said, and thought: *dammit*. She poured herself one small glass of Chilean Shiraz and savoured its rich, oaky taste. 'You're right, of course. Too much time together isn't a good thing. We're not married after all.'

Sara got up to go. 'Think about what I said, please. Don't live so dangerously, love.'

Ten minutes later Miles was back, looking ruddy-faced and pleased as punch. 'You could take on the world with that thing, old girl. Boy, does it make a bang.'

'No fatalities, I presume?'

'Not a one. Although I don't give your pal the pheasant much chance of surviving the year. Stupid thing watched me banging away at the treetops and scarcely blinked.'

She thought about the half-witted bird, with its beady eye and comic gait. It didn't need to be smart to survive. It just needed to be less stupid than the other pheasants.

'Do you have to go up to town tonight?' she asked, feeling guilty for pressing him like this.

'Oh God.' He was downcast on the instant. 'I don't have a choice, darling. If I did, I wouldn't think twice. This is the big meeting. We rubber-stamp the deal. And my job too.'

'Of course,' she said, and poured another half glass of wine, unable to work out why she felt so depressed. 'Stupid of me to ask.'

He left the drive at five thirty. She watched from the living room window. After he'd gone a perfect Beulah night fell, the sky clear and pierced by winking stars. The vernal equinox was under way. Night would equal day at the turn of the season, and, from this point on, there would be more light than dark in the world. Until the celestial cycle turned again at the autumnal equinox, Burning Man, when the great cogs and chains of creation would make them equal for one day again, then reverse direction into cold, bleak winter. Somewhere in Sterning Wood, Marjorie Tyler and her followers were marking this pivotal point in the earth's annual journey. With an unfilled space in the ceremony where the initiate should have stood.

In desperation, she phoned Justin. There was no reply. She didn't know whether to be grateful or disappointed. Sara had a point, as always. But Sara hadn't lain in his embrace in a damp chestnut bole, listening to the wild creatures of the wood, feeling the heat of ecstasy run through her body. Sara didn't know or care what it was like to need or be needed. For her, practicalities had superseded emotions. Sara's world excluded danger, and with it went love and passion too. To be safe, Alison reasoned, was to be merely half alive. To live only for the future was to deny the present.

'Damn them,' Alison said to herself, and thought that a few glasses of red wine could hardly pose a problem. *Damn them all.* Marjorie and her favours. The beastly quack and his seasons. And men, for all the complexities they introduced into the messy business of living.

She went to bed at ten, feeling a little queasy from the drink. But it was impossible to sleep. The night seemed full of odd sounds. The distant, unexpected screech of an owl. Cars on the Minnis. Drunks stumbling out of the pub. Something, a mouse or a squirrel, scratched its way across the roof space, its talons scraping the ceiling.

With the lazy, involuntary roll of the half drunk, Alison fell in and out of sleep, dreaming in a random, narcoleptic fashion that mingled reverie with reality and never let the seam show. Miles blasted the broad, blue sky and feathers fell like rain. Marjorie Tyler and Bella Cartwright danced naked in a clearing of newly harvested leeks, nuzzling each other suggestively. And Arnold was there, with all the sadness of the world on his ancient shoulders. He sat weeping wordlessly in the old armchair in the study, staring at her, shaking his grey, dead head.

There were two Alisons in this place. The first awake, in light; the other dreaming, in the endless folds of the velvet night. One of them – and she didn't know which – sat bolt upright in the big, empty double bed, looked at the bedside clock flashing two fifteen at her and thought: *there is someone in the room.*

Then turned to the big Georgian window overlooking the

Minnis where, so many months earlier, a different Alison, new to the village, had unwittingly shown her nakedness to the long-dead Harry Blamire, busying himself on the bright-green cricket pitch, peering through the windows of Priory House, nosing his way into everybody's business.

The curtains were open now. Harsh bright moonlight poured through the open window with a chill, alabaster power that sucked the heat out of the room.

A man stood there. A powerful, stocky figure, staring out onto the Minnis. He held a long, narrow implement in his hand and raised it to the light. Alison saw the reflection it made on his face, a brief spark of radiance on a single dead eye. There was a scar on the skin, a lightning flash cut that glowed deathly white. The knife turned and caught the full reflection of the moon. Something viscous dripped from the blade.

A ragged cloud rolled across the sky, obscuring the lustrous moon.

'Say something,' she stuttered, loathing this sudden nightmare with every cell of her being. The dreaming Alison sat upright and put her hand in front of her face. There was nothing there to see. The room swam in an opaque, inky blackness that concealed everything. Even the incubus by the window. 'Say something, you bastard.'

The words echoed off the distant walls with a queer, dead resonance. Alison put her right index finger firmly in her mouth and bit hard. There was pain, the ache of teeth on bone. Did this happen in dreams? Her head, still drowsy with wine, pondered the question and had no satisfactory answer. In dreams, it said, anything can and will happen. The hidden strings and pulleys only reveal themselves afterwards, in the grateful light of day.

Then, while her head still debated this, something came close. Foul, hot breath fell upon her cheek and a hand, strong and sudden, grabbed the back of her hair, jerked it painfully backwards once then let go. She cried out and knew, on the instant, how pathetic the sound was. The dream Minnis was deserted. There was nothing outside but the creatures of the feral darkness, owls and badgers, foxes and crawling, snapping rodents. To cry out to them was to invite their interest. Predators roamed this world.

'For God's sake, say something,' she repeated.

And he laughed. Slowly, cruelly, a hoarse, tobacco-stained laugh that came from somewhere near her right shoulder, close to the window. It was as if the thought transferred itself invisibly between them. He moved and there was the swishing sound of the curtain. Now they would stay in darkness, even when the moon was free of the obscuring cloud.

'And you thinking we was dead,' the voice said, and immediately Alison closed her eyes, refused to see the flashing scar, livid on his cheek. The harsh Kentish accent brought it all back: the fire, the agony, the running, stumbling brawl in the stinking interior of Paternoster Farm. 'You *thinking* . . .' He fell into silence.

She shook her head from side to side. You can dream the pain of teeth against bone, she thought. You can dream anything you like.

'I'm sorry,' she sobbed. 'Harry, *I'm sorry, sorry, sorry.*'

He moved again in the darkness, so close to her face now, but still she couldn't work out the direction as his presence shifted through the gloom.

'Sorry?'

'*Sorry, Harry.*' You could apologise to a phantom in a dream, she thought. There was nothing inappropriate about this. Spectres didn't blab. Dead men didn't rise from the

254

ground, extract confessions, then walk down to the police station and ask for justice.

'Well,' the ghostly Harry said, half cheerfully. 'Then that's all I need to hear now. Ain't it?'

'I . . .'

He pounced, strong hands took her head, turned it round to him, rough, unshaven skin brushed her cheek.

'*All I need to hear!*' This phantom was laughing at her, could squeeze the dream life from her veins if it wanted.

A single hand came to her mouth, took her lips painfully, made them purse in a round, circular shape, like a cruel parody of a kiss. Something fell onto her tongue and she thought: *pills*. Dreams could have pills. Dreams could have anything.

His hand clamped roughly over her mouth then, strong fingers squeezed her nostrils. She felt something warm inside her nose. *Blood*. Some dreams led to blood, always, and this was one of them, this was the blood dream to end them all.

She held her breath, ran the cold, reliable logic through her head, waiting for the nightmare to lift. When it did she would walk downstairs, make herself a cup of tea, sit, quietly shaking, until the real world returned, and with it some semblance of sanity. In dreams there was no such thing as breath. Time was its own master, ran as long or as short as it thought fit. And sometimes ran out. Her lungs felt ready to explode. The veins pulsed painfully in her temples. Alison swallowed and discovered another new dream sensation too. *Taste*. The pills had been crushed in her mouth. They were bitter and vile on the back of her tongue, slipped painfully down her throat. She swallowed again and again, dream body mirroring the automatic responses of her waking one, until the foul smack of chemicals was just about gone.

The powerful, coarse hand came away, disappeared into the blackness, then patted her painfully on the back.

'Good girl,' he said. 'You takes your medicine. You makes your peace. All things get equal in the end.'

She swallowed again. The pills were working in her stomach, feeding something into her body. Air rose inside her. A feeble belch, the odour of vomit inside it, slipped from between her trembling lips.

'Almost,' he said, 'anyway.'

Something flashed past her face. There was a sudden breeze, the hint of silver in the blackness. A strange sensation. Not painful at first, more like a coldness on her cheekbone, then something warm, flowing unexpectedly down her face. The blade sliced through her flesh, in a single, swift rush and was gone, leaving her gasping for breath, arms starting to flail in the black empty air. She coughed. Bile spilled out of her mouth, her stomach began to revolt. He was on her again. She felt the presence of the knife in front of her eyes, knew, in a sudden, time-halting moment of revelation, what it was like to face extinction, and found herself screaming for the life of the child inside her.

'Take it,' the old, familiar voice said out of nowhere. The shaft of the knife, warm wood, damp with sweat, pushed against her hand. Her fingers extended automatically to grasp it. Then, with the weapon firm in her grip, she swept the blade through the blackness, searching for his unseen shape.

There was blood in the air, more blood than could come from a simple line of gaping flesh on a woman's cheek. And something else too, something soft and warm, feathering in front of her face, held there, deadening the blows of the knife as she flashed it towards the spectre that invaded this sacred space of her life. The frenzy consumed her, screaming, flailing, sobbing.

And he was gone. No noise, not even a footstep. His presence simply disappeared, the way fog lifted suddenly from the raw downland scarp. Through the curtains a dim silvery light filtered slowly back into the room. The *dream* room, Alison reminded herself, and wondered, almost calmly, what strange event, back in the waking world, had wound its way through her sleeping consciousness to be transmuted by her subliminal imagination like this.

Deep inside, some primal constituent of her being began to move. She dropped the knife, her dream fingers clutched frantically down beneath the sheets, felt at the dampness growing, seeping between her legs.

In the half dark she snatched the wetness on her nails into her mouth. The taste of blood and salt entered her head. She reached forward, clutching at the bedclothes, and recognised this softness she had ripped apart with the knife. Loose fur, damp and fleshy, covered the bed, familiar fur, that had once borne the name Thomas. She coughed, retching mindlessly onto the sheets and felt a sudden, sharp twinge in her stomach. The process, inevitable now, she knew, was under way inside her, moving, like some subterranean shifting of the earth, sparking into the familiar, fatal cycle.

BELTANE

In the six weeks between Easter and Beltane, bitter anger and despair fanned mutual flames in Justin Liddle's soul. They burned incessantly, alone. The day after Alison was taken into hospital he had sat outside the ward at the William Harvey, pleading to see her, trying every excuse, even his uniform, to find a way to her bedside. It was useless. She refused to allow him one minute's admittance. Then she was gone again, physically recovered but shipped – of her own volition? – to some distant nursing home to 'recover'.

She left an aching, physical absence in his life. In its place, guilt wormed its inevitable path into his head, slyly offering to rationalise what would, he knew, always remain irrational. Nothing could explain the tragedy. Yet the idea that this was some kind of punishment was always there, for both of them he imagined. It was unfair, deeply wrong, and still it gnawed at his consciousness.

There was nothing to sate the pain but work. Alison wasn't crazy, not completely anyway. There was something going on. He could smell as much in the sharp spring air of the village and the way the word 'Beulah' brought knowing glances in odd corners of the police station. He had hung around the plain-clothes people for a while, listening, gently probing. Rumour had it that once or twice in the past year they had taken an interest in the village. Not, he soon gathered, of their own volition. They were as reluctant to work their way up Vipers Hill as he was. Someone outside the station, perhaps even outside the county, had tipped them a wink. A few discreet inquiries had been made. And nothing had come of it, not even a whisper outside the tightly closed ranks of CID about what had prompted the activity in the first place.

Then a low-key notice had come through from the immigration people at Dover docks. It said that someone looking like one of the Blamire brothers had passed through the port twice, once just before Christmas, again in February. Typically, the individual was long gone by the time immigration had spotted his face on the security videos. On both occasions he had entered the country on a cheap overnight coach from Brussels. A long way from Bangkok, Justin thought. Was either of the Blamires sufficiently well versed in the ways of the world to indulge in this kind of globe-trotting without some assistance? He doubted it. Something was afoot in Beulah, and it was connected to the fire at Paternoster Farm.

Spring blossomed. Hares danced on the Minnis. The first cuckoo sounded its duotone in the spinney of hawthorn beyond the cricket pitch. Bluebells shot through the newly coppiced areas of Sterning Wood and disappeared as quickly as they came. Barley rose from the ruddy clay earth that topped the chalk scarp. And Justin Liddle quietly went about his business, talking to people, asking casual questions, making notes, and, in the black, empty depths of the night, cursing the world for her absence.

When time allowed, he would drive around to the dismal, burnt-out site of the rendering plant, stare at the muddy, seared ground, trying to assemble the possibilities in his mind. But the pictures always returned: the two of them together in the wood, their frantic, desperate couplings in Priory House at Christmas. There was something about

Alison, something strange and enticing, that was impossible to let go. It wasn't just that she was beautiful, that her face came to haunt him in the oddest, most unexpected of moments. She was an electric mixture of toughness and fragility and that brought out a baffling fusion of emotions in him. One side of her was delicate, brittle, in need of protection, as much from herself as anything else. The other had strength, the power to put him under her spell, make him do whatever she asked, without question. There were, he judged, two Alisons, and he loved them both, in equal measure.

And he loved the dead child too, spent restless hours at night trying to imagine what it would have looked like if some vicious, dark twist of fate had not conspired to take it from the world. The sense of duty he felt towards the unborn infant was, he knew, a living, seamless element in his love for her. This was their mutual loss and it grieved him that they could not share it with some mutual pain.

He had been off duty when the news about the 'accident' came through, and cursed himself for the fact for weeks after. The story emerged fitfully. Alison had miscarried again, and the loss of the child had triggered some bout of self-destructive frenzy. She had taken a knife and cut herself. For reasons no one understood she had, into the bargain, taken the blade to Thomas, the cat she loved so much, and savagely cut the hapless animal into pieces. In the bedroom, a place that still lived in his imagination.

John Tyler had found her on the doorstep of Priory House when he drove to work at eight the next morning. She was covered in blood and had already lost the child. Cataleptic schizophrenia was the grim phrase Tyler had casually used when Justin had caught up with him. Late that night, shocked, still in uniform but now off duty at his little flat in Ashford, he had looked it up and thought that, perhaps, he could begin to understand. Alison would say nothing to anyone for weeks, and was swiftly whisked to a private nursing home to recover. Yet this was an illness, not the reproachful, self-inflicted thing that the unthinking herd liked to label 'madness'. There was a real, physical disorder involved, an excess of some strange, insidious chemical called dopamine in the brain. Alison had found her way to this personal version of hell through some unfortunate coincidence of alchemy inside her head.

In the middle of April, when she had turned him away, unseen, at the nursing home for the fourth time, he called on Sara Harrison. Her bulge was huge and made her walk with an awkward, burdened gait. Sara's dress sense was as individual as ever, but somehow she looked less the ageing hippie these days, and more the middle-class mother-to-be. Her hair was more kempt, her face sadder, showing lines he hadn't noticed before. Alison was more than a partner. She was a friend. It was only to be expected.

She listened to his tentative inquiries then asked, rather coldly, 'Is this business or pleasure, Justin?'

He fumbled for the words. 'I don't know what you mean.'

'Don't you now?' She sat on the ancient, battered sofa and glared at him. 'You leave her alone. She's got enough on her plate without more complications.'

He wished he could be more frank with her. Somehow the uniform stood in the way. 'I don't want to make anything more complicated for her. Honestly. I just want her to be happy.'

'My, we are generous.'

'I don't think you're being fair, Sara.'

'She's my friend. You're not. Why should I be fair?'

Sara was smart, he thought. And resilient with it. 'Point taken. I just wondered how she is. Whether she'd talked to you about what happened. Whether she's . . .'

He couldn't say it. The idea was unthinkable.

'Barking?' Sara offered. 'Is that what you mean?'

'I don't know what I mean.'

She grimaced and, for a moment, he wondered if she was going to cry. 'How she is . . . What do you expect me to say to that? She lost her baby, Justin. That was all she wanted in the world.'

'I know. I care for her, Sara. I care for her sanity. All these stories she tells . . .'

'You leave her sanity to us. I can't say you've helped much. If she'd just settled down, we'd never have had this nonsense.'

The idea had occurred to him, repeatedly, and it was, he knew, utterly wrong. 'You don't know that,' he objected. 'None of us knows why this happened.'

'Screwing around didn't exactly help put her head back on, Justin. Not to put too fine a point on it.'

'It wasn't like that.' He didn't dare close his eyes. She would be there in an instant, in that familiar, heated embrace.

'Maybe not,' she said miserably.

'Does he know? Miles? About us?'

'Search me. What does it matter now anyway? I haven't told him if that's what you're asking. But if you will make a habit of getting your kit off in the wood in the middle of the day I don't think you can be surprised when people talk. How could you do that to her? Didn't you know she was only just out of one breakdown?'

He had assumed that was behind her. Alison had, for the most part, seemed smart, on the ball. He remembered the first time they met, at the hospital after Sara's car crash. There was nothing remotely crazy about her. Nothing obvious anyway.

'Men,' she said sourly. 'You haven't a bloody clue. You don't even recognise what's in here.' She stabbed a finger at her rotund belly. 'It's just some physical blemish until it pops out into the world and starts bawling. And then, if you're lucky, one of you might take a peek at it and say: *mine*.'

'Of course,' he said dryly, 'all men are bastards. Let's take that as read. What I was asking was: is she sick again? Is that what's going on?'

Sara's mouth became a thin, bloodless line while she thought about her reply. Then she said, 'She didn't try to kill herself. I don't care what John Tyler says. She lost the child and went mad for a while. Got the knife. Hurt herself a bit. Killed the poor sodding cat. It doesn't mean she needs locking away.'

He still couldn't make sense of it. 'She told you that?'

'No. I'm guessing. She's saying nothing. Just blanked it all out. "In denial", as her compatriots across the pond would say. She won't talk about it at all. Not to me. Not to Miles even.'

'But why didn't she call someone?'

'*I don't know!*'

She was trying to help. He understood that. These were just difficult questions.

'Perhaps,' she suggested, 'it all happened so quickly. She's been there before. Maybe, once it was over she just . . . oh, work it out for yourself. Alison was very focused on that child. She cared for that more than anything. A lot more than for herself.'

He did follow the line of reasoning. There was, at times, something close to self-loathing inside Alison.

'So that's it?' he asked. 'She lost the child. Did some stupid things with a knife? Then sat on the doorstep, in the freezing cold, waiting for the world to wake up? It doesn't make sense.'

Sara was silent. Something stirred inside Justin Liddle, something, he realised with a twinge of guilt, that had to do with police work, not Alison Fenway.

'Well?'

'I don't like telling tales,' Sara replied slowly. 'Too many get told in this place as it is.'

He waited.

'She had an argument,' Sara declared in the end.

'Who with?'

'Old Mother Tyler.'

This puzzled him. Marjorie Tyler was an oddball, but not, as far as he knew, someone prone to village spats. 'I don't understand the significance, Sara.'

'There isn't one, of course. Forget I ever said it. I talk too much.'

'You're being exasperating.'

She rested her hands on her great tummy and gaped at him. 'I know. It's stupid. It can't have anything to do with it.'

'Go on.'

'Alison won't let on about what happened. It's not what I said before. Denial. She *won't*. Do you understand the difference?'

He thought about it. Women could be so vague at times. 'You mean she's scared?'

Sara nodded. 'I think so. It's probably just my hormones talking, but that's what I think.'

Beulah was too thick with conspiracies sometimes. Perhaps this was what had turned Alison's mind. 'Why? And what would some row with Marjorie Tyler have to do with it?'

Sara stared at him. He felt there was something he should have understood. 'Don't you know who Marjorie is, Justin? Don't you know what she does around here?'

'Village eccentric who grows a little pot in her conservatory.'

'You know *that*?'

'Of course I do. And I'm not stirring up any hornet's nest by bringing the drugs squad down on her either. Not so long as she keeps it to herself.' He tried to see all the links in his

head. 'I still don't get it. What's that got to do with Alison?'
Sara was on the brink of some revelation. He could feel it.
'Sara, she's your friend. If this is more than some horrible
personal tragedy, it needs to be looked into.'

'Maybe. Don't ask me because I don't understand it
all fully myself, nor do I want to. And even if I did, I
wouldn't tell you because you'd be down there like a
shot, pumping Alison for information just when she least
needs it.'

'Give me some credit, please. And anyway,' he added
bitterly, 'she won't see me.'

'Quite right too. You're a copper, Justin. You never take
that uniform off.'

That did offend him. 'That's unfair and untrue. You don't
have to like me, Sara. I don't care one way or another. But
understand this. I love Alison. I believe she loves me. If
something was done to her, that's my business for no other
reason.'

She looked a little ashamed. 'I'm sorry. I get defensive.'

He knew that. There was something he didn't like about
Sara, but she was, he guessed, a good friend. 'And by the
same token,' he added, 'I don't want her head filled with
nonsense. If it is nonsense. Beulah baffles me, it always has
done. I don't want it making Alison worse.'

Sara refused to meet his eyes. 'I've told you everything I
know, Justin. You're the copper, you make what you will
of it. If something did happen, my guess is Marjorie had
something to do with it. And I repeat my earlier question:
do you know *who* she is in the village?'

Justin Liddle's brow furrowed in puzzlement. 'Sort of the
Queen of the May or something, I imagine. She always seems
to be leading the charge when the dancing begins.'

Sara looked pale and downcast. 'You're going to hate this.
Marjorie is the witch. The white witch, she'd say, I imagine.
But the witch all the same.'

He laughed. He couldn't help it. 'You mean like broomsticks? And casting spells and stuff?'

'No,' she replied in a flat monotone. 'I don't mean that at all. You townies can be so bloody stupid sometimes.'

'Right,' he said, a flash of anger in his eyes. 'I'm the one not talking about witches and I'm stupid. So what you're saying is that Marjorie cast a spell. And Alison lost her baby, went mad with the knife. Went mad full stop.'

'A spell? Depends what you mean by a spell.'

'Mumbo jumbo. Pins in a piece of wax. That kind of thing.'

'Oh, Justin,' she sighed. 'You really can be clueless, can't you? Marjorie is the boss here. In Beulah. Our own little world. Where no one talks to outsiders like you. She doesn't need spells. Not to get poor old Mary Wethered out of the way. Or to make sure Miles Fenway gets the top job instead of the sack just to get Alison on her side. And, when that goes wrong, she doesn't need spells to get her revenge on poor old Alison either. She just goes out *and does it*, you dunderhead. Or gets it done, more likely.'

He suddenly felt cold in his thin, regulation police shirt. 'Bullshit, Sara. People wouldn't stand for that. Even here. And you shouldn't be encouraging her to believe that kind of stuff.'

'You think so?' she said smartly. 'And you've no suspicions of your own?'

He shuffled uncomfortably on the chair. 'Suspicions – what the hell do they amount to?'

'Maybe nothing,' she answered. 'Maybe a lot. Let me tell you one other thing. When I first met Alison – shortly after, to be precise – she thought someone had been inside the Burning Man last September. *A person*. Whatever . . . no one said a thing. No one *saw*. I thought she was crazy. Now, I'm not so sure.'

He felt as if he'd wandered into a madhouse. 'Dead

people in bonfires. It's a load of bollocks. This isn't another universe. The same rules still apply.'

Her eyes twinkled. 'Really? So why is Marjorie Tyler growing pot under your nose and you daren't do a thing about it? Isn't that some kind of spell?'

'No,' he replied gruffly. 'It's just me being practical.'

She shrugged. 'Same result. How do you think Marjorie sees it?'

He felt cross, insulted somehow. 'Frankly, I don't give a bugger. The plain fact is, if you think something's wrong here you should come out and say it.'

'And then move somewhere else? That's what it would mean, Justin.'

He picked up his radio and his cap and rose from the chair. This conversation was going nowhere. 'If it's so bloody awful here, what's the problem?'

Through the window he could see it was a glorious day. The Minnis was glistening green under a bright spring sun. A pair of partridge flew low across the grass in perfect formation, their tiny wings a fuzzy blur of feathers.

'The problem, Justin,' Sara said slowly, trying to explain this to him, 'is I *like* it here. It's my home. These rules of theirs, whatever they are, *work*. Provided you keep to them or just stay out of their way.'

'Well, in that case, you'd better learn to live with it. You'll give Alison my regards? If she wants to see me about anything – personal or otherwise – that's fine. If not, I won't bother her.'

'Liar,' she said immediately.

He knew now what he disliked about Sara Harrison. She was too direct – and too perceptive – for her own good.

'I shouldn't tell you this, Justin. But Alison really did have something going with you. If she wasn't married, if she didn't need to settle down right now . . . who knows?'

'Thanks,' he said bitterly. 'That makes me feel so much better.'

He stormed out of the cottage door, breathed the clear, chill air. It wasn't the same in Beulah. There was no carbon monoxide at the back of the throat, no sense of soot entering the lungs. Everything seemed different sometimes. And it dared him to intervene. For one mad moment he even considered barging into Marjorie Tyler's boring middle-class house and calling in the drugs squad. As if that would make the world a better place.

The radio sounded. He picked it up and took the message. Marjorie Tyler could wait. Mitch Blamire had called the station asking for him. He wanted a meet at the Devil's Kneading Trough at three. Justin Liddle went to his car, pulled out a pad, and tried to scribble down every last question he could imagine.

A solitary skylark hovered in the sky over the chalk escarpment. Black-faced sheep grazed on the hill. Beyond them, waving in the wind, was a stand of quaking grass and fescue, the pale, nodding heads of pyramidal orchids just visible among the waves of green. This was a popular beauty spot on warm, summer weekends. Today, in spite of the bright, bleached sun, the wind was blowing hard, chilling to the bone anyone foolhardy enough to brave the heights. Only a single car stood beside the regulation police Peugeot in the lay-by.

The day was so clear he could see the giant chimneys of the power station at Dungeness, far away across Romney Marsh. Beyond that, the grey, lifeless waters of the Channel stood between England and France, little more than thirty miles away. In the far distance was a tantalising shape that might have been cloud or land, the bare, rocky outcrop of Cap Gris Nez.

He thrust his hands deep inside the pockets of his black police parka and headed for the escarpment edge and the deep, crater-like indentation in the ground that the locals called the Devil's Kneading Trough. Justin walked around the edge of the vast, circular blemish. He had never liked it, and it had nothing to do with the name. The feature seemed out of place among the gentle, undulating curves of the Downs.

In a minute, he reached the end of the path, stood on the small, paved viewpoint and stared ahead. On days like this the distance between Beulah and the rest of the world seemed enormous. From the outlook at the very edge of the hill, with its ancient, worn compass, pointing out distances and directions to local towns and villages, the visitor felt like some kind of angel, surveying the flat, everyday world from a point of lofty, exalted grace. And weren't devils really just some kind of angel too? Ones that had simply fallen to earth? Justin Liddle shook his head in wonder. The crazy talk of Beulah could become infectious. And Sara was one of the saner ones.

The wind picked up speed, blew an icy blast into his face. He cursed and looked around. It was an odd spot for the returning Mitch to choose. Why not the cottage down from the Green Man which had been the Blamire residence for as long as anyone could remember? Justin marked that as one for the notebook. One day, perhaps, there would be sufficient evidence to ask for a warrant to search the cottage. Perhaps Mitch wanted time to hide the evidence . . . of what? He thought about Alison's suspicions, and wondered why she only saw fit to share them with Sara. There was a simple, logical answer to these mysteries somewhere, and part of the answer lay in her head.

'*Mitch!*' he bellowed into the swirling air. The single

skylark rose suddenly higher in alarm. A stupid black-faced tup took to its heels and scuttered away towards the low beech woodland, with its carpet of seasonal anemones, that stood at the village side of the scarp.

A familiar, stout figure came out from behind a mound of hawthorn and bramble, buttoning his fly. Justin nodded at him, swore again, and then stared at the lumpen mass of Ashford, a few miles away, on the spreading plain beneath them. *Ashford*. Where there were no witches, no Mitch Blamires and no deep, encircling mysteries. And no Alison Fenway either. He closed his eyes and could see her instantly, naked, in the chill spring air of Sterning Wood, tight in his embrace.

'Damn,' Justin Liddle muttered, then opened his eyes and almost jumped out of his skin. On the cheek of the approaching figure, unmistakable and livid white in the piercing brightness of the day, was a scar, the shape of forked lightning. Justin did a double take, staring at the man, staring at the scar, trying to dredge some once-familiar memory out of the dusty cellar of his head.

'Mitch?' he asked, feeling stupid. This was Mitch, surely. But, on his cheek, the tell-tale scar that Harry wore with such pride.

'Aye?' the man said, stopping in front of him, blocking the view down to civilisation.

'I thought . . .'

'Scare yer, uh?' Mitch grinned, and it was him. There was just the question of the physical blemish, and Justin couldn't take his eyes off it.

'I don't understand.'

Mitch stabbed a finger at his cheek. 'What? Me birth-mark here?'

Justin shook his head. 'I don't think my memory's playing tricks.'

'Lots of tricks get played hereabouts, copper. Story I'm

telling is that after Harry was gone it just *grew*. Woke up one morning in Bangkok and there it was. Harry's present, uh?'

Justin looked at him. Mitch was always the quieter, the more decent of the two. Although this was, of course, comparative. 'That's bollocks, Mitch. You did that to yourself. Why?'

Mitch Blamire gave him a sour stare. 'Why not? He were my brother. Why can't I remember him how I want?'

The Blamire boys loved their little knives, he thought. Pen knives, sheath knives, a flick in there too, not that they'd take that out while he was around. A few quick slashes with a couple of drinks down the hatch, and there it was. Mitch had erected a memorial to Harry, a living one, for all to see.

'You're sure he's dead then?' Justin asked.

'You're the copper. You tell me.'

Justin nodded. 'Someone was killed when Paternoster went up. Nothing we can identify, but you can put two and two together.'

'Did that already. Did that the night it happened. We was identical twins, you know. Twins got a link.'

'So you knew?'

Mitch rubbed his chin, wondering. 'Knew that very moment. I'd had a few down the Green Man. Woke up, still pissed, and he was gone. I *saw* it.'

'Saw what, Mitch?'

'Him dying and that. What else?'

Justin wondered whether to dignify this drivel with his notebook, and decided against. 'So what happened?'

'Thing blew up, didn't it? Like a big bonfire. Like Burning Man, only ten times over.'

'You don't think there was something suspicious?'

Mitch was almost laughing in his face. 'Suspicious? Like what? We was playing with dynamite in there. You got to expect a few explosions now and then.'

'And so you disappeared.'

He shrugged. 'I was upset. And what was there to hang around for? Weren't going to be no funeral now, was there? Some money came through quick from the insurance. Why not bugger off for a while? Have some fun for a change?'

'Why'd you come back?'

'Skint,' Mitch admitted. 'And besides, it's cricket season soon. No one but me knows how to deal with that pitch now, do they? Can't have a bunch of middle-class wankers going in and ruining all that work Harry and me put in over the years.'

It was all, in a sense, plausible. Even the scar. 'So how long have you been back?'

Mitch laughed unpleasantly. It wasn't just the scar. Something of the late Harry seemed to have rubbed off on him now. 'How long? Longer than any of you know. I been back and forth since before Christmas. Those who I wanted to see me saw all right. Just didn't want to talk to nobody else. That's all.'

'Been working then? Doing jobs for Mrs Tyler?'

The piggy eyes narrowed, full of suspicion. 'Marjorie's the Queen of the May. We all work for her in one way or another now, don't we?'

'Really? How?'

Mitch lost his smile. 'However she bloody wants, mister. Got to earn a living. If old Marjorie wants her garden doing, her rubbish moved, whatever, I'll do that for her. I'd do it for you, if you paid me.'

'Gardening . . .' Justin Liddle thought of Paternoster Farm. He'd driven past more than once when it was working. The smell was so putrid he'd never even considered taking a closer look. Not exactly on a par with sorting out a herbaceous border. 'You're a real handy man, Mitch, aren't you?'

Mitch's cold eyes glinted at him. At that moment he could

have been Harry. 'Oh, I'm handy all right. Don't you go forgetting it. Anything else you was wanting to know? Only I got things to do. Harry and me used to come here when we was kids. I want to get me memories straight.'

And plenty more besides, Justin guessed.

The stocky little man eyed him eagerly. 'We done here? You going to stop hounding me now? That's why I asked to see you. Don't want no little police dog sniffing at my ankles day in, day out.'

Justin ignored the bait. 'You're not off on your travels again, Mitch, are you?'

'What? Leave this place in summer? You'd need to be off your trolley. As mad as that Yank bint of yours. Beulah's me home. You get to know that when you're on the other side of the world banging some Bangkok whore and wondering why you bothered. You got a home, Justin? You figured out where that is?'

'Not here, that's for sure,' Justin said softly, then stuffed his hands deep in his pockets and went back to the car. He glanced back once. Mitch was in the centre of the crater, flat on his back on the damp grass, hands behind his head, staring at the sky. Justin followed the direction of his gaze. A premature horned moon had appeared in the blueness. The lone skylark danced against it, singing wildly. From the beech stand came the sudden, unmistakable screech of a muntjac.

He took a deep breath, then drove, too quickly, down Vipers Hill, and back into the smog of Ashford.

The nursing home had been a farm once, back in the days when the flat, arable land north of Sevenoaks had supported agriculture. Now it stood marooned in an ordered field of neatly tended lawn by the side of the bustling M25. If she sat in the garden, beneath the chill spring sun, with her back to the motorway, looking at the ancient farmhouse and the stately oaks that shaded it, she could almost believe this was somewhere close to Beulah. Provided she stopped up her ears, to keep out the constant, droning roar of traffic. Provided she never took a breath, and let the heavy, tarred stench of carbon monoxide fumes penetrate into her lungs.

They let her have one of the most expensive suites, paid for by Miles's medical insurance. It was in a wing that had been made out of a former oast complex. She slept beneath the ancient cone, pointing upwards to the stars, trying to believe this had some magical property, like a pyramid, focusing the healing power of the sky into her ragged, shaken body. But the truth was that this was just a fancy hotel for the temporarily barmy, handily situated for the lunatic diaspora shaken out of London and looking for respite. She did not need to be healed. What had happened, *had* happened, although she failed to understand exactly how. It was only fate that prevented her from spilling the beans, fate that made her silence take on the guise of a mute disorder of the mind. And so Alison Fenway waited, passing her time in the nursing home library, with its shelves and shelves of ancient, leather-bound classics: Dickens and Dumas, C. S. Lewis and the rollicking, ridiculous adventures of John Buchan. For this brief period of time, quiet in an armchair in her room, she became part of a world where there was, for the most part, a visible dividing line between good and evil, darkness and light.

One week after Justin Liddle had stood by the side of the Devil's Kneading Trough, talking to the newly scarred Mitch Blamire, a small, bright-red Alfa Romeo crunched over the gravel of the nursing home. Miles was busy and Alison had no complaints about that. It was unfair, she knew, but somehow she held him responsible. So she had seized the opportunity and asked for Sara to come and pick her up instead. It was too early to think about men. Every time her thoughts drifted towards Miles and Justin one word – 'torn' – came into her head. She didn't want to face choices. Somehow it was inhuman even to think of there being some kind of contest between these two men in her life, a tournament in which she decided the winner. Fate, chance and destiny had their part to play too.

So this day she stood outside the door of the home, a quiet, impersonal nurse by her side, holding her bag, and watched Sara manoeuvre into the last remaining space in the car park.

Time, Alison thought, watching her friend roll awkwardly out of the driving seat. It moved with such relentless certainty, oblivious to small human tragedies. In the few weeks she had spent in the home, letting her head search for some kind of quietus to its ills, Sara had grown so large. Some pregnant women become fat and struggle to shrug off that excess of flesh for years after the event. Some bear the child as if it were a kind of physical extension, tacked awkwardly onto their body in a jerry-built, temporary fashion that will disappear almost the moment the hidden burden enters the world. If it ever came to pass, she would fit the first category; Sara, undoubtedly, was in the second. Growing larger made the separation between the hump and the person become more marked, not less. She looked like a woman carrying a pillow stuffed up her flowery cotton dress.

Sara came up the steps, planted a kiss on her cheek, and Alison, without warning, burst into tears, laughing nervously all the time.

'Oh God,' Sara mumbled into her ear, holding her tight. 'It's all right now, love. We'll get you out of this bloody place. Back home. And heal you good and proper.'

Alison snivelled and wondered just how pathetic she looked. 'I'm sorry . . .'

'I'll take that,' Sara said severely to the nurse and grabbed the bag.

The woman coughed, gave her a nasty look, and went back through the big, white double doors.

'Sodding hospitals,' Sara cursed. 'Who do they think they're kidding?' Alison clung to her tightly, feeling the hard bulge between them. 'I don't know why you checked in here, love. Everyone knows you're not potty.'

Alison relaxed her grip and peered into Sara's clear blue eyes. 'Do they?' she asked, then pressed a ragged tissue to her nose.

''Course they do. Why do we have to have these fancy explanations? Something horrible happens and all these big words appear. They put you in homes. They give you drugs. It's rubbish.'

'Good old sensible Sara,' Alison said, smiling, aware of how damp her face was. 'You always stick up for me, don't you?'

'That's what friends are for, in case you've forgotten. And, by the by, it's selfish too. I'm getting fatter and more stupid by the day. I need you. The business needs you. Now can we go back to living our lives please?' She paused nervously. 'You are coming back, aren't you? You won't give up on us because of this?'

Alison was surprised by the question. The thought of abandoning Beulah, of trying to make her own way in the world outside, had flitted through her head for only an instant. There was work to be done. There was a need for some kind of resolution. Some decisions she had reached already. There would be no obsession about getting pregnant for a while, not until she knew where her private life was headed. The constant, aching urge for a child was, in some way, responsible for her present position. She needed to avoid this kind of fixated behaviour.

'You don't get rid of me as easily as that,' she said. 'I'm not the quitting type.'

'Good for you,' Sara exclaimed, hugging her again, and

looking as if she was the one about to burst into tears this time. They walked to the car. Sara dropped the bag by the boot, stretched upright and put a hand to her back. 'Ouch.'

'Are you all right?'

'No, I'm not. I'm trying to pursue a modern lifestyle trapped inside the carcass of a sperm whale. Oh, be a darling, will you? You do the driving?'

Alison stared at the flashy new car.

'I know, I know,' Sara said apologetically. 'It's a stupid little boy racer. I bought it when my hormones were performing the Floral Dance around my reasoning faculties. Three weeks ago it felt lovely. Now I can't squeeze bulge here under the steering wheel. It's a doddle to drive. Honest.'

Alison nodded. There was something so transparent in this little ruse of forcing her to do something, take some responsibility. She loved Sara for it all the more. But the car was odd. It was so brash, so expensive. Nothing like the battered 2CV which had been a part of the Sara she had first come to know.

'It must have cost a fortune,' she said.

Sara patted the gleaming paintwork. 'Dead right, love. You're not the only one with relatives, you know. An old aunt popped her clogs and left me a surprise present. Probably thought I'd spend it on a nursery. But bugger it. I deserve a treat now and again.'

'An aunt? You never mentioned her.'

Sara sighed. 'You don't know everything about me, Ali. Thank God. What do you think of it?'

She hated the beast. It had a slick, harsh beauty and possessed a definite male aggression. It was the last thing she expected Sara to buy. Money, she thought; we all seem to be rolling in dough, and never noticing the changes it brings.

'Cool,' she lied. 'Can I see how fast it can go?'

'Within reason, my dear,' Sara replied. 'Chuck her around too much and I'll be throwing up on your lap, I warn you.'

On the road she didn't want to drive fast at all. It came to her that she had hardly taken her own car beyond Ashford in months. The motorway seemed foreign, a roaring monster of aggression where deadly metal objects flew at her from all directions. After a brief attempt at overtaking, and finding that even 90 mph was too slow for most of those around her, she settled into a steady 55 in the slow lane, and trudged gently down the carriageway.

'Gossip,' she said to break the awkward silence that had descended a few miles north of Maidstone.

'Oh, let me see,' Sara answered, scratching her head. 'A pint of beer has gone up five pee in the Green Man. Someone demolished the post box in a van or something the other week *and failed to 'fess up*. Yappy has been trying to knock up the Downings' stupid poodle bitch again, and failing miserably. 'Bout it really.'

'I don't know. You turn your back for one second and the place is falling apart.'

'You're telling me.'

A huge articulated lorry stormed past on their right, so quickly the draught from its wake shook the car. 'And . . .' Alison wondered, 'the people?'

'People. Yes. There are still people. Keep the car still, will you, love? I had baked beans for breakfast and they're pigs to get off the upholstery.'

'Sara. Talk to me.'

Sara sighed. 'Well, there's Miles. Your husband. He's been working his bollocks off as far as I can gather. Either visiting you or doing something in London. Scarcely been seen at the bar of the Green Man, if that's what you're wondering.'

'Not exactly. I *know* about Miles.'

Sara stared at her. 'Do you? It's been tough for him too, you know. He's terribly worried. About you.'

'I was terribly worried about me. For a while. Then you just have to get up and get on with things.'

Sara took a packet of Polos out of her bag, offered one, and they both sucked on the sweet mints for a while. 'That's the spirit, girl,' she said. 'Stiff upper lip. You will come to me when you want to drop the façade and have a good cry, won't you?'

'Of course.'

'And you won't give up? Trying for the baby, I mean.'

Alison paused. The car and Sara's sudden wealth continued to bug her. There was a limit to the secrets she was willing to share. 'No. Not in the end. But I'm taking a break for a while. I'm not even going to think about it.'

'Best thing. Send him off to the bathroom with a copy of *Playboy*. You could come around in time for Burning Man. That's a good few months away. Worked for me.'

'Yes,' she said quietly. 'And Miles will be fine, trust me. He just wants peace and quiet. He's got enough on his plate with the job.'

The majestic profile of Leeds Castle passed. The line of the Downs was now quite apparent to her left, though this was still, she felt, commuter belt territory. The steep chalk spine would run like this all along the motorway until it dipped into the flat, glacial valley of the Stour, close to Ashford, then rose again, in the wilds, beyond the White Horse, beyond the Devil's Kneading Trough, to Beulah. And home. There were such memories, such mysteries, and it was still difficult to work out what was real and what imaginary. The bedroom would be a problem. She would sleep next door in the guest room for a while. But Priory House *was* home. She needed to be there. That internal argument was the shortest of them all.

'And our friends the Tylers?' she asked.

'Same as ever,' Sara groaned. 'Weird. And miserable, too. He *is* a doctor. He takes that so seriously. I think he feels responsible for you in a way.'

'He's not my doctor any more. And her?'

Sara thought about it. 'Marjorie's not been herself really. I don't understand what's going on. It's as if she feels threatened by something.'

Alison said nothing.

'You're not thinking of doing anything silly?' Sara asked.

'Wouldn't dream of it. Is Justin still around?'

'Ever present, I'm afraid. Asking a lot of questions too. About Paternoster Farm and all sorts of things. Don't you dare show him that little bone of yours. You'd never get him off your back.'

'No.'

'And one other thing,' Sara added. 'He still has the hots for you. Big time. Be warned. Do you mind if I say something?'

'If I do, will it stop you?'

'Of course not. Don't make things more complicated than they already are, love. Let's just settle down, get everything in order, and have a little peace for a while.'

'Naturally.'

'That came out a little too glib, darling. Think about it. I have a brat to spawn. All this stuff affects me too, you know.'

Alison suddenly felt full of self-hate. She had scarcely given Sara a thought. Yet here she was, trying to run a business, have her first baby, face life as a single mother and mend a crazed chum at the same time. She took her left hand off the wheel and touched Sara on the arm. 'I'm sorry. I can be so selfish sometimes.'

'You've got the right to be. After what you've been through. But a period of tedium would be appreciated, until the bawling starts my end, of course.'

'Agreed.'

They were almost home now. The next junction would take them onto the Canterbury Road, then to Wye, and, finally, the long climb up Vipers Hill to the village.

'One last thing,' Sara said, suddenly serious. 'I thought you ought to know this in advance so you don't get any unnecessary heebie-jeebies. Mitch has finally come back. The Minnis is getting mown again.'

'Mitch?' The year seemed to be turning full circle. She could picture summer again. Cricket on the green. Lazy beers outside the pub. 'Where's he been?'

'Bangkok, like everybody said, although the word is he may have been coming back to the village unannounced, and keeping it secret, a couple of times since Christmas. Justin gave him the third degree, naturally, but he's done nothing wrong. Hightailed it after Harry popped his clogs. Now he's back to normal. As normal as a Blamire gets at any rate. If he can do it, gel, so can you.'

'Good,' she said, and felt that way too. Black deeds could sink to the bottom of one's memory. Time could heal everything.

'The bugger is,' Sara continued, 'what he's done to himself, which is why I wanted to warn you in advance.'

'Done to himself?'

'Only gone and carved a scar in his cheek, just like Harry's. In a dim light you'd be hard pressed to tell the two of them apart. If Harry wasn't dead, of course.'

The bright, clear stretch of motorway suddenly darkened in front of her. Alison felt the wheel slip from her grasp, the car move gently out of her control, drifting across the carriageway. Horns blared. Vehicles swerved around her, tyres screeching, livid faces yelling through windows, all at the periphery of her vision. Sara was screaming. There was the sound of metal on metal, something shaking the car violently.

The Alfa Romeo slid along the crash barrier of the central reservation for a good fifty yards. Then Sara managed to get control of the wheel, steered the vehicle safely to the left and got them on the hard shoulder. It came to rest a couple of hundred yards from the Ashford turn-off. Alison sat in the driving seat, a queer smile on her face.

'Jesus,' Sara gasped. 'That was deeply stupid of me. I'm sorry, I don't know what I must have been thinking.'

Alison was still smiling. She felt as if some weight had lifted from her head. 'No. My apologies. I seem to have wrecked your car.'

They got out and surveyed the damage. There was a long dent marking the right hand side of the vehicle. It could have been a lot worse. Sara took the keys and drove them home. Alison never said a word.

She stepped through the back door of Priory House with her heart in her mouth. This was the scene of so much joy and more than a little agony. It was the age-old question: which would win in the end. In the nursing home she had toyed with the idea of a fresh start. No men. A new place, perhaps back on the other side of the Atlantic. But always the memories of Priory House came back to her and they were, in the main, sweet and powerful: Arnold lording it at the Aga, Miles tackling the thick snow of the Minnis on his tractor. And Justin, strong, loyal Justin.

There was a bouquet of roses on the kitchen table, lazily spilling lush, red petals on the polished pine. The house smelled of flowers and fresh paint. Sunlight streamed through the windows. It was smiling for her, she thought. Saying: *this is home, this is where you belong*. With all the little secrets.

She made tea for both of them, got the number of her car insurers, and they chatted idly about the business, calming down all the time, letting the soothing, undulant rhythm of the village seep inside them. An hour later, when Sara left, she went upstairs and sorted out the spare room, her head whirling all the time.

At five o'clock, forty minutes before Miles was due to return home, she went into the kitchen, found the small hiding place above the Aga, and thrust her hand inside. The matchbox was still there. She pulled it out and opened it. The small bed of cotton wool was pristine white. The bone was gone.

The absence of proof was a kind of evidence itself. Alison laughed out loud into the echoing emptiness of the kitchen.

'More flowers,' Miles said, beaming, and presented a bouquet of white chrysanthemums. She kissed him, found a vase, and placed them above the kitchen fireplace. He touched her cheek and it took her a moment to realise why. He was running the tip of his finger lightly along the faint yet discernible scar left by the knife.

'I don't know what happened then, Alison,' Miles said, suddenly serious. 'I do know we can put it behind us. Make something fine out of our lives. And I won't rush you. Everything happens at your speed. The way you want it.'

This was a speech, she thought, something he had prepared. Something very Miles: short, to the point, and sincere. She touched the nape of his neck, brushed her lips lightly, briefly against his cheek. 'You're so kind, Miles. And you're right. Things will work out. In their own time. Be patient with me.' She hadn't even mentioned the minor accident on the motorway. It seemed irrelevant.

He reached for a bottle of expensive burgundy and started to uncork it. 'I'll be as patient as you want. We mustn't let this destroy us, love. I can't imagine this place without you. It feels like a morgue when you're on your own.'

She accepted the glass, tasted the deep, red darkness of the wine, and decided he was wrong. Priory House was big, with high ceilings and faraway, unused corners. But it never felt morgue-like, not even after a few weeks away. The house had too much personality for that. Miles was just being Miles. Trying to be nice. He probably appreciated a little time away from the mad wife.

He had arrived home at seven, more than an hour later than planned. Being boss of Mersons was, she guessed, a time-consuming affair. All Miles's ideas of detaching himself from London, of focusing his life more and more on Beulah, seemed to be receding. The one grain of comfort in this was that the time he spent at home seemed to be gaining a fresh, intense quality she had never seen before. Miles adored the house. In his frantic, last-minute visits to the nursing home he had told her how he was back on his little tractor now, whizzing around the garden whenever the grass gave an excuse. Without a spot of help from anyone, least of all the Blamires, he had pruned the errant apple trees and turned the espalier pear that ran across the back of the garage into a neatly trained system of well-kempt branches. She had looked at the garden when she returned and it was impressive. The espalier now sprouted buds. Summer was returning, and with it a new, surging renewal of life.

Miles had money too, and was not unwilling to spend it. In the nursing home he had helped bring her out of her shell by introducing an interior decorator, getting them talking about ways of sprucing up the dining room, with its tatty furnishings and ancient paint. When she chose the scheme, he had ordered it immediately. She arrived home to find the room immaculately decorated, so perfect it seemed an impertinence even to walk into it. A fine oval walnut table sat at the centre, with six matching chairs. A new, thick wool carpet felt soft underfoot. Just the thing to host dinners with visiting directors.

It must have set him back thousands, and there was still plenty more where that came from. Marjorie Tyler's favours did not, it seemed, work in small measure. Miles's salary had climbed to the 500K mark. With bonuses and a decent year's trading behind him he would be pushing the million. Options and sundry various perks were gathering around his wallet. They were no longer simply well-off. In the space between her 'accident' and her re-emergence into the world, the Fenways completed the transition to the realms of the truly rich. Money would never be a problem again. It had come out of nowhere, like Sara's mysterious legacy. To question its provenance would be to tempt fate.

Were she and Miles still the same people who had made their way, half in fear, half in wonder, up Vipers Hill less than a year before? Logic dictated she answer no. Yet they looked the same. Miles seemed not a day older. The country air, when he was there to enjoy it, suited him. Incidents – from Burning Man to the affair with Justin – had wormed insidiously into their lives, even if the latter remained, as she hoped and believed, secret from Miles. Still it was difficult to feel that, beneath the skin, the newly wealthy Fenways had changed at all. She felt older and – not wiser, that was the wrong word – more knowledgeable about the ways of the world. The Beulah world in particular. In essence, however, they were still the same people, the same flesh and blood. The instruments had not changed, only the tunes that were played upon them.

'Look,' Miles said, grinning like a child. He went over to the Welsh dresser and picked up an ancient sepia photograph in a battered frame. There was a date hand-written in an illiterate scrawl in the corner: 1908. And next to that the words *Beulah Village CC, Fine Gentalmen All!* A team of ancient cricketers stood there, the front row kneeling on one leg, the rear standing upright, gloves and bats and balls in their hands. Facial hair appeared to be the fashion of the day. All but three of the men wore bushy, obscuring beards that made them look like spear-carriers from some Gilbert and Sullivan opera. She peered at the clean-shaven faces. Two were horribly familiar.

'You spotted the Blamires then,' Miles said. 'Probably their spelling too.'

'What is this, Miles? Some kind of a joke?'

'Not at all. That's the team we fielded in 1908. The club is one of the oldest in the country, you know. They've been playing on the Minnis since the late eighteenth century at least. Got photographs back into the 1860s.'

'And are the Blamires in those too?'

'Probably. Those two are . . .' He struggled to remember. 'Oh, I don't recall. One of them's Mitch and Harry's granddad. The other bought it in the First World War apparently. As did most of them in that picture I guess.'

She stared at the men there. All dead. And the Blamires, whose gene pool seemed destined to flow through Beulah for ever, sometimes through the most unlikely of channels. These ancient faces were, in a way, still alive. Conventional wisdom dictated that they would end with Mitch, poor, womanless Mitch, living on his own, a bachelor wedded to the barren green mistress of the cricket pitch. But conventional wisdom was worthless in Beulah. Mitch, and Harry before him, doubtless had their secrets. Sara had found a father somewhere . . . and both Mitch and Harry looked remarkably happy the day after Burning Man. She shook her head and gave the picture back to Miles. There were some things she didn't want to face just yet.

'Why do you have this, Miles?'

'I'm in the club. Well, not quite. They invited me to

audition. Quite an honour, you know. Apparently I have been quietly assessed while at the bar, so to speak.'

'Assessed for what? Your cricketing abilities? Do you even *play* cricket?'

'Used to,' he answered, a mite offended. 'At school. Not great at batting but I can bowl a bit. Straight and fast, although I lack consistency. There, it's best said. The first three of the over always go like billy-o but I fall to pieces after that. If the batsman's any good, he just defends the beginning, and whacks the hell out of the rest. And besides, beggars can't be choosers. When they took that picture Beulah was a bigger, livelier place than it is now. They had any number of people to pick from. Now – well, work it out for yourself. If we didn't poach players from outside we'd never make eleven men.'

She tried to remember the games on the Minnis the previous summer. And the women, in their floral dresses and hats, wandering around with vast plates of sandwiches and jugs of beer for the men. 'I don't see myself as a cricket widow, darling.'

'No.' This amused him. 'I don't see you that way either, actually. I think you can steer safely clear of the egg and cress sandwich rota. It would be nice if you could prop yourself in a deck chair and watch me bowl the odd cove out. *If* I get a chance, of course.'

'We'll see.' The idea sounded quite attractive.

'And I do want to belong here, darling. Just like you. John Tyler asked and I thought it would be churlish to refuse.'

'Tyler,' she repeated flatly.

'That's right. He's the chairman.'

'And Marjorie?'

'Social secretary or something, I believe. Which basically means organising the egg and cress rota.'

'Do we ever escape their tentacles?'

He sighed. 'Look. I know they're a couple of odd bods.

But they mean well. Apparently he was an absolute hero when he found you. After . . .' He fell into an awkward silence.

'My *turn*?'

Miles looked cross for one moment. 'I don't know what to call it. I'm sorry. Look, love. I am a traditional English male. I do not enjoy opening up about these things. If you want counselling, for both of us if you like, just say so. You can have anything you want.'

She laughed out loud and liked the way it lit up his face. 'Oh, my God, Miles. Could you see the pair of us in counselling together? You squirming like a cornered rat? Me laughing at the psychobabble?'

It was Miles's stiff, English sang-froid that attracted her to him in the first place. It was his plain, focused practicality that made the marriage work.

'I would be a bit of a prat, wouldn't I?' he said, with just the hint of a blush. 'We're not made for that kind of thing over here.'

She poured them both another glass, enjoying the wine. 'Quite. No counselling for either of us. Just time. And space. I'm sorry. I shouldn't have embarrassed you like that. You don't need to call it anything, Miles. It's in the past. Gone.' *It never really existed beyond the first flash of insanity.*

'I know.'

'And the Tylers . . . well, you'll excuse me if they don't go top of my favourite people list. I don't like them, I'm afraid.'

'It's a village, love. You can't like everyone. You've still got to live with them.'

That much was certainly true, she thought. 'So when do you audition?'

'Tomorrow. Practice in the nets, weather permitting. First match of the season is on May Day. Against Wye. A real local derby apparently. You'd almost think there was bad blood between the two. But if you want to do something instead . . . ?'

Talk about loaded questions. Miles was itching to play cricket with his blokey friends. It would have been cruel to have denied him.

'I just want to settle back in,' she said. 'Look at the new decorations. Work out which room to improve next. You play your games. I'll get us something decent for supper. And we can sink a bottle or two.'

He raised his glass. 'To us, old thing.'

'Less of the "old thing", if you don't mind. I feel . . .' Was she just saying this? No, it was true. 'I feel fine.' She'd examined herself in the mirror. The scar apart, which gave her bland features a touch of character that, perhaps, they needed, she looked fine too.

'Chiz,' Miles said, in deliberate, estuarial fashion.

'Chiz.'

The two glasses met beneath the great kitchen light. She thought of the pine table and another time. Of mistletoe berries tumbling from the ceiling, fake velvet antlers on blond hair.

'Miles,' she said. 'I left something by the cooker. Something I found. It was in a matchbox.' She walked over and took the box from the ledge by the cooker where she had left it. 'Did you see it?'

He shook his head. 'No. Why?'

'It's gone.'

'Was it valuable?'

'Not really. Who's been in here while I've been away?'

'People,' he said, unhelpfully. 'All sorts of people. Those cleaners from Canterbury you found for one. I let them in. Sara let them in. Don't know why we bother locking the place really. No one else around here does.'

'Hmmm.'

He hesitated. 'Alison. Are you *sure* it was there? I don't recall seeing anything.'

'I'm sure,' she answered. He looked so guileless. 'Never mind.'

Three hours later, when Miles was propping up the bar of the Green Man, inveigling his way into the team a little further, she phoned Justin Liddle at home and suggested they meet the following day, in the hidden lay-by behind Sterning Wood, on the narrow, little-used single-track route that led, after many winding diversions, to the old Roman road of Stone Street, then on into Canterbury.

She had reasoned this out. The bone had been removed openly and deliberately from the kitchen. Someone knew and feared her suspicions. The nightmare of the miscarriage was a warning. And a mechanism too, to prove to anyone who listened that she might be crazy just like they said.

Meeting Justin again would acknowledge that the mystery lived outside her head, in the real world, alive and malevolent, and was not the creation of her own twisted thought processes. And more, though she tried unsuccessfully to suppress it. Miles's quiet, interior support was welcome and generous, and just a touch diffident. There was, she thought, something detached and distant about Miles, as if, in his heart, he feared that everything – the loss of the child, the mysterious missing finger bone – was the product of her own, fevered imagination. Justin listened. He cared, blindly, without asking too many questions. She missed him. There was no avoiding the fact.

'I am *not* some crazy old woman,' Alison whispered, her eyes rising to the fake chandelier above the table, her memory returning to the sight of a single, pearly berry falling under some unworldly, ponderous gravity.

These flashes came out of nowhere, with a sudden vicious intensity. Sometimes they procured delights, sometimes nightmares. She blinked and the berry was gone, in its place the boiling cauldron of fat inside Paternoster Farm and a single, severed hand sliced free by the closing cover, falling to earth like a dying bird.

'To hell with it,' she hissed, and ached for his touch.

The old saw had it wrong: April had not been a month of showers. A fair weather system sat over most of southern England, never much wanting to go. The days were bright and sunny, the nights, in the main, crystal clear, with a light scattering of ground frost, like icing sugar gently sprinkled upon the earth. With the weather, too, came the occasional fog and it was unlike any Alison had encountered.

In Beulah, the fog was white, a luminescent, glowing white through which the sun tried to peer inquisitively for hours on end until its heat managed to dispel the moisture and pour some radiance down from the sky. The atmospheric effect was also purely local, dictated by the altitude of the village and a curious, complex meeting of local breezes, from the sea near Folkestone and the damp marshlands of the Medway to the north.

When it descended, she knew that on the plain, in Ashford and Wye, where ordinary people were now yawning, getting out of bed, and slowly making their way to work, the sun was bright, the morning radiant with life. Justin Liddle, who was now thinking about driving up Vipers Hill, would see the billowing cap of cloud on the top of the Downs as he approached the village. The police Peugeot would slow as it reached the summit and find itself engulfed by the opaque, close billow of vapour. Then, hidden from view, lights vainly trying to pierce the all-embracing whiteness, it would slowly work its way down the zigzag, along the avenue of poplars that marked the entrance to Beulah, around the Minnis, and park in the covert lay-by to await her arrival.

In the fog, she thought, everyone was equal. Incomers and locals alike.

Miles had wandered off to the Minnis around ten. Through the thick cloud of white she could hear, from time to time, the now familiar sound of a ball being played against a bat. She wondered at their enthusiasm. Even in the 'nets' – one, to be precise – any kind of practice must have been hard. But this was a male ritual. After the warm-up, they would retire to the pub, for lunch and beer and, ostensibly, a heavy round of planning for the summer. She wondered what cricketers talked about. Strategy? Who got to wear the wicket-keeper's gloves? The captain of the team, Jim Barnes, who farmed a scruffy-looking patch just behind the Devil's Kneading Trough, was vaguely familiar from the pub. A big, ruddy-faced man in his late forties, he had a kind of authority about him. The rest of them, from what she remembered the previous year, were just half-recognised faces. Men from the surrounding villages. Even a couple from Ashford. Beulah was dying in a sense. The inability to field a truly local cricket team was just one of the symptoms of its slow demise.

But there was work to be done. The financial records of the partnership had been largely untouched for two months. She sifted through the sheaves of purchase orders and sales records and considered the financial health of their joint enterprise. It looked to be in its prime. While she had been 'away', Sara had gone into overdrive, selling like crazy to compensate, Alison guessed, for any slump that might occur due to the impending birth and the flaky state of her partner. According to the records, the two of them would turn over more than half a million pounds in the coming year: a lot of 'crap' to shift, she reckoned.

A sudden guilty thought rose: perhaps that explained the new car. Perhaps there was no odd legacy from an unannounced aunt. Sara had her secrets too. Could one of them be that she was raiding her share of the partnership proceeds before they had got around to dividing them formally when the accounts were through? There would be nothing strictly wrong in that, although good manners would dictate that one half tell the other. Even if the second partner was trying to find her sanity in some nursing home outside Sevenoaks? She stared at the numbers on the page and wished they could speak. It would be legal for Sara to treat herself. Feeling ashamed of herself, Alison flicked through the bank records, one by one, found nothing, and felt wretched about these treacherous thoughts. Sometimes it seemed as if she suspected everyone in the village.

She glanced at her watch. There was still time before she went to meet Justin. No point in delaying it any longer. At some stage she had to face Mitch Blamire, the new Mitch, with a lightning-shaped scar on his cheek. The thick, enveloping fog proved as good an opportunity as any. She pulled on her green Barbour jacket and went outside.

The cold, white cloud obscured everything. The sound of the practice session, a leisurely thumping of leather against wood, was mangled by the weather in some mysterious way too. She knew how to get to the nets where Mitch, the eternal club hanger-on, would surely be lurking. You opened the front gate, walked across the narrow road, then ten yards to the clubhouse, and ten yards to the left. Today, she could not be so certain. The fog seemed to change the nature of sound, as if the general laws of physics had become fallible, temporary codes of behaviour, mutable at will. The sounds of the day – low, unintelligible voices, the occasional grunt of action, the hard ball smacking willow – lost their shape and sense of direction in the dense, impenetrable brume. The small, well-defined heart of the Minnis was engraved upon her memory. Yet now this interior map was meaningless. She felt she

293

could become lost in an instant if she veered from her chosen path.

Alison strode in a dead straight line, across the road from her front gate, onto the long grass at the edge of the green, then the shorter turf that led to the pitch. She felt in the pocket of the jacket and pulled out a small pen torch, flicked the switch, and saw a thin, useless beam of yellow penetrate the cloud in front of her. She walked on, and something became apparent through the fog. They had turned on the spotlights by the nets. The powerful shaft of artificial light cut through the mist just enough, she guessed, for the men to make some semblance of action. Ghostly figures moved like slowly dancing shadows in the eerie light. Their cries came to her, muffled and incomprehensible, across the green. Then a strong hand took her arm, Alison swung the torch beam round, and found herself staring into the smiling face of Mitch Blamire. Scar and all.

'Morning, Mrs Fenway,' Mitch said pleasantly.

She shook her arm free of him and tried to smile back. He'd come from the clubhouse and gripped a heavy shovel in his right hand. 'Morning, Mitch. Nice to see you again.'

It was impossible to look at him, with the scar now vivid on his cheek, and not see another image rise dutifully from her memory, of a figure at the window in Priory House and the glinting of a sharp blade in the spring moonlight.

'You too, Mrs Fenway. That's for sure.'

It was hard to tell in the diminished light, but he seemed, she thought, older. And it wasn't just the scar.

'You're better now?' he asked.

'Never finer. In a way I wasn't sick at all, was I?'

'I'm no doctor. What would I know?' Mitch said, nodding. 'Life don't run on straight lines, do it? Everyone loses things along the way, then gets up and breathes the air again.'

The Blamires were never short of a bucolic cliché for

the occasion. She stared into his eyes, marking the way he flinched from her. 'I guess so,' she replied. 'You lost Harry. I lost . . .' What? It was impossible to imagine.

'Yeah.' He'd pulled his face back from her. It could have been Harry now, she thought. The most visible part of him was the white outline of the scar.

She reached out and touched it. 'How'd you do that, Mitch?'

He came forward again, suspicious of the question. 'How? Most of 'em ask "why".'

'How?' she repeated.

He dropped the shovel, pulled something out of the pocket of his grubby brown trousers and held it in front of her face. There was the sound of something metallic, then the long, slim blade of the flick knife flashed out of nowhere.

She reached up and touched the straight, thin line on her own cheek. Then held his hand, pulled the knife closer to her face. He resisted. He looked scared.

'We've both got scars now, Mitch.'

'Yeah,' he grunted. 'And we done 'em ourselves, eh? Guess the two of us is both mazed. You and me are the village idiots, Mrs Fenway. How d'you like that then?'

She took the shaft of the knife, pulled it from his hand and held the blade between the two of them, aiming the sharp, slender point at the mark on his cheek. 'I don't want to be scarred again, Mitch,' she said slowly. 'Do you understand that?'

'Guess no one does,' he replied, and he was nervous.

'Does she understand that?'

'And who might that be, Mrs Fenway?'

She nodded at the opposite side of the green. 'Jardis, the White Witch over there. The Queen of the May. Old Mother Tyler.'

He grinned stupidly. 'You know sometimes you clever folk just lose an old yokel like me.'

She tried to remember the book she had read in the great white room they gave her in the nursing home. 'What was it Mr Tummus said? "Always winter and never Christmas".'

Mitch shook his head. 'We had lots of good Christmases here, Mrs Fenway. Not that I was around for the last one, but I heard that were a good 'un too. You and your husband's loss notwithstanding. His father was a fine man, I gather.'

Alison was not about to be distracted by Mitch's mysterious sympathy. She handed him the knife. 'Make sure she understands, Mitch.'

He took it from her and carefully folded the long blade back into the body of the weapon. 'Got work to do, thank you. Season starts at Beltane. Can't have molehills and shite all over the wicket for that. Now can we?'

'Are you OK?' Justin sat in the driving seat of the police Peugeot, staring into her face, registering the scar, she guessed, yet afraid to bring it into the conversation. Outside, the world was completely opaque. Someone could have stood a yard from the car and never known they were there.

'I'll survive.'

He touched the line on her cheek, running a single finger its length. 'I didn't know what to do, Alison. It was all so awful.'

'Yes,' she replied and took his hand from her skin. 'But it happened. And it's over. You didn't need to do anything. This is my battle. *Mine.*'

Something crackled on the radio in his jacket pocket. He reached up and turned down the volume. 'There's nothing wrong with asking for help, you know.'

She lit a cigarette, half opened the window and blew the

smoke out into the dense cloud of fog. Old habits returning. It should have occurred to her, while she thought through matters in the nursing home outside Sevenoaks, that Justin would be in agony. 'I'm sorry. I ought to have got a message to you somehow. I'm sorry. I just wasn't ready to see you.'

'I didn't mean that. I just didn't understand what happened.'

'Join the club.' Would there come a day, she wondered, when she could tell someone everything? Of Harry in the furnace? Mitch, with his newly scarred cheek, exacting a terrible revenge? It was unrealistic to expect that kind of deliverance. The events of Beulah and the fast-cycling seasons seemed to conspire and envelop her in a strait-jacket of lies and deceits.

He folded his arms on his chest. 'Alison, I don't want to force you to say anything you don't want. If you want to tell me something, do it in your own time. No ties. Nothing expected in return.'

She looked into his eyes, knew he meant every word, and stifled the urge to kiss him. 'You're a hero, Justin. Why are you hanging around a mad old trout like me?'

'You called,' he replied with a weak grin.

'Ah yes.' She gave him a nice smile and didn't dare to take this particular line of the conversation any further. The thick blanket of fog gave them an odd sensation of privacy. 'I thought a lot when I was getting better. I had the space to do that and I need to tell you something, though you're going to think I'm crazy.'

'Most people in Beulah are one way or another.'

'Nevertheless . . .' The moment seemed pivotal, for both of them. This was the start of a conversation she could never have with Miles. There was no guessing where it might lead. 'They killed someone, Justin. On the night of the Burning Man. They built this big straw figure, put it in the bonfire *and there was someone inside.*'

He didn't burst out laughing, which was something. He didn't even look much surprised.

'Well?' she asked, to break the silence.

'I was sort of expecting it,' he admitted. 'Sara told me about you finding something. A bone.'

'Hmmm.' She wished Sara could be a touch more circumspect at times.

'So where is it?'

'Gone. I came back from Sevenoaks and looked at the place where I left it. Somebody had been there. It could have been anybody. I don't know.'

'Oh.'

'Could you not be a little more forthright and tell me I'm out of my mind or something?'

He shuffled in the tiny driver's seat of the car. 'If that's what you want. Is it?'

'No,' she replied firmly. 'I want you to agree with me, say there is something going on here, and find out what the hell it is.'

'Well, in that case, I need to know: are you asking me as a friend? Or as the local plod?'

'That's not a fair question, Justin.'

He gave her a chilly stare. 'Oh, but it is. Because the answer depends on who I am. As the local plod I'd have to ask you what evidence you have. And we both know the answer to that. None.'

She stared silently out into the fog. Justin was very on the ball. It was a mistake to think otherwise.

'As a friend,' he added quickly, 'I'm with you all the way. Something about this perfect little place stinks to high heaven. I can't put my finger on it, but it's there. CID have been looking at this place for one thing, not that they've let anything slip to me. I still think that fire at Paternoster was fishy too. Why the hell did Mitch run like that? How did it happen in the first place? And now you're telling me something happened in that bonfire. I don't know . . .'

'Justin,' she said emphatically. 'Something *did* happen. I know. I saw it.'

'OK.' He tried to look sympathetic. But she wasn't sure. Maybe some doubt still lurked there. 'Let me be the first to say something's up. Whether it amounts to murder I don't know. But it's there, written in their faces. They're waiting for something to happen. And sometimes I think . . .' He stopped, uncertain of himself.

'Go on,' she said.

'Sometimes it's in your face too. I'm not stupid, except in a few understandable ways. There's something here I'm not being told. I need you to be frank with me.'

Alison looked him in the face and said, as honestly as she could, 'I can tell you what I know. Nothing else, unless I'm certain about it myself. I don't want anyone else around here thinking I'm crazy. And I want to be sure it won't hurt you as well.'

'I'm a big boy,' he said without thinking. Then, 'What do you mean "as well"?'

She folded her arms and tried to think her way through these dangerous waters. 'I mean there is a reason behind all this, Justin. A reason I'm here. A reason things happen to me. You have to let it lie at that for now. In the end, I promise, there'll be no secrets between us.'

It was not the answer he wanted. 'Let me understand exactly what you're saying,' he continued. 'You think that what happened to you wasn't an accident? That someone was behind that too?'

She reached over and held his hands. 'I'm not ready for this, Justin. It's too painful and I can't explain why that is.'

He looked deeply offended. 'Dammit, if you don't trust me, if I don't know the truth, what's the point?'

There was only one way. She leaned over in the car and kissed him slowly, chastely, on the lips, touched his hair, and was taken aback by the sudden surge of electricity that ran through them. 'I trust you, my boy,' she said. 'More than anyone. Poor, naïve Miles. Sara even. But we have to do this one step at a time. And we have to be careful. We have to watch. And listen. And think. Like I said, there's a reason, a mechanism to all this, and when we see that, we have them.'

His hair was longer, she realised. It felt soft and delightful underneath her fingers.

'And do I have you?'

He looked so desperate. At that moment, she needed his help so badly. 'I'm nearly ten years older than you, Justin. Damaged stock.'

'*No*. You're the best, Alison. You're . . .'

'The Queen of the May?' she asked, with a laugh, and felt like crying. No man had ever been this devoted to her, she knew. Justin was so special, and it couldn't possibly work.

They sat in silence, his hand on her knee, staring out into the fog, and she toyed, for a moment, with the idea of moving across and straddling him, sitting above him, head crushed tight against the roof of the tiny police Peugeot, moving towards some slow, cathartic act of devotion.

Then he looked out of the side window and exclaimed, 'Sod it.'

A dark figure had emerged from the gloom. It was wearing a trilby hat. A long walking stick waved in one hand. Justin wound down his window. 'Morning, Sir Frank.'

The ancient, craggy face of Frank Wethered peered at them through the window. 'Morning, Justin. Mrs Fenway. Bloody awful weather, eh?'

The two of them nodded glumly.

'Don't know how they expect to practise cricket in this,'

Wethered babbled. 'Still, got to get their eye in for Monday. Big day, Beltane. I gather your husband will be playing.'

'So I hear,' she replied.

'Hope you'll be there to watch that. I'm club president so I have to be there, of course. Not that I'd miss it for all the tea in China.'

She tried to smile. 'Me neither.'

'Well.' He doffed his trilby in a comical gesture. 'Must be going. Leave you two to your own devices.'

'Thank you, Sir Frank,' Justin said icily, and they watched the old, frail figure disappear into the mist.

He looked at her, miserable and exposed again. 'Well, that's that. It'll be all round the place by lunchtime. Village plod is shagging the townie woman again. And this time in uniform, in a lay-by.'

For some reason she could only find this amusing. The locals thought her crazy; why should she care what they saw? 'You might look a touch flattered.'

He wriggled awkwardly in his seat, an obvious case of priapic discomfort. 'Oh, I'm flattered all right. But you know that. So where first?'

She beamed at him. 'Beltane, dear boy. We watch their rituals. We learn.'

'I'll be in the thick of it,' he said miserably.

'Policing a village cricket match? Surely not.'

'No, they don't need that. I'm playing. Got roped in to turn out for Wye. The desk sergeant runs the team. He's a batsman short.'

Her head whirled. The thought of Miles and Justin facing each other across the vast, green expanse of the Minnis was deeply disconcerting. These were the two most important men in her life. In a way she loved both. 'How sweet,' she said. 'You'll be playing against Miles.'

'The demon fast bowler, I suppose. Any tips?'

She tried to remember what Miles had said in the house. There could be no harm, no treachery, in passing on the comments. 'His first three deliveries are good ones. After that, he goes to pieces. He says the smart move is to play safe at the beginning and knock the crap out of him at the end. Does that make sense?'

He looked naïvely grateful. 'It could do. Thanks.'

She kissed him again and found the thought of the two of them locked together in the front seat of the car coming to the fore of her consciousness once more.

'Gotta go, Justin,' she said, and within the minute was striding through the thick, dense fog, back to Priory House.

The cricket practice ended at one thirty. Then the team and its assorted hangers-on retired to the long main bar of the Green Man. Miles Fenway knew the pub and its regulars well by now. He had a familiar space close to the coffee machine. Norman understood that he preferred his pint of Spitfire in a jug with a handle, not the plain glass favoured by regulars. No one joked about him drinking from a flower vase any more.

Jim Barnes, everyone said, was a hopeless farmer but not half bad at running a cricket side. A big man, with huge, bristling mutton-chop sideburns and slicked-back hair, he carried a brutal, domineering kind of authority. As captain, he had a ready, incisive grasp of the real abilities of his players and no qualms about upsetting someone with an over-inflated ego. He knew, too, when to turn up the heat. Beulah, quite deliberately, and for reasons Miles did not fully understand, refused to play in any of the local minor leagues, restricting itself to 'friendlies'. Of them, the most important – and the least friendly of all – was the local derby with

Wye which opened the season, this year on Beulah's home ground.

Just the mention of the word 'Wye' was enough to start even the most faint-hearted of Beulah players ticking. There existed between the two sides a bitter, entrenched rivalry so deep-rooted that no one could explain, or even remember, its cause. Mitch had a theory: Wye resented Beulah because the village team had proven antecedents a good thirty years older than those of the larger community down the hill, formed around the well-manicured pitch maintained at great expense by the agricultural college. It was, in Mitch's view, ancient versus modern, hill folk versus townie (Wye, with a population fast rising past the two thousand mark, clearly counting as a metropolitan area, in his opinion).

To Miles, this seemed overly complex. The truth was that the season began, always, on May Day, with the match against Wye. To win the opening fixture of the summer was to set the tone for the games to come. Cricket was, in essence, an arcane form of tournament, conducted according to ancient ritual. The tenor of the summer would depend, to an important extent, upon a fair showing against the bigger, stronger side from Wye. And rivalry that bordered upon hatred was one possible route to success. *Demonise your foe.* There were, he thought, lessons to be learned on the bumpy, queer-shaped expanse of the Minnis pitch, lessons that could apply to life in the cut-throat world of the City too.

Barnes stared over the table, a blank expression on his ruddy face. 'You think you can bowl better'n you can bat then, Miles?' He had the local rolling 'a' in his voice. Bat came out as *ba-at*.

'With practice, Jim.'

'You can get in them nets every weekend? Wednesday nights too? That guaranteed? I know you City blokes. You promise the sky and deliver sod all when it suits you.'

'If I say I'll do it, I'll do it.'

John Tyler, who seemed to act as a non-playing coach at Barnes's side, sipped a tomato juice mixed with a large fino sherry. 'Got to give the man a chance, Jim. He *is* village, you know.'

'Lives in village,' Barnes conceded. 'I'll say that much for him. But has he got the commitment? That's what I wonder. Or is he just one of them fellows that ups and offs the moment he gets bored?'

'Commitment is commitment,' Miles said forcefully and thought: *getting the job running Mersons wasn't half as hard as this particular interview.*

'Even if that barmy wife of yours goes barmy again?' Barnes asked with a glint in his eye.

Miles said calmly, 'My wife is fine, thank you, Jim. I'll make the time.'

'Maybe.' Barnes's gaze was fixed on the empty glass.

Miles took the hint and pulled out a twenty-pound note. 'Let me buy this one. Let me buy one for everybody.'

'He's a gent!' Mitch yelled.

Barnes didn't move. 'You shut your gob, Mitchell Blamire. I'm the captain around here. I says who's buying.' He glowered at the twenty on the table. 'Tell you what, Mr City Man. You and me gets out there this afternoon. I'll test your mettle. From what I've seen, if you don't let yourself go or nothing, I'll put you in the team. You can bat at the dead end of the list where you belong. You may even get to bowl if we get short. That a deal?'

Miles beamed and held out his hand. 'Done!'

Barnes stared at his fingers, and didn't take them. Instead he picked up the note, gave it to Mitch, and said, 'Make yourself useful and get them pissing beers in, Blamire. A man's spitting feathers here.'

A ripple of cheers ran around the narrow tables where the team had congregated. Tyler leaned over, laughing and slapped Miles on the shoulder. 'Congratulations. You're in.'

'That's nice,' he said, and finished off a good third of a pint of Spit in one go. More beer arrived on the table, and bowls of hot roast potatoes from the kitchen. Norman rang the bell for time and was greeted with a cacophony of jeers.

'I think,' Mitch observed, 'we could be poised for a lock-in.'

Tyler shook his head. 'More business for me. I should be a liver specialist by now, you know. I think this is one occasion I will forgo.'

He stood up and Frank Wethered, still wearing his top coat, fresh from his walk, took the seat next to Miles. 'A new cricketer, eh?'

'On probation,' Miles replied. 'I have to prove myself to Jim here, and he seems a tough taskmaster.'

'As I should be,' Barnes said, then prodded his neighbour with a fat forefinger and launched into a dirty story.

Frank Wethered gave Miles a wan smile, then said, 'Do you mind if we have a private word, old boy?'

Three hours later, when Norman's patience became sufficiently exhausted for him to close the pub briefly in order to clean the bar, Jim Barnes and Miles Fenway stumbled out to the nets once more. In the foggy light of the late afternoon, arms rose in anger, bats swished through the air, like the weapons of ancient warriors at swordplay.

With seven pints of Spit and a couple of whisky chasers, Miles Fenway was inducted into the playing ranks of the Beulah cricket club and duly scheduled for the forthcoming fixture with Wye on the Minnis, wickets pitched at two in the afternoon on May Day.

He stumbled home at six, feeling bloated and decidedly

drunk. Alison surveyed him swaying by the kitchen door, looking a little pathetic.

'You smell like a beer can stuffed with dead ciggies, darling,' she said sweetly. 'Upstairs for a bath, now. If you're sober I've got some pheasant in cream and cider on the go.'

'Bacon sandwich'll do,' Miles said, slurring his words. She bought wonderful bacon these days, from Coopers down the hill. It sat in the frying pan and *sang*. No mess of water and white, plastic-looking foam.

'Your wish is my command. I'll try to steer clear of vegetables or anything else that might mop up the beer.'

Miles stumbled and clutched the big pine table for support.

'God,' she said, 'you are slaughtered, aren't you? Do try and stay upright. I don't want beer running out of your ears and staining the new carpet.'

'Boglocks.'

'Boglocks indeed. Now run along.'

He didn't move. Miles looked different. Frank Wethered had blabbed, she guessed. And Miles was just too drunk for an argument.

'I'm in the team,' he said in the end.

'Surprise, surprise. Did you ever doubt it?'

'Don't be so bloody cynical,' he mumbled sourly. 'Someone's got to make an effort here.'

'Sorry.'

'You still sleeping in the spare room?' he asked.

'Oh yes. For a little while. Be patient.'

'Spend all my fucking life being patient. That's the truth of it.'

She wanted to kiss him on the cheek and send him packing. But it would be like planting her lips on an ancient, overflowing pub ashtray.

'Just a little longer.'

'Huh,' he snorted, and shuffled off to the stairs, his head alive with dreams of flailing bats and tumbling wickets.

May Day was special. Beulah rose while the rest of East Kent slept. At three thirty in the morning, lights were on in the houses around the green. The bar of the Green Man, still fuggy from the previous night's tobacco, had a steady stream of visitors, men and women in country green, sipping coffee and brandy, devouring the bacon sandwiches and kedgeree, devilled kidneys and angels on horseback, that sat atop the long oak bar.

Beulah, it seemed to her, surveying them, was oddly childless and, on the surface, almost seemed to enjoy this strange status. The perfect green of the Minnis was rarely littered with crisp packets. Only visiting townie yobs turned the signposts ninety degrees in the wrong direction, sending stray visitors off to Folkestone when they hoped to arrive in Canterbury. Yet this was a pretence. All of them, from the Tylers to Frank Wethered, had a heightened sense of order and delineation. Without children, Beulah was in danger of becoming what it so closely resembled at first glance: an image on a picture postcard, artificial, two-dimensional, deprived of the continuity and energy of successive generations. The Cartwrights alone seemed to deliver the goods, and, the fragile Bella apart, their offspring seemed only too anxious to uproot themselves and head for the plains as soon as they could.

Bella was the youngest in the room, quietly sipping an orange juice in the corner, by an ancient collection of corn dollies nailed to the wall. Beulah's one current hope for regeneration, Sara, was absent. Alison could hardly blame her. There were better places for a near-term woman to be on a cold May morning. The pregnancy, too, had started to assume an urgency of its own, as if it possessed a singular, proprietary version of time itself, and could race forward or slow the pace of each passing minute at will. When they last spoke, the previous day, Sara had sounded down in the mouth, almost scared. It was still nearly eight weeks until the baby was due around Midsummer's Day, but the event had now entered the fevered zone of uncertainty. Each twinge, each ache and physical discomfort would be analysed, examined, peered at for clues to its provenance. It was a time, she knew, when Sara needed her more than ever, and both Justin Liddle and the Beulah mystery would, when the great event came, have to take second place.

John Tyler's long, pale face appeared, peering into her eyes. 'Penny for them,' he said.

She watched Marjorie, who had been by his side, slink off to the far end of the bar and felt satisfied, childish as it was. Miles was there, listening to Barnes hold court.

'I was wondering,' she said casually, reaching for a small kidney speared with a cocktail stick, 'what dumb British habit meant you had to crawl out of bed at this godforsaken hour. And why?'

'Tradition,' Tyler said with deliberate pomposity, mocking himself. 'You Americans just don't understand, do you?'

She thought about it. 'This is some kind of ceremony designed to prove you're all different. That everything out there' – she pointed to the darkness beyond the pub window – 'doesn't really matter. Trains and boats and planes. TV and waiting in line at Tesco. All the things that happen to most people. What counts here is the ritual because that makes you special.'

'Hmmm. Tradition as snobbery. It's a point of view, of course. I'd agree with a lot of it. All that stuff in London. The changing of the guard. Beefeaters, for God's sake. All that nonsense the tourists love so much. But there's a difference here. Who's here to see? We don't even invite the local rag along to take pictures. There's nobody to impress but ourselves.'

'Worst sort of snobbery,' she observed. 'So high and mighty you don't even deign to share it with someone else.'

He eyed her slyly. 'Ah. Now you *are* taking the piss. You don't believe that for a moment.'

'I don't know what to believe any more,' she replied without thinking.

'But you will.'

'So,' she said, asking the question she knew he expected, 'if this isn't about snobbery, what is it about?'

For a moment, John Tyler looked lost for an answer. 'Literally? A good old pagan festival, of course. You remember the calendar I once drew for you?'

'Vaguely.'

'Tut, tut. You really should pay more attention. Beltane – May Day if you like – is one of the four great points of the year. The birth of summer, and the diametric opposite of Halloween. The reign of the king of light begins, the lord of darkness retreats in defeat.'

'Of course,' she said, stifling a shudder. 'But what's that got to do with cricket? Or standing around in a bar at four in the morning drinking . . . God, what is that?'

There was a glass of what looked like liquid mud in his hand. Tyler shrugged. 'Norman's house special for these occasions. Chilled miso soup with a large slug of vodka in it.'

'Good grief,' she gasped, wincing.

'Tastes better than it sounds. And never forget, the Japanese are the most long-lived folk on the planet. Still, back to your question. Some things are impossible to explain. But let me ask this: do you think there's something special about Beulah?'

'Naturally. It's . . .' The words refused to come when her mind whistled for them.

'Unspoilt?' he suggested.

'More than that,' she replied, wrestling with the idea. 'It's *apart*.'

'Good,' he said with a sudden smile. 'I couldn't have put it better myself. And we'd like to keep it that way. Now, shall we go?'

The crowd at the bar was moving, downing the dregs of coffee, grabbing the last morsels of food. They walked out onto the Minnis, pulling torches out of their pockets. It was still pitch dark. The air was fresh and invigorating. A beam flashed briefly in her face.

'Miles?' she asked.

'None other,' he replied in a lifeless monotone. The weekend had been punctuated by awkward silences. She had waited for him to ask about her assignation in the little police car but all he spoke about, on the rare occasions they conversed, was the forthcoming cricket match. She wound her arm through his, nudged his big, dark body and they headed off across the pitch, out towards the edge of the escarpment and the White Horse, tagging at the end of a crowd of no more than thirty.

'Want to talk?' she asked.

'Not particularly.' She wished she could see his face in the gloom. It was unlike Miles to sulk.

'Is this going to go on for long?'

'As long as it takes. You're my wife, Alison. That means something.'

'I know,' she said, then unhooked her arm and felt like screaming at him, filling the air with everything she knew about Harry Blamire and the toy box in the cupboard. Trying to make sense of it all. But there was a time for everything.

'Give me some space,' she said, and strode to the front

of the pack to walk alongside the Cartwrights. Bella grinned shyly at her. The girl looked different today, older, more worldly. She wore an ankle-length, flowing shift and her long hair was clean for a change, tied carefully into braids with narrow ribbons threaded through them.

'This your first, then?' the girl asked.

'First what?'

'Beltane, of course. Better than Christmas, if you ask me.'

'We get presents, Bella?'

'Some have had ours already. Might be getting a few more before the day's out too.'

Alison didn't need a history book to understand Bella's drift. May Day had a reputation, she knew that already. Maidens in the woods, hands on the tall, upright maypole. But why was Bella so excited? The revellers were so small in number, and middle-aged almost to a man.

Then they came to the edge of the Minnis and passed through the rough scrub and the tangles of blackthorn and field maple. In the east, beyond Canterbury, a faint yellow corona announced the impending arrival of dawn. There was the sound of voices ahead, the scraping of a fiddle. Alison recognised the voice of the strange girl from Yule, the one with the witch joke. In the darkness she made out costumes, men in Morris outfits, with bells on their arms and legs. They made a soft ringing sound as they walked through the chill morning air.

The sun rose slowly on the horizon, a sliver of golden fire, and a gasp ran through the people on the hill. Somewhere, another fiddle struck up a slow tune. Men began to dance, slow, dignified movements, in the growing light. Torches were extinguished. An excited chatter rose through the ranks of people sitting on the damp, hillside grass.

She felt a hand on her shoulder, turned and found Mitch Blamire leering into her face. He was holding something in his hand: a trowel. 'You'll be needing that, Mrs Fenway. No spectators allowed here.'

'But I don't know . . .' she objected.

'You cut, gel,' he said, and made a stabbing action towards the ground. 'You know how to do that now, don't you?'

There was a general movement along the hill, towards the pale outline of the White Horse. The music grew louder, accompanying the growing day. Morris men danced. Figures moved over the white edge of the gigantic chalk figure, all of them women, heading towards the long, priapic horns. She followed them and watched. Slowly, painstakingly, on all fours, they were renewing the edge, taking out the rye grass and weeds that had encroached over the previous year, revealing again the pristine white of the chalk.

'Come on,' Bella said, beaming, and the two of them got down on the ground and began to worry at the stubborn carpet of growth. The Horse, she realised, was huge. There must have been a good thirty or more women working at the job. Even so, they covered only a small part of the chalk outline's perimeter. There was still a vast amount of spoiled edge to improve.

'This is going to take ages,' she groaned.

'That's why you need a good breakfast inside you,' Bella replied, yanking at a dogged dandelion with her hands. 'You just put your back into it now, Mrs Fenway . . .'

'Alison. Please.'

'Very well then, Alison. You work at it and then we'll be done. Can't expect the men to tire themselves out now, not with the game this afternoon.'

She did as she was told and, to her surprise, found some pride in the neat, white line in front of her. Bella took advantage of a lull in the music and started to sing, in a loud, clear, melodious voice, 'I danced in the morning when the world was begun . . .'

The melody ran around the line of cutters, and soon the

sound of song filled the hillside, rose up to drown the trilling of the skylarks hovering over the scene. She had never seen the girl look so happy, and like this – clean, delighted, prepared somehow – she was extraordinarily pretty.

'Magic!' Bella said excitedly, breaking from the chorus. 'You not singing then, Alison?'

'Don't know the words.'

'You're learning now, aren't you?' she said pleasantly.

'Perhaps. Bella? Why are we breaking our backs like this when the men are lounging around?'

''Cos it's our job, ain't it? You see that handsome chap with the hurdy gurdy?'

Alison looked down the hill. A tall, dark-skinned youth with long, curly hair was turning a medieval-looking instrument, making a wheezing, only partly musical sound.

'I see him.'

'Reckon I'll be stroking his pole before the day's out. If you'll pardon my language.'

'Pardoned,' she sighed.

'And mebbe you'll be doing the same with your copper, eh? If your hubby doesn't pull his finger out at that match. Don't want to get bedded by losers now, do we?'

Alison stabbed her trowel in the loose chalk and closed her eyes. 'Bella. *Please*.'

'Oops. Sorry. Gob running away with itself again.'

'It doesn't matter. There are no secrets in Beulah, are there?'

'Only important ones,' Bella said, eyes twinkling.

'Such as?'

'That's for you to find out now, missus, ain't it?'

Alison groaned and looked at the men lounging at the foot of the figure, their silhouettes wreathed in cigarette smoke, coarse, ribald laughter floating on the fresh morning air. The light haze was lifting. It was going to be a glorious day, a true portent of the coming summer. The bleached-out hues of the winter sun were gone. In their place was the bold, confident radiance of summer. She realised, with a shock, that she had never really appreciated this change before. The seasons seemed so marked in Beulah. It was impossible to escape them.

'Who are all these people, Bella? Your chap with the hurdy gurdy thing and the rest?'

'Friends,' she said coyly.

'From where?'

'Places like ours. You don't think Beulah's on its own in the world, do you? We got friends in other villages. One in Sussex. Another down Winchester way. They help us out.'

She stopped digging and stared at the girl. 'And you need it, don't you? That help? If they weren't here, this wouldn't be much of a celebration at all. There'd be nobody's pole to stroke.'

Bella cast a long, deliberate glance down the hill in the direction of Miles, who was standing with the rest of the team, hands in pockets, chewing the fat. 'Oh, I should cocoa. That husband of yours is a fine catch. And there's no harm in a bit of variety, specially on holidays.'

Alison stared at her in silence.

Bella looked worried. 'I haven't offended you again now, have I? It was only a lark.'

'No,' Alison said, thinking. 'Take him if you want. He's not much interested in me right now.'

'Thanks but nah. Not my type really. Too posh.'

Alison wondered. She had never seen Miles as a philanderer. 'Shall we change the subject?'

The girl nodded. 'Probably for the best. Shagging's such a little thing and it causes no end of trouble. That's why Beltane's so good. It don't matter what you do. Tomorrow it's all forgot. Just like that German beer festival thing.'

Alison caught her eye. 'And just like Burning Man too?'

'How do you mean?'

314

'You can do anything you like. Swap partners. Whatever.'

Bella stopped digging and wiped her grubby hands on the nice clean dress. 'You're fishing now.'

'Just asking, Bella.'

'Well, in that case all I can tell you is that it's like Burning Man and it's not like it.' She surveyed their work on the hillside. The long, rigid horns of the chalk figure were now pristine, a clean white line defining them against the verdant grass. 'Beltane's fun. And Burning Man's serious. Dead serious. You get me? God, I wish you'd give in and join us. It'd be nice to get closer.'

'Yes.' The musicians had struck up again, a rowdy jig. The Morris Men danced, clashing long sticks, shouting as they met and re-met on the isolated hillside.

''Nuff talk, Alison,' Bella said firmly, and plunged the trowel back into the hard, white chalk.

The Horse was renewed by ten in the morning and a magnificent sight it was too. The women stood back from their completed work to a round of applause from the men, and a fresh bout of music and dancing ensued. The gigantic figure seemed to shine from the hillside, horns pointing upwards, into the depths of Sterning Wood. The sun was king of the day now. It stood, a bright yellow orb, radiant in a cloudless blue sky. Below them, along the path of the busy A28 trunk road, a haze of pollution hung like a low cloud over the earth. On the Downs, atop the winding hazard of Vipers Hill, the air was clean, undefiled. Alison, exhausted from her efforts with the trowel, filled her lungs and felt thoroughly elated.

Bella looked at the pair of them and laughed. 'What a couple of scruffs. Reckon I'll be heading for the tub before anything else.'

'Take a shower at our place if you like. It'll save you the walk back to the cottage.'

'Don't mind if I do,' the girl said, then picked up both the trowels and slung them across the grass at Mitch Blamire. 'There you go, Mitchy boy,' she yelled. 'You can stick them up your arse for another year.'

Mitch glowered at her. 'Cheeky bitch. You should mind your elders.'

'Oh, I'll mind you, Mitch,' the girl replied. 'One day I'll be dancing on your grave. Only way you'll ever get to look up my skirt.'

He wandered off, cursing. Alison watched him retreat. 'He's a hard man to cross, Bella,' she observed. 'I'd be careful.'

'Mitch? He's a poppet. Just does as he's told. Always. We going now?'

They walked back to the village, ahead of the rest of the pack, admiring the day. Trellis tables were already out on the Minnis. Bunting decorated the roof of the cricket pavilion and the windows of the Green Man. The pitch was a perfect plateau of grass, albeit one with a distinct southerly slope. Bella stopped outside Priory House and stared at the driveway. 'You sure about this?' she asked.

'Of course. It's crazy going all the way to the cottage just to freshen up. Take some of my things. You're welcome.'

The girl wrinkled her nose. 'Never been in the big house before. Feels funny.'

'It's a house, Bella. That's all,' Alison said, and led the way to the back door, walked into the kitchen, and filled the kettle. The girl followed, wide-eyed. She stopped in the kitchen, staring at everything, and said, 'It's *beautiful*.'

'Yes,' Alison conceded. 'I guess it is. We're lucky. Now, do you want a coffee or something first or would you like to head straight for the shower?'

'Got a Coke?'

Alison shook her head. 'Will orange juice do?'

''Kay.'

They went upstairs and entered the guest bathroom. Bella stared at the large, white whirlpool unit, with its buttons and shower fittings, and exclaimed, 'Blimey. Does it come with instructions?'

'Just climb in, dear. Play with anything that comes to hand. You'll get the idea.'

The girl put down her glass of orange juice and pulled her dress over her head. She looked skinny and so young in a tatty T-shirt and old underwear. 'What about you?'

'We have an en-suite in the bedroom.'

'Bloody hell! Another one of these?'

''Fraid so,' Alison said, then removed some towels from the cupboard, and threw them on the floor. 'See you in the bedroom. I've got something you can wear if you like.'

'Cor,' Bella said, then shuffled off the last of her clothes and started to fiddle with the taps.

Alison retreated to her own shower and let the stream of warm water remove the grime of the White Horse, then lull her into a dreamy, relaxed state of semi-exhaustion. She threw on a robe, lay on the bed, lit a cigarette and stared out of the window, thinking of nothing in particular except how warm and lazy the day felt after the morning's exertion. The Minnis was busy once more. The Morris Men were taking a break, supping early pints of beer outside the pub, the musicians playing idly on the seats next to them. The wickets were up on the pitch, tiny wooden totems to the ancient religion. In the nets, the team was warming up with a lazy determination. On the far side of the green, close to the Tylers' house, was the upright, rigid outline of the maypole, garlands of streamers wrapped around the shaft.

She remembered the first time she had stared out of this window at the odd bustle of activity on the Minnis. It was the day of Burning Man when, without thinking, she had let the

317

late Harry Blamire see rather more of her than was sensible. Could everything stem from that single act? The thought was dismissed on the instant. There had been a bone on the ground. Yappy had found it, and now the evidence was gone, spirited away from the kitchen by hands unknown. There could be no discernible link between Harry's greedy gaze at her nakedness and the mystery of the fire.

Nevertheless, she thought . . . and reached forward to pull the curtains closed. Bella walked in, a towel around her, and stared in surprise at the window. 'My, Alison,' she said, 'we're the prudish ones, aren't we? You think that lot are interested? Nothing on their minds except cricket if you ask me.'

'Perhaps . . .'

Bella threw herself on the bed and grinned. 'Perhaps nothing. You won't see any of them, least of all your Miles, this side of closing time. That's the way it goes. Mind you, with a bath like that who needs a man? You just twiddle those buttons and . . . kazoom!'

Alison finished the cigarette and reached for another. 'Want one?'

'Nah,' Bella said, then reached forward and took the unlit cigarette out of Alison's hand. 'And neither do you. Horrible smelly things. Why d'you bother? You don't even look like a smoker to me.'

'Habit,' she replied.

'Well, it's a bad one.' Bella rubbed the towel vigorously against her body, then threw it off the bed, turned over onto her naked stomach and gave Alison a knowing look. 'You kill me, you really do. You got all these things here. Mr Fenway. This big house. Them baths. A bedroom bigger than our kitchen. And it's still not enough, is it? You're still a bag of nerves, smoking them fags you don't really want.'

'Thanks for the analysis. Is there a charge?'

'Nope. You get it all for free,' Bella said, smiling innocently. 'Some fresh togs for the day could come in useful, though they'll hang a bit on a bag of bones like me.'

Alison waved at the wardrobes. 'Help yourself. And by the way, I haven't had much of a great time recently. I get to smoke if I feel like it.'

Bella didn't move. 'You just need a spot of healing. That's all. Turn on your side.'

'What?'

'You heard,' Bella said. 'Turn on your side, with your back to me. I done massage at night school.'

Alison did as she was told and a pair of thin, strong hands came down on her neck and started to pummel deep into the muscle.

'Ouch!'

'Sorry,' Bella apologised. 'Hurts a bit to begin with, but you're so tense, Alison. Like you got a bundle of knots in there. Just try and relax, will you?'

'OK.' Alison closed her eyes and wondered what Miles would make of this scene: his wife being mauled in the marital bed by a naked teenage girl. But Miles was in cricket mode; Miles was jealous of men.

'Don't you worry,' Bella said, her fingers working ever harder, more subtly. 'He won't come disturbing us. He's got other things on his mind.'

'What?' she said, astonished. 'How did you know I was thinking that, Bella?'

'I'm a witch. Didn't they tell you? Nah. It's obvious, isn't it? First thing townies do when they're starting to have something nice happen to them. Feel guilty about it. And what's there to feel guilty about?'

'You should be a psychiatrist,' Alison said, and closed her eyes, enjoying the rhythmic massage that had now spread to her shoulders.

'Seen enough of them. I reckon you're right.'

The girl moved Alison's robe gently off her shoulders, reached forward and kissed the back of her neck.

'Bella . . .'

'Sorry.' The hands became still, and immediately Alison felt an ache at their absence.

Alison didn't turn around to face her. She didn't want that pressure yet. 'I don't want you to get the wrong idea. That's all.'

'The wrong idea being what?' Bella's voice suddenly sounded petulant, adolescent. 'Me making you feel nice? About the only bloody thing I'm good at, missus. Don't get many complaints.'

'I did like that. It's just . . .'

'Just what? You don't have to have a man to make you happy. 'Cos they always got a price, and it always comes with pain. Agreed?'

'I guess so, but . . .'

'But nothing,' Bella interrupted, and went back to Alison's naked shoulders with a sweet, painful vengeance. 'Women are different. We just give because it's nice giving. You know the trouble with you lot? You spend all your time looking for things to make you happy. You don't ever know enough to wait and let it come to you.'

Alison closed her eyes and said nothing. Bella's warm damp legs were against hers now. The two of them lay locked together in a half embrace. She felt the girl's lips on her neck again and the warm, rough dampness of her tongue. A hand came from her back, reached round for the front of her robe, untied the belt and then slid, tenderly, first to her groin, then, measure by measure, up the taut, hot skin of her stomach to take a firm grip of her left breast.

'Don't,' Alison whispered, without conviction.

'Say that once more and I *will* stop,' Bella warned. 'And then you will be sorry, my love, this being Beltane when all the rules get broken and nothing ever matters afterwards.

These are just little, sweet things, Alison, and I'm good at 'em. And you and me, being women, know that. We know how to love one another, better than any man ever can.'

Bella took Alison's robe in both hands and gently helped her remove it, then threw a leg over hers, leaned half upright, smiling into her face. 'Here's a pretty thing,' the girl said. 'Here's a May Day to remember.'

'Bella . . .'

'Shush, my darling,' Bella said, and reached down to kiss her long and hard on the mouth, tongue probing, hands moving through her hair. After a long, sweet interval, she broke for breath. 'You just shush and feel the goodness come.'

Which it did. Slowly, sweetly, with a rising crescendo of pleasure, pure, unsullied, quite different from the bittersweet experience she got from a man. Bella's lovemaking was so strange and adventurous that Alison knew it could be experienced once only; to return to these curious, exotic places would be to spoil such vivid, entrancing memories.

She closed her eyes and let Bella's feverish fingers and inquisitive mouth do the rest, firing her imagination, quickening her breath, turning the world in on itself until the entire universe consisted of nothing but these two panting, damp bodies, writhing with an ecstatic languor on the softness of the bed.

A flood of heat and dampness soaked this shared world and Alison cried out, a long, rapturous moan. Bella lay in her arms, giggled like a child, then kissed Alison playfully. 'You wait,' she said, 'and the goodness comes in the end.'

'Yes,' Alison said, eyes still closed, relishing the afterglow.

'You was so far gone there, love, so far you didn't even notice.'

'Notice what?'

'Company,' Bella giggled.

Alison opened her eyes in sudden shock. Miles sat at the end of the bed naked, aroused. He reached forward, took her foot in his hand, Bella's in the other.

'Miles,' she stuttered. 'I didn't hear you . . . How long?'

'Shush,' Bella cautioned. 'Beltane comes, things happen. Not just goodness for you, my selfish little dear.'

'But . . .'

He climbed onto the bed, kissed both of them, snuggled up behind Bella, stared over her shoulder.

'I . . .' Alison said.

His body moved. Bella gasped, a tiny spasm of pain on her face, then surprise, followed by pleasure. 'That's how posh likes it, eh?' she said, smiling. 'Country habits catching for you too . . . *ow*!'

Alison rolled out from beneath her. Miles stared at the back of the girl's head, then turned her face down, held both her arms with his hands and arched his body, over and over again. Bella's face was half hidden by the pillow. It was impossible to tell whether she was in agony or rapture.

'Miles,' Alison said, very seriously.

His hand came free and pushed her away. She lost her balance, fell slowly, awkwardly out of bed. Miles adjusted his position, raised his speed, pulled the girl back by her haunches and let out an animal roar. Alison looked at her again. Bella was transported. This was her goodness, coming out of the blue.

Trying to ignore them, trying not to hear the grunting on the sheets and the counterpoint of the bedsprings, she picked up her clothes, walked naked into the guest room and dressed. When she went downstairs, the sound of activity was undiminished but had taken on another tone. Bella was giggling. Miles seemed incapable of anything but animal grunts. And the bedsprings sang, constantly, beating, beating.

In the kitchen she glanced at the clock. It was nearly

eleven. May Day seemed destined to last for ever. Not that Bella and Miles would mind.

She walked to the back door, opened it and found Sara standing there in a vast floral maternity smock, beaming.

'Alison,' she said. 'You look wonderful. And I feel like shit. What's the secret?'

From upstairs came the unmistakable sound of Bella and Miles reaching a mutual climax, primal teenage scream mixed with guttural caveman grunt.

'My God,' Sara exclaimed, eyes wide open. 'We are starting to assimilate fast, aren't we?'

Norman had put the summer chairs and tables outside the pub. They grabbed the last spare set and set down their drinks and sandwiches. Sara patted her vast stomach and said, 'Eat up, son. The time for drip feeds is fast disappearing.'

Alison watched Miles and Bella leave the house, not even looking at each other. He ambled over to the cricket nets and joined in the casual banter and half-hearted practice. She was away to the Morris Men and the musicians, clean, fair hair flowing in the wind, ribbons twined through the locks once more, wearing a long cream linen shift Alison had bought, during a different lifetime, from Banana Republic on Fifth Avenue. She looked ecstatic.

'You know the sex?' Alison asked, suddenly realising the import of Sara's words.

'I couldn't stop myself. Sorry, I'm not the patient sort.'

Alison sipped on a half of beer. The day was getting hot. 'And what about Dad?'

Sara looked disappointed. 'Yellow card, darling. You know that subject is off limits.'

'Of course. I wasn't asking you to nail him. Just whether he knew. Or cared.'

'I care,' Sara said firmly, and downed her orange juice. 'And that's all that counts. Bed stories are best kept behind closed doors. Yours certainly are, as far as I'm concerned.'

Alison laughed dryly. She couldn't help it, though the memory of the bedroom remained deeply disturbing. 'Jesus Christ, Sara. What's happening? I've just had my first experience of lesbian sex, with a teenage girl at that. She then goes on to get screwed by my husband. And it's still not lunch time. I never even used to think sex was such a big thing. All of a sudden my morals got turned upside down and I'm as crazy as the rest of you.'

Sara poured her second bottle of Britvic. 'To hell with morals. This is May Day, dear girl. Or Beltane to be precise. Don't worry. It passes.'

'But I am worried!' She watched the team stroll over and take a leisurely look at the wicket. 'No. Take that back. I'm not. Not that much. And I feel I should be.'

'Ah. You *want* to feel guilty, and it fills you with guilt that you're not.'

Bang on target as usual. 'That's about it.'

'Poor Alison. You have such high standards. You expect so much of everyone. You don't think you're alone, do you? In messing around a bit once in a blue moon? Falling for Bella's little lines?'

She was puzzled. 'Little lines?'

'Don't tell me.' Sara put on a passable impersonation of Bella's Kentish inflections. '"I done this at night school, missus. Just you lay back and relax."'

'How the hell . . . ?'

Sara just smiled wanly at her.

'Oh,' Alison gasped, as the idea began to dawn.

'Like I said. You're not the only one. And Beltane does come round once a year.'

'Quite.' She felt like another drink. Something stronger.

'Did you enjoy it?' Sara asked frankly.

Alison thought about her answer. 'I guess so. Hell, I was out of control. Enjoyment's not the word. It happened. And I don't think it should.'

Sara shook her head. 'You do like to complicate things, love, don't you? Just go along with the local view for once.'

'Meaning?'

'Darling, people here have appetites. When they're hungry, they satisfy them. That's it and that's all of it. And, besides, it won't happen again.'

This was something else she failed to understand. 'Why not?

'Because Bella's done what she had to. As far as they're concerned, you're on message. In the team. Part of the club. Could be worse. You could have got Frank Wethered instead. And Miles might have been lumbered with Mad Marjorie, though I find that a touch hard to imagine.'

'Too much for me,' Alison exclaimed and headed for the bar for refills. When she returned, John Tyler was at the table with a cheap white cotton hat over his bald pate, trying to keep off the sun. He and Sara were already deep in conversation. Alison listened with mounting horror.

'The one thing I don't understand, John,' Sara was saying, 'is the timing. It's all very well people bonking like bunnies in the morning. But what about the Warriors of the Willow? We hate losing to Wye. What's this going to do for their cricket?'

'Ah,' Tyler said, erecting a long, pale finger. 'Medically speaking of course, sex before battle is distinctly bad news. The laws of physics naturally apply. Energy expended cannot be quickly replaced. But, as I frequently have to point out to you newbies, literal explanations do not always tell the whole story. That great fraud Aleister Crowley, for example, who died in Hastings by the way . . .'

'Excuse me,' Alison interrupted, glaring across the table, 'to what does this conversation refer?'

Sara looked at her knowingly. 'I was just asking the good doctor here whether, if it's true the team likes a bonk on Beltane morning – no names, no pack drill – it doesn't ruin their game. I happen to put a lot of store by village pride and I don't see why a bunch of blokes should blow it just because they fancy getting their end away.'

'*As* I was saying,' Tyler continued, 'Crowley, who was, of course, an utter mountebank, puts forward this theory in his Thelema garbage that the act of orgasm itself – male or female – has innate magic properties. That's magick with a "k" in his version, but still a load of balls. Nevertheless, this is not a new notion. The fashion for sex *after* military conquest . . .'

'You mean rape?' Alison interrupted.

'Normally, though not always,' Tyler replied, unabashed. 'Post-victory intercourse, that's a habit well documented. However, there are ancient cultures – in Greece, China, the Middle East – that practised a kind of religious, organised orgy *before* battle in the belief that it released some kind of mystical force from within the body. Reich had much the same idea as Crowley of course and called it orgone energy. But there's also the Hindu *prana*, meaning the body's vital airs, of course, as does the Taoist *ch'i* . . .'

'Just a minute,' Sara objected. 'You've rattled through two complete shysters and a couple of world religions in one breath. It's a bit much to swallow.'

Tyler looked impatient. 'I am, dear lady, merely trying to answer the question to the best of my knowledge. Physically – in the world of Newton – it follows that they must have less energy to expend on victory. *Meta*physically, there are those who believe the act of orgasm releases some other form of energy which may, or may not, more than compensate for this loss.'

326

Alison looked sceptical. She slapped her purse down on the table. 'That is absolute bullshit. A fiver says Wye will win. I bet that lot haven't been dancing the jig-a-jig all morning.'

'Ah,' he smiled, 'a wager. You know my weakness. Done. For the remaining duration of the match, however, I advise abstinence from now on. Particularly,' he said, staring at Sara, 'for you, my dear.'

'Believe it or not,' Sara replied, aghast at the idea, 'I had not been considering joining in with that little ceremony.'

'Good idea. You'd be amazed how many early deliveries are down to sex, even as late as eight, nine months into the game. And people still believe we do it just to reproduce. Ah well. You take care. I suspect the time draws near.'

Sara reached out and patted Alison affectionately on the arm. 'Don't worry. I have a friend. And a partner. Ali's been a marvel.'

'Good,' Tyler murmured, and for once Alison felt she had done something that met with his approval.

There was a noise on the far side of the Minnis. A coach drew up next to the cricket pavilion and disgorged a gaggle of men dressed in white. Next to the motley crew of Beulah they looked remarkably fit and organised. Justin was there, Alison saw, smart and upright in neatly pressed whites. He positively shone under the bright May sun. By contrast, Miles, with his dark olive skin and duller clothing, seemed somehow a lesser man: older, weaker, more in doubt.

'Ah,' John Tyler said, beaming, 'the sun kings arrive, looking fine and fair and wholesome. All ready to conquer. I don't suppose you'd care to change that bet?'

'You mean now you've seen the cut of the Wye team's jib you want to drop out?' Alison replied, with narrowed eyes.

'No. Let's make it a tenner. Make it my little contribution of *ch'i* to the proceedings.'

She watched Justin limber up, long arms swinging lithely,

looking strong and confident. 'Done,' Alison said and looked around the green, feeling happy, relaxed, almost free of the nagging doubts and worries that had dogged her when she first left the house and joined Sara. Suspicion was a kind of disease sometimes, one that fed upon itself.

It was Beltane. The White Horse now stood pristine on the downland scarp. A small flock of disputatious swifts swung through the air overhead, chittering constantly, like tiny black scimitars carving their paths across a perfect blue canvas. White figures ambled around the flat, close-cropped grass of the pitch, casually stomping down the odd bump, picking up a stray twig, puzzling over the odd bare, brown patch of earth. There was a crowd too, a small one, as much musicians and dancers as locals. Perhaps, she thought, that was how they preferred it. This event was no village fete. There were no stalls, no raffle tickets. It existed for the game, and, above all, the day.

Alison Fenway tried to see the whole of the Minnis in one glance, to freeze it for ever in her memory: the verdant common, the line of cottages by the pub, Priory House, large and grand, and, on the opposite side, well behind the perimeter road, the white outline of Granny Jukes's windmill.

On the vast, green pitch the first ball of the day careened through the warm air. Winter's grip was loosening. Summer, hot feverish summer, was coming out to play.

It was an hour into the game, which was both impenetrable and fascinating, that Alison finally managed to recall the old joke in its entirety. She slapped John Tyler on the arm, a little too hard – the beer had been flowing by this stage

– and said, 'Listen. I remember. An American definition of cricket. It goes . . .'

Tyler blinked, put down his tomato juice, and said, 'Don't tell me. "You have two sides, one out on the field and the other in. Each man in the side that's in goes out. When he's out he comes in and the next man goes out till he's out. When the side that's in is all out, the side that's been out comes in. Then the side that's been in goes out and tries to get out the one that's coming in. Sometimes you get men still in and not out when the side that is in is finally out. When both sides have been in and out, including those who are in and not out, that's the end of the game."' He paused. 'Was I close?'

'Swine,' she complained. 'It took me ages to remember all that.'

'Oh dear.' He looked genuinely sorry. 'I'm a bit of a smartarse sometimes, aren't I?'

'Damn right.'

Sara had disappeared, waddling off to the loo complaining of an overstocked bladder, then offering to refill Alison's glass of Spit. Alison had come to the view, somewhat against her wishes, that there was no animosity between her and Tyler. As the distance grew between the strange events that had occurred on Miles's birthday, so did her grasp of them. Were Marjorie Tyler and the now revealed Mitch Blamire really responsible? Was it possible she had, as most everyone else believed, simply gone crazy while locked tight inside a nightmare? With a half-gallon of best Spit inside her, nothing seemed certain any more. Beulah, she felt, did that to its inhabitants, one of many favours. Nestled in its oddly warm bosom, they became apt to forget the harsher turns of life. Or, as John Tyler would doubtless put it, saw them in their proper perspective.

'I apologise,' Tyler said, very sincerely. 'Will you and Marjorie ever be friends, do you think?'

This was another village trick. Reading your thoughts, sometimes before they had crystallised properly in your own head. 'I don't think so. We're not ... *simpatico*.'

'No. Shame really. But I understand. Still, everyone does want you to feel at home here.'

'I am at home. I do belong. Believe me.'

He gave her a frank glance. 'I do, actually. Marjorie really must call off the recruitment troops.'

'Why? Because you think I'm in the team already?' Inducted twice over according to Beulah terms, she thought, once with Harry, again with Bella, who had, perhaps, passed on the news to Marjorie. Yet Bella had no need to make the effort, which, in itself, gave pause for thought. Marjorie may not have been party to the trick on Burning Man.

John Tyler gazed at her queerly, with an expression that was preciously close to sympathy. 'I never make assumptions. Not on important matters anyway.'

'Tempt me,' she blurted, conscious of a slur in her voice. 'When do I get to hear secrets?'

'When do you care to ask?'

'Right now. What happens at Burning Man?'

He puzzled over that. 'One step at a time, I think. Or rather one feast at a time. Ask me what you like about Beltane.'

'But ...' It seemed desperately unfair.

'No,' Tyler said firmly. 'I am breaking any number of unwritten rules already.'

Sara returned from the pub, bearing a tray laden with glasses and packets of crisps. Alison leapt up to take it from her. Sara seemed to be getting heavier by the moment.

'Did I miss anything?' she asked. 'Anyone out?'

'We haven't been talking cricket,' Alison replied. 'I'm about to filled in on Beltane. So what happens next? After the match? Some games in the wood? Will Marjorie be doing the dance of the seven veils?'

'Not at all,' he said, half disappointed with her. 'Don't you get it? The match *is* the thing. The music. The dancing . . . They're just side shows.'

He waved over towards the maypole, where a group of women, Marjorie looming large among them, continued to prance around the upright shaft, entwining ribbons, laughing, looking, to Alison, like a page from an ancient children's book. Beulah were batting. The scorecard next to the little pavilion read 143 for 8. The Wye side stood stock still, scattered around the pitch, as an unidentifiable figure almost strolled down the wicket to deliver a ball that wound its way lazily through the air, bounced once in front of Dickie Cartwright, then, with a puff of dust, lurched mysteriously to the right of his bat and removed the off stump.

'Oh bugger,' John Tyler groaned. 'Not so good now. Hope your husband can put up a bit of a stand.' Miles walked slowly out from the pavilion, bat tucked under his arm, cricket togs a distinctly off-white colour.

'Miles is no batsman,' she objected. 'He never said he was.' The game seemed so slow. 'You mean this is *it*?'

'Yes,' Tyler replied impatiently, eyes fixed on the wicket.

'Sometimes,' Sara offered, 'cricket is more than a game. Your American roots are showing I'm afraid.'

'Best bleach them out,' Tyler added quietly.

'But . . .' Her head was full of questions, none of which formed quite correctly. Then she fell quiet. Something was happening on the pitch. Justin was coming in from the far boundary, close to the maypole, and talking to someone she assumed was the Wye captain. A red-haired player near the pavilion threw him the ball. Justin bobbed it up and down in his hand knowledgeably then started to amble towards the wicket.

'Yes,' Tyler announced. 'Change of bowler. Change of tactic. They obviously think your husband is the weak point, dear woman. Can't blame them. We've still got Barnes in at the other end. So . . . ?' He turned to stare at her. 'Do tell. What are our friendly plod's predilections? On the field that is?'

'I beg your pardon?'

'Spin, swing or pace? Googly, yorker, flipper . . .'

She waved a hand at him. 'Whoa! I don't have a clue what you're talking about.'

'Hmm,' Tyler grunted. 'Well, I guess we'll find out. Looks like a long run-up to me.'

Justin had walked well past the southern wicket, halfway back to the boundary, and was polishing the ball on his groin in what looked, to Alison, a very professional manner. To her surprise, the dancers had now stopped. They stood with the musicians on the far side of the pitch, watching Justin's run-up, yelling at him, words she could only half hear. Mitch Blamire was there too, making unmistakable obscene gestures with his right arm.

'That's not goddamn cricket,' Alison protested, feeling suddenly offended by the way Justin was being taunted. 'They're supposed to stay quiet. Not yell at players like that.'

Sara glanced at her sympathetically. 'As the good doctor said, dear, today the game's the thing.'

'Wherein we'll catch the conscience of the king,' John Tyler mumbled into his beer.

'Right . . .' Alison took a mouthful of Spit. This was quite exciting. She couldn't help but feel it.

Justin began to lope slowly down the pitch. Miles, his back to the pub, stamped his bat on the ground in an obvious gesture of nervousness. Then Justin's big frame picked up speed. He was thundering down the grass, arm crooked and at the ready. In a flash, faster than the eye could follow, the upper half of his body went into a sudden spastic rictus, his hand spun round in a 360-degree arc and the ball rocketed down the pitch, bounced a good six feet in front of Miles, then flew high into the air, missing his head by no more than an inch.

The small crowd went wild, shouting, jeering, screaming obscenities. Mitch Blamire was marching up and down the boundary making quacking noises, arms akimbo, flapping like wings. These jibes were, she realised, aimed as much at Miles as at Justin.

'Whose side are they on?' she asked.

'Oh, ours, ultimately,' Tyler replied, looking red-faced, almost excited. 'That doesn't stop you appreciating an opponent's skills now, does it? And your plod has a fair turn of pace on him, I'll say that. Damn near took Miles's head off with that one.'

'He's not my plod,' she said, and realised no one was listening. The entire population of the Minnis was fixed on this encounter between Justin and Miles, as if it were some kind of a jousting match. And almost as dangerous too. She had seen the way the ball had torn down the pitch. Miles should have worn some kind of protection, she thought. On the TV cricketers did just that. But this was Beulah. Helmets and face guards were probably thought of as wussy.

Justin was back near the boundary, polishing the red leather urgently again, feeding it with spit so that the stain of the ball created a long, dark mark on his perfect white trousers. He seemed oblivious of the catcalls from the tiny crowd. She couldn't work out whether they were trying to distract him or urge him on. Justin turned even closer to the boundary this time, to give himself a run-up longer than the wicket itself, then came racing down the grass towards them. The ball left his hand so quickly she failed to follow it. Then a red flash soared down the wicket, bounced once, closer to Miles this time, leapt up from the ground as if it had received an electric shock, found some impossible gap between pad and bat and removed the middle stump. She watched in awe as the long stick of wood, torn from the ground by the force of Justin's delivery, performed somersaults back towards the wicket keeper before burying itself back in the earth.

'Well done!' John Tyler yelled. On the boundary now, Mitch's impersonation had reached new heights. Squatting, quacking, making gestures which looked suspiciously defecatory, he wove a path through the jubilant dancers, only breaking off to point an accusing hand at the wicket, a gesture accompanied by a raucous, avian squawk. Miles had his bat under his arm and was walking, deeply disconsolate, back towards the pavilion. Alison realised she felt deeply, deeply sorry for him. What had occurred was some kind of ritual public humiliation and one visited, as everyone here appeared to know, by a significant party. Miles had been both cuckolded and bowled out for a duck. She could take the blame for one, but not both.

'I need to go to him,' Alison said, and started to get up from the table.

'Sit!' To her astonishment it was Sara who took hold of her arm. 'Alison. This is a game. Miles hasn't lost it.'

'Yet,' Tyler interjected, with what appeared to her to be glee. 'And even if he does, remember: every dog must have his day.'

'Wye go in now,' Sara continued. 'Justin will have to bat, in all probability. And Miles can bowl. It's not over.'

'Not at all,' Tyler agreed. 'I've watched your man. Miles, that is. The plod there has a lot of strength but he was lucky, in my opinion. Miles can outbowl him, on a good day. You'll see.'

She watched the hilarity at the boundary, where Mitch was still clucking his way through the crowd. 'Why are they doing that to him?'

'Perhaps,' Tyler suggested, 'they recognise pride and are waiting for a fall? Miles is a nice chap, but he's very full of himself, you know.'

'I think,' she said icily, 'I know my husband better than any of you.'

'Quite. Then perhaps they see two men fighting over a prize they both wish to possess. It's a possibility.'

'Oh, do be quiet, John,' Sara spat at him. 'He's winding you up, love.'

Tyler tried to look conciliatory. 'This is cricket as it used to be, my dear. Raw. Uninhibited. Forget about Lords and W.G. Grace. That was a Victorian invention. Cricket, true cricket, is about primitive combat. It's like all true sport. War wearing the flimsy threads of civilisation.'

White threads, she thought. In Justin's case so very white. 'Well,' Alison observed, 'I hope Beulah come out in the second half, or whatever you call it, and knock the living shit out of them. Even if it does cost me a tenner.'

'That's the spirit,' Tyler said, giving her a playful tap on the shoulder.

And Alison was very nearly right. After tea, with the sun losing some of its pre-summer power, Wye came in to bat. The two men in her life were on the margins of this early game. Miles fielded at the very edge of the boundary, behind Dickie Cartwright as wicket keeper, trying to sweep up any errant balls that escaped Cartwright's gigantic gloves. Justin sat in front of the pavilion, watching the play. She felt like wandering over and talking to him, but it was somehow inappropriate. There were sides here and she was determined to stay absolutely in the centre.

Wye opened badly, losing three wickets for twenty-five runs, and still Miles didn't bowl, still Justin sat on the sidelines. Then the visitors found their pace, settled into a steady rhythm, not spectacular, but effective, taking runs when they had the chance, keeping a weather eye on the overs and the run rate. She understood, from what Tyler said, that there had to be a resolution to the game. This was not like one of those big events at Lords, where men played for three or five days and still walked away with a draw. Wye and Beulah were playing a fixed period match. In the space of forty overs, one or the other would score the greater runs or be bowled out. And slowly, Wye was getting there, edging over the century, seeing victory in their grasp.

In the thirty-fifth over, Beulah rediscovered some of their spunk. Jim Barnes bowled two vicious yorkers that dismissed both of the batsmen who had done so much damage. Wye had started the over looking certain winners. At its close, they had just twenty-four balls left to make the twenty-one runs needed to win. The small crowd was silent now, but expectant, as much a part of the game as the players on the pitch. One of the Cartwright boys came up to bowl and had his man caught out with his first delivery. The next five balls saw the visitors down a further wicket, for only three more runs. Alison followed the arithmetic. Beulah was on course for a win.

She looked at the fielding side. To her horror, Miles was stepping up to accept the ball. 'What's happening?' she asked. 'Why are they choosing Miles? Hasn't he had enough rotten luck already?'

'Limited overs,' Tyler replied with a grimace. 'You can't just leave your best bowlers on all the time. You have to share it out among the team. It's the rules. I imagine Barnes thinks it's time for Miles to pull his weight.'

Sara let out a moan. 'Oh wonderful, John! And if he makes a pig's ear of it?'

'If he fights the good fight . . .' Tyler said. 'This *is* a contest, you know.'

Miles tore down the grass and delivered a scorching ball that caught the Wye player full in the chest. Alison winced. It must have hurt like hell. The crowd was howling again, mocking the pain.

'Damned barbaric,' Alison complained.

'Cricket, my dear,' Tyler replied, and they watched Miles

thunder towards them again, launch a curving delivery down the wicket, one that swung tremendously, in ways that defied the law of physics, then deftly removed both bails and downed the outside leg stump.

'Whoa!' Tyler yelled and punched the air. The dejected batsman hobbled back to the pavilion. He seemed to be in real physical pain.

Miles fluffed the next two balls. The fifth delivery went wide. The sixth got well and truly clobbered for a four that clattered straight up the wooden steps of the pavilion. Tyler harrumphed. Alison remembered what Miles had said, and she had duly passed on to Justin. The first three balls were good ones; the rest just went to pieces. She prayed the two of them would never face each other across the pitch.

The Cartwright boy took the next over and got knocked all over the Minnis. Wye needed sixteen runs to win at the start. The doughty Ashford fireman who faced Cartwright for most of the over duly reduced that to just six with a couple of fours and two singles. The last ball left him facing Miles for the final over. A slower, surer delivery tempted the batsman out of his crease, he swept wildly at the veering ball and was caught trying to hook it behind.

Alison closed her eyes, knowing what would happen next. When she opened them, Justin was walking to the crease, looking nervous. Miles stood, a distant figure in off-white, tossing the ball up and down in his hand.

'Is he good?' Tyler asked. 'As a batsman, that is?'

'I don't know,' Alison hissed, and watched Justin try to settle in at the crease. In the distance, Miles began to run. He looked wild-eyed, like a charging bull.

The ball came out of his hand like a missile, streaked down the pitch and hit Justin full in the stomach without bouncing. He doubled over in agony. Alison screamed in anger. The tiny crowd was roaring again.

337

'I say,' Tyler objected. 'That's really not on. I wouldn't have expected that of Miles.'

'Dammit,' Alison yelled. 'He might be hurt. You're a doctor. Go take a look.'

He put up his hand defensively. 'If I'm asked. *Only* if I'm asked. No pain, no gain, as they say. Plod is the last man, you know. If he retires, Wye have lost it.'

They watched Justin drag himself to his feet, wipe his face with his shirtsleeve, and face Miles once more. Alison whispered to herself: *don't touch it, don't touch it.* The ball whizzed down the pitch, so close to the off stump that the bail appeared to move. The crowd whistled in disappointment, John Tyler with them. Mitch was back doing his duck act again, quacking up and down the boundary. Beulah scented success.

Miles's fourth ball thundered into the earth in front of Justin then rocketed up from the grass. He ducked swiftly, avoiding being rendered unconscious by no more than a couple of inches, Alison judged.

'This,' she said, 'is ridiculous. He's not trying to bowl him out. He's trying to cripple him.'

'Nothing outside the rules, you know,' Tyler observed. 'Although it's not exactly sporting, I'll agree. Still, two balls, six runs to go. It's pretty much a foregone conclusion, isn't it?'

The penultimate ball followed the same path as its predecessor, but connected this time. Justin was caught on the side of the head and went down with an audible yell that rang across the common. The crowd clucked with glee.

'John . . .' Alison said firmly. 'This has got to stop.'

'Why are you telling me? All he has to do is walk, you know.'

Justin lay curled on the ground. One of the umpires, a sheep farmer in Stowting, walked over and spoke to him. Slowly, he rose to his feet. A chorus of catcalls came from the crowd, Bella's drunken, high-pitched tones leading the voices. A fiddle played a short snatch of jig and was then silenced. One ball, six runs short, Justin Liddle faced Miles Fenway on the bright green sward of the Minnis.

It was, Mitch Blamire averred later, a perfect ball. The final delivery, launched after a long, deliberate run-up, swung through the early-evening air to bounce six inches in front of the wicket, its eye already set firm on the centre stump. By this stage the stricken, aching Justin was moving. Something in his memory stirred, something that recalled the laws of physics and how they applied to the racing, force-filled mass that is the cricket ball. There was no energy left in his body, by this stage, to take that surging missile and turn its momentum around with a sudden, powerful stroke of the bat. Justin had decided, before the ball was even out of Miles's hand, to take the altogether riskier route.

As it flew towards him, he moved forward and to one side, arcing the bat to his shoulder, trying to synchronise its motion with that of the ball. When the speeding missile shot past on its path to the stump, Justin's arm was already falling, the bat before it like a scythe cropping ripe corn. The willow swept backwards, picked up leather before the wicket, hove it into the air, conjoining the power of both fast-moving objects.

The ball rose over the stumps into the air, flew out over the Minnis, out towards the pub. The crowd was silent. Every figure on the pitch was still. Nothing seemed to move in this frozen world except the racing red orb that Justin had lifted from the earth, ripped free of gravity and sent spinning through the air.

John Tyler stared at the pitch, with its still figures, and assessed the object growing before them.

'Fucking hell,' he gasped, wide-eyed. *'Duck!'*

All three of them dived beneath the cover of the bench table. Something spun over their heads, whistling as it cut through the air, then broke noisily through one of the arched windows of the pub and shattered into tiny pieces Norman's favourite bottle of Laphroaig before dropping, spent and fatally scratched by broken glass, into a newly opened carton of cheese and onion crisps on the floor behind the bar.

On the pitch, the umpire gave the sign: *six*. Wye's tiny team of supporters jumped up and down from their position by the coach.

'Behold,' Tyler said, astonished. 'The sun king in his ascendancy.'

No one heard him. Sara felt too ill, was holding her stomach, wondering what was happening there. Alison was racing across the grass, heart pumping, seeing the way the crowd had erupted, set its eyes on Justin, and dashed across the pitch towards him. She remembered Burning Man. She recognised the look in their eyes, and her voice was fighting to form the words, to scream, *'No, no, no . . .'*

They got there first, Mitch Blamire at their head, Bella and the dancers not far behind. Even Granny Jukes was following, her electric wheelchair running gently across the Minnis grass.

The Beulah team was leaving the pitch. Miles was a distant, miserable-looking figure, almost on the pavilion steps. Wye seemed baffled by their reception. Chaos was loose in the world.

Feeling faint and short of breath, Alison watched Mitch race up to Justin, leaning now on his bat, pull back his great, thick arms, like tree trunks, and throw them round Justin's pained, exhausted frame. Then heave him into the air, with others coming to the fray.

Justin's long, white body rose above them all, onto their shoulders. He smiled and made a drinking gesture. She slowed, trying to work this out. A cheer went up, and it was from the Beulah mob and the Wye crowd. Both were saluting him. Justin was the hero and looked the part. They paraded him along the wicket, a raucous, happy rabble.

Alison drew to a halt next to them, too shocked, too lost for words to try to take part. There was a mechanical sound next to her and Granny Jukes hove to her side, a bottle of brown ale lodged in the lap of her ancient dress.

The old woman looked at Justin, gave a great grin, then stared at Alison, something like pride in her eyes. 'There,' she said over the row. 'Didn't I say he'd won yer? And you thinking I was off me head. There'll be mischief tonight, me girl.'

'No one wins me,' Alison said, as much to herself as the old woman. Justin was loving it. But there was blood on his face, where Miles had struck him with one of those vicious deliveries. In a sense, she thought, there was more than a tournament here. There was a sacrifice too.

'Well, aren't you the clever dick?' Granny observed, in a light, pleasant way. 'You should come see my windmill some time, young 'un. Might learn something.'

Everything was fine. Everything would work out, she felt sure of that. Alison tried to straighten her wayward hair, tried to feel respectable. 'I'd like that, Granny. Some time soon.'

'Mebbe,' the old woman said. 'But not so soon I reckon. You ought to be looking after yer pal.'

The two of them looked back at the pub. Sara was flat on her back close to the front door, legs open, mouth moving, Tyler by her side.

A long howl of pain drifted across the Minnis, rending the soft, early-evening air.

MIDSUMMER

On the second Monday of June, Alison Fenway stood in the front room of Crabtree Lodge, beaming into the plump, rosy face of Jamie Harrison, newborn of the parish of Beulah. Mother and son were in the very peak of health. Sara seemed set to shrug off the excess weight in record time. The child was simply perfect, a tiny bundle of pink-cheeked life, with Sara's pale skin, a random fuzz of unexpectedly dark hair and a face that teased her. Was Harry Blamire in there somewhere? She dismissed the thought. It was wrong even to admit it into her head, though there was a resemblance, perhaps. And with it came dark, subterranean possibilities, the memory that, if this was the case, she had, unwittingly perhaps, despatched young Jamie's father to a fiery, agonising end. They had lived in Beulah for almost a year now, yet the place seemed thick with dark, encircling memories.

She held Jamie in her arms, feeling the natural curve of his tiny body against her breast, wondering what it would be like to cradle a child of her own like this. Sara watched her, thoughtful, uncertain.

'I'm sorry,' Sara said quietly.

'For what?'

'That it's just me. I hoped we could do this together.'

'You don't need to worry about me. I'm a survivor.'

Those penetrating blue eyes peered at her again. 'Yes,' Sara said finally. 'I think you are, really. You'd have to be, all the wars you go through.'

'Ah,' Alison said, nodding. 'The wars. There are a lot, aren't there?'

'Too many. Do you think we can have a year off, please? You and Miles might settle down again, get you in the family way and breed a playmate for little Jamie there.'

Alison looked into the child's bright eyes and passed him back to his mother. He was wriggling, hungry. Sara opened up her blouse in an instant and Jamie fixed himself to the offered breast. The sight of it made Alison wince inwardly with pain.

'Alison,' Sara continued, pressing. 'You and Miles will be all right, won't you? This nonsense with Justin won't come to anything?'

Alison resented being pressed. 'I don't want to talk about this. Not now.'

Sara's eyes flashed with barely repressed fury. 'Well, I do. So you're saying it's not over?'

Alison felt a headache coming on. This was not the time for an argument. 'I'm not saying anything. Can we change the subject, please?'

'Not until I've had my say. Will you think about this for a moment, please? Are you really prepared to wreck your marriage, wreck your place in the village, just for some good-looking plod?'

'Dammit, Sara,' Alison barked back instantly. 'Don't sit in judgement on me. I've got two men in my life. You've got none. Maybe it's easier for you in some ways.'

Sara backed down a little then, Alison thought. The point was a sound one. 'I'm still worried about you and Miles, love. I still think you need to be careful.'

That was good advice and she knew it. 'To be frank,'

Alison admitted, thinking out loud, 'I'm no longer absolutely sure *what* Miles thinks. After that goddamn cricket match he sort of went to pieces. He spends more time in London than he did before, even though he promised he'd be there less. And, I don't know how to put it, he's just given up somehow. As if he's waiting for something to happen. For his time to come round again. I'm sorry I shouted at you.'

'Men,' Sara exclaimed firmly, back on the women's side again. 'It's hard to work out whether they're impenetrable sometimes. Or just plain thick. But at least he's waiting. Not many would do that.'

'Miles isn't thick,' Alison objected. 'He's off balance. Upset somehow, and it's not just about me. Hell, I don't know.'

'You could ask.'

'I could. But I don't think it would do any good. Miles is *terribly* English. We don't have that kind of soul-searching conversation.'

Sara took her by the arm. 'Then try, love. Don't just drift apart. You'll regret it. Miles is the one, you know. Not Justin.'

She looked at the two of them, mother and child, wondering what gave Sara, a woman who had chosen such a strange route to motherhood, the right to make this kind of pronouncement. 'Don't worry about us,' Alison replied. 'One way or another it'll work out. I spent too much damned time working to make things happen these last couple of years. Now I'm just going to sit back and ride the wave for a while.'

Sara eyed her suspiciously. 'Meaning you won't do anything silly?'

'Hope not. You know what's most odd? That this should happen here, of all places. I lived in Manhattan for more than ten years, most of them married to Miles. We thought we had such sophisticated lives. Out on the town. Watching

344

our friends fall in and out of affairs. And we never got caught up in that, not once. And then he inherits that funny old house and we come to Beulah. One year later it's like I've lived my life ten times over.'

'Yes,' Sara said quite seriously, 'but you see the difference? Manhattan is merely a city. Beulah is an entire world. The possibilities are endless.'

'Of course.' And Sara was right too. People didn't get ceremonially incinerated in New York, not in her experience at least. The city was wild by design and intent; Beulah merely incorporated savagery into the exotic richness of its own identity.

'You must make it up, my dear. You must put the past behind you – the rest of us did – and get on with your lives. There's really no alternative.'

'There is,' Alison replied grimly. 'But I've been there twice already, and I don't want to go back.' It was necessary to get this straight in her own head too. 'And I won't, either. I . . .'

She stopped speaking. A deafening noise had built up from nowhere outside the cottage, roared over them with a force that rattled the crockery on the flimsy sideboard, then disappeared as quickly as it came.

'Bloody RAF,' Sara complained. 'Seems like the low-flying season has started early this year. Why do they always pick on us? Why can't they go and pretend bomb Ashford or somewhere?'

'I guess even paradise can't keep out the armed forces. Perhaps they're envious.' Alison watched the tiny shape in amazement. Jamie hadn't even stirred. 'God. He's such a poppet.'

Sara unfastened the baby from her breast. He was sound asleep and snoring, blowing tiny white bubbles out of his mouth. 'Amazing, aren't they? You were saying?'

It seemed unimportant somehow. Alison wanted to lose

this fixation with herself, if she were allowed. 'When I came to Beulah I knew this *was* the place. *Home.* I never had anywhere like that before. Home was just a roof and four walls. Beulah's more than that. I can't explain.'

'You don't need to, love. It was the same for me. A perfect paradise. Except perfection isn't quite what you expect, not when you meet it face to face.'

'No.' Alison picked up the sheaf of papers they had been discussing. The partnership was going from strength to strength. The profit and loss account was steadily rising in the black. No mention had been made of the mysterious aunt again. The bright shiny new car that stood outside Crabtree Lodge still disturbed her, but this was not a time for further complications. Economically, if not emotionally, the future seemed secure. Beulah protected those it embraced. 'But what's the price?'

'Pardon?' Sara looked pale and tired all of a sudden.

'I couldn't help wondering. If we get so much from Beulah, don't we have to put something back?'

The baby woke up and gave a sharp, piercing squeal. Yappy joined in from the hearth with a pathetic howl. 'Bugger,' Sara cursed. 'Nappy time and I bet it's a gruesome one.'

'Sorry. I was just babbling.'

'That's true,' Sara replied, working on Jamie's all-in-one suit.

'I'd best be going. You've got your hands full. Don't feel the need to rush back to work. I'm doing fine. I just wanted to keep you up-to-date with the figures.'

Sara struggled with a forest of writhing arms and legs, 'God, you're an angel. One day soon, when he's behaving, we'll pop over to the Green Man and down a few.'

'Done,' Alison said, and with one last, lingering look, was out of the door, out into the fresh air of the Minnis. Summer was racing fast to the Downs now. Swifts and swallows danced above her head. The hedgerows were alive with sparrows, chaffinches and the darting shapes of robins. Balsam grew rampant near the blackthorn thickets: thick lush stems bearing the promise of a torrent of pink blossoms. Down on the distant plain by the main road to Canterbury the fields of rape made brilliant yellow patches in the hazy blue fug of traffic fumes. Here, high up on the Minnis, it was impossible to smell either the pollution or the harsh, cloying scent of the distant crop. None of the hill farmers grew the damned stuff. For them, the crops were traditional: wheat and barley and pasture for the flocks of tubby sheep that grazed idly on the rolling meadows.

Puffs of cumulus sat in the blue sky looking like cotton wool. Beulah was immaculate, impregnable in her isolation. Alison strode out, back towards the empty cricket pitch. It was nearly noon. The first cars had arrived at the Green Man, incomers looking for lunch. She breathed deep of the clean, sharp air, feeling how it cut through the cobwebs in her head. Then her eyes settled on the tall white shape of the windmill, set back from the common, down its own gravel track. May Day was a confused jumble of memories, some good, some uncertain. Among them was the wrinkled, perky face of Granny Jukes issuing an invitation, for the first time.

She changed tack, veered away from the path by the perimeter of the pitch that led to Priory House, crossed the road, strode quickly past the Tylers' house then turned down the lane that ran to the windmill. Close up, it seemed much smarter than she had expected. The woodwork was in fine condition, recently painted a brilliant white. The downstairs windows were edged in glossy black. A small extension had been added at the rear so that the living space was now more sensible; without it, the mill would, she guessed, have been no more than forty feet in diameter. Above her the arms of the sails were still intact, but bare, wooden stumps, devoid of fabric. On the big, primitive gearbox that joined the contraption to the body of the mill someone had affixed a vast metal circlet, locking the turning mechanism in place. It was now rusty, orange and disfigured. Many years had passed since the Beulah mill had ground the tough, gritty local barley.

Alison raised her hand to the large, brass knocker in the shape of a horned imp, then withdrew it. The door was opening already and behind, in a wheelchair, all smiles, revealing rickety, yellow teeth, was Granny Jukes looking rather smart in a clean white cardigan and floral print dress.

'Been expecting yer, gel. Come in, come in.'

'You're a witch, Granny,' Alison said, bemused, and was further amazed when she stepped inside the mill. She had been expecting something close to squalor and the dank, close smell of a home that rarely benefited from fresh air. In fact, the room was delightful: spotless, well aired and, just like Sara's cottage, packed to the gills with furniture and bric-a-brac.

'A witch?' the old woman cackled. 'You daft ha'porth. I saw you coming down the track. I may be eighty-nine and scratching at the casket but my eyesight's as good as when I were seventeen. Now you go get that kettle on and we'll have a cup of char.'

She did as she was told, watched all the time from the wheelchair. The kitchen was in the extension, with all the mod cons including a microwave. Everything about Granny Jukes's windmill seemed impeccable.

'Old Marjorie does it.'

'What?'

'The cleaning, of course. That's what you was wondering. How come an old crone like me keeps everything spick and span? Marjorie, that's how. She can be quite sweet when she feels like it, though I hear you think contrary. And to be frank with you, there's things I find less than satisfactory about her. We all do.'

Alison poured the milk into two teacups and placed the pot on the table, waiting for it to brew. The great Beulah tea ceremony . . . all the proper rituals had to be followed.

'What do you hear, exactly?'

'Like I said. You two's mortal enemies. Which makes no sense to me at all. Not unless you're planning on becoming the cat that gets the cream yourself. Well, are you?'

Alison couldn't help laughing. 'Granny, I don't even know what you're talking about. And even if I did, the answer's no. I'm quite happy just being in the background.'

'Can't do that in Beulah. You're either in or you're out. No halfway houses here. Thought that townie friend of yours would have told you that. How she doing then, her and the young 'un?'

'I just came from there. They are . . . in tip-top condition.'

The old woman picked up the teapot, poured and said with a grin, 'Well, ain't that dandy? Got digestives in the kitchen if you be wanting them.'

'Not for me . . . but if you'd like some?'

'Nah. You lose your appetite when you get older. Nothing tastes of much. Like eating straw. You mind that. One day you'll wake up and see it's all gone, just in a flash, and you'll be left wondering at what you missed.'

Alison sighed. 'Thank you, Granny. That piece of advice always sounds sensible every time I hear it.'

'You bet. So what do you think of my little home?'

Alison gazed around the smart, circular room, with its planked walls, full of old photographs and chinaware. A set of steps led up the far side to what she guessed were two further floors above.

'Not much use to me now,' Granny Jukes said. 'Can't make them stairs any more, so the social paid for me extension. Now I got a little bedroom right next to the kitchen over there. Right handy. I get around on me frame, make a cup of tea when I want it.'

Alison couldn't help but be impressed. By the mill, and its owner. 'It's beautiful,' she said. 'How long have you owned the place?'

The old woman shook her head. 'How long? What you talking about, gel? Jukes has always owned it. Lord knows how long it's been in the family.'

'I should have guessed. You must have seen a lot of changes around here, I imagine?'

Granny Jukes wrinkled her ancient nose. 'Changes? Not more than you could count on a hand. Motor cars mainly, blasted things. Me dad had it when it still *was* a mill, of course, and we lived in one of them tenants' cottages by the boozer. Money went out of that between the wars, of course. He went to work casual, on the farms, and we moved in here.'

'And after . . .' It came out so easily until Alison checked herself.

'After?' The old woman's eyes twinkled. 'You mean when I'm gone? No need to be shy about that. Everyone pegs it in the end, don't they? When I go, I go, and they'll have all the fun in the world reading out Beth Jukes's will and finding out I leave it all to the dogs' home in Canterbury. That's our secret, by the way. No regrets. I may look like a shrivelled old prune now, but I had my time here. Was Queen of the May long before Marjorie Tyler, or that poor cow Mary Wethered come to that. You just see this skinny old body now, but these bones have seen their share of life, believe me. Just 'cos I never thought a man worthy of marrying don't mean I never got the best thing they have to give a girl, do it?'

Alison smiled, not indulgently. Granny Jukes was as sharp as a razor. 'Queen of the May?'

'Or whatever you choose to call it. Not the name that matters, is it? What it stands for.'

'And,' Alison asked, a little excited, 'that is?'

'Respect. Keeping the village together, from generation to

350

generation. You don't get places like Beulah these days, and you know why that is? They forgot the ways.'

'What . . . ?'

Granny Jukes waved her into silence. 'Questions, questions. Stop asking, start listening. And feeling too.' She glanced down the path. 'Old Ma Tyler on the way here, gel. Why don't you pop up them stairs and take a look around the top floor? The view from the window's best in the village they say. You can peer right at the Froggies on a clear day. And you can give old Marjorie the shock of her life when you come back down.'

'Who am I to argue?' Alison replied, and walked across the neat, circular room, then started to climb the curving staircase. Judging by the amount of dust, it was scarcely used these days. The steps ran around the walls, through the empty middle floor of the mill, then opened out into the topmost part, a small, round room where the gear machinery of the sail mechanism stood at the centre like the silent, shrivelled corpse of a deformed giant. A long, narrow window replaced the opening where the original beam of the sails entered the mill. She stood on the metal box of the gears and peered out through the glass, out beyond the village looking south. Sure enough the distant curve of Dymchurch Bay stood in the mid-distance, a glorious blue under the summer sky. On the horizon, the distant outcrop of France was clearly visible through the haze. Alison stood at the window, feeling she could launch herself into the warm air from where she stood, open her arms and fly. Downstairs, the front door thunked and Marjorie Tyler's loud voice drifted into the room.

The top of the mill was a kind of attic, full of junk. Alison stepped down from the window and walked around the great mechanical hub, noting a ramshackle collection of old cupboards, tables, boxes of photographs, plates, papers and albums. The place seemed a physical representation of

Beulah's memory. If she could peer through every box, examine every photograph, read each word, she might, perhaps, begin to understand.

She ducked past an ancient, battered grandfather clock, stood up and was, for a moment, terrified. Something had enveloped her, a ghost, white and feathery, that came out of nowhere and descended on her face. It smelled of dust and flowers, its long arms flapped against her cheek, feeling like dead skin, and she would have screamed, as loud as she could, if something at the back of her head hadn't checked the sound, argued for reason, ordered her eyes to look again.

What had scared her was, when she regained her senses, nothing more than a dress. Long and white, with ancient flowers attached to the chest and shoulders, it was made out of soft, thin silk, almost transparent with age. It fell from a hanger attached to a beam, shifting in the light wind that came through the patchy tiles of the mill. And Alison knew, on the instant, what it was, knew with a certainty that defied explanation. Once, years ago, a younger Beth Jukes had become Queen of the May, before Marjorie Tyler, before Mary Wethered. This was the dress she wore on the day she was transformed. She touched the fabric. It felt deliciously soft and sensuous in her fingers, as if some power remained from across the years, a charge that had deserted its owner who now sat old and wrinkled in a wheelchair downstairs. The attic was full of gewgaws and baubles, books and memorabilia, that could speak more directly. But nothing, it seemed to her, had the power of this single, delicate piece of ancient clothing.

She walked down the rickety stairs, hand carefully on the rail lest she stumble. Granny Jukes was in her wheelchair, sipping at another cup of tea, looking beatific as Marjorie bustled around the room, dusting with a cloth, whistling an unrecognisable tune.

'You was a while,' the old woman said triumphantly. 'Enjoying the view?'

Marjorie turned and went bright red.

'It's a lovely view, Granny,' Alison replied. 'It's a lovely home.'

Marjorie stared at her, stony-faced. 'I wasn't aware . . .'

'Half deaf as well as half daft,' Granny Jukes interrupted. 'I heard her clumping about like she had boots on. Fair intake of breath at something up there too, if I'm not mistaken.'

The old girl was cunning. She never missed a trick. 'The dress scared me, I'm afraid,' Alison explained. 'Bumped straight into it.'

'Ah, the dress.' The ancient eyes twinkled with the same bright merriment she had seen in those of Jamie Harrison, just a while before. 'Stories that could tell if it could talk, eh?'

Granny Jukes looked her up and down, smiling broadly. 'Reckon that'd fit you, young 'un. You want to go fetch it?'

Alison scampered up the stairs without thinking. Behind her she could hear voices rising, Marjorie beginning to complain bitterly. The dress lifted easily off the hanger. A shower of thin dust came with it. The thing couldn't have been moved in years. She walked downstairs with it over her arm and stood in front of the wheelchair, feeling like a girl again.

Granny Jukes was in mid-lecture to Marjorie. 'Don't you be going on at me about gratitude, woman,' she yelled with glee. 'You do it 'cos you have to. I passed everything on to Mary Wethered good and proper. Bet you reckon that Cartwright gel ought to be doing the same for you too one day. If that ever comes to pass.'

Marjorie's face was redder than ever. 'But it's a village heirloom,' she complained, half stuttering. 'Not yours.'

'Arseholes!' The old girl was loving it. 'Me mam made it, I christened it. So to speak. You see them blossoms?'

Alison touched the shrivelled flowers on the dress, felt the crisp dry texture of the petals crumbling in her fingers.

'Picked them meself. Blackthorn and dog rose, summer of 1940 when those bleeding Germans was up in the sky getting knocked about good and proper by our boys. Don't need the likes of you, Marjorie Tyler, to come telling me what's mine and what ain't.'

'All the same . . .' Marjorie whined.

'Splendid!' The old woman's face was rent by an enormous, gap-toothed grin. Unconsciously, Alison had let the dress fall in front of her, as if she were trying it for size in a store. It was a perfect fit. 'Wear it. Just for me.'

There was a battle going on, Alison thought, and it was not one that concerned her. 'I couldn't, Granny. It's yours and it's precious to you.'

'All the more reason why I gets to say where it goes. Do as you're told. Indulge an old woman.'

Alison took off her jacket, then her blouse and jeans. She stood in her underwear, undoing the old, covered buttons at the back of the dress.

'Look at her!' Granny Jukes crowed. 'You think you'd get your fat frame in there, eh, Marjorie?'

'This is wrong,' Marjorie Tyler said firmly, the colour rising in her face. 'This is wrong and you know it. You can clean your own damn sty if you go on like this.'

'I'll help,' Alison said immediately. 'If it's a burden to you, Marjorie, I'll do it.' Then she slipped the dress over her head. The smell of old dust and ancient flowers was overpowering. Yet the fabric felt delicious against her skin. It shifted, clinging to her like gossamer woven from wispy spider web, as she took a few steps in her stockinged feet up and down the room.

'*Look at her!*' Granny Jukes bellowed. 'Now there's a Queen of the May.'

Marjorie swore vilely and swept her hand along the sideboard, sending an old blue and white Delft plate, kept carefully on a stand, to the floor. It shattered noisily into a thousand pieces.

'Ignorant cow,' the old woman yelled at her. 'You pick that up or all the world'll be hearing about your thieving ways.'

'I'll do it,' Alison said immediately, and went into the kitchen for a brush and pan. There were words behind her, harsh words on both sides.

When she returned, Marjorie was in the doorway, glaring at both of them. 'What I got, I got by way of right,' she said, quite calmly.

'Stolen,' the old woman repeated. 'Like some toerag from down the hill, and look where that got us. What one person thieves, another can take back. You remember that, Marjorie Tyler.'

The door slammed with a deafening noise. Alison took off the dress, folded it carefully, then put it on a chair.

'You take it, gel,' Granny Jukes said. 'I meant every word of that. You'd make a far finer Queen of the May than that old cow, any time.'

'I don't want to be Queen of the May, Granny. I don't want to be anything but me.'

Granny Jukes nodded. 'Well, in that case you just take that frock as a gift then. From an old woman who's grateful for all the help you're going to be giving her from now on. Marjorie means that, you know. She won't be back, and I'm not having those buggers from the social in Ashford poking around my home when they feel like it.'

Alison felt the lovely fabric, the warmth of the silk. 'Thank you. I'll cherish it.'

'You bet you will. Now get your clothes on and be gone. I'm watching *Countdown* in a couple of minutes and I like doing that on me own.'

Alison picked up her clothes from the floor and slowly put them on. Granny was right about one thing. She was in good shape. Whether it was the spell in the nursing home or Beulah, her body felt tauter, fitter than it had done in years. Without thinking, she bent down and gave the old woman a light kiss on the cheek, said goodbye, and, with the dress over her arm, headed for the door.

'You're too kind,' she said with a smile.

'Nonsense. That slip of a thing was made for the likes of you.'

Justin Liddle sat at a spare desk in Ashford nick, staring at the paperwork in front of him, hand poised on the phone. This was a stupid way to do things. The police hierarchy had been casting a suspicious eye over his clear-up rate in any case. Paternoster Farm had come to nothing. A couple of burglaries down the hill at Wye were still unsolved. They seemed dimly resentful that he'd found nothing to throw at Mitch Blamire too. If they recorded every incoming and outgoing call, as some of the lads suggested, it could be awkward.

He stared at the drab room and realised, with a rising, choking anger, that he hated this place, hated this life. What he wanted was a new existence, with Alison Fenway at its heart. And if her presence was impossible, then he'd go anyway. Alison had opened his eyes. There was, he now understood, a world beyond the one he had previously inhabited, a world where the only limits were those of the imagination. In her arms, with the taste of her in his mouth, Justin Liddle was free of duty, free of everything but the pursuit of some sharp, bright ecstasy beyond reason, beyond the everyday life that previously entrapped him. Like Eve, she had cast the scales from his eyes and filled him with a lust for this new world of wonder.

The clock turned seven fifteen. Miles would be gone to work. He dialled the number and heard, with a flutter of the heart, her warm American tones.

'We need to meet,' he said, and listened to the wordless hesitation on the line.

'I'm not sure, Justin,' she said after a while. 'I don't think this is good, for either of us.'

'I *need* to see you.' His voice rose in the empty room and echoed off the peeling paint of the walls.

'That isn't a good reason,' she replied coldly. 'Not for me.'

'You're not thinking, Alison. I've found things out. Things about Burning Man. You need to know.'

The line went quiet again. His heart skipped a beat. Was it possible that she had changed her mind? That she would bury these memories, these suspicions, and fall into line with the Beulah way of thinking?

'Alison.'

'I heard you. Why do we need to keep unearthing these corpses, Justin? Maybe it's better we just forget. About everything, you and me included.'

'You don't mean that!'

Her voice shouted at him out of the earpiece. 'Dammit, Justin! You don't know what I mean. You don't know the first thing about me.'

'That's wrong,' he said in a quiet, measured voice, thinking this through, understanding how to hook her. 'I know you better than you know yourself. I know you're not crazy. I'm staring at the evidence. I know you're scared too, with good reason. Does Miles understand that, love? Can you tell him?'

There was silence again, but this time hope lived inside it.

Justin Liddle looked up from the phone, triumph in his face. Through the glass door Vinny Bennett, the duty sergeant, was biting into a bacon sandwich, giving him a sour look. Personal calls on station phones. Not a good idea. Justin didn't give a damn. Alison was coming back to him. Nothing else mattered.

She drove into Ashford at six, noticing the way the smog placed a thin film of grime on the back of her throat when she reached the bottom of Vipers Hill. This was a mistake, she guessed, but sometimes mistakes could be educational. Justin had understood how to push the right buttons; he was learning too.

The flat was spotless, kitted out with furniture straight from Ikea. It was on the first floor of a modern block overlooking the busy old road to Tenterden, half a mile from the decrepit town centre. Only the rumble and roar of the passing Eurostar express spoiled the effect. It was that, she imagined, which put such a bijou place in the range of a junior policeman. She coolly accepted his embrace as she entered, then settled into a soft, overstuffed chair, with a glass of Scotch.

'I shouldn't be here,' she complained. 'Life's too complicated.'

'No argument there,' he nodded. 'But you stumbled on something, love. And one way or another we need to understand what it is.'

He pushed a pile of print-outs across the small glass and metal coffee table that separated them. 'These are missing persons records going back ten years. All for the first two weeks of September. Quite a popular time for people to go walkabout actually. Kids go back to school and hate it. People go back to work after the summer holidays. Ordinarily I wouldn't read too much into it . . .'

Alison stared at the long list of names on the paper. 'Wouldn't read too much into it? How many names are there, Justin? There must be fifty or more.'

'Thirty-two in east Kent, to be precise. And remember these are the reported cases. Probably a third of people who go missing never get logged with us. Either it's a family thing or they're pretty much on their own and no one gives a toss.'

'That's a comforting thought,' she muttered.

'That's life. It wouldn't happen in Beulah, of course. Nothing goes unnoticed there, though whether even a missing person would get notified to the nick is a moot point. These figures are pretty much in line with national averages. What gets interesting, though, is when you look at the detail.'

He leaned forward and, with a yellow highlighter, ran through seven names on the list. 'These are odd. They're all men and women aged between twenty-two and thirty-five. They all go missing around the middle of September. And they're real mysteries. All the families of missing people say they can't understand why they should have taken off, of course. Some of them are even telling the truth. But these people really do seem the genuine article. And every one of them had a job that took them away from home. Lorry drivers. Couriers. Travelling sales staff. An air stewardess. So it took a while for their absence to be noted.'

She looked at the dates. 'It was last year I saw someone on the fire, Justin, and you don't have a name for then.'

'No. That's just the way the paperwork pans out. There was a fair on at Folkestone. When it packed up and moved on to Hastings one of the ride attendants never turned up. They reported him missing to Hastings, not to Kent, so he's not on our files. Took a little detective work to track that one down. Mark Horrocks, twenty-three, originally from Bromley. Never seen since.'

She tried to remember what she had seen in the fire. 'A fairground attendant? Surely they just drift about all the time?'

'Perhaps. But the fair people say this one was dead straight and absolutely reliable. That's why they reported him in the first place.'

'So what are you saying here? Is it really what I think?'

Justin shrugged. 'If they're capable of killing one person in the way you suggest, they're surely capable of killing more. And here's something else.' He pointed at five consecutive years. 'If the theory holds and the ones I've outlined fit the bill then maybe they alternate, male and female, in consecutive years.'

She thought rapidly. It was a man she'd seen in the fire. There'd been the fight. These two had to be connected. So this year by rights it ought to be a woman. Perhaps Marjorie was already measuring her for the part; the thought chilled her but had some missing thread of logic within it too. The dead man of the previous year was a stranger. Even Beulah would not sacrifice one of its own. 'Too fast, Justin. I found it hard enough to believe someone died last year. Now you're telling me they do it annually, like a village fete? Why, for God's sake?'

He had his incisive expression on. 'You know the answer to that. You know it better than I do.'

He was right too. 'Because,' she suggested, 'that's the real ritual. The one that matters. All the rest is a prelude. Burning Man keeps the village whole. It protects Beulah from the poison of the outside world.'

She felt breathless. If there were even a grain of truth in the idea then something was amiss. Burning Man had not cured Beulah. Some darkness was abroad, sending Harry

Blamire, and later his brother, into her bedroom, despatching the more vicious of the twins to a fiery death at Paternoster Farm.

'I think that's what I'm getting at,' Justin said quietly. 'It's serial murder, deliberate, cold-blooded. And maybe it's always been like this.'

She found it hard to squeeze all the possibilities into her head. 'You mean going back to our old friend Prior Fenway and those guys in the Middle Ages?'

'No!'

She wished Justin would stop looking at her as if she were stupid. Then it dawned, and the idea seemed much worse than anything she had previously imagined. 'Oh, my God. You mean right back from for ever?'

'Precisely.' He nodded. 'How old could something like this be? You look at what we like to call primitive cultures and they have rites going back to the Stone Age. We don't because we're civilised. Beulah isn't, not precisely. As John Tyler always points out, the Church just ripped off a load of old pagan rituals. Why shouldn't Beulah have kept the oldest of all?'

The thought horrified her, horrified Justin too judging by the pale, wary look in his face.

'They had to adapt it, of course,' he continued. 'From time to time they got caught, even when Prior Fenway was around. But you could probably hide that pretty easily for most of the time, until recently. And then, what do you know? Some company happens to build a disposal plant on communal land. It adds some money to the parish coffers *and*, just as importantly, allows them to get rid of any incriminating remains.'

She did not want to believe this. 'Someone would see, Justin. Someone from outside. They couldn't get away with it, not year in, year out.'

'Really? You said yourself that whatever was inside the

Burning Man was very well hidden. You only saw it because you were in an odd position, and perhaps something went wrong. Even then, you'd have thought you were mad if you hadn't found some evidence to suggest otherwise the following day. And remember. This is Beulah. Where there's never any trouble. We don't police the event. We don't police *any* events up there.'

Something still didn't make sense. 'There's a much easier explanation.'

'Which is?'

'Perhaps this did go on. Perhaps even after all that trouble way back when. But it stopped. These are odd people but they're not murderers. I spent some time with Granny Jukes yesterday. She's a sweetie. She was chief prefect once, handed it on to the late Mary Wethered who had it snatched from her by Marjorie. Sure, Granny went along with the dancing and the wild ways. I don't doubt that. But I don't see her killing people on an annual basis.'

Justin sighed. He was as uncertain about his original hypothesis as she. 'So what did happen?'

'You said it yourself. John and Marjorie Tyler. The village has been dying for twenty years or more. They offered the radical alternative. Killed Mary Wethered and instigated the old regime. Midnight naked dancing *and* the sacrificial rota. Look at your own records. These missing people happen under Marjorie's reign. Did you go any further back?'

'Only a little,' he admitted. 'It starts to get a little fuzzy beyond that.'

She patted the back of his hand. 'Occam's Razor. The simplest answer is usually the right one. The Tylers are fundamentalists. They think the only way they can pro-tect their precious piece of England intact is by reviving the old ways. And now people are too scared to speak out, probably because the Blamires were strong-arming on Marjorie's behalf. Then Miles and I turn up and suddenly an alternative's on hand. Marjorie's crazy enough to think I might oust her and put things straight again.'

Justin shook his head. 'But why you? It doesn't make sense.'

'You should have seen Granny Jukes fitting me out with her old ceremonial dress yesterday. And the way Marjorie went white when she understood what was going on. As far as the Tylers are concerned, their kingdom's under siege. You know it's mad. I know it's mad. But, as you remind me perpetually, Beulah rules aren't the same as ours.'

'Why not Sara or someone?'

She tried to shape the words carefully. The conversation was approaching dangerous ground. 'Sara won't do it. So who might that someone be, Justin? Beulah is dying. Look at it from their perspective: Paradise is being depopulated.'

'All the same,' he insisted. 'An American, of all people?'

'Thanks,' she said with a grin. 'It's not me personally, although maybe that story I told them about my witchy ancestors helped. It's Miles. The Fenway line. My guess is that Emily left him the place deliberately in the hope that the rest of the village would grasp the opportunity to set things right. Marjorie tried damned hard to head this off at the pass by enrolling me as her number two. And, not realising what I was doing, I pissed her off no end by refusing the job. What other explanation can there be?'

'So she thinks that one day you'll be the new Queen of the May?'

She nodded. 'That's the long and short of it.'

Justin stared at the papers on the table, avoiding her eyes. 'Does Miles know? Does he understand she's threatening you?'

'Miles is . . . so busy,' she stuttered.

'Too busy to be told his wife's in danger? Or that she miscarried with what he thought was his child because Marjorie Tyler arranged it?'

363

The room was hot. The purple wallpaper seemed livid. A Eurostar train passed by with a deafening roar, shaking the walls. Justin got up, came and knelt beside her and took her hands in his.

'Miles . . . is my husband. He cares deeply for me. He'd die for me, Justin. There are things I can't tell him. Such as us.'

'He *knows* about us,' Justin said, and ran his fingers through her hair. 'And that's no reason not to tell him about this.'

Lies did not come naturally to her. She lacked the glib mental agility necessary for successful deceit. 'Sometimes you just have to trust me,' she said lamely.

'But I don't, not on this.' He kissed her softly on the mouth. She closed her eyes and there, right on cue, praying to be released, was the memory of that night in Paternoster Farm, Harry Blamire disappearing into the flaming maw of the vat. 'You haven't told Miles because you daren't. There was another death last autumn.'

'No,' she said slowly, drawing away from his embrace, aware that her eyes were streaming now. 'Not now.'

The small, neat, antiseptic room swam lazily in front of her eyes. She felt breathless, the guilt rising in her gorge like bile. Justin bent forward and kissed her damp cheek once more.

'You have to tell me,' he whispered. 'I'm not Miles. I can listen. I don't think you're crazy.'

Sometimes there was nothing to do but find the impulse, stare it in the face, ride it back to nowhere.

She stood up and went through the open bedroom door, kicking off her shoes, unfastening the buttons on her blouse, filled with some desperate urge to be naked in this small, hot room, because this was a state of innocence and sweetness, a place beyond lies and thoughts and visions that rose like bile from some dark corner of her memory. A dim phosphor light shone orange through the thin curtains. Somewhere in the night car tyres screeched. This was, she sensed, a moment when it was possible to turn her back on Justin Liddle and the world of the plain, shrink into some quiet, obedient Beulah shell and let events run their course. But Harry Blamire would not allow this; his was a demon that needed to be exorcised, in the oldest and most direct of ways.

At the bed, naked now, she turned and saw him following hungrily, something like victory in his eyes.

'Alison . . .' She placed an urgent hand on his mouth. No time for words. Alison Fenway clawed at his shirt, tore it from his chest, and mounted his struggling body. Astride him in the orange light, feeling for that urgent solidity to coax it to its natural location, she fell into the old ritual, arcing, writhing, seeing nothing in her head but Harry Blamire's death, understanding that this was the first step towards its banishment from her head.

There was a form of release in this outpouring of heat and sweat. Later, panting from the effort, struggling for the words, his head nuzzling her breast like that of some giant child, came the second.

The night was the colour of a raven's wing. Soft, insistent drizzle fell gently from the cloud-covered sky. While the world slept, while Alison Fenway twitched dreaming in the arms of her lover, two figures walked slowly out of Sterning Wood and onto the Beulah Minnis. A lone, furtive badger fled from their approach, smelling on the night air something it recognised and feared. The stench of modernity, of complex hydro-carbons poised between stasis and chaos, sloshing inside a metal can, accompanied these two as they walked, silent, but not unnoticed. A barn owl rose pale and ghostly from a low tangle of bracken and field maple, dropping the struggling shrew from its talons as the strange, noxious smell attacked its nostrils and spoke of that other earth, beyond the Minnis, on the plain. The racket of its wings beat up a vixen, crouched, low and silent, behind a thicket of wild marjoram, fighting to decode the night's blackness with its twitching nose, listening for the tell-tale thump of a buck rabbit trying to warn the warren or the measured rattle of a wakeful pheasant.

The animal bolted, brush erect, dashing beneath the bracken, fleeing this foreign stink and the unwelcome presence of the intruders. They moved on, across the deserted common, passing the still, dark shape of Crabtree Lodge where every light was out, where mother and child slept in the same small room. Sara Harrison lay dreamless in an ancient double bed with an ornate metal frame and a soft, down duvet where, almost nine months before, the beloved infant was conceived in a short, passionless frenzy of physicality. Jamie twitched and turned in a wicker Moses basket by the bedside, dreaming dreams more inchoate than any that had previously entered his head, seeing images and faces he could not begin to understand, sensing, on the chill early summer air that blew in through the cottage's patchy tiling, the same foreign scent that had dispatched the fox across the Minnis, sent the owl scuttering for the invisible moon, its talons bare save for the worthless stain of animal blood. The child awoke, screaming incessantly, a cry that brought his mother back into the world, hushing and tutting, offering her breast through the open-fronted gown, wondering at the suddenness of his urgent, terrified squeal, wondering too why he pushed the breast away, became calm, then fell asleep almost as soon as she was there.

The figures and their stench moved on. Past the Tylers' house, past the empty, neatly tended pitch. Here there were more houses, more people, but these were adults, their senses flattened, coarsened over the years. No one heard the velvet footsteps on the grass, no one noticed the alien reek they carried with them into Beulah's universe, not until it had transformed itself, sought another state of chaos, and by then it was too late. The transgression, the rape of Beulah's sanctity, had begun.

Fresh, white paint caught the stench of petrol. And, with an aching, final inevitability, the two conjoined, atom upon atom, molecule upon molecule, married in a metamorphosing heat.

Alison Fenway awoke, screaming, leaping out of her lover's arms. Her head was full of fire, the fire of Burning Man, a blazing, angry fire that consumed and transformed everything in its path.

Thirty minutes later, while she was still disconsolate, despite all the comfort he could offer, the phone rang. Justin Liddle, white-faced, confused, reached for his uniform.

The trail comprised ashes, blood and lives. It began at eleven in the evening when a Land-Rover parked in a pub car park in Folkestone had been stolen. In the back were three cans of petrol used for farm machinery and a set of heavy duty tools: wire clippers, a forester's saw, log spikes and mallets, scythes and hammers. It ended in Beulah, around four in the morning, after a zigzag path of havoc and terror.

Near Shakespeare's Cliff, at the southernmost tip of the Downs, where England met the Channel and a mythical Lear once leapt into nothingness, they had come across an ancient, high-beamed barn, the wood like tinder, scarcely needing the petrol to feed the flames. The blaze killed a new-born litter of pigs inside. They had listened to the high-pitched squeals until the racket brought an irate farmer out of his bed, shotgun in hand, screaming vehement threats, carrying a useless bucket of water.

This was, Beulah came to judge, the city mentality and its hatred of everything country: calculating and heartless, unwilling to let go until the dread round of deeds was complete. Eight miles on, after a measured, calm drive through the narrow, serpentine lanes of the desolate hill country, they stopped in the flat, high valley of Elham, entered a field full of Romney sheep, ripped open the bellies of three that were too slow and stupid to run away from the bright, dashing beam of their torches. Five miles further on, close to the dead straight Roman road of Stone Street, they parked the vehicle close to a riding school, hopped the fence into the nearest paddock and, with the hammer and the log spikes, blinded a mare and her six-month-old foal.

Beulah was next and it was almost as if they knew the village. The Land-Rover was parked in the lay-by close to Sterning Wood where, weeks before, Alison Fenway and Justin Liddle had sat, awkwardly rekindling a relationship that both had believed dead. From there, they walked, can in hand, across the Minnis, to the windmill, pale in the night, the smell of fresh paint still on the white, wooden exterior. It was close to dawn now. The first presentiment of light was on the horizon, rising in the east, beyond the scattered lights of Canterbury. The petrol co-mingled with the paint, spreading the flames, eating into wood that was dry and dead after two centuries of braving the gales atop the Downs. While the old woman slept, the mill around her became an upright, blazing coffin, flames licking from its foot to the tip of the ancient blades in under a minute. By the time she was awake, choking, gagging on the fumes, unable to get out of the small single bed by the kitchen, they were gone, back to the lay-by, heading for the plain, laughing uncontrollably, wondering how best to cover their tracks.

It was an hour before Dickie Cartwright rode his bike

across the Minnis on the way to work. By that time the mill was a blackened stump, like an old decayed tooth, and the flames had precious little left to consume. He called the police and the fire brigade from the public phone box outside the Green Man. Fifty minutes later – it took so long for the engine to navigate the narrow lanes from Ashford and work its way up Vipers Hill – a disconsolate crew arrived and found the man who had called them standing in the smouldering remains of Granny Jukes's living room, weeping, babbling, incapable of rational speech. By what remained of the kitchen, on a twisted pile of charred metal and cloth which had once been a bed, was an unmistakable shape, grotesquely deformed, looking like an ancient mummy recovered from some distant pyramid. Dickie Cartwright stared at it and cried like a wild animal. The firemen quietly damped down what flames remained and waited for the police. The smell of burning, and something darker, more sinister behind it, lingered over the Minnis, staining the boughs of haw blossom. Flecks of soot and motes of carbon floated in the soft morning air and descended upon the ancient cricket pitch, like snowflakes from hell.

No birds sang, not a single lark. Beulah was tainted.

'Justin.' Alison wished she could stop crying. He was in uniform, watching some more senior colleagues from Ashford walk through the rubble of the mill, turning blackened objects over with the toes of their shoes. 'Justin, this isn't what it seems. I told you. Granny had this terrible argument with Marjorie Tyler. You can't ignore that.'

He looked at the rest of the villagers, standing in a mute, angry gaggle by the ambulance. Marjorie Tyler was among them, looking uncertain, maybe even scared. Voices were raised. The little crowd was shocked and angry, and some of it seemed to be going in Marjorie's direction. John Tyler was nowhere to be seen.

Justin took out a neatly folded handkerchief and gave it to her. 'You shouldn't jump to conclusions, love. Whoever did this seems to have left a string of nastiness behind them. We've got reports of stuff outside Folkestone. We've found the Land-Rover they nicked burned out down on one of the industrial estates in town. They were just a bunch of joyriders out for what they consider fun. Maybe it all got out of hand. Maybe they didn't even know someone was inside the mill. It doesn't look like a house, after all. Particularly in the dark.'

'That's what they want you to believe. Trust me. Marjorie's losing her grip here and Granny was helping to twist it from her. She takes her revenge. I told you.'

'Possibly,' he sighed. 'But where's the proof? If we catch the louts who did this and they finger Marjorie, all well and good. But without that, it's just guesswork.'

He was right, she knew it, but that didn't make things any easier. 'You could search their house.'

'Why? We'd need a warrant. I'd have to go to a magistrate and ask for one. On what grounds? That she's a vengeful witch? That's going to work, isn't it?'

She stared at the tragic remains of the mill and said, simply, 'Shit.'

'Look. I know how you feel. But we need to take this one step at a time. We need information. So why don't you go over there with the rest of them and listen to what's going on? There's something up, believe me. It may be just what we need.'

Alison walked over to the small crowd by the ambulance, went straight to Sara, who was holding Jamie to her tear-stained face, and hugged the two of them. The baby, wide-eyed and baffled, seemed to be the only individual in the vicinity who hadn't been crying.

'This is wrong,' Sara said, very firmly. 'This is completely wrong. Things like this don't happen in Beulah.'

Dickie Cartwright, looking half mad, heard her and bellowed, 'Bloody right there, missus. Not ever.'

The crowd gave a mutual murmur of support. Justin was right, Alison thought. The mood was ugly, and it was not just directed at the anonymous thugs who torched the mill.

Frank Wethered, his eyes pink and watery beneath the ever-present trilby, pointed an accusing finger at the wrecked shell of the building. 'It was different when Mary was alive,' he said in an indignant, high-pitched voice. 'And when Beth was in charge, not that most of you can remember *that*.'

Sara stamped her boots angrily on the dry earth. 'Funny to think of it now, but she never was a granny, was she? Not strictly speaking. And yet . . .' The tears welled up again. 'Oh, bugger.'

'Moreover, Marjorie,' Frank Wethered continued, 'this is not a unique occasion. Beulah has been tainted too many times in recent years. I suspect . . .'

'Oh, shut up, Frank!' Marjorie Tyler yelled at him. She was red in the face, a bright, florid red, but her eyes were white and sharp and piercing. 'Stop talking such absolute bollocks. Are you saying I'm responsible for this?'

Wethered looked daunted by the vehemence of her response. 'I . . . I didn't say that. All I'm saying is something's wrong here. We should *not* have to put up with this kind of thing.'

'So what am I supposed to do?' Marjorie demanded. 'Erect a border around the place? Issue us all with passports? We live in the modern world, Frank. We can't avoid it. The horrible little bastards who did this pinch cars, cause havoc. They hate us because we have something they envy. And now and again they come in and get their revenge. We keep to the old ways. We do our best. It keeps us safer than most.

It doesn't make us impregnable, Frank. What do you think this is? Magic?'

Alison listened to her rant and the lacuna in her logic was so obvious it had to be challenged. 'But it is a kind of magic, isn't it? At least it ought to be. If it isn't, what's the point?'

They looked at her in silence, interested. Bella Cartwright gave her a secret, knowing wink.

'And you can shut your gob too,' Marjorie bellowed. 'What does some Yank incomer know about us? Huh?'

Alison left Sara and the child and walked over to stand directly in front of Marjorie, not cowed by her vast physical presence. 'Enough to understand when something's wrong. To know that the Queen of the May, or whatever you are, doesn't stride around like some tinpot South American dictator.'

'Hah!' When Marjorie laughed, she looked half deranged. 'You *know* these things, do you? All you know, girl, is how to nip into the woods with your tame Mr Plod.'

Alison extended a hand and, very deliberately, prodded her index finger into the flab of Marjorie's shoulder. 'My business is *my* business. What I do concerns me alone. You shouldn't judge things you can't understand, Marjorie. I'm no saint. I don't think Beth Jukes was either. Are you judging her too?'

Frank Wethered gave a laugh that sounded like an old mare whinnying. 'Beth was *no* saint at all, dear girl. She picked plenty of cherries hereabouts when she was younger, mine included. More's the pity none of us was good enough to wed.'

Marjorie glowered at him. 'Be quiet, old man. Your time's past.'

'But,' Alison interjected, 'everyone's time passes, Marjorie. Beth's. Frank's. Yours. Mine. The question is what do we do with the time when we have it. And Beulah's bleeding, isn't it? You're right. I'm just an incomer. A Yank. I don't understand the half of what goes on here. But I can see when something's wrong. I can *feel* it.' There was a loud murmur of assent from the crowd. 'Why can't you? Or are you just going through the motions?'

Alison felt a hand on her shoulder. It was Sara, trying to hold her back. She shook herself free, and the old saw – in for a penny, in for a pound – rose in her head. 'I think you are responsible, Marjorie. I don't understand how. There are people here who probably know that better. But you led us here somehow, and Beth Jukes knew that too.'

Marjorie's eyes narrowed. 'She had her innings. She was a senile old woman. Not worth the time I spent on her.'

'Are any of us, Ma?' Bella asked cheekily from behind Marjorie's vast bulk. A whisper of rebellious laughter ran around the crowd.

'Know your bloody place, Bella,' Marjorie spat back at her. 'And as for you . . .'

It came so quickly and she wasn't expecting it. Marjorie Tyler moved her vast bulk with an extraordinary turn of speed, pulled one arm back and punched Alison hard and low in the stomach. 'Any of your plod's seed up there we'll soon have it out,' she hissed, then stood gloating, hands on vast hips.

Alison had stumbled to the ground, desperately short of breath, vision disappearing behind a tumbling wall of blackness. The vast shape of Marjorie Tyler now loomed over her. A stiff boot kicked at her midriff, came back and stabbed at her cheek. There was the salty, iron taste of blood in her mouth, and voices, rising, crying, screaming.

Marjorie's presence retreated; a male voice, familiar through the hubbub, railed at her attacker, a harsh, admonitory tone of aggression behind it. Gasping for breath, racked with pain, Alison was too shocked, too confused to put

373

a face to it. She rolled herself upright, sat on the ground, trying to think straight. Uniforms were coming to her, policemen and firemen, and someone was holding Marjorie tightly by the arms, yelling at her, holding off the violence.

Alison felt grateful and looked at the man. It was Miles, loyal, faithful, predictable Miles. He must have heard something on the radio in London, she imagined. Heard of the trouble, understood the pain it would cause, and simply abandoned his desk, driven home where he belonged. To his faithless wife, to a cold, empty house.

'Miles,' she said, beginning to weep again. 'Miles.'

His familiar hand came down and patted her head. 'It's OK, darling. This nonsense is done.'

The policemen were with them now. She didn't even want to see Justin's face there.

Alison Fenway mustered all her dignity, and stood up. On cue, the tiny Jamie Harrison let out an exultant yell, registered her presence, and held out his arms, demanding to be taken. Alison laughed, and tasted again the blood in her mouth. Sara offered up the child. He came willingly, gurgling, and nestled in Alison's arms.

'From the mouths of babes,' Dickie Cartwright said quietly. 'You all see that, then?'

The crowd was silent, even Marjorie, who stood speechless, red cheeks glistening with sweat, a hint of apprehension in her eyes.

It was, she thought later, as if a gauntlet had been thrown, straight onto the verdant grass of the common. But by whom? Alison leaned on Miles for support, never once turning back to see the charred stump of the windmill or wonder what Justin was doing just then. Events had shifted into some new, unforeseen conjunction. And there was mourning to be done. For Beth Jukes, and for Beulah itself.

On the morning of the funeral, she opened her wardrobe and stared at the clothes inside. The white silk dress was back from the cleaners. It seemed almost new now. The ancient flowers had been removed. The fabric felt fresh and sleek, not something spun into being more than half a century before. Granny Jukes – Beth, as she now thought of her – provoked more mysteries dead than she ever had alive, and that made her absence all the more frustrating. There were so many questions she could have asked the old woman. No one in the village was better placed to answer them.

And, more. She *missed* her. In their all-too-brief friendship some bond had been forged, some recognition of kinship. Perhaps neither fully understood it, though Beth Jukes was a lot further down the road than she was. Her absence left an ache, and the manner of it made the pain a general one. Beulah had been shaken, harmed by this violent, murderous intrusion from outside. It was impossible for the village not to turn to Marjorie Tyler and ask the simple question: *Why?*

She chose a bright, patterned dress, sleeveless, modestly cut at the neckline. Beth would have hated being surrounded by black during her last journey on earth. Miles watched her in silence. She was still in the spare room, there was still this separateness between them. Yet a truce had been struck. In the inevitable comparisons her head made between the two men in her life, one truth had become unavoidable. Miles, poor, loyal, dunderheaded Miles (except when it came to money), was more than a husband, more than a lover. He was a friend, constant and true. It was Miles who had seen the opportunity Beulah offered to put her life back together again. It was Miles who stood firm when she wavered.

Gratitude could, she thought, be a more enduring emotion than love, and no less worthy either.

'Two funerals in six months,' he said. 'God, we're getting old.'

She remembered the day Arnold was cremated. Slushy rain in Godalming, a sanitised service in a crematorium that reeked of municipal efficiency. And thought, but did not mention it, that there were three deaths in the family this year. 'What a way to go,' she said quietly.

Miles seemed thoughtful. 'You can say the same for Arnold. But . . .' He fiddled with his black tie, reluctant to go on.

'What were you about to say?'

He shook his head. 'I don't know. These things happen and it makes you realise one day your own turn comes. And is it any stranger lying in a bed in some godforsaken nursing home counting the hours? I'll be damned if I'm having that.'

'So what do you propose?'

'Perhaps I'll take up hunting, jump the wrong fence and wind up in a combine harvester. Or get felled out there on the pitch by a stray yorker from your demon copper. Alive one moment, dead the next. It's the only way, really.'

She walked over to him, touched his face with her hand. 'Try to avoid it for a while yet, Miles. We've a long way to go.'

Hope left a faint flush on his cheek. 'You'd miss me?'

'Of course I'd miss you! What a thing to say.'

'I thought,' he added delicately, 'that perhaps I'd passed my use-by date.'

'Oh God.' She kissed him lightly on the lips. 'Miles, you are married to a bitch.'

'A *perfect* bitch,' he corrected her.

'Very well then. A perfect bitch. I apologise. I am not the faithless hussy you think. Really. It's just that . . . things get complicated sometimes.' And you, she thought, are the last person I can tell. Confessing to Justin was one thing; the complicity bound the two of them together. An admission of her guilt in Harry Blamire's end was entirely different. It would unleash all manner of demons, on her side and on Miles's, and if that happened there could be no going back.

'You belong here, Ali,' he said firmly. 'You belong with me. In Beulah. In this house.'

'Maybe.' This was, she felt, a time for caution.

'No. Absolutely. You just don't know it yet. It's not my time. But that'll come. Why do you think I'm here? I'm waiting. I'll wait as long as it takes.'

'I know.' And it might be easier if he wasn't so patient, she thought. A touch more anger, a little more fight could at least clear the air. 'That doesn't mean it will happen, Miles.'

'But it will. Like night follows day. Everything here is part of your healing. Part of *our* healing. The pain. The joy. The discovery. Even you and Sara. Don't you ever think about that? You left New York thinking you'd never work again. Now, between the two of you, there's a business, a sizeable one too. You've got a role. Things are falling into place.'

Something about his optimism was deeply depressing. 'I wish that child had fallen into place, Miles. I wish I'd woken up that morning and it had all been a dream.'

Miles took her face in his hands, chastely, to press home the point. 'And I wish I hadn't gone up to London that night. I spent weeks in agony over that. But don't you see, love? It doesn't matter. If it hadn't happened then, it could have happened any time. That's one of the things Beulah taught me. Life isn't something we can just plan, write down on a sheet of paper and wait for the events to unfold. You've got to live it, every day, because none of us knows what lies around the next corner.'

She tried not to laugh at the huge gap in his logic. 'But I thought you did, Miles. *I* lie around the next corner. The loyal, faithful wife.'

'Now,' he said, not offended, 'you are teasing me.'

'I'm sorry,' she replied meekly. 'Let's give it till the end of the year, shall we?'

'If you like, but it's not going to take that long. And until then, until you come back to me, you're your own woman. Do what you like. Find something inside yourself that you can hold onto. I can wait. It hurts, but when this is over, when we're together again, it's going to be the best thing we've ever known. Promise.'

Alison toyed with some jewellery on the dressing table, avoiding an answer. Perhaps she was pushing Miles too far. Perhaps he really believed what he said.

He looked at his watch. 'We need to be going, love. It wouldn't do to be late.'

And so, at eleven in the morning on Midsummer's Day, in the tiny hilltop churchyard of Elmleigh, beneath the shadow of the boxy Anglo-Saxon steeple, Beth Jukes was laid to rest. Alison had never been to Elmleigh before. The beauty of the place took her breath away. The churchyard was a narrow rectangle bordered on two sides by fields in which huge, ginger-coloured cows munched lazily, eyeing the mourners with a bored, familiar gaze. The patch was dotted with headstones, many cock-eyed and ancient. A ragged line of yew trees protected the northern side of the plot by the road. The coffin, unnaturally pale and shiny in the bright summer sun, came in through an ancient lych gate covered in lichen and ivy. This must have been one of the highest points in southern England, higher even than Beulah itself, which was now a distant, picture postcard image a couple of hundred feet beneath them and several miles away. Yellowhammers danced through the yew branches, flashing brightly between the dark-green needles. A lone bird of prey, a buzzard perhaps, wheeled overhead, caught in a torpid thermal. A pair of larks broke the silence, dancing noisily in the blue, cloudless sky.

Almost the entire village had turned out for the funeral, a measure of the respect the old woman carried. Norman, now in an old, creased suit that showed its age, had closed the pub for lunchtime and invited all comers to an afternoon-long wake behind closed doors. Frank Wethered wore a new black trilby. John Tyler was similarly funereal and alone. The Cartwrights were out in force, Bella silent, thoughtful, in a flowery top and jeans, while Dickie Cartwright looked like a man lost, his eyes awash with tears, bawling uncontrollably as the wooden box was laid next to the neat, geometric cavity that had been dug into the red earth.

Alison Fenway stared at the grave they had prepared for Granny Jukes's tortured frame, then turned her mind to the day: the bright-blue sky, the animals, the birds and, most of all, the people of Beulah, so strange sometimes, yet so certain of their place too. There were worse spots to lie in the ground. She could imagine, when her own time approached, feeling some comfort at the thought that there might be somewhere like this for her too. Beneath the grass, embraced by the shroud, the dead might sleep content and dream of resurrection. Then she closed her eyes and, with a cruel suddenness, saw the alternative: fire, all-consuming, merciless.

She blinked awake again and forced her mind to wander, lazily taking in the churchyard, with its ancient stones, like loose teeth in a shaky jaw. Names and dates surrounded her, births and deaths, the brief narratives of existence, the celestial jester's anecdotes that began in the womb and ended in the grave.

Yet even this peace was not inviolate. Out of nowhere the sky was brutally rent by a deafening roar, so loud it shook the entire earth. A gigantic, low-flying warplane thundered overhead, bucked and reared as it reached the hill, filling the world with its furious noise, raining the stench of paraffin down on them. The flowers around the grave tumbled across the grass, collided with the ancient headstones under the powerful wake of the aircraft. In the adjoining field the ginger cattle stampeded in a panic, their large, round eyes rolling in fear.

Dickie Cartwright waved an impotent fist at the plane as it veered off into nowhere, off to the next unfortunate waypoint on its journey through the ether. Alison Fenway breathed in the fumes of the other world, thought about Beth Jukes and the shattered sanctity of Beulah and began to cry.

MICHAELMAS

This was, they all knew, the poisonous summer. After the killing of Beth Jukes, Beulah and its people lost their mutual sense of balance. The season and the earth seemed out of order, waiting for something that would bring concord back to their realm on the hill.

This disequilibrium spread into the physical fabric itself. In the fields, by the hedgerows, in the lawns of the village houses, the earth seemed to fester, become dissolute, destroyed from beneath by rampaging armies of tunnelling moles, attacked from above by badgers and the frantic, destructive assaults of green woodpeckers, stabbing at the ground with their sharp beaks, fleeing in a caw of neurotic laughter the moment a human being approached. The gorgeous landscape was scarred. The livestock looked scrawny and feeble in the fields. The barley grew short and mean, deprived of rain, starved of some precious nutrient it had come to expect.

And over everything hung a close, enervating heat, trapped between the parched earth and the low, flat summer sky. The still, airless high-pressure system drifted in at the beginning of July and refused to budge. Capping the high ground like an invisible seal, it locked Beulah in a parched, atmospheric amber, forcing the carbon monoxide and chemical stench of the plains into the sweeter, purer upper air to make a cocktail that choked the lungs and left a dank, metallic stain in the mouth. Nothing prospered, save for racking coughs, relentless headaches and attacks of breathless, aching asthma. Few birds sang. Even the migrant swallows and swifts seemed to have deserted the village for fairer prospects, though the miasmic air was rank with food. Aphids and blackfly, winged beetles and vile, insistent bluebottles thronged the day. Thirsty mosquitoes and biting bugs disturbed the night, droning noisily out of view.

Yet no one moved. No one fled the village, even for a week of holiday. This was the waiting time, and it took its toll on all. Miles Fenway threw himself into his work with a vengeance, spending more time than he liked in the City, solidifying his position at the very pinnacle of the newly merged Mersons, thrusting the memory of the fateful cricket match out of his mind. While Sara moved slowly into the daily drudge of motherhood, Alison Fenway continued to master the conduct of their business, ensuring bills were paid on time, tax accounts filed, the revenues kept on a steady growth curve. Between the chores, between the nagging, new-mother worries, Sara still found time to work her particular magic: a consignment of Moroccan rugs bought here, a container of hessian wall hangings there. But all this happened down the discrete, disjointed medium of a phone line; nothing passed between their hands except pieces of paper. To Sara, who seemed the very mistress of the entrepôt concept, this was nothing odd. Yet there were times when Alison felt so distant from the process – never seeing these wares, never knowing whether they were, in truth, as lousy as Sara made out – that the very cycle itself, of supply and sale and the endless round of money, became quite unreal. This was a time, Alison thought, when they needed the tangible touch of labour, of life, and all that arrived were numbers on paper.

Dickie Cartwright became a man possessed, leaving for the

barren, desiccated fields at five in the morning, hitting the bar of the Green Man at the end of the day. Drunk, mute and inconsolable, he would return home most evenings around ten, physically awash with beer, incapable of speech. Angie took on cleaning work from miles around, even though they had no real need of the extra money. Day after day she would drive miles, out to Woodchurch, Chartham Hatch and beyond, to scrub someone's toilet or vacuum a dusty carpet, anything but to be in the village, with its nervous air of anticipation. Bella stayed in her room, playing Invicta Radio at full volume, thirteen hours a day. Frank Wethered took to walking his dog across the bare, yellow grass of the Minnis for hours on end, stomping blindly through the dead bracken, doffing his summer canvas hat to all comers, saying nothing, thinking nothing. The cricket team performed miserably. Jim Barnes announced he'd be giving up playing the next season, and no one made a move to take his place. July ran through all their fingers like sand. Lammas passed at the beginning of August, and there was no dancing in Sterning Wood, no lone couples entwined beneath the dank, yellow moon that leaked through the stagnant night sky.

Beulah was counting the days to Burning Man. Marjorie and John Tyler tried to maintain appearances. Each day, he would drive to the surgery. Each weekend, he would attend the cricket match to watch Beulah lose. Few spoke to him. The Tylers' reign was in jeopardy. Marjorie knew it too. She was scarcely seen outside the house, except for the one time, the single occasion when the village got a welcome morsel of gossip to break the hot, tense monotony of the season. It was a Thursday. Anyone close enough to the Tylers' conservatory would have recognised the pungent odour of marijuana, overlaid with the oily fumes of gin. A storm was breaking inside their lives, between them, spilling out into the world. Fierce words, bitter recrimination, and, in the last event, some physical encounter which, Beulah rumour had it, only Marjorie could possibly win.

That night, drunk and unsteady with drugs, she had wandered out onto the deserted Minnis, stood beneath the waxy moon and bayed imprecations at the world, at everyone in Beulah and beyond who had set in train the cycle of events that was now working its way towards the pivotal point of the season, the autumnal equinox, the night of harvest home.

No one came. No one called the police. The next morning, Dickie Cartwright saw her vast, unconscious body slumped face down on the damp grass by one of the bench seats just outside the boundary of the cricket pitch. He swore and pumped the pedals of his bicycle harder, heading off towards Vipers Hill and a day on the combine. Come breakfast time, Marjorie was indoors, back in her lair. John Tyler went to work with a black eye. 'Walked into a door', he told Norman when he drank a large Scotch, ignored, at the bar of the Green Man that evening. No one said a word. The poison was extant in the village, in all of them. And beyond.

One week after Beth Jukes died, the police in Folkestone had arrested those responsible: two youths on a spree, high on cheap cocaine, full of fury against the world. They knew nothing about Beulah. Only the chance turn of events, the cruel god of circumstance, sent them and their can of petrol to the odd, unfamiliar windmill on the Minnis. In the plain light of day, Marjorie was innocent, as innocent as any of them. Yet innocence seemed to be an absent concept that year, and not just for Marjorie Tyler.

Down on the plain, where the choke of traffic smog never really went away, Justin Liddle went about his daily business like a man trapped inside some permanent, ever-tightening nightmare of the soul. The source of his poison was different from the rest of them, more personal, more painful. It was the guilt of complicity, running, breeding, racing through his blood, like a virus without an antidote, a fever without a cure. It carried the scent, the fleeting, holy fragrance of Alison Fenway in the very cells that coursed through his veins.

Detective Chief Superintendent Barry Wills was a short, stocky man with beady eyes, an unruly head of greying red hair and a permanent vile temper. He crossed his arms, nodded at the sheaf of paper on the plain, grey office table and said, in a grunty Northern voice, 'Bloody mess, eh, Liddle. An' it's all on your front doorstep.'

There was something wrong with the station heating system. It had triggered, even though it was another scorching, airless day outside. Hot air was pumping out of the vents, turning the inside of the building into an oven. With the foresight of all 1960s architects, the creator of Ashford police station had, thoughtfully, ensured all the windows were sealed tight shut. So everyone was in a bad mood that day, everyone was looking for a dog to kick.

'Those lads that torched the old woman's place are out of the way, sir. That's good news, surely?'

Wills let out a tobacco-stained sigh. 'I wasn't talking about that, Liddle. I was talking about this place of yours. It's a bloody mess.'

Justin shuffled uncomfortably in his seat. 'I'm not sure I follow, sir.'

'Sadly, I can believe that. Look. Last year this Blamire character goes missing, dead apparently. Some woman claims she's run off the road deliberately. This year there's some mysterious incident where a woman is found injured, apparently self-mutilation. Then murder, pure bloody murder . . .'

'I think that's going to be hard to prove. More like manslaughter, sir. They were out of their heads. We don't even think they knew Beulah.'

Wills exploded. 'That's not the point I'm trying to make.'

Justin didn't reply. There was, he sensed, danger here.

'The point is: what the hell is going on? You've got this pretty little village patch. The worst thing you should be dealing with is a spot of petty vandalism and the odd cat up a tree. That's why we sent you there, for God's sake.'

'Thank you, sir,' he replied icily.

'Oh, don't get on your bloody high horse with me, son. No one's got any illusions about your future hereabouts, least of all, I trust, you. Village plod material, Liddle. Nowt else. And I'm not sure you're up to that, frankly. Not with what you've given us so far.'

There was a flicker of righteous indignation in Justin's head. 'Sir, you assume these things are connected. There's no evidence for that. You assume Beulah is my only responsibility. It isn't. I'm there part time, and for most of that there's nothing to do anyway.'

'I assume nothing, lad. Those yobbos aren't connected, for sure. But something's up there. If I believed in statistics – and I don't, by the way – I'd be pointing out to you that a little hamlet like that just doesn't get that level of serious crime. Not unless some of it's coming from within. But bugger statistics. It just *feels* wrong. And if you don't understand that, you're in the wrong job entirely.'

'I thought,' Justin replied very deliberately, 'we were supposed to rely on evidence, not hunches. At least, that's what I was taught.'

'Don't be smart with me, Liddle. You can catch joyriders like that. What's going on here is something much more subtle, mark me. Don't you get it?'

'Apparently not.'

'Huh,' Wills grunted, and took a swig of lukewarm tea. He sifted through the papers in front of him then threw one across the table. It was a short report; attached was a snatched photograph of Alison. 'You know this woman, Liddle?'

'Alison Fenway, sir,' Justin replied. 'Wife of a local banker or something.'

'I asked: *do you know her*?'

'To speak to.'

'What's she like?'

Justin tried to think quickly. It paid to be straight. 'American. Pretty. A bit neurotic. But then you can hardly blame her. She went a bit crazy when she lost the baby. I think she had a stability problem once before. When she lived in America.'

Wills pushed another photograph over to Justin.

'Sara Harrison,' Justin said, trying not to sweat. 'Village hippie. Works from home. Just had a kid.'

'She and the Fenway woman friends?'

'I believe so, sir. I think they run some kind of small business together.'

Wills's ginger eyebrows rose up a wrinkled forehead. 'Small, eh? They formed a legal partnership a few months back. Too early for any accounts, of course, but they have filed VAT returns. Looks to me like they're going to turn over half a million quid or more this year. *Small*?'

Justin looked at the report from Customs and Excise. The figures were startling. 'I don't know anything about their business, sir. Sorry.'

'"Sorry,"' Wills repeated. 'Sounds like you should have that word tattooed on your forehead, doesn't it, lad?'

'I don't see what this has got to do with these events.'

'Me neither. But it's *interesting*, isn't it? Amazing where a bit of gossip gets you. Now,' he said, pushing a third photograph over the table, 'this pair of oil paintings.'

John and Marjorie Tyler were pictured, from some distance, walking across the cricket pitch. They looked foul-tempered, as if they were arguing.

'It's the local GP. He works in a practice in Wye. And his wife. She's . . . a character.'

'A character, Liddle? Now tell me. How does this character get on with these other people here? With our Mrs Fenway, for example? And the late Jukes woman?'

There was too much to think about. All he could do was keep it plain and simple. 'No love lost, I don't think. Not unusual in a small village.'

Wills looked interested. 'Any reason why?'

'Marjorie . . . Mrs Tyler is sort of head of the village committee or something. I think she suspects Mrs Fenway has her eye on the job – wrongly, from what I hear. But things sometimes get out of proportion.'

'And Miss Harrison?' Wills would not let this one go.

'I think she's pretty sensible. Sits in the middle and tries to calm everyone down. Nice woman. Very bright.'

'Right.' Wills took the papers back, put them neatly into the manila envelope in front of him and folded his arms. 'So do you have any questions for me, Liddle?'

'Sir?'

'Jesus Christ, man! Aren't you going to ask me why I've had people up on your patch photographing the locals? Or do you know already?'

'I . . .' There was an explanation here, he thought, and remembered Alison's injunction: *Occam's Razor.* Choose the simple one. 'I did put in the book that I suspected Marjorie Tyler was growing wacky baccy for her own personal use. I discussed this with Superintendent Johnston and it was agreed we would take no action provided it never extended beyond her own home.'

'Ah yes,' Wills said, nodding. 'A little smoke before bed. That's where it begins, you know, Liddle. A little light relief, and then some more. Before long, you're into heroin and crack cocaine. Before long, you can feel the very pillars of society beginning to quake under your feet.'

Justin stifled a sudden, nervous urge to laugh. 'I don't think there's crack cocaine in Beulah, sir. I would have noticed.'

'Would you now?' Wills replied dryly.

'Yes, sir.'

Wills turned up the ends of his mouth in what was meant to be an ironic smile. 'We're done, Liddle. Unless I've missed something here. Unless there's something you would like to tell me?'

Justin inserted a deliberate pause before his reply. 'Not that I can think of, sir.'

'Good.' Wills kept smiling.

'So . . .'

'So what, Liddle?'

'So what do you want me to do?'

'Be a good village plod, lad. Keep your eyes and ears open. Tell me anything that matters.'

'About what, sir?'

'Search me, Liddle. Search me.'

Wills watched him leave the room. The young copper was sweating by the end. The perspiration stood like translucent pearls on his forehead. Detective Chief Superintendent Barry Wills knew the signs of guilt when he saw them. Beulah could no longer be left to the attentions of Justin Liddle alone.

It was Saturday morning. Alison stood by the back door of Priory House, fuming with anger, close to tears. In the middle of the lawn was a tangle of feathers, red and brown, pale down and long display plumage. There had been a commotion during the night: a brief squawk fighting for attention through the hooting of the tawny owls. Now the source was obvious and, stupid as it seemed, this could only be another sign of Beulah's growing dissolution. The pheasant, much-loved and so tame it had come to feed from her hand, was gone. The pompous, idiotic creature, that had survived at least one shooting season and probably more, had been snatched in the darkness by a roaming wild animal. The ridiculous venom of her rage worked its way into a loop of self-defeating frenzy. The bird had become part of her personal landscape, funny, alive, individual. And now all that was left was a pile of scattered feathers and a few traces of bloody tissue.

Miles came to the back door, looking a touch worse for wear from the night before in the pub. 'Oh dear,' he said kindly. 'You were rather fond of that old thing, weren't you?'

She felt like kicking something. 'Shit! Why now? It's all part of the sodding mess, isn't it?'

He tried to smile. 'I don't think you can blame Marjorie Tyler for the loss of your pet pheasant, love. Lots else besides, but not that.'

'All the same . . .' She leaned her head against his shoulder and wondered whether Miles had a point. It was just a question of waiting. For whatever would make them right, make Beulah right too.

'Tell you what,' he said brightly. 'We'll deal with it. Let me go get cleaned up first and then we're off.'

'Deal with it?'

'It's just a fox. And you gave me a nice, tight shotgun that's just the job for Mr Renard.'

She stared at her husband as if he were a stranger. 'Miles, it's a wild animal. I hate the damn thing, but it doesn't mean I want it killed. It belongs here.'

'Now there, my dear, you are wrong. That scruffy little

monster has been hanging round the village for three weeks. I saw it with Barnesey last week when we were out popping pigeons.'

'*Clay* pigeons?' she asked cautiously.

'Not exactly.'

It was too early in the morning for this kind of revelation. 'Miles, I bought you that gun because I thought you needed a hobby. I didn't think you'd go around killing things with it.'

He patted her on the shoulder, with a measure of open condescension. 'Oh God. You are so innocent sometimes. This is the country. Things get killed. Pests in particular.'

It seemed deeply odd to her. She had never once thought that Miles was capable of such an act. 'Well, let's leave the pigeons to one side. This is a fox. Four legs. Big, bright bushy tail. I hate the bastard thing, but no.'

He shook his head. 'It doesn't belong here. We saw it. It's downright mangy. It's a town fox, love. All the tree-huggers in Camden catch the blasted beasts, refuse to kill them, and drop them on our doorstep instead. They spread disease and pass it on to our native foxes. They're deeply bad news.'

'A town fox? Are you having me on, Miles?'

He looked instantly serious. 'Not at all. I wouldn't dream of joking about anything with you at the moment. This thing is a pest. I should have done something about it before. I know exactly where it hangs out.'

She hesitated and realised, immediately, she was lost.

'Look,' he said, 'we'll track it. When we find it, you decide. If it isn't the mangy, scruffy beast I say, then we'll let it go. I don't want to go killing local foxes. Not without good reason anyway.'

'Track it? When did you become the great white hunter, Miles?'

For some reason that seemed to offend him. 'I don't spend

391

all the time in the pub. We've been shooting almost weekly ever since April. I picked up a lot.'

'Obviously,' she replied. 'You promise? Only if I say so?'

'Scout's honour,' he said, crossing himself.

Fifteen minutes later, with the Purdey High Deco broken beneath his arm, they were walking down the garden, towards the copse that marked the boundary between Priory House and the raw, bare scarp that fell steeply away to the plain behind.

She looked at the gun. 'Do you like it, Miles?'

'Like it? It's *beautiful*. You've no idea how . . .' He stopped, unhooked the thing from beneath his arm, took a shell from his jacket, popped it in the breech, snapped the barrel shut and held it out for her. 'Take it.'

Alison looked at the weapon and remembered why she'd picked it. The Purdey was beautiful, a work of deadly art. Not a big, bulky, masculine prop at all. Gingerly, she took the weapon from him and wondered at its lightness in her arms.

'Point the barrel away from us at all times, it's loaded. Aim over the trees, out down the hill. When you feel ready, just squeeze the trigger. Don't pull.'

'Miles,' she said, 'this is ridiculous.' But the gun had a life of its own. When it was in her hands it seemed to move naturally to her shoulder, the twin barrels rose of their own volition until they pointed above the line of hawthorns at the bottom of the garden.

'Squeeze,' he said.

'Is this going to hurt?'

'Not at all.'

'But what about the fox? He'll hear us.'

'Let me worry about that. *Squeeze*.'

Her index finger wound its way around the finely sculpted trigger. She pulled gently against the measured weight of the mechanism, backwards, backwards. Then the air was rent by a loud explosion, the barrels jumped skywards and Alison felt a sudden sharp pain in her shoulder.

'Ow!'

Miles was beaming at her. 'That was good. Really. You didn't jerk it at all. Most people do.'

She lowered the gun and handed it back to him. 'That hurt, Miles. You should've told me.'

'Then you wouldn't have done it.'

That much was true. 'All the same . . .'

'All the same, nothing, love. You could be a natural shot, you know.'

She rubbed her shoulder. 'Bullshit . . . And, anyway, I couldn't kill anything. I'm not like you men.'

He was still beaming. 'Really? What if that mangy old fox walked in front of you now? Feathers on his chin?'

She kept on rubbing and said nothing.

'What,' Miles continued, 'if those murdering toerags who killed Granny Jukes were standing there? Grinning all over their faces, knowing they'll probably be out of the detention centre and back on the streets by Christmas?'

'Now that,' she said firmly, '*is* ridiculous. A mangy fox is one thing.'

'And murdering toerags something else, eh?' He broke the gun, ejected the smoking shell and put it in his pocket. 'I suppose so. Let's get him, shall we?'

They climbed over the fence at a gap in the rambling hawthorn hedge. The field behind was plain pasture with scrawny grass. Sometimes sheep grazed there. She could hear their low, baaing grunts from the kitchen. Today it was empty, just meagre upland meadow on a steep bank that pointed south west, out towards Romney Marsh and the distant, ugly outline of the power station. Thanks to the constant still weather, the view was hazy and thick with pollution. On a clear day the bright, sparkling waters of the Channel formed the distant horizon, with France beyond.

Today there was nothing much to be seen beyond the sprawling shape of Ham Street, with the railway line cutting through the middle.

'This could take ages, Miles,' she said, suddenly starting to think a fox hunt was not a great idea. 'And what if there's someone around?'

'Give it an hour and we'll see. As I said, I think I know where he hangs out. I'll watch for any people but there's no public footpath here. I've never seen anyone walking the dog or suchlike.'

She thought of Mitch and Harry, and the way they wandered through anyone's garden, peered through any window they liked. 'Right. As if people in Beulah really need public footpaths to tell them where to go . . .'

Miles gave her a withering glance. 'Think positive, dear. Trust me.'

She followed him to a thicket of low, half-starved black-thorn and they parked themselves on the dry ground. A scattering of shrivelled sheep droppings betrayed its former role as a windbreak for the flock. Alison wrinkled her nose in distaste.

'Shush,' Miles cautioned. 'We need to get close if we're going to get him with the shotgun. A rifle would be much better for the job.'

'Now you tell me . . .'

'Shush!'

And so they waited, for almost fifty minutes, not speaking, just listening to the faint breeze and the very occasional burst of birdsong. It was the height of summer, Alison thought, and there was only one word to describe this bare patch of ground on the Downs: *bleak*. It was an adjective she never expected to apply to anywhere close to Beulah.

Finally, when she was wondering whether to prod Miles and persuade him to go, his body came stiff with anticipation, his face fixed itself on a point where the hill gave way to sky, some ten yards distant. There, like the tip of a tattered paintbrush, stood something orange and erect, moving slowly, jogging across their vision.

Miles passed her the gun. She looked at him. And hesitated.

He lifted the barrel and laid it gently in the vee of the misshapen bush that hid them from sight.

'Wait until I say,' Miles whispered.

She mouthed, 'No.' And didn't move.

Ahead of them, through the branches of the bush, the fox emerged. It was, she saw instantly, an intruder. Its fur was matted and revealed dun patches of bare skin. It limped along, head hunched towards the ground, eyes half open, adopting a sickly, furtive gait. She'd watched foxes before, many a time, out on Vipers Hill, on her long walks beyond the Minnis. The native creatures were magnificent, a fiery orange colour, tripping across the fields, free, wild animals, facing the dangerous day, wondering whether they would hunt or be hunted. This thing seemed to belong to a different species, a mongrel, half-breed lesser fox, a kind of vermin that spoiled the natural order.

Around its muzzle was fine down, pale and soft, stained with blood. A long, reddy feather clung to its cheek. She felt the weapon come automatically to her shoulder, the trigger fall beneath her finger.

Miles, by her side, stared into her eyes, and she wondered what he expected to see there. Hesitation? Fear? She felt none. The fox was mangy. It did not belong. This was not a question of revenge for the dead, much-loved bird in the garden. It was a matter of symmetry, of equilibrium.

Miles scanned the scene once, out from the bush, out towards where the creature was approaching, on a diagonal path, and said, in a low voice, 'Now.'

The gun roared, made the same, familiar pain in her shoulder. Something squealed. The two of them shot to their feet. She had to look. The animal was a heap of fur and blood on the short, spent grass, its head half removed, its interior parts a tangle of flesh and sinew exposed to the air. Overhead a crow squawked, hungry.

And – this wasn't a dream – the dead fox was screaming, in a woman's voice, shrill and loud. The sound came straight out of the bloody hole that was once its neck.

Alison blinked twice. Miles said, 'Oh shit.'

A large, angry figure appeared over the lip of the hill, waving its fist. What looked like tiny spots of blood dappled Marjorie Tyler's flapping cheeks. The huge woman raced over to them, only stopping when Miles took one pace forward to check her. Alison held the gun guiltily and found it was impossible not to smile. Marjorie was not hurt, not seriously anyway. The peppershot must have carried over the hill, caught her as light, lead rain, barely pricking the skin. She was lucky it hadn't hit an eye.

'You could have fucking killed me,' she screamed, her voice high with rage, hands feeling at the damage to her face. 'He'll have to pick these fucking pieces out one by one.'

'Sorry,' Alison said flatly.

'Sorry?'

'It was an accident, Marjorie,' Miles intervened. 'We were after the fox. You can see that. We didn't know you were there.'

'We thought no one was supposed to be there,' Alison added. 'It is private property, after all.'

Marjorie Tyler raised a big, muscular fist. Alison burst out laughing, she couldn't help it.

'Oh dear,' Miles groaned, taking another step between the two women. 'Marjorie,' he said, 'you seem a little distraught. Would you like me to drive you down to the surgery? Get someone to take a look at that?'

The big woman glowered at him but there was defeat in

her face. 'I can drive myself, thank you,' she hissed. 'You haven't heard the last of this.'

She barged past, headed back towards the fence and the boundary with the common, public ground of the Minnis where she must have entered the field. Alison looked at the dead fox. Beulah was better without it, she believed. Then she looked at the receding figure of Marjorie Tyler, raised the empty shotgun to her shoulder, aimed and said in a quiet voice, 'Kapow.'

'Bad girl,' Miles said. 'Bad, bad girl.'

Between the end of July and early September, Alison Fenway and Justin Liddle met just twice. On both occasions it was late in the evening, in the little lay-by close to Sterning Wood. They talked. Once, the first time, they made love, crushed together on the cramped back seat of the Peugeot like furtive teenagers, neither knowing quite why they went through this ritual.

Intimacy was difficult. Alison's confession had changed the balance of their relationship. She wondered if Justin resented the weight of guilt she had passed to him. If that was the case, he didn't show it. Justin seemed preoccupied, and not just by the untangling of the mystery. Two days after they met for the second time, he called again, while Miles was at work. She was busy on the accounts. The numbers kept climbing and climbing. There was some serious juggling of cash to be done, and the complexity of the business was getting beyond her.

It wasn't the best of times to call. Curtly, she rejected his offer of a tryst. Alison was tired of the lay-by, tired of the needless deception. She wanted answers still. Wanted to know how Marjorie Tyler – and perhaps the downtrodden

John too – had engineered these misfortunes in her life. But Justin had few idea beyond those he had already proposed. Once a year, at Burning Man, someone went missing, perhaps alternately male and female. Miles, unwittingly by blood, and she, by marriage, appeared to be the rightful heirs to Marjorie's crown. Yet these were just motives and shadows, not the precise, cold facts she expected of the police. There was precious little anyone could do with them.

In some odd sense, too, this failed to concern her. Beulah was going through its waiting period, and the unravelling of the mystery was a part of that. Burning Man loomed on the calendar. This was Marjorie's opportunity to regain the momentum. She had to act, and when she did, Justin would surely be there. Watching, recording everything in his little notebook. In some unseen, inexplicable way, the solution lay within the ticking of the clock, the constant revolution of the seasons. It was a question of patience, and being prepared.

Then, just over a week before Burning Man, when the date was starting to nag in her mind like a distant migraine, Justin called once more, asked for a meeting with her and Sara, and the world turned again.

It was a Thursday morning and the weather was particularly vile. The sky had turned dull and oppressive. The atmospheric pressure was palpable, a constant, aching presence on the skull. Low murmurings of thunder rolled unseen overhead, unable to work up the energy to pierce the torpid heat and reach the earth. As she walked across the Minnis to Crabtree Lodge – Justin's chosen location for the meeting – she noticed how ill-kempt the cricket pitch looked. The grass that, last year, had been pristine green, as close-cropped as a skinhead's pate, was now dry and brown, with the occasional molehill disturbing the surface. The sky groaned and a few meagre drops of rain fell on her head. Alison felt as if she were walking beneath a floating ocean of physical tension that strained to burst on the world, drowning it in an instant.

Justin was there already, in a T-shirt and jeans, his private Ford Escort parked outside the house, the equivalent of a sign declaring 'off duty'. He and Sara were drinking tea in silence side by side on the sofa while Jamie slept, an angelic bundle, in a basket near the kitchen. Alison looked at them and felt cold. Never, in all the time she had known them, had Justin or Sara seemed as deeply miserable as they did that day.

'Well?' she asked.

'I came to warn you,' Justin said. 'I just want you to be aware.'

'Aware of what?' Alison asked. 'Justin, you're the policeman here. Can't we expect a little protection from you?'

He frowned. 'I don't think I'll be in the force much longer. I'll see Burning Man out of the way and then I'm off. I thought perhaps teaching . . .'

Alison wished he would just look her in the eyes once. 'Justin! What's happened? Why are you behaving like this?'

'I'm not this person, Ali.' For a moment she thought he might burst into tears. 'I can't live like this. Lying. Hoping for something that's never going to come.'

Sara put a hand on his knee. 'Justin. I can see you're upset but I think this is a private conversation between you and Alison. I can't help. Please.'

'This isn't about how I feel,' he said coldly. 'I came here to warn you. And to say I won't be around much longer to play these games.'

Alison watched the nervous, knowing glances they were exchanging and, in desperation, pleaded, 'Will someone enlighten me here? I'm not getting the joke.'

'There's an investigation going on,' Justin said. 'CID, I think. Perhaps from outside the force, I don't know.'

'Good.' Alison stared at them, still uncomprehending.

'You mean they're taking these disappearances seriously? Linking them to Burning Man?'

'No.' He sounded tetchy, impatient with her. 'I told you. I've no evidence of anything about Burning Man. They're keeping me in the dark, quite why I'm not sure, but I think it's to do with drugs.'

Alison looked at Sara for a reaction and failed to gauge the emotion running across her friend's face. 'You mean Marjorie? Fine by me. Hang her as easily for a horse as a sheep, I don't care.'

'I thought that originally,' he replied. 'But I was wrong. Tell me, Sara. Exactly what is it you buy and sell through this company of yours?'

'I do the books,' Alison interrupted. 'I can tell you down to the last damn number. Rugs and fabrics and gewgaws, bric-a-brac, curiosities, treasures from around the world, rare exotic delights, knick-knacks and . . .'

Her mouth went dry. Sara's head hung down and there was a stream of tears coursing down her cheeks.

'Crap,' Alison added lamely.

'Oh, stop it!' Sara scowled at her with a strange, intense ferocity that might even have contained a thread of hatred. 'Please, Ali. Stop it. He knows. Can't you see? *He knows.*'

'Knows what? Am I the only one outside this secret?'

'I think,' Justin said as tactfully as he could, 'that what Sara is saying is that you've been selling a little more than that. You do the books, Alison. You know the kind of money you've been turning over. Didn't it ever occur to you that it's an awful lot?'

She thought about the numbers, the strings and strings of numbers, and realised how deeply, stupidly wrong Justin was. These figures were abstract, distant entities, with no true meaning. All she had done was ensure that they stayed on the right side of the page and never wandered towards the danger zone that had to be written in red ink. Both of them took out a modest salary; the extra noughts on the figures were the distant cream on the cake, something to be thought about tomorrow.

'You mean . . .' She remembered going to London, the odd little scene in Camden Market, the hidden bundle of dosh. And meeting Marjorie Tyler on the train back. 'You mean you've been peddling dope, Sara, and I've just been your stupid, goddamn bookkeeper all along?'

'Don't say that!' The volume and ferocity of Sara's voice woke Jamie from some inchoate infant dream. The child mewled. Sara raced to the basket, gently plucked him from the tangle of sheets and held him to her chest. Alison watched the expression on his face and it almost tore her apart. There was such unspoken love within their shared genes. Jamie gave a single burp, went back to sleep. With a tender, easy precision, Sara laid him back in the basket, gingerly tugged the sheet over his tiny frame.

Then she came back to the sofa and, with fierce, tear-filled eyes, stared at Alison. 'You don't know what it's like, love. I'm not complaining. I'm not envious. But you don't know what it's like, being on your own. No husband. No money. No hope. I spent years flogging all that crap that's in the books. Working my fingers to the bone. And sometimes it worked. Sometimes it didn't. Two years ago it didn't work, not at all. I was in so much debt. They wanted to repossess the cottage. They wanted everything I owned. I didn't know where to turn.'

Justin peered at her with a remoteness Alison found distastefully professional. 'So,' he asked, 'you started shifting drugs instead?'

'Oh, yes, Justin,' she spat back at him. 'Just like that. Cheap Moroccan rugs one day, fine crack cocaine the next. What do you think?'

Alison thought about it and knew she was right. 'I think, in those circumstances, you'd do what anyone in Beulah would. You'd go to the person who's supposed to help and ask her. You'd go and ask Marjorie Tyler.'

Sara looked relieved she didn't need to name names herself. 'It's why she's there. What else could I do?'

'Quite a lot actually,' Justin said demurely. 'You mean Marjorie arranged all this?'

'She knew people. She's just an old hippie herself. She and John are always popping over to Amsterdam for whatever. And she got her cut. Oh, yes.'

Alison examined her emotions. They were shifting so rapidly. 'You got me involved. If all this comes down around your ears, it comes down around mine too. And I knew nothing about this, Sara. You could put me in jail.'

Sara stared at the Moses basket. 'Don't even talk about jail, please. I'm not stupid. I've been working out how we can ditch this whole thing. Just deal in what we're supposed to be dealing in. It'll cut the turnover but we can survive. In a couple of weeks, after Burning Man, after the village found itself again, I was going to tell you. Not everything. Just enough to make sure we got through.'

'Thanks,' Alison replied, not minding the hint of sarcasm in her voice. 'I'm really grateful.'

Justin watched the two of them and Alison was startled. Suddenly he did look like a policeman; something was running through his head. 'Why did you get Alison involved?' he asked.

'She knows. I needed the help.'

He said nothing, waited.

Please! Sara looked as if she were in agony.

Alison stared at her friend, in shock, but in sympathy too. 'Marjorie told you to, didn't she? That was all part of the plan. To get her talons into me.'

'She could kill you, Sara. She could kill any one of us. Believe me.'

The long, convoluted chain of events began to unravel in

Alison's head, and there were so many complex possibilities. 'She told you to wrap me up in the business. And what else? The accident?'

Sara closed her eyes for a moment and, in spite of the betrayal, Alison hated herself for pressing these questions. 'I ran off the road, Ali. That's all. There was no other driver. Marjorie just wanted you scared. Scared and dependent, so that you'd rely on her for security, protection, just like the rest of us. That's why she wanted me to wind you up about Paternoster Farm. Invent anything I could to make you more likely to see her as your guardian. She was frightened when Miles and you came to the house. Miles may not have a clue what's going on here, but you're smarter, you can see.'

That's right, Alison thought. Blame it on me. Blame everything on me.

'You wound Marjorie up,' Sara continued. 'All that stuff about you being one of the New England Parkers. Ancestors burnt at the stake and the rest. She went on and on about that. Marjorie's got no sense of humour. No sense of irony. She took you at face value. You either became an acolyte like the rest of us or you got destroyed. You don't believe this now but what I did was, in part, to protect you. And I hate myself for all this, more than you can ever know.'

She did, Alison knew that. Something inside, some deep, formless logical process, told her that friendship was too important, too sacred to be ignored in these circumstances. Some relationships needed testing in the fire to judge their worth. 'And she persuaded Miles, good old dead-drunk Miles, to let Harry Blamire into the house, in his bed? How did she do that, Sara? How?'

Sara was horrified. *'What?'*

'I never told you,' Alison said softly. 'I couldn't.'

This was the worst for Sara, she knew. Worse than being found out.

'It's too awful,' Sara said. 'That woman . . . Jesus, she

terrifies me. Don't take it out on Miles, love. Marjorie can make you do anything. Hurt, betray someone you love. *Anything*. That cow is a witch. I believe that, with all my heart.'

The two of them stared at each other and fell into silence. Finally, Justin said, 'Get out of it now. Burn all the records. Destroy as much evidence as you can. They can't have a lot to go on otherwise they'd be taking a sledgehammer to the door now. You might get lucky. I can't promise much but I'll do what I can.'

Could it have been just one short sentence that began it? Alison was unsure whether she could live with that thought. A few words unspoken, a silly boast about an ancestral myth that was probably untrue. Could everything stem from that? Perhaps, she thought, but only in the sense that the words were a catalyst. It was Marjorie Tyler, her vast shadow hanging over the village like a cloud, who was the protagonist. It was her thirst for control, her despotic nature that had brought disaster upon them all. Nor was it quenched. She thought about the incident with the shotgun, the stand-up argument over Beth Jukes's body. To see the world through Marjorie's eyes was to see a Beulah replete with menace, and only one means available to deal with the threat.

Justin got up, thrust his hands in his jeans and stared at her. 'I'll be here for Burning Man but that's it. Let's hope we can settle this once and for all then. It might be wise if you stayed away, Sara. Can you make an excuse?'

'The best excuse,' she said, looking at the baby.

He stared at Alison. 'And you?'

'What do you want me to do?'

'I'd like you around, Alison. I can call people in if I need it. But it would help to have witnesses. It could help both of us.'

'I'll be there.'

'And also . . .' Justin looked so sad, she thought. As if his world were disappearing in front of his eyes. 'I can't see you again, Alison. Ever. It's not that I don't want to.'

The words eluded her, and not for the ordinary reasons of guilt and embarrassment that went hand in hand with the act of adultery. The relationship with Justin had turned out wrong in more ways than one. The brief, ecstatic moment at Yule should have been the beginning of something that bloomed during the summer, after May Day and the cricket match, before reaching its natural end. What happened instead was this arid, poisoned season where everything seemed out of joint, in Beulah and the lives of its inhabitants. His time had never really come and gone as it should. Now he was fading from her life and would, she knew, be gone from it entirely when the nights turned chilly and the blackthorn on the Minnis began to sport the deep, misted blue fruits of autumn.

'I love you,' he said. 'I don't know why. I wish I didn't, to be honest. I never knew it could be this painful. I just know I do and it was fated, there wasn't a choice, not for me. Not ever.'

She stepped up and kissed him once on the lips. 'I know,' she said again.

They watched him leave and Alison, to her relief, felt not a moment of regret. The season was changing already. Sara sat on the sofa, dry-eyed now, as miserable as sin.

'You must hate me,' she said. 'I don't blame you. I can't say sorry enough. I can't . . .' The tears came again, thick and fast. Jamie awoke on cue, as if Sara's sobbing had carried through the ether on some invisible thread of despair.

Alison stood up, walked over to the Moses basket, and took out the writhing, forlorn child, kissed him once, then returned with him to the sofa. She sat next to Sara, passed her the baby, then wrapped her arms around both of them.

'You,' she said resolutely, 'are my friend, my best friend.

You both matter to me more than you'll ever know. And anyone who has hurt you is my enemy.'

'Sarge?'

Vinny Bennett looked up from the desk. He was a kindly, stupid man who would never progress beyond the rank of sergeant. Justin liked him for his innocence and honesty. The station was empty that night. People were on holiday, coppers and customers. The place had the air of sullen boredom about it.

'I got this event up at Beulah tomorrow night. What if something happens? What if I need back-up? How long will it take?'

'Beulah, Beulah. All I bloody hear about is Beulah,' Bennett moaned. 'You and your village. Those buggers from CID are still sniffing around, you know.'

'They found anything?' Justin asked hopefully.

'Nah. You can see it written on their miserable faces. Not that they'll let on. Pissing in the wind, as usual.'

'Understood. But, like I said, what if I need help tomorrow night?'

Bennett's big, bucolic face looked puzzled. 'Back-up? For Beulah? What you got on up there, boy? Sheep-shagging *en masse*?'

'Nothing . . . I don't know. It's just that I wonder sometimes. What if I did need help? How would I get it? And how long would I have to wait?'

'Amazed you have to ask. You ought to know the answer already. How long did it take when that poor old woman got burned to death? Best part of an hour, I recall. And what do you expect? Bloody place is stuck up there on the Downs, middle of nowhere. Nothing happens. Doubt they'd call us if it did. What are we supposed to do? Stick a couple of cars down in Wye waiting for them to pick up the phone?'

'An hour?' The closer Burning Man got, the more fuddled he became when he tried to think his way through the evening. Marjorie, with the aid of Mitch Blamire and who-ever else was in her ring, would attempt to place someone inside the straw man, of that he now felt sure. There would be an attempt to disguise the fact before the figure was dragged to the bonfire. They could drug the victim. They could wait until the flames were at their very height, then hurry out, throw the effigy straight into the blaze, do every-thing so quickly that the ordinary bystanders wouldn't notice. There had to be some kind of disguise. It was impossible to believe that everyone around the fire – ordinary people, like Sara Harrison – knew what was going on too.

But this train of thought had such implications. There had to be somewhere they could keep the intended victim beforehand, render him or her unconscious, and then hide the body inside the straw figure. It was this place that he needed to find. Waiting for the fire itself would be such a risk. He had to catch them in the act of preparing for the murder. And when he did, he had to contain the situation long enough for help to arrive. He thought of Mitch and those strong, muscular arms, like stubby tree trunks. At least this year there was just one Blamire boy to deal with, and whoever else had been roped into the game. All the same, it was not an encouraging prospect.

Bennett was looking at him with a touching degree of concern. 'If you're worried, lad, say so. We can sort something out.'

'It's just an instinct,' Justin replied with a shrug.

'An *instinct*? Cripes, I can't help you there. Guvnor wouldn't like me committing resources on instinct.'

'It doesn't matter. It's probably nothing.'

Vinny Bennett watched the young copper shuffle off down

the corridor, back towards the CID offices and the coffee machine. They all knew the gossip in the nick. Justin was on the way out. *Unsuitable for service*. And maybe a cloud hanging over him too, though Bennett found it hard to believe Justin would get involved in anything seriously bad. 'Kids,' he said to himself.

Down the corridor, mind racing, Justin Liddle walked into the toilets and settled in the first cubicle. He stared at the obscene graffiti scratched on the wall and listened to the heaving and grunting coming from someone three traps down. This was his life, locked inside some tiny, stinking cell, alone, with no horizon, no hope. He thought of Alison and his heart rose in passion and despair.

If there was one reason why he had lost this game it was, he judged, a lack of decisiveness. There was no going back. Alison was lost, for ever. But he could still leave her one last talisman, one final gift.

He took out a ballpoint and a plain, civilian notepad, wrote the message with his left hand, folded it over once, and scrawled the name 'Detective Wills' on the front. They would check the paper for prints. Wills would wonder about the handwriting, and how the unknown informer had come to know his name. But by that time he would be gone.

Then he waited, for more than an hour, alone in the toilet, his head becoming clearer, seeing a path through these problems. After the change of the ten o'clock shift, when the nick was good and empty, he walked down the corridor to Wills's office and left the note on his desk. Quickly and efficiently, he rifled the filing cabinets, took out every piece of paper that had some relevance to Alison and Sara and stuffed the haul into a plastic supermarket carrier.

With a satisfying sense of finality, he walked out into the clammy town air at eleven, drove to the Eurostar station and bought an open one-way ticket, usable on any train, any day, for the fast service to Marseilles, changing at Lille. He knew nothing about his destination but the name sounded promising. This was a port. Boats came and went from all over the world. There were horizons, blue and bold and empty, stretching in every direction.

A mile down the road, in a lonely cul-de-sac, he parked the car at the old, abandoned railway works, poured lighter fuel on the pile of papers and touched them with a match. Blackened flecks lifted on faint flames towards a fusty yellow moon. For the first time in his life, Justin Liddle felt ready to run.

The night was close and airless. It was 8 PM and Miles was about to drive to the station for the Eurostar to Paris. One business trip. She watched, wishing he would stay.

He stuffed his washbag into the case. 'I'll be back tomorrow, love. Promise. It's the big night after all.'

'Oh yes. The big night. How could I forget?' Poor Miles, she thought. He had such a short, narrow focus. The past was past. The future unknown. It was a simple, down-to-earth attitude she wished she could share. 'You won't let them keep you?'

'Of course not. Why?'

'I don't know. I want you here, that's all. Last year was so . . . It was as if everything bad started then.'

He stopped packing, came over and put his hands on her shoulders. 'In that case let's make a vow. After Burning Man tomorrow we start again. No looking back. No recriminations. Just a fresh beginning. And it will be all right, Ali. Promise.'

He kissed her, once, full on the lips. She felt a tremor, something of the old Miles, young, strong, never waning, never giving up the fight. 'I don't know if I can do that, Miles,' she said. 'I don't know if it's fair on you.'

'You can. And let me decide what's fair or not.'

She watched him go. Priory House felt big and cold and empty after he left. The place needed people. More than anything, she thought, it needed children, the sound of young voices bouncing off the walls, laughter tumbling down the wide Georgian staircase. Pipe dreams, fantasies, they seemed to return with the season. Life was changing, radically. In a matter of weeks she could be labelled a drug dealer, could be facing prison, Sara alongside her in the dock. Unless Burning Man did work some miracle this year and there was some kind of magic in the flames.

In front of the Aga she made herself a coffee, pouring a stiff slug of brandy into the mug. Then she walked into the study, took down the long wooden case from the wall, opened it and stared at the elegant object inside. The shotgun possessed some primitive, intrinsic power of its own. In a sense, she felt, it was alive. Sufficiently so to scare the living daylights out of Marjorie Tyler. Or end a life, if its natural course was run. She stroked the polished wood of the stock, remembered what it felt like pressed to her cheek, the sudden jerk of the barrel, the painful explosion of the blast. And the flea-bitten rag of matted fur jumping, suddenly formless, gouts of blood in the air. The transition from consciousness to dark – an endless, all-consuming night without fear or shame or sentiment – was instantaneous. If she closed her eyes, she could imagine holding this thing in reverse, feeling the awkward press of the trigger against her finger, the barrel at her mouth, and . . .

Alison Fenway shook herself out of the dream, put the gun back in its case and returned to the kitchen. The black dog of depression could steal on a person so easily, and for no reason at all. The game was not begun. Justin had plans, deeper, broader ones, she suspected, than he was willing to reveal. Miles, naïve as he was and lacking in certain important details, would never give up hope. Above all, Sara possessed a reason, a bright, lively reason why they should all survive intact, in spite of Marjorie Tyler's machinations.

She looked into the garden. Night was falling. The moon cast a dull, waxy light on the apple trees, now full of unpicked fruit. Tall necks of hollyhocks and delphiniums nodded in the herbaceous beds. The thick, cloying scent of stock blossom drifted in through the half-open back door. The evening was airless and oppressive, but the beauty of Beulah was still there. Beth Jukes would have breathed deep on a night like this, chuckled at the erratic improbability of the world, and then proceeded with the perennial problem of living.

Alison swore inwardly at herself, put on her walking shoes and stomped out of the house, out onto the Minnis, determined to lose the mood through the simplest of remedies, physical exertion. She stopped by the deserted cricket pavilion and nearly abandoned the effort. Across the Minnis, in a recognisable shape close to the pub, the foundations of the bonfire had begun: planks and old timber, brush and scrub lay like the base of a spent volcano waiting to be replenished. She waited a moment, wondering if the strong, squat figure of Mitch Blamire would appear out of nowhere, a pile of scrub, or something worse, tight in his strong arms. But the Minnis was still. It was close to nine. What activity there now was took place at the bar of the Green Man where, in the distant, harsh illumination, she could see the customary line-up of regulars motionless over their beers.

'Men,' she said softly, and, on the instant, laughed at her own predictability. On another night, Miles would have been there with them, and she couldn't blame him. When she thought about the women of Beulah – the faithless American harpy, the murderous giant, even Angie Cartwright, with her scared brand of neurosis, there was scant wonder the men took refuge in the bar from time to time. And, the old voice said, 'at least you know where they are'.

She dug in her heels and marched directly across the pitch, over the short, parched grass and the cracked earth that had seen so little victory this season. A light burned in Crabtree Lodge. There was the shape of Sara's head, behind the thin curtain, her body in the unmistakable pose of nursing, a small figure close to her chest.

Alison stomped on, over the rough grass, through the dry bracken. The horns of the White Horse appeared before her, glowing beneath the moon. Far off were the lights of Canterbury and the great bulk of the cathedral. Sterning Wood lay like a dark stain to her right, a pool of inky blackness beyond the chalk figure. She stopped, lit a cigarette with a shaking hand, and sat down on the brittle grass. There were such memories here. Of Bella Cartwright, bright and sparkling on a joyous summer day, and an encounter afterwards which still burned a fiery hole of pleasure in her memory. And another Bella, crazed to the point of violence, pointing the righteous finger of accusation in the chill winter woods. Events intermingled in her imagination, formed relationships with each other which made no sense in the logical, linear light of day. This, she believed, was part of the challenge, part of the test. To face them down, to see them for what they were: distant happenings in the past, shadows without substance.

She walked to the end of the ridge, to the small sundial that stood on the spur above the steep drop down to the plain. The incline was almost a cliff here. If she launched herself off from the edge, she would roll and roll, tumbling head over heels for the best part of half a mile before the low, barbed-wire fence at the foot of the hill brought her bloody body to a halt. *Lover's Leap*. Someone in the pub had called it that once. It seemed utterly inappropriate. Beulah simply did not embrace a universe where life had such little value that it could be thrown away on a whim, without meaning or purpose.

Holding out her arms, as if they were wings that could lift on the hot night air, she walked to the very edge, stared down into nothingness, and did not feel afraid, was aware only of a sense of achievement, of stillness.

She turned and, with a brisk stride, marched past the head of the horse, past the shining horns, into Sterning Wood. It looked like the hinterland of Hell. The coppicers had been at work, felling the sweet chestnut, saving the best for timber, burning the brush in small fires scattered around the cleared forest. Every ten feet the glowing embers of their work stood like low, red beacons, crackling and hissing. She hurried on, past the coppice work, on into the untouched part of the wood.

An owl hooted.

'Owl,' she said out loud.

Vast wings flapped, and a distant, ghostly body rose through the waving branches of the chestnut trees.

She laughed. Something stirred in the woodland floor, rustling the leaves, racing to escape the speed of her approach.

'Fox,' she said. Then, 'Or badger. I don't care.'

She pushed skinny branches of sweet chestnut out of the way, heedful of their habit of whipping back into the face at the slightest opportunity. The leaf cover grew thick; the moon receded. She reached into her pocket, pulled out the little torch and cast a thin, pale beam through the Stygian dark in front of her.

Then the nature of the wood changed. The smell, too. Beneath the bosky odour there lurked something of Paternoster Farm still, a fetid chemical stench that rose up from the ground and assaulted the nostrils. The light returned, fainter somehow, as if the moon itself were frightened of this spot.

The clearing was smaller than she had expected. The demolition men had done their work. Nothing remained of the charnel house where, if her hunch was correct, the Blamire boys had neatly imprisoned their victims before their grisly deaths, then disposed of the inconvenient remains after. She had, she thought with no small measure of pride, disrupted Marjorie Tyler's monstrous regime considerably in the past year.

More importantly, there were no terrors in this place. The dismal, meagre clearing was nothing more than a space in the great expanse of Sterning Wood. Harry was but a memory, a distant one, disappearing down the vast, flaming maw of the contraption he had tended.

'And you deserved it, Harry,' she said softly into the clearing. 'Whatever I feel about that night, however I look at it, you had this coming. I will *not* apologise.'

In the trees behind her something stirred.

'Badger,' she said. 'Or fo –'

The word never formed. Something dark and enveloping came down over Alison Fenway's head, stifling her breath, stifling her screams.

A fist, hard and bony, stabbed into her rib cage, sent her reeling to the ground, choking, gagging, trying to think. Then a rope cut across her hands, her arms, binding her tight, trussing her like a turkey on the ground. She screamed, but only for a moment. A piece of vile-smelling fabric forced its way into her mouth. She gagged once, felt sure it would work its way into her throat, suffocate her from the inside.

Breathe.

Easier said than done. It was a big thing, like some great and ancient hankie pulled from the long-dead Harry Blamire's dirty, dusty pockets.

BREATHE.

The dark grew dimmer still. She could feel her consciousness narrowing to a point somewhere between her eyes, dissolving to a faint blur of perception, without form or reason.

Alison Fenway coughed once and sensed the night slipping from her head. From somewhere beyond her reach, a place outside the scanty physical dimensions that now formed her universe, came a sound she recognised.

Marjorie Tyler laughed.

This Burning Man the world forgot that the calendar had reached September. The sun stood high in the smoggy sky. Small pinnacles of cumulo-nimbus rose out of a scattering of cloud, stained black beneath, the faint rumbles of thunder in their bellies. The day was unbearably close and hot. Even approaching six o'clock it was sufficiently powerful to give Barry Wills a headache beneath the sweaty crop of straying hair. Wills looked at the Minnis and the bonfire rising from the earth, Mitch Blamire and Dickie Cartwright working away at its construction.

'I hate the fucking countryside,' he said to no one in particular. 'It smells. The people are weird. There's muck everywhere. What makes this lot tick, Liddle? You're supposed to know them. You tell me that.'

The six-strong team of CID detectives stared at Justin mournfully. The day was not going well.

'They like to keep themselves to themselves, sir,' he replied weakly. He felt uncomfortably hot in the uniform. And useless too. These men thought they knew what they were looking for. His presence was unimportant, unwanted. None of them guessed that it was his note that had brought them out on the promise of hard evidence against Sara and Alison. And, Justin reasoned, would keep them in Beulah long enough to provide him the back-up he needed.

Wills was essentially stupid. Too stupid to realise that all the important Beulah files were missing, except those that pointed a faint, suspicious finger at Marjorie Tyler's narcotic predilections. Justin wanted a swift resolution. The open ticket to Marseilles burned a hole in his pocket. If Burning Man went well, and luck was on his side, he would be sitting on the train at seven the following morning, leaving this worn-out life behind, like a snake shedding its skin.

But that depended upon Wills sticking around. And, more than anything, Alison being saved. They'd been to the house and she was out. No one had seen her since the night before. It was eminently possible that she had decided she couldn't face another Burning Man in Beulah. Something about the idea was unconvincing, however. Alison was, above all, bold. Given the opportunity, she would, he judged, face Marjorie Tyler down as certainly tonight as she did on the morning after Beth Jukes's death.

Ringing through his head, like an alarm bell refusing to be quiet, was the grim, relentless suspicion that his search for Alison and the intended sacrifice were focused upon the same target. He wondered, for one brief, fateful moment, if he dare tell Wills of his fears. Of Burning Man, and what had happened the previous year. Inwardly he could hear the CID man's laughter. Nothing would send them speeding down Vipers Hill, back to civilisation, more swiftly.

He watched Wills light a cigarette and stare miserably at the tail-end of the cricket match on the green. Beulah was playing a friendly against Sellindge. Once again, they were getting thrashed.

'Had enough of this,' Wills grunted. 'Some bastard's been wasting my time. Wait'll I get my hands on him.'

'Sir . . .' Justin tried not to sound too desperate. 'Just because we haven't found anything yet, it doesn't mean something won't turn up.'

'Really?' The detective's face was the very picture of

sarcastic disbelief. Justin realised that he found Barry Wills a very unpleasant man indeed. 'And you're the expert in these things, are you, Liddle? You know about CID work?'

'No, sir, I just . . .'

The other CID men glowered at him.

'We turned over the Harrison woman, Liddle. We turned over the Fenways' house, not that anyone knows where Madame Fenway is. Don't suppose you can help there, can you, boy?'

'No,' Justin answered coldly.

'Well, we found nothing. No drugs. No evidence. Nothing. If I didn't have that tip-off and the fact of those accounts to the contrary, I'd really think those two were a couple of nice middle-class women with a fancy line in mail order. For Christ's sake, maybe they are. Maybe we are being fed a line here. What do you think, Liddle?'

Justin shook his head. 'I don't know, sir. I'm just a village plod.'

'And not that for much longer,' one of the CID men noted. 'What's it next, Justin? Postie?'

A low rumble of laughter ran between them. Justin looked at the pub. A gaggle of figures were sunning themselves on the table at the front. 'You could always have a beer. Good beer in the Green Man, I'm told.'

There was, he thought, a certain inevitability in conversations involving policemen and pubs. One of the DCs looked at Wills hopefully and said, 'No harm in a beer is there, sir? Not if you stand us down.'

Wills ran a hand through his sweaty scalp and licked his lips. 'Never any harm in a beer, son. Best suggestion you've made all year, Liddle. Though not for you. Can't have men in uniform drinking, can we?'

'Certainly not,' Justin said, looking suitably shocked. 'And anyway, I'd like to fish around if you don't mind . . .'

But no one was listening. The group of detectives was

walking at an eager pace across the Minnis, eyes fixed collectively on the bar. Justin tried to collect his thoughts, scanned the cricket match and saw Miles Fenway there, sitting it out on the batsmen's bench. Miles had been dragged from the game when Wills and his crew had descended on Priory House. He was already out, caught on a miserable hit which Justin had witnessed during the first over of the match. Miles's response to the CID visit ranged from wide-eyed disbelief to mute fury. He was as much in the dark about Alison's absence as anyone. Justin thought about Alison's husband, swallowed hard, and walked around the perimeter of the pitch.

Miles looked up wearily from the bench. 'No more stupid questions, constable. Please.'

'Mr Fenway . . .'

He gave a wry smile. 'You can call me Miles, old chap. I think we are . . . close enough for that.'

Justin felt deeply confused. There was something about Miles he liked a lot. This should not have been surprising. Alison felt the same way. It didn't make things any easier.

He sat down on the bench and stared at the bunch of plain-clothes men hunched over two tables at the front of the Green Man. 'I guess that's right. *Miles.*'

'There. That wasn't hard now, was it?'

'Look,' Justin said. 'This is pretty awkward for me. As it is for you, I'm sure. But it's important we talk.'

'Is it?' Miles seemed genuinely foxed on that point. 'Try to see things from my point of view, Justin. You lot have been all over my house looking for evidence my wife is some kind of drug dealer. And manifestly failing to find it. You don't know where she is. I don't know where she is. And now her boyfriend is sitting next to me going on about I don't know what . . . Why is it important?'

'She's missing, Miles.'

He shook his head. 'Tell me something new. Sometimes . . .

418

she does this. I've known her a lot longer than you, Justin. Ali is a complicated person. Sometimes she just needs to be on her own.'

'I take your word on that. And I'm not asking out of self-interest. Alison and I are over.'

Miles laughed. 'Of course you're over. You don't think I'd be talking to you if you weren't, do you?'

'No,' Justin answered, wondering how he could be so stupid.

'You're yesterday's man, Justin. In a sense you always were. Everything that's happened here in Beulah, with Ali and her life, has been about her finding herself. Finding some cure. And I think we're almost there. I think she's coming round. Maybe she's gone away because that's part of the process too. I don't know. Ali's strong, you know. She has to be.'

She always said Miles was naïve. Justin was shocked to see it for himself. 'There could be another explanation.'

Miles picked up a spare cricket ball, tossed it up and down in his hand, watching the desultory game slipping towards inevitable defeat. 'Such as what? She really is a drug dealer and she's on the run? What about Sara? I don't see her fleeing.'

'She's not a drug dealer. Not knowingly, Miles. But things are a touch more complicated than you think. Those CID blokes are not completely in the dark. More to the point, I think Ali could be in danger.'

The word had some magic property. Miles dropped the ball. 'Danger? What kind of danger?'

'I think . . .' Where was it possible to begin without sounding ridiculous? 'I think she saw something last year. At Burning Man. I think some people believe she's got ambitions in the village. Ambitions that could threaten someone like Marjorie Tyler. I'd just like to know where she is. That's all. And where Marjorie is for that matter.

I've looked everywhere and I can't find hide nor hair of her.'

Miles stared at him and Justin tried to convince himself there was nothing idiotic in the gaze. Alison always said Miles was a genius at money and an innocent at everything else. Justin hoped, prayed, this was only true up to a point.

'This is that murder nonsense again, isn't it? All that ridiculous notion she got into her head about someone being inside the fire. For Christ's sake, Justin, I was *here* for Burning Man. Don't you think I would have noticed?'

'Were you sober? Were you looking? I talked to her about that. She was in a different position from the rest of you. And she found something. A finger bone.'

Miles's face was immobile, unreadable. 'Did you see it? This finger bone? I just thought . . .' He hated to admit it. 'Oh, all right. Alison's no stranger to the condition. I thought she'd gone off the rails again.'

'No. She said it disappeared. Someone took it from the house. But who?'

Miles's head dropped forward. He glowered at the dry earth and said, vehemently, 'Shit . . .'

'Pardon?'

'Come with me.'

They got up from the bench and walked the few yards across the green towards Priory House. Miles cast a glance back at the pub. 'Your friends are going.'

'What?' Justin turned and saw the detectives approaching the car park, heading home. 'Damn.'

'A problem?'

'I thought they could help. I pulled a very stupid trick to get them here. Otherwise I'm on my own if something happens.'

They walked up the drive. 'You mean you tipped them off about something? That's why they've been going through the drawers in my house? Turning over poor old Sara too?'

Miles could be smart too, he thought. 'Partly. Sorry. But I had my reasons. And they didn't take much pushing. There's not time now, Miles, but I have to tell you Alison was in trouble before today. Badly.'

The back door was open. Another Beulah habit Justin had tried to curtail. Why did no one lock their doors? More importantly, why did no one ever get burgled?

'That can wait,' Miles said grimly, and led the way into the study. He stood before a big antique desk, opened the roll-up front and pulled out a tiny drawer of paper clips and elastic bands. Behind it was another compartment. Miles reached in and extracted an envelope.

He gave it to Justin. 'I don't know why I kept this. I should have just thrown it away.'

Justin opened it. Inside, on a small mat of white cotton wool, was a bone, charred and still stained with ash. 'I don't understand.'

'No,' Miles interrupted, and sounded a little sour. 'I imagine you don't. I didn't until Sara let on. She was obsessed with this thing, Justin. It was as if . . . everything started with it.'

They stared at the bone. The more they looked at it, the more it resembled a human artefact.

'God, I'm a bloody moron,' Miles said bitterly. 'I thought it was part of the problem. I thought, if I took it away, we could go back to normal. *I didn't believe her.*' He gazed miserably at Justin. 'And you did, didn't you? All along. That was what she needed, more than anything. Someone who believed. What an idiot! I've been.'

'It's just . . .' Justin wondered if Miles were about to break down completely. 'You have to pull yourself together, Miles. We don't have time for this. Something's wrong. We need to find Alison.'

He wouldn't collapse under pressure. Miles, beneath the financier exterior, was a good bloke. 'You really think Marjorie's involved?' he asked.

'Probably,' Justin replied cautiously. 'Oh, dammit. I *know*. I just can't prove anything. And where the hell is she? I've looked everywhere.'

Miles glanced outside. The cricket match was over. The light was failing. Most of the players had dispersed. No one was working on the bonfire any more, which seemed smaller than last year's. 'I don't get it,' he said. 'Where is everyone?'

Justin followed his gaze onto the deserted Minnis. 'What do you mean?'

'Last year . . . I was a bit pissed, but there seemed to be so many people. It was a party, for God's sake. And now look. I don't even recognise any of them.'

The two men gazed at the Minnis. It was virtually deserted. There were more people around of a good summer evening than seemed to have turned out for Burning Man.

'Bugger.' Justin cursed himself for being so stupid. They were right. He was a lousy copper. 'Why the hell didn't I think of that? What an idiot!'

Miles peered at him, baffled. 'How do you mean?'

'They're not going to do it outside the pub, in front of everyone. Not this year. They know I'm around. They know people are sniffing.'

Miles blinked and looked slow again. 'You've lost me.'

'There's nothing in the rules that says they have to use that bonfire. It's just there to fool us. They're all somewhere else.'

'But where?'

It came back to him. Naked bodies flying through the night. The clearing beyond the White Horse.

'In Sterning Wood. Where else?'

Miles rose from the desk and took down the long wooden

422

case from the wall, opened it and gently withdrew the Purdey. Justin felt the temperature of the room descend several degrees. 'No,' he said firmly. 'No guns, Miles. They're not needed.'

'Aren't they?' There was some hard, unthinking fury in Miles Fenway's eyes.

'Please.'

Miles looked intently into his face. 'She's my wife, old boy. *My* wife. No one lays a finger on her again.'

Before she opened her eyes, Alison was aware of the smell. This was Paternoster Farm all over again. The air was thick with a dank stench of earth and animal, as if something were slowly rotting in the room. The place was unnaturally warm. And she was not alone. Close by was the sound of breathing, quiet, controlled and rapid.

She waited until she was fully conscious, fully aware of herself and only then, eyes darting in the half darkness of the place, began to scream. The sound died almost on the instant. She had struggled and it was useless. Something bound her to a small, hard chair. Her hands, tied tightly at the wrist, sat on her lap. In front of her, mimicking her every move, was an image from a nightmare: a face, stricken with terror, head covered in flowers, buttercup and rose, lily and heather, woven carefully through her hair.

Alison looked at herself in the mirror and felt her sanity briefly desert her until the pain and the anger forced it to return. Bella was seated by her side on some kind of low stool, looking at her through the mirror too, although they could have been no more than a foot or two apart.

'She said to make you pretty. Not that you're not already. They said you should look like you was made of flowers.

Like the Queen of the May's supposed to be.'

They were in an ancient caravan, somewhere deep inside the wood, she guessed, close to what remained of Paternoster Farm. She was wearing something foreign, a tight shift, decorated in a lurid floral print. Bella caught her staring at it. 'One of mine. Sorry. They said you had to wear something bright, and I didn't know what to do. Didn't let that dirty old bugger Tyler undress you, mind. That would have been a bad thing.'

'Bella.' It was hard to think through the entire range of possibilities. They each kept tripping over one another. 'What the hell is going on here? Let me go, please. I don't find this amusing.'

'Oh shit.' Out of the blue Bella buried her face in her hands and burst into tears.

'Bella. Please . . .'

'I don't want no part of this, Ali,' she blubbered. 'You do believe that, don't you? It's old Ma Tyler. She's hopping mad. She says you killed old Harry. You betrayed Miles for someone out of the village. It's you that made everything go wrong, going after her like that. And it's that time. They got to burn someone.'

The maze of possibilities suddenly narrowed to a single certainty. Alison almost found the process, the elimination of the detritus from her mind, comforting. 'Bella. Listen to me. It doesn't matter what you've done. Just untie me. We'll both go out of here together, go home and forget this ever happened. Nothing will come of it, trust me. Tomorrow we just go back to living like we always did.'

'Can't do that,' Bella said and picked up a pair of long, narrow scissors to snip at an errant rose that hung down over Alison's neck. 'She'd kill me if I did that. And that's not all. She's got the village scared up the same way. God knows what she'd do.'

'Bella! You cannot let this happen!'

There was a sound from behind them. A thin draught

of fresh air came in through an opening door. Bella cast a terrified glance in its direction and then, very carefully, slipped the pair of scissors into the pocket of the shift, felt Alison's arm, pressed it against the handle to make sure she knew it was there.

'Can't do nothing, missus,' she murmured, then retreated.

There was the smell of sweat and the sound of a heavy body. Marjorie Tyler's vast form hove into view, a triumphant smile on her face. Alison looked into her eyes. They seemed heavy, dead. There was the flowery smell of gin about her.

'My,' she said, her voice a touch slurry. 'We do look lovely. You can get going now, Bella. Go warm your hands on the fire. We'll be along soon.'

Alison felt the heat of fury rise inside her. 'Piss off, Marjorie. You don't imagine, for one moment, you can really do this, do you?'

Anger, bright and vivid, flared in Marjorie's eyes. 'This is my village. I can do what the hell I like.'

Alison wanted to say something more, wanted to taunt her. But this seemed a juvenile gesture. And something else too. She was afraid. Scared in an entirely new way, quite different from the terror she had known inside Paternoster Farm or the dreamy, unreal nightmare of Mitch Blamire, impersonating his brother, pouring some dread concoction down her throat to rid the world of Justin's child.

'Cat got your tongue?' Marjorie crowed.

John Tyler came up on Alison's other side carrying a small black medical bag. He opened it, reached in and came out with a syringe and an ampoule. 'No need for unpleasantness, Marjorie. This is unusual enough as it is. A resident indeed.'

He stared at Alison with a piercing gaze. 'You look lovely,' he said.

'My. Thanks.'

'No.' He seemed cross. 'You never did listen. You never even tried to understand.'

'Understand *what?*'

'The story. The allegory. I told you. In the *Mabinogion*. The lord of winter, betrayed by his wife so she could sleep with the lord of summer. Light and dark. Heat and cold. And you. Blodeuwedd she was called in the story. It means she was made of flowers. But she might have been Guinevere too. It's the same old story.'

The tale did ring some infuriating bell in her head. 'And I'm her?'

Tyler looked as if he were trying to understand this himself. 'Sometimes I think life is just a myth, running around itself, cycling through the centuries. One more Blodeuwedd. One more Guinevere, betraying Arthur for Lancelot. And, in a sense, Miles won in the end, didn't he? In spite of the treachery. Not that I'm being judgemental about that.'

Perhaps there was some ancient, atavistic triangle between the three of them. In Beulah anything was possible. 'So what happened to her?' Alison asked, desperately trying to delay the needle. 'The woman made of flowers?'

Tyler's gloomy face looked a little dreamy. Maybe they were both on the chemicals. 'She was turned into an owl, of course. Shunned by the creatures of the day. Better fate than Guinevere, of course. Poor cow was despatched to a nunnery.'

Alison looked at John Tyler and wondered how Marjorie had subverted him. What force had put him under her spell? 'John,' she said. 'You know this is ridiculous. You know Justin and his pals are sniffing around here. You can't think for one moment they won't find out.'

Marjorie roared with laughter. 'Coppers? Justin? The cavalry coming across the hill? Oh, Alison. You can be so deeply, deeply stupid sometimes. *We are our own people here. This is our realm.*'

'Justin will see to it . . .'

Marjorie leaned down, leaned into her face so closely that she could smell the gin on her breath. 'Well, you won't have to worry about that now, will you? Not when you're coming back as an owl? Or dust, more like.'

'Marjorie,' John Tyler said primly. 'This is not appropriate. We are not common murderers. We do not take pleasure in this.'

She cast him a viciously withering look. 'Oh, shut up, John. I take my pleasure where I want. As do we all. She had her chances. If she'd listened, if she'd been obedient, we could all be getting along swimmingly by now. Miles and her in the big house. Us running the show. Some hapless tramp old Mitch picked up in her place instead.'

'This is not about vengeance . . .' Tyler continued, and plunged the needle deep into the ampoule.

'Put that away!' Marjorie barked at him.

'What?'

She reached over Alison, grabbed the syringe from his hands and threw it back in the bag. 'I said, put it away.'

Tyler looked shocked, offended. 'We don't want a repeat of all that trouble last year. It'll make it easier if she's drugged for the straw man. We don't need to be unnecessarily cruel, Marjorie. No one's ever suggested that. Not in all the years . . .'

'Cruel?' Marjorie stared contemptuously at him. 'Do you think they did it like this a hundred years ago? Five hundred? It's all these modern measures that are our undoing. We stick to the ritual, pure and true.'

Tyler blinked rapidly, trying to come to terms with this. Alison saw her opportunity. 'John,' she said, 'you have to stop this. Now. She's mad. You know that better than any of us.'

Marjorie pushed her hard in the chest. The chair toppled backwards. Alison fell painfully to the floor. From there she could see what happened so clearly. Marjorie's vast bulk moved swiftly across the room, her trunk-like arms came up, one of them clutching a long, shining knife. She held it tightly to John Tyler's throat. He looked utterly terrified.

'Do we argue, boy?' Marjorie hissed. 'Do we dare?'

He shook his head.

'Good. No drugs. No straw. We go back to the old days. We give them a night to remember. And after that Beulah's ours again, for as long as we like.'

Then Marjorie's gigantic hand came down, wrenched Alison to her feet, and untied the rope that bound her to the chair.

'You can walk, all right,' Marjorie said. 'You probably think you can run, too. But where to, Mrs Fenway? You think of that? You start bolting and you get this . . .' The shining knife rose and threatened Alison's throat. 'And my, I'd like that.'

She paused, trying to think, then stared at Alison with an odd expression. 'Good girl, that Bella, eh?'

Marjorie reached down into the pocket of the shift and extracted the scissors, held them triumphantly in front of Alison's face. 'Giving you ideas, was she? Thinking maybe you'd get away?'

The silver knife flashed. Stunned, Alison watched the blade sever the rope at her wrists. Marjorie unwound it as a single length, then grabbed her by the hair and tied the rope around her neck like a noose.

She tugged once on the end then led her out into the night. The air was heavy and close. There was the smell of burning wood, the crackling of fires from the forest. And above them all the low, guttural growl of thunder.

By the time Miles Fenway and Justin Liddle reached Sterning Wood, the weather was already starting to change.

The endless high pressure was reaching its expected climax. A storm was on the way, rolling around the guts of the sky, pondering where to break.

Justin had talked, as he drove furiously around the Minnis, spoken of burned files and how suspicion could, with a little work, be shifted from one person to the next, like some gigantic boulder that can be tipped sideways with the push of a finger. Then he parked in the lay-by close to the woods where, what seemed a lifetime before, he had once wooed Alison with vague, unfulfilled promises. Miles took the gun out of the boot, passed the big police torch to Justin, and the two of them set off into the thickness of the coppice, with its leafy smell, its unseen creatures.

It was hard to judge directions, to think about which way to proceed. Before, at Christmas, the wassaillers had approached from the Minnis side of the wood, past the White Horse. Now, Justin had to discover the opposite way, trying to work out which path through the slender chestnut woodland before them would be best.

Miles stood behind him, the gun beneath his arm. 'We're wasting time. We need to find her.'

'I know. It's not easy.'

Something stirred in the trees. The dun shape of a tawny owl lifted out of some low branches in a flurry of feathers.

Then there was another, louder sound, closer to them, and it was Miles who was swearing, cursing like a trooper, arms flailing, groaning as if in pain. Justin jerked the torch beam wildly through the sea of branches. There was a dark, squat shape there, immediately familiar.

'Mr Fenway! Mr Fenway!' Mitch's Blamire's voice laughed at them from a few feet away.

Justin turned the torch on Mitch. The gun was firmly in his arms. Miles lay breathless on the ground. 'Bastard came out of nowhere,' he moaned.

''Course I did,' Mitch laughed. 'You get to learn that when you're poaching. That what you gents doing, now? A little pheasant or a partridge for the pot? Nice gun, sir. Nicer than any I'm ever likely to own.'

'Mitch,' Justin said carefully. 'Don't do anything stupid. I've got other coppers beating the woods too. They'll find us all before long. Just be smart this once. Give us the gun. Take us to where Mrs Fenway is and we'll deal with this quietly in the morning.'

Mitch Blamire guffawed. 'Others in the woods? Don't insult my intelligence, boy. I could live 'neath these trees if I wanted. I could hear you a mile off, smell you too if truth be known. Nobody here but us, mister. And a few of my friends. Who I imagine you'd like to meet.'

He came up to Justin, thrust a fat hand into his police jacket, took out the radio threw it to the ground and stamped on it. 'Don't want you talking now, do we?' He waved the gun down the path. The two men went in front. Mitch Blamire followed behind. It was no more than three hundred yards and then they were in the clearing, with fifteen or more people, the Beulah hard core, Justin guessed. Among them was Frank Wethered, behatted as usual, the Cartwrights, Norman from the pub, and Sara Harrison, looking wild-eyed and terrified. And, held captive at the neck by a rope which Marjorie Tyler gripped tightly in her hands, Alison, her head covered in flowers. She looked at Justin and Miles and said nothing. Marjorie held her close to a bonfire some ten feet tall, wigwam-shaped with a gap in the middle where a sizeable tree trunk was rooted in the ground. The air stank of petrol.

'Visitors, Ma,' Mitch said from behind them. 'Armed too. Now why d'you think nice blokes like this would be wandering around the woods at night with a gun in their hands, eh?'

John Tyler lurked behind Marjorie, solemn, apprehensive.

They all looked scared, Justin thought. Maybe that was where the opportunity lay.

He stepped forward, in front of the semi-circle they made, and held out his arms. 'This is enough. It stops . . .'

It was Frank Wethered who lashed out at him, thin arm whipping through the air to strike Justin on the cheek. 'Shut up, you stupid oaf! You don't understand a damn thing.'

Mitch Blamire crooked the Purdey beneath his shoulder and laughed. 'Right there, Frank. This is Burning Man. We got a job to do.'

It wasn't working. They were more under Marjorie's spell than he expected. Miles glanced at him, eyes darting back to the woods, then kicked hard at Mitch, sent the squat figure reeling towards the ground.

'Run, Justin,' he yelled desperately. 'Get help, for God's sake.'

The circle was broken, uncertain. Justin hesitated, almost for too long, and then took to his heels, racing into the encircling night, through the forest of slender chestnut. Dickie Cartwright and two other figures raced through the dark to rugby-tackle Miles to the forest floor where they struggled in a flurry of curses. Then Mitch stumbled to his feet, cursing, and pointed the gun at the heap of flailing bodies until they were quiet.

'You keep your peace, Mr Fenway.' Mitch was wheezing, hurt. 'We'll get that bastard. He can't run far. And he weren't a friend of yours either.'

They let Miles rise from the ground. His face was bruised. There was blood on his cheeks and the low note of defeat in his voice. There must have been ten men against him. 'This is insane, Mitch. You can't think you'll get away with it.'

'Watch us,' Marjorie barked. 'We'll deal with you and the plod after.' She jerked on the rope. Alison stumbled forward, eyes shining in the dark, and fell to her knees. 'Mitch, you tie her. Have done with it.'

The crowd was silent. Alison tried to see Mitch Blamire's face in front of her. He was grinning, but unsure. The fire was unlit. Justin was free. And she was not about to go easily. This was not over, she thought.

The rope flew over her head, thrown to him by Marjorie. Mitch took it, wrapped the end around his free arm, gave it a gentle, tentative tug, like a farmhand toying with a young bull. 'Nothing personal, Mrs Fenway,' he said. 'You understand that? We just got to do things right here. Otherwise it all goes to pot.'

'Then do it, Mitch,' she said calmly. 'I'm awake now. I can see you.'

In the end, she thought, it was Mitch who was afraid here. She had despatched his twin to the grave. She had spilled Blamire blood. Mitch was, she felt, in awe of her. At this final juncture, fear and hesitation coursed in equal measure across his face.

Expressionless, he walked slowly towards her. Counting the seconds in her head, trying to choreograph this last desperate dance, she seized the moment, grasped the rope and pulled. Mitch, caught by his own momentum, stumbled. The gun danced like a silver charm in front of her. Alison fell forwards, rolled on her right shoulder, desperately reaching for the weapon in his hands, felt for the wooden stock and tore it firmly from his grasp.

There was no true time in this place. No difference between a second or an hour. The Purdey was tight within her grip, the familiar shape against her shoulder. Somewhere in her reeling imagination the filigree dragons on the metalwork shone with a radiant luminescence. And Marjorie had the rope again, had snatched it from the felled Mitch Blamire, was pulling, pulling, from behind, such agony on her neck.

Alison tumbled towards her, easing the strain on the rope, then pushed herself to her feet. She flailed out with the gun, expecting Mitch to pounce any second. But he was somewhere else, beyond reach. The twin barrels rose, struck something soft and human. Marjorie cried out, letting loose the long, flashing knife, which disappeared into the blackness of the wood. The rope fell loose. Alison was standing now, free. The Purdey sat in her shoulder as if it were part of her body. On the ground, fat and helpless, face bloody, rolling, screaming imprecations, Marjorie Tyler struggled to get upright.

'Bitch,' Alison said quietly, to herself, not to this small crowd of onlookers, who didn't move, didn't say a word behind her, made no noise whatsoever, knowing the power that rested in her hands.

The vast figure thrashed about on the ground, alone, no sign of John Tyler anywhere. Marjorie's piggy eyes glinted at her, full of hatred, and in that glance Alison saw every venomous deed that had been done to her these past twelve months, each odious act replayed, full of pain and misery and a dark, malevolent intent.

'Bitch,' she repeated softly, and the weapon jerked twice making a sound like thunder, a rolling, roaring explosion that brought some deep, growling counterpoint from the thick and threatening sky.

It was, some observant, rational part of her mind came to judge, a simple, instantaneous transition. One second, Marjorie rolled on the earth, a living, thrashing heap of fury. The next she was gone and in her place was flesh and blood, mere corporeal remains, the pumps and girders of the body's mechanics, still twitching, but out of some lingering electrical spark alone. What had been Marjorie, the essence of her life, had disappeared, ripped from the world by the force of the weapon and Alison's single-minded will. The sky roared again, a fulminatory row above their heads. The first few drops of ponderous rain touched her face. She was aware now of the throng around her, bodies mingling, rushing, shouting.

There was Miles shaking himself free from the gang that surrounded him. Somewhere in the wood, racing for help, there was Justin. Two men, her men, against the mob. It was, she knew, insufficient. Alison Fenway closed her eyes, let the smooth, comforting form of the Purdey slip from her fingers to the floor and waited for their anger to descend.

Even then, the night was closing in. Her consciousness grew hazy. In the loud, frantic frenzy, someone touched her, and it felt more like an embrace than an assault. She held up her arms, not knowing why. They rushed around her. In the throng she saw so many faces, people she knew, laughing, screaming, cheering. Frank Wethered's hat was off, which was, it seemed to her, an odd memory with which to leave this life. Bella Cartwright's face dipped down briefly from view, down to the shattered remains of Marjorie, and then she returned, waving hands smeared in blood. Close by, singing a happy, nonsensical song, Mitch Blamire danced a jig, round and round, all on his own, like some muscle-bound genie released from the bottle. Beyond him, thoughtful, hand on white, pale face, faintly smiling, stood John Tyler, looking at them all, mulling over the proceedings.

She wanted to speak, but the words wouldn't come. Her vision was failing. A long dark tunnel lay ahead, racing up to her consciousness, racing to greet her. The night bellowed at them. It had ceased to possess a form she recognised.

John Tyler's face hove into view and it was friendly, even though the syringe was back in his hands.

'Good girl,' he said. 'Brave girl.' She felt the needle enter her arm, behind it the deadening force of some overpowering anaesthetic. Someone was singing a song, a familiar song, from a movie she could no longer remember, from a time when the past was warm and sunny and safe. She knew these words. Her lips moved with them, automatically.

Quietly, with no perceptible melody, just busking along

with the chorus around her, Alison Fenway whispered, 'Ding dong, the witch is dead, the wicked witch, the wicked witch . . .' Then fell in a lifeless heap to the ground.

She woke alone in the big bedroom overlooking the Minnis. The sheets were ruffled on one side of the mattress only. Alison was wearing a plain nightshirt and felt clean. There was the dim memory of someone bathing her the night before. A pinprick in the arm. Then nothingness again. No dreams.

The Minnis showed evidence of overnight rain. Now it was clear, crystal clear, the horizon so distant it strained the eye. The welcome break in the weather had transformed Beulah. The grass was a happier shade of green than it had been in weeks. There were people on the common, walking dogs, smelling the fresh, clean air. The sky had lost its aching tension. It possessed the diminished blue of approaching autumn, with the occasional puffiness of pure white cumulus on the horizon. The sun had the lazy, golden glow that came with the end of summer. Someone, on the far side of the common, was starting to rebuild Granny Jukes's windmill, fresh pale wood rising from the scorched base. A small detail, but one that seemed to make so much difference to the composure of the scene. Beulah was coming alive again, after its long, strange interlude of disharmony. She remembered staring out at the place little more than a year before and feeling, with a keen, private intensity, its secret sense of wonder, the precious, flawless harmony that ran through everything. In the rush of events, from Burning Man onwards, her appreciation of the village had, to some extent, disappeared. Now it returned in a flood of memories and fresh observations: something perfect. Something to be preserved. And something better understood too. There was clarity in this new day, lines of logic racing around her head, answers to mysteries that had once seemed impenetrable.

Mitch Blamire whizzed around the perimeter of the pitch on his little tractor. Further away, outside the Green Man, people were clearing up the remains of a bonfire. *Two?* She had no idea what time she had fallen into the black pit of unconsciousness, deep in Sterning Wood, the night before. There could have been a second fire. Everything might have been a dream. Then she touched her neck, felt the sore marks left by Marjorie Tyler's rope. On the far side of the Minnis two police cars stood outside the Tylers' ugly modern home. *No dream.* She had, she thought, understood that implicitly from the moment she awoke and stared at the perfect alabaster ceiling in the bedroom.

Alison peered outside again. Miles was with the people near the bonfire. Sara was there too, with little Jamie in her arms. There was laughter. It seemed a jolly, natural scene. She dressed quickly, and went outside.

Mitch had stopped mowing the pitch. Now he was working by the cricket pavilion, and his face lit up when he saw her striding across the grass towards him.

'Mrs Fenway!'

He was beaming. She smiled in return. 'Mitch?'

'Such a morning, eh, ma'am. All that rain done washed the world clean. Brought us back to life again. Fresh as a daisy out here.'

She sniffed the air. It was glorious. Mitch continued to gawp at her like an idiot.

'Listen,' he said, ducking behind the pavilion porch. 'Bit of moisture does wonders for the Minnis. Got mushrooms coming up everywhere overnight. Not just your common stuff, neither.'

He held up an ancient wicker basket. It was full of blewits and chanterelles, penny bun ceps and pure white field mushrooms. 'I been minded to take a couple of partridge this morning too, missus. It'd be an honour if you'd let me leave 'em by the back door. Give you and Mr Fenway a treat tonight.'

There was such an air of deference about him, Alison thought. Mitch was a changed man. This was a changed world. 'That would be lovely, Mitch,' she said, and examined the brown, taut skin of the ceps. 'Can I borrow that knife of yours?' she asked.

Mitch blinked nervously, then, without a word, reached into his pocket and slowly pulled out the long, slim shape of the blade. She took it from him, pressed the small, worn button at the side and watched the silver shaft spring out, catching the sunlight. The ceps were perfect, as if they had just come out of a baker's oven. She carefully sliced the brown skin and admired the creamy flesh underneath.

Alison beamed at him. 'You're a sweetie, Mitch.' The sharp blade sparkled in the sun. So much power in such a small object. She shivered, a long, painful convulsion that ran the length of her spine, then gave him back the weapon and set off across the Minnis.

Frank Wethered, with his lively little terrier yapping at his heels, strode through the outfield, lifted his hat and bade her a bright good morning. Bella skipped past, grinning foolishly, face newly scrubbed, yammering nonsense, a long, gabbling stream of words that rattled from her mouth so quickly, one over the other, making no sense.

'Bella,' she said finally. 'Slowly. Please.'

'Oh.' The girl was suddenly upon her, planted a damp kiss on her neck. 'I love you, Alison Fenway. We all love you. More than ever.'

'That's kind.' She stared at the remains of the fire on the common ahead. There was just Miles there now, with Sara by his side, the baby in her arms, both of them talking idly. 'You had a fire, Bella?'

''Course we had a fire, Ali. Later than usual but it was Burning Man after all. Some Burning Man too.'

'Quite. And you're all . . . at peace now?' Alison asked.

'That's a way of putting it.'

'What happened?'

Bella's eyes flashed with the old evasiveness. Not everything changed, Alison thought, and found her head going into overdrive, measuring possibilities against each other, weighing the likely outcomes.

'Best you ask Miles about that,' Bella replied carefully. 'He's your man.'

'I guess he is,' she said, and kicked into her stride, walked briskly over to the remains of the fire. Miles watched her approaching. Something glinted in the grass, caught the lazy fire of the sun, briefly dazzling her eyes. Alison blinked and then it was gone. Miles had moved his foot over the small, reflecting object, and he now stood in front of her, face full of admiration, arms open wide.

She declined, choosing to stay away from him. Sara watched, mutely, a little worried perhaps, Jamie writhing slowly in her embrace.

'Welcome back,' Miles said. He looked older, somehow. In this new, clear light the faces of everyone in the village had some added depth, as if they were images from some ancient painting recreated in the flesh.

'Isn't that presumptuous?' Alison walked over to Sara, took the baby from her, held out his ample frame and compared the two faces. The child was exquisite. He stared at her with a quiet, patient dignity.

'I must be very stupid sometimes, Miles,' she said. 'He's so obviously yours. How couldn't I tell?'

Sara walked up to her and, very slowly, threw her arms around Alison and the child, kissed them both. 'Ali,' she said. 'It's painful when the scales fall from your eyes. Be patient. This hasn't been easy for any of us.'

438

She wanted to laugh but it was impossible. The day was unreal. Some kind of battle was being fought inside her head. 'You all lied to me.'

'No,' Sara said firmly. 'We hid from you a truth that would have hurt you. We had no choice.'

There was something close to a laugh then. 'You did this for me? All this deception? All these things I thought were spontaneous?'

'We all had to plan, love,' Sara replied flatly. 'I needed a child, and I had to pick the best. What do you expect?'

'Loyalty?' she wondered.

Miles shook his head, as if she were a slow schoolchild trying to pick up on a difficult idea. 'We're loyal to each other, Alison. All of us. Not to some false morality.' He stared in the direction of the police standing miserably outside the Tylers' house. 'Not to them.'

No, she thought. That was not what she meant. It was hard to string these thoughts together. She held the child tightly, wondering what answers he might possess. 'Why, Miles?'

'Sara needed me. And it was Burning Man. Why not? I couldn't give you a child then. It wasn't our time.'

'And Harry?'

He didn't look proud, she had that to say for him. 'None of this comes for free, you know. We don't keep Beulah by accident. The Blamires have always been the same. They work for whoever pays them. They stick with the winning side. But you have to meet their price. Without them, we'd have been lost. It pained me too.'

'But it was Burning Man,' Sara said, swiftly intervening. 'It was . . . allowed.'

The memories were too numerous, too powerful. They crowded out everything else in her head. 'And you made me think it was Marjorie all along. Right from the beginning. Just for last night.' The line from the song rang through her head. The witch really was dead, by Alison's own hand.

Sara looked at her severely. 'I told you,' she said. 'These things are either passed on willingly or they're taken. Marjorie wasn't giving anything up. We couldn't win it for you. Marjorie would have killed you in the end, Alison. Just like squashing a bug.'

'And you'd have watched? If I failed?'

Miles took her by the shoulders and stared into her eyes. 'You didn't fail. You couldn't fail. The end was never in doubt. Beulah is ours. I'm a Fenway. Emily knew what she was doing when she left me that house. It came with plenty of hints. And there were people here who wanted to help too. They understood Marjorie's time was over.'

She laughed dryly. 'So that's it, Miles. You're the Lord of the Dance. I'm the Queen of the May. And every year we pick some stranger off the street and burn them alive just so Beulah never gets tainted by the outside world, just so they never build more bungalows on the Minnis and spoil our precious paradise.'

He looked almost cross. This was the new Miles. Or, it occurred to her, the *real* Miles. 'Don't judge what you don't yet understand. It's not as simple, or as brutal as that. Beulah is precious. It was going to pieces. Look what happened to Beth Jukes. Just because some animals from the plain felt like some fun. This is paradise. *Our* paradise. We have to defend it.'

The tears came out of nowhere, bitter and full of fury. 'You took my child, Miles. *You took my child.*'

And he was smiling, the kind of easy, indulgent smile that always came on these occasions, when her head was running ahead of itself, when her mind whirled with bright, insane possibilities. 'There are things that are meant to happen in the world,' he said confidently. 'You and me. And things that aren't. I'll give you children. Now that everything here is right and in its place. These will be the best times. We've earned them. Can't you feel that?'

'No!' Jamie Harrison was disturbed by the noise. He stared at her with an expression of frank puzzlement tinged with fear. 'Oh God,' she moaned, and handed the child back to Sara. 'I don't feel anything. I don't even have the energy left to hate you.'

She looked at the lazy police activity outside the Tylers'. Every one a man. 'I could walk over there. I could tell them everything.'

Miles shook his head. 'Do you think they'd believe you? Ali, as far as they're concerned, you weren't even in the village last night.'

They had so many answers. She found it impossible to think ahead. 'Then who shot Marjorie Tyler?'

Sara cast a knowing glance at Miles. 'There are things you need to know, and quickly,' she said. 'Justin got into a fight with Marjorie and she wound up dead. At least, that's what they think. He's doing what he planned to do all along, carrying the can for you, love. We can all get away with this, don't worry.'

No one, she thought, could believe that. Not for a moment. Justin was incapable of such an act.

'Alison,' Miles said firmly. 'You have to listen. You have to get the story straight for when they do ask. Justin . . . let's just say he's quite a chap. He'd been aiming to leave for days, and get you two off the hook with that drugs thing at the same time. We talked about it and concocted the story that he and Marjorie were in the drugs venture together. They argued. There was a fight and the gun went off. He told me he'd fixed some of the paperwork so that the police will believe at least half of that. Justin's fine, long gone to the Continent by now, with enough money for a new passport. I'll see he doesn't go short wherever he lands up. He deserves that much.'

One of the police cars drove slowly away from the Tylers'

house. She watched the uniformed driver yawn at the wheel. 'No one will believe that, Miles. No one who knows him.'

'Of course they will,' he said sharply. 'They're just stupid coppers. There are witnesses. John Tyler who says Marjorie and Justin were thick as thieves over something. He knows which side his bread's buttered on now. John's been a brick all along. He wanted Marjorie gone, in the right way, as much as the rest of us.'

Justin had wanted to flee, she knew that. 'I could run,' she said.

'Where to?'

'To Justin, wherever he is,' she said, and knew how pathetically juvenile it sounded.

Miles was unhurt by the barb. 'You don't meant that, love. Justin. Sara here. Even the Blamire boys. They were part of our initiation, part of giving us our rightful place. We don't need them any more. We're ourselves at last. And besides . . .' There was a note of sudden practical determination in his face. 'If you try to run from me again, Ali, you just fall off the edge of the world. You know that place. You've been there already and I don't think you want to go back. We belong together, love. We're nothing apart.'

Forty-eight storeys over Manhattan. Flames licking at her bloodied ankles. The street beckoning from below. That was another realm, she knew. That was a kind of hell.

'You made me your goddamn pawn.'

He took her face in his hands. 'I made you my queen, Alison. I did this for you.'

She looked at Sara and the child. He was the very image of his father. He would grow up a Fenway bastard, well versed in Beulah ways. The line went on, would continue, always.

Miles kissed her once on the forehead. 'Go back to the house. Wait for me. I'll make this up to you, promise. This is the beginning of the best of times. Outside this place, when we go to London, we're them. We follow their ways. We abide by their petty rules. But here, in Beulah, we're our own masters. This is our world. We own it.'

When she was past the cricket pavilion, past seeing, close to the footpath to Priory House, Miles moved his foot, reached down and picked up the solitary object that had shone in the late summer sun.

The partridges lay in the wicker basket, perfect in death, two compact bundles of soft, brown down. She picked them up, walked in through the unlocked back door and placed them on the kitchen table.

It was hard to think, hard to separate the two Alisons now. One quiet, settled, ready to accept, to be subjugated, give Miles the child he wanted (and this could come now, some interior sense told her so). The other still rebelling, still fighting the memories and the pain.

She walked upstairs into the big bedroom and found what she wanted. Beth Jukes's dress lay on the hanger, perfect and pale. Alison threw off her clothes, slipped it over her head and felt the cool, clinging silk take on the form of her body, lock itself to the curves of her breasts, the taut form of her torso.

She surveyed the Minnis once more. Miles was alone, standing by the remains of the fire, a large, powerful figure in the landscape, one that could not be ignored.

A house, she mused, was full of the instruments of death. Knives and skewers. Hammers and saws. Sharp or blunt, they could take a life, they could change the relentless passing of the world, with all its minor tragedies, for ever. All it required was the courage.

He was walking across the grass now, looking taller,

stronger than she had ever known him. Perhaps this was the true Miles all along and she had failed to see it. Perhaps it was Beulah that gave him the strength. Or there was something in the air, something in the very atoms of the place, that transformed Miles. And would now transform her in turn.

Alison watched him and felt this second, mutinous part of her detach itself, float free of her being, out of the window, out into the late summer air, with its crisp freshness and its promise of the long dark days to come. This other Alison rose high on light, feathered wings, beating, beating, beating, and hovered somewhere over Beulah, still and powerful. There was a moment when she was both it and the person standing at the window. A moment when each looked at the other and saw some mute form of recognition. Both watched Miles approach and, for the earthly Alison, the dress was like a second skin, tight and electric on her flesh. She could feel the hairs of her body standing on end. The hardness of her nipples ached through the silk.

Above, in the sky, with her doubts and her spreading wings, this other Alison gazed down on him, saw him take the silver object from his pocket. It was covered in ash. Soot and dirt blocked the mouthpiece. Miles puffed away the debris, spat on the metal and rubbed it with his hankie, clearing the channel. Then he put the silver police whistle in his mouth, tasted the smoke of the fire and something more organic, like burned meat, and blew hard. A sound, long and piercing, filled the Minnis, then rose into the glorious sky.

Startled, the pale, hovering bird flapped its wings once. Then it was gone for ever, feathers dissolved in the brightness of day, sharp, dun beak turned to a memory the colour of the fading sun.

Miles Fenway looked up at his wife in the window, a slim, expectant figure in the radiant white dress, watching him, transfixed. And, with quick, anxious steps, covered the path to Priory House.